I0679333

TIMELINES

Rory Haymont

TIMELINES

Rory Haymont

This is a work of fiction. Names, characters, places, and incidents either are the product of the author's imagination or are used fictiously. Any resemblance to actual persons, living or dead, events, or locales is entirely coincidental.

Copyright © 2025 by Rory Haymont

All rights reserved. No part of this book may be reproduced or used in any manner without written permission of the copyright owner except for the use of quotations in a book review. For more information, contact rory@roryhaymont.com.au

IBSN 978-1-7636363-6-1 Paperback

IBSN 978-1-7636363-7-8 e Book

Also by Rory Haymont

Books

The Dreamer

Zen

Bruja

Kirby

Three Shot Stories

Proximity

The Hand of Tæranon

The Survivor

Nance

The Blue Groper

Names

The Baker's Dozen

Short Novels

The Girlfriend Experience

Reaper

The Blue Groper

Proximity

The Reputation

Continued over......

Prologue 1

Elouise and her father had reached an agreement about some of their research outcomes and inventions. Those discoveries with the potential for use by government or those seeking to spread terror to control or harm human populations would be destroyed. It was a risk of greater concern to her father. However Elouise appreciated the intent. They arrived at this conclusion via a formal meeting because that was the way they operated. A necessity for Elouise as she had few casual conversations. It was necessary to codify this because neither wanted to constrain pure research. Their investigation might lead to an undesirable outcome however this may not be apparent until the outcome was reached. And Elouise's mind had to release what it generated. They also knew from experience that some piece of an innovation might be segregated and able to be sufficiently quarantined from a larger outcome to contribute to some other result for the greater good. Final outcomes were then configured to be commercialised by the market, to maximise profit, which was used for Elouise's primary objective. The Graceland Project which all relevant science disciplines assured the world; was impossible.

However on this one occasion she did not faithfully adhere to the intent of the agreement though she believed she met the letter of it. Prodigious as her intellect was, to generate what may be a highly complex research outcome and then destroy all trace of it was inefficient. Although she could recreate it, it would take time which would displace the time she could be working on her great endeavour or the commercialisation of ideas to support that. She did the first thing her unprecedented genius would create that all her peers would say was impossible. And it would, in a narrow interpretation, satisfy her agreement with her father. It was a bubble, though she would not dream of calling it that. She didn't give things names. It was not located in any specific position in space nor in any era of time except for the second she went in and the second came out. A process unobservable because she always came out before she went in. All the outputs of her genius that might be misused by humanity was kept safe as was her one precious possession One of the only two physical objects she cared about. The other being the spaceship she was building, which she would also never give a name.

Prologue 2

Kirby had left an enormous legacy. The greatest of which were events she'd catalysed. Without which the safety from merciless marauders and the equality among the various genders for the trillions who lived in the far flung Nautilus Galaxy, would never have occurred.

Kirby saw her legacy differently. Bringing surfing to the exotic beaches of Li, creating a taste among the locals for the spirits and beers she produced, creating an art movement based on cartoon characters and being a mother to two inter-species children, while sharing her life with a squirrelesque partner she loved deeply. These things; and making it through the Graceland Challenges, were what she was most proud of.

Unfortunately she also left a legacy that would not reveal itself until long after her death.

The Ageless One

'What I received in The Passage is not an Infallible.' Chrona allowed that to hang there. Hoping that she'd been inadvertently provided a working version rather than the final. However what she saw in the Renewal Plan was too intentional. Too strategic. Though *very* well concealed. Anyway there was no such *thing* as an Infallible. She'd led the Sisterhood *believe* that such a thing existed to make the whole process more dramatic. Ritualistised. Now she was tired of dramatic. It had all happened so many times. But this was different.

This was dangerous.

Basilica had recently been designated Renewing Envoy for the end of the Age. An honour to be sure. Especially when conferred on such a young member of the Suffragaito. It was a largely ceremonial role acting as the Bridge between the Ageless One and the Renewing Assembly. A specialist Department which linked to many Departments all of which had been working to ensure an Infallible Renewal had been prepared and would be executed. This Infallible was built under the auspices of the Authoring Envoy. Under her leadership, the Renewing Assembly also made the assessments and selections from a large field of hopefuls to become Bearers of the Renewal. It was not uncommon for a Sororibus, always young, to find her Peace if she failed to be selected after such a great effort, and then to be consigned to be one of those left behind.

The Authoress had provided her work to the Suffragaito for the Passage of the Infallible to the Ageless One. Only the Suffragaito, governing body of the Sororibus, were appraised of the details. The geographical centres for the Renewal were a novel arrangement and the sources of diversity selected for the Bearers were both wider spread than the in past, yet with local intensity based on the settlement nodes, some, never before settled. The Capital would be smaller than had been the case in other Renewals relative to the regional cities. Which were spread at a greater distance across the continents. The Authoring Envoy had built a Renewal that would lead the Sororibus towards greater diversity which would stimulate ever more creativity, science and breadth of thought than had been the case to date. Marvellous as the achievements of the Sisters who preceded them were. She was believed to be the greatest Authoresses through the Ages and it was expected that those in the coming Renewal would sing her praises for generations.

For the Ageless One there had never been a problem. Under the Authoresses guidance, the Renewal was designed over a period of decades and checked and rechecked for a year before its Passage to her. She had started to feel bad that the whole thing had got so out of hand. She would take the Renewal provided to her, pick out some ideas she liked. And then do whatever she wanted. No one survived from the Suffragaito who Passed it to her, so there was no one to notice that the Renewal she received and the Renewal the Bearers began were different. It had even given her a laugh now and then when a particularly pretentious Authoress droned on and on at the ceremony of the Passage about the marvels of her Renewal. Which the Ageless One watched from her ship. She was far too mysterious to attend. Laughs had been getting thin on the ground over the past fifty or so thousand years as she'd really started to tire of the whole thing. And there was also the memory issue.

The Renewing Envoy had minor interactions with The Ageless One, as did all Envoys. A more senior member of the Suffragaito ran the Renewing Assembly and was Basilica's contact and behaved as her Manager. Though not technically so in the Constitution. As those who considered her a mere gesture to the younger generation were about to find out. When not an Envoy to the Ageless One, Basilica was a junior member of the Suffragaito. To some, including Basilica, these small interactions with the Ageless One were worth a lifetime of preparation and the loss of an opportunity to be one of the Bearers in the Renewal. Envoys were ineligible for this, though they must have been *selected* for the honour first against a field of

5

hundreds of millions. And then relinquish it. Hence their sacrifice for these few meetings with the Ageless One was great indeed.

The end of the Timeline for most of the Sororibus was a time to cease to focus on the acquisition of wealth or power or any duties except those that were gratifying. There was only ever a modest gap between what any individual could aspire to compared to what the least powerful and wealthy had. Theirs was an egalitarian society. Now most of the population turned to the enjoyment of the time remaining. Stores of everything for a pleasant life, staples and luxuries, had been laid up for over a century purely for the last decade of this final generation to enjoy. It was a decade of festivity and an opportunity to focus on the intimate relationships of friends and family. To some it was the culmination of lifelong efforts. Some of these, not engaged by intimacies or celebrations, or perhaps suffering some ailment or having had their primary purpose in life draw to a close; took their Peace in the traditional ways. Some of the population, as always at the end, had to sacrifice some or nearly all of their lifespan because the Horizon had the final say. Entreaties to the Ageless One had been made to delay the Renewal of the Timeline and she had shown grudging understanding. However all now accepted that the end of the Timeline and it's Renewal ran as close to the Event Horizon as possible. Too close some thought. This was the first matter Chrona chose to complain about, pointlessly, to her new Envoy.

Basilica realised she had been thrown a hand grenade rather than having an honour bestowed upon her. The honour was conferred on her, part through her tireless efforts to demonstrate worthiness. Also it was a demonstration, at that very late hour, that youth was valued in leadership. The Authoring Envoy and Precipt of the Suffragaito, both very long serving, made the selection having given very few advancement opportunities to the younger generations elsewhere. Now this token appointment confronted a serious problem. Not of her making and initially beyond her understanding. Her predecessor, the Authouring Envoy, had access to the intellect of millions over the course of decades to craft a unique Timeline. Infallible to any risk of a failure but certain to produce a peaceful and enduring society. A lifetime searching through the millions of Fallibles to produce an Infallible for the Ageless Onc to approve. This occurred once every fifteen hundred years. This Authoring Envoy had performed the ritual of Passage to the Suffragaito and then taken her Peace.

'I have been accommodating.' Said Chrona. 'Far *too* accommodating.' Basilica realised she was going to be the subject of an unprecedented rant by The Ageless One, followed by the task of taking very unwelcome news to Suffragaito whose duties were expected to be light in the ten years before the Horizon. The great majority were all very senior to her as elected representatives. 'The petitions I received to allow more of the last generation to persist again and again has led to a point that we come perilously close to the Event Horizon by the time the Renewal is complete. And that means *nothing* can be allowed to go wrong. Which has *never* happened. Hence my disappointment in myself to be swayed so. And now to be presented with a Fallible, buried deep in what was Passed to me only a few days ago. Need I ask of the fate of the Authoring Envoy?'

'She has taken her Peace Ageless One.'

'You'll address me as Chrona.' She smiled. 'I don't envy you.

Last Envoy. Overseer of both Renewal and Horizon. Planned to minute detail and requiring little by way of direction. Was that not the expectation of you? Now we're dealing with what might become a disastrous Time Loop or worse.'

Basilica was sincere. 'In our relative positions…Chrona, it is likely you cannot conceive the honour it is for me to be the Renewing Envoy. However, my immediate concern is that I am unfit to resolve this matter due to the experience I lack.'

Chrona appreciated the values of this young Sororibus, who had cast away everything to have a few minor conversations with her. Even though she had scaled the competitive mountain to *first* be named a Renewer and also won the confidence of her peers to be elected to the Suffragaito. She would cast it all aside. To the Ageless One, this level of commitment, more than experience, was what would be needed. 'That means you'll need to learn quickly. You will need the capacity to be *very* decisive and uncompromising in dealing with the Suffragaito who have grown accustomed to having nothing of much import to manage, regardless of how they view themselves. A situation thanks to the work of all those billions that went before them. You will have an authority which is not usually exercised by an Envoy, and I will be revealing things to you never to be retold. I may give you capabilities via the Sharing only I am aware of. I have assessed your mind, and you are fit for the tasks, otherwise our conversation would have been brief.'

When she was gone the Ageless One felt the guilt she tried to supress. She was tired of the whole undertaking. It had gone on so much longer than intended. All she had wanted to achieve was to give at least a few of those she encountered on a planet long ago salvation from their awful circumstances. A renewal. An opportunity to colonise a new world she would help them establish and then she planned to return to her wandering ways. Which were as often about trade as charity. Hence the vast cargo section of her spaceship. But she stayed long enough for the Sororibus to further develop the technologies those before them had left behind to identify the Event Horizon in their future. It had challenged her to find a solution. It reminded her of something she'd seen. A fascinating thing. She went back in time to recover something the greatest genius the earthlings ever produced left behind which was never supposed to be found. It stimulated her own prodigious genius, and she did something remarkable with it. Unprecedented. And dangerous.

This Renewal threw the risk into sharp focus for her. This 'Fallible'. For all its subtlety and elegance had not been able to conceal its objective. *Someone* knew what she had done. What she had created. And they wanted it. They'd fled into a population which made them like a tree in a huge forest, and she had to find them. She knew this entity would take her ship here on Sororibus if it could. But she had more protections than she had revealed to any. And she began at once to make the great Orb and the Cargo section it rejoined very fifteen hundred years, impregnable to attack.

A failure of the Renewal might draw an end to the Odyssey of the Sororibus. Timely perhaps and her healthy expediency would help her cope. She'd welcome it if she was honest with herself. However to lose control of the ship; or allow a replica to be made was to imperil galaxies. All across time.

The Suffragaito

'It's unusual to be called at short notice, outside of our scheduled meetings and summon us here. Some travelling a great distance, from the fruits of life all have earned as some prepare for the inescapable Peace and some Renewal.' The Princep of the Suffragaito had served in the role for half a lifetime. And some believed that was half a lifetime too long. She was elected again and again for her steady conservatism in the leadership role. This had led to some egoism. Though not as much as there might have been. More importantly she earned the valid accusation of the younger Sororibus that they had been given few opportunities for meaningful advancement. Now it hardly mattered so she could make concessions. The greatest concession to youth, the Renewing Envoy, stood before her now.

The Envoy didn't need a preamble from the Princep, all were aware of the precedence of the summons. 'That is true. This situation is an emergency. The Ageless One…'

The Princep cut across the younger Sororibus immediately. She would likely have done this no matter what Basilica said. 'The word *'emergency'* has never been uttered in this Chamber Envoy. Your youth and devotion to the Ceremonial relationship you enjoy with the Ageless One needs to be respectful of the protocols established in the Suffragaito over the passage of so many millennia.'

'The word is for me to choose. You have interrupted an Envoy. Which is an *actual* precedent by my calculation. I will now take the opportunity to explain as to why the word was chosen and you will *not* interrupt again.'

There was a stony silence. This Envoy was going to be torn to pieces in the media once leaks, which were never supposed to happen, trickled out of the Assembly. A rare occurrence in their culture. Expected to be inevitable in this case as during her long career none had used such a tone with the Princep.

'You have been assembled as an emergency sitting because a *Fallible* Timeline has been Passed to the Ageless One. This Timeline prepared by the Authoring Envoy and approved by the Princep had a Fallibility *intentionally* buried within it. A solution must be found quickly.'

'Let me be clear so that time and energy is not wasted discussing it, we cannot resort to any of the many previous Infallibles. All of our history since its inception would be repeated and always bring us here to this point. Again and again in an endless loop. There would be no new diversity, merely a repetition of what has occurred.' This was an entirely ridiculous premise, however the Ageless One, even in what she saw as a dire circumstance, would be amused to observe if any believed it. She was gratified when her Envoy, with a little trepidation, had pointed out to her that reusing an Infallible could not produce a perfect replica of what went before. She was further gratified to note that her Envoy knew exactly what she was up to. The Princep believed what was said because she was focused more on the challenge to her authority than whether what was being said was plausible. 'We need to resolve this matter now in the Timeline we abide in. And there is little of it left. This may be complex and difficult. Hence, I withdraw my earlier characterisation and I will describe our circumstances as a *dire emergency*.'

A nod by Basilica gave the Princep an opportunity to speak. 'My presumption regarding the language within which your message was couched was improper and I ask your forgiveness.' Her apology was necessary however communicated with residual dissatisfaction with the way the Envoy had provided her message. What followed was imparted with complete confidence. 'I'm sure you'll agree it will be prudent to determine who is the most experienced and capable Suffragette among us to be Envoy to the Ageless One to navigate this unprecedented situation. Naturally your ongoing strategic advice will be valued.' This last was so patently disingenuous it eased the way for the young Envoy.

Chrona wanted Basilica to be blunt and authoritative. Basilica supplied that 'No.' She left a pause she expected to go unfilled, and it was. 'I will continue as Renewing Envoy. However, your observation has merit with respect to the suitability and capacity of those in the Suffragaito, including its leadership in these circumstances. The Ageless One has mandated that each member of this Chamber will consider whether she believes she would best suit retirement or make her contributions to the navigation of the difficulties we face. She has recommended Incumbents who believe alternates would be better placed to make such a contribution, shall select the individual they consider most fit to fulfil the role.'

To the Ageless one it made no difference who was in the Suffragaito but in her mind some of the old fossils might as well go off and do whatever they did for enjoyment and let some younger ones in. A situation she now realised she should have been making interventions into long before. She'd been spending too much time in stasis these days. Basilica was the youngest Envoy ever appointed and now Chrona realised what she'd been missing. Also, she wanted to start examining the minds of any of those who might hold clues as to who conceived the strategy with the Authouring Envoy. These well-connected politicians would be a good place to start.

The Princep restrained herself from interrupting again during Basilica's missive. 'Envoy.' She looked at Basilica with a penetrating gaze. Developed over forty years of unassailed authority. 'This issue can hardly be couched in terms serious enough. However, you have significantly overreached your authority. An Envoy does not override the will of the Sororibus in the Assembly of the Suffragaito irrespective of the seriousness of the situation. Our civilisation has avoided autocracy for aeons, and this will not be the point at which it commences. Retirement and appointments without elections is unconstitutional. This being only one concern with your…missive.'

'You will do what has been asked of you or the Ageless One will take to her ship and depart within twenty-four hours.' Chrona had the young Envoy toss this in case they chose oblivion, so she finally could *leave*. Blamelessly. The complex strategies of that tree hiding in the forest would come to nothing if its life was torn to shreds across the Horizon.

The Ageless One has never made a threat of any kind. This was of the worst imaginable at the worst imaginable moment. The Princep was now more conciliatory. 'Emergency committees of the Sororibus Representatives will be established within the hour. And a plan made for you to present our strategy to the Ageless One.'

'No.' Another pause not to be filled. 'And as to your concerns that an Autocracy might emerge, as you are aware an Envoy might assume emergency powers if directed by the Ageless One. Even though this has never been invoked. The other members will make their choice as to retirement and nomination of a second. None older than thirty. A further mandate of the Ageless One is that if a single word uttered in this Chamber is released to anyone not residing in it, the source should find their Peace within the *hour*. Following an Open Sharing. Princep, as leader of the of Sororibus you are as of this moment retired. The Ageless One passes on her gratitude for your long service.'

'For those who wish to retire from their posts, along with the retiring Princep, monitors will be called to where you now sit to make a recording of your Sharing. This may take some time. You'll then be rewound to the commencement of this meeting. The Ageless One expects many to continue. Especially those more recently elected. Those remaining will stay in your accommodations in the Precinct until the day after tomorrow when those new appointees will have arrived, and we will re convene. I will not take questions.'

There were no *questions*. However the pronounced arrogance of the Envoy would not go unchallenged. One made a loud call expressing concerns. Soon more followed. Then silence. On a large screen usually used for individual Suffragette's reporting on a region or portfolio lit with the visage of the Ageless One. Few had ever seen her. She was known only via the descriptions of some of the Envoys. And here she was. Unexpectedly youthful in appearance at least. And magnetic. Immensely powerful and authoritative. And something more. 'Are these the representatives of a people I have so long poured my heart into. Descendants of those rescued from misery and shepherded for aeons to blossom to fulfil a remarkable potential. Will you resort so quickly to anger and aggression. I watch your proceedings when there may be some matter of contention.

These are usually resolved *adequately*.' She looked at the outgoing Princep. 'Accept my determinations with good grace or careen into the Event Horizon. Should you wish to continue our long association, accept that the Envoy speaks on *my* behalf, irrespective as to whether I give exacting instructions or not. Remember this *always*.' The Ageless One's voice cut a very sharp edge. 'Follow her edicts or find your *collective* Peace.'

The screen went blank. A quarter found their Peace that day after a recording of their Sharing was made. Half of those remaining provided their best recommendation as a replacement. Based on merit and youth. The role had little in the way of prestige anymore and those departing could enjoy the fruits of the celebrations before the end, whatever its duration. Most had served their constituency with faithfulness and dignity and their decision was respected. They received sincere expressions of gratitude for their labours. The Sororibus were conscientious, civilised, intelligent, creative and could also be tolerant of a wide variety of lifestyle choices. That was the real reason the Ageless One had supported them through what to her had become interminable cycles. They ultimately earned her devotion.

Basilica

'You went very easy on them.' Said the Ageless One. Basilica wasn't sure how to answer. 'Yes. I have a sense of humour Basilica. Or at least I have what I think is a sense of humour. I'm not often called upon to be interactive so perhaps not. I was pleased with some of your innovations. You did what you knew I wanted. Not to the letter of my instructions. You have embedded yourself more deeply in what, I fear, will become a most unpleasant affair.'

Basilica wasn't sure to endorse the observation as to whether the Ageless One was in possession of a sense of humour or not. So she moved on, which the right decision. 'I struck a tone based on my interpretation of the threat.'

'And it was the right tone. You have completed the most urgent task?'

'Yes Chrona. The Authoress's full recorded consciousness has been examined.' All Envoys provided their entire consciousness to be retained in case some detail was needed in the understanding of decisions made and the strategies that informed them. Right down to the minutia of these processes.

'And the news is not good would be my guess.'

There was a pause. 'It's unprecedented. Entire periods, months, were lived and deleted. Daily at least half the waking hours missing. Monitoring advises they have no experience of such a thing. The gaps were filled by a recapitulation of earlier times which she some-how projected to cover her actual thoughts and experiences. They point out that making such a survey has never been a requirement of the stored Sharing. I asked them to find a hundred volunteers to submit to such a survey to understand if these anomalies are more commonplace than realised or if the Authouring Envoy's is unique.'

'I applaud the initiative. A program which might be difficult to get willing volunteers for. Who was the first.'

'I was Chrona.'

'The Princep and Authoring Envoy chose well for the

wrong reasons.'

Basilica ignored this and said. 'I've advised any of those Sororibus taking seats in the Suffragaito they are volunteers for the initiative. In addition to the one hundred. All those who choose their Peace are having their full consciousness examined.'

'You looked further into the details of your predecessor?'

'Yes Chrona. She never formed a bond with another Sororibus. Citing the need to devote her time to her work. However, she maintained several servant and companion Adules in her household. Now that the records have been examined, her life away from her tasks was unusually private. This was concealed behind relationships with those she cultivated whom perhaps believed they were experiencing friendship however my review of the Sharing suggests relationships were formed for the purpose of...'

'Strategic influence.'

'Yes Ageless One. And a broader subterfuge. Her relationships with any one Adule commenced earlier and lasted longer than is typical.' Basilica was a little reluctant to impart the next statistic. 'Careful examination of records, intentionally shrouded with what can be seen in this light as omissions and falsifications, reveal she...interacted with significantly more Adules than might be usual in our culture.'

Basilica got the sense that Chrona knew something she didn't. 'And how many is that?'

'About five times the number a...youthful and energetic Sororibus might maintain as a part of a household. But she resided beside a Botanic Garden she convinced a philanthropist to build. It had a large workforce with whom, on examination of the rudimentary

Sharing of the Adules who work there, appear now to have been interchangeable with those in her household.'

'No wonder she looked so worn when we met. Which was on a handful of occasions only. She suggested her tasks were exhausting but fulfilling. I'd assumed this was a refence to Authorship.' Basilica smiled. A sincere but still reverential acknowledgement that her idol since childhood was indeed possessed of a sense of humour. Chrona now became suddenly grim. 'The *Author* has been sharing the Sororibus mind with Adules. *All* of it. And worse I fear. I believe now we saw only a fraction of the genius we are dealing with.'

'An Authoring Envoy not part of the Sisterhood. A male.' Basilica knew too little of the individual to fully grasp what was a risk. 'A… child of a Sympathetic? Risen to such a place of authority and influence. It's unthinkable.'

'Deliver everything to me. Every trace of data you can find associated with *him* and *his* Adules. From all the Author's associates you consider it necessary, gone to Peace or not, I will need to have *their* full consciousnesses to interrogate. And have all the private moments unlocked. Unique over millennia for such an invasion of privacy to be contemplated. I alone will have access to these passages of their lives. And your next tasks Envoy?'

'Redouble and widen the investigation into the…Author, such that every detail that can be found will found. Bring together the best Timeline auditors in their hundreds and map the anomalies you have identified. I assume the fact that the Authoress was one with a concealed gender is not to be made known.'

'We must do all we can to keep the Author, who *abides still* Envoy, from knowing the depth of our understanding of what he contrived. I regret now my approach to the Assembly as we may have been better served had we abided in silence for a time. However my knowledge was imperfect.' Basilica was processing the fact that the Author was somehow still at large. 'Execute your plan. We will meet after the next sitting of the Suffragaito.'

Buddhists

It was awkward. And Helen didn't do awkward. Usually. Unless she caused it, in which case she thrived on it. But this old Buddhist Monk had outsmarted her and now her array of probing questions evaporated in the face of a kindly old man. The Bastard. And he had brought out his entire monastery arrayed around him to watch the interview. The interview was supposed to be with a stratospherically successful Futures Trader who had suddenly decided to become a Monk. He had been worldly a year ago. *Very* worldly. Helen thought it would be interesting to joust a little on the interface between the worldly life he had left behind, and, though she would not say it in so many words, the boring as batshit life he had chosen for himself. He'd seen her interviews. He said he thought it would be fun and handled to tour of the monastery segment of the interview. And then handed it off to an old man. Bastard.

Now she was confronted with creating the most boring piece of television she had ever been responsible for. However the old monk smiled. 'You think I have caught you in a net. But the net is of your own making.'

'Ooookay. To hell with it.' she thought. *I'll stick with questions, with an adjusted emphasis, rather than try to make up some insipid ones as I go along.'*

Helen could never fully grasp the impact she had on people. It even stirred in a man who thought he could love nothing more than the teachings of the Buddha. 'My research has been sufficiently inadequate to have left me unable to know how to address the…guy in charge of the monastery.'

'There are a number of honorifics that might be used. I appreciate your desire to find out. Bhante is how I'm called here.'

'And you came to be a monk early in your life?'

'My parents where poor. Peasants is a word that might have a negative connotation, but that's what they were. They were honest, hardworking and dignified. But very poor. They fled the Chinese invasion of Tibet, experienced great hardship and…adventures before settling in Northern India. At the age of seven I was discovered as the reincarnation of a much-revered lama. I left my family forever and moved to the Monastery in Sikkim. I resided there until some visitors from your country, this was back in the nineteen sixties, convinced me to found a monastery in North America to bring the enlightenment here to this beautiful city.'

'Which wasn't enlightened prior to your arrival?'

He laughed. 'I cannot make a judgement on that because I wasn't here. It was remiss of me not to have said that their desire was to bring the enlightenment of the teachings of Buddha to your city. I abbreviated it to see if you were planning to go easy on a feeble old man.'

Helen laughed. 'Having met you Bhante, feeble is not an adjective that springs to mind.' This sincere observation was followed up by. 'Is it enlightened to choose to marry, have a child and abandon them.'

The old man had to think a while before answering. 'My response is that the Buddha made this great sacrifice to seek the enlightenment desperately needed by mankind to demonstrate a pathway to peace and an end to suffering. But I find that answer unsatisfying. Because for a wife to lose her husband, and a child to lose a father means that he was the cause of suffering while also on a journey to find its remedy. And so, you would ask if, today, a man or a woman leaves their partner and children to find enlightenment are they not being selfish in wanting to possess this enlightenment for themselves at the expense of their family.'

'That was indeed my follow up question.'

A voice an into her earphone said. *'Christ Helen. What is this guy a hundred.'* There was laughter from her producer as there almost always was. *'Give the poor old guy a break.'* He knew Helen had quite a bit of material to get though. All of it crafted for a Futures Trader 'playing dress up for a while' as she'd put it.

Helen was sure if she was interviewing the Dalai Lama he would slay her on every question she had while she and everyone else would love him for the answers and the way he delivered them and feel good about themselves. All unawares however, it was she that had melted the Bhante's heart. She changed the subject, convinced the Bhante would go off and meditate on the issue of family abandonment and in all probability come up with a satisfactory answer. For him at least.

'So monks Bhante...the celibacy thing. Does it get... hard sometimes.'

He laughed. This was firmer ground. 'There are many many worldly things which seek to come between a monk and the path of enlightenment.'

'And so how does a monk handle that.'

He laughed again. 'It's handled by monks and nuns as it has been since humans were confronted with such a predicament. The mind is restored to a placid state and the frequency of the struggles with celibacy reduce as one becomes more and more adept at the practices of the Buddha.'

'Buddhists are of course atheists. Right?'

'Yes. But it's important to point out that worshipfulness and spirituality does not need to suggest a god or creator being. We worship the Buddha in the manner of awe, and deep gratitude.'

'Although some might call it a philosophy, Buddhism looks more like an organised religion. Do you think that was the Buddha's intention.'

'Frankly, it's my belief that humans like to organise in a variety of ways. To come together in a monastery is one of them. And so, as Christ did not specifically recommend the formation of monasteries, some people find more success in pursing their spiritual journey in this kind of fellowship. Others in different arrangements. I believe the Buddha would be satisfied with all of them.'

'Even boys as young as six are sent to monasteries. In many countries the authorities have an 'age of consent'. Even though this is for a different purpose, do you think these boys have any real opportunity…sufficient maturity…to decide to devote the rest of their lives to a religious practice.'

'Although a very valid concern, some of these boys receive food and an education which they would not have if they stayed with their parents. And some young men leave the order to pursue secular lives. And this is a welcome development. Often they retain some of their practices or their love of the Buddhist path.'

'Would it be close to the bone to suggest Buddhist monasteries in poor areas should take up advocacy for family planning in the villages.'

He laughed. 'Nothing is close to the bone for Buddhists Helen. And who knows, your ideas might be the seeds for reflection on this matter, although I'm not in a position to say. Most of the monks here were once Futures...market people.'

'Do you believe in Reincarnation.'

'Yes.'

'However it can be neither be proven nor disproven.'

'I would need to reflect on that. We believe in the Wheel of Life from which one must transcend to Nirvana.'

'It's always intrigued me who organises all of that. On the one hand Buddhists are atheists and on the other there's this ladder to be climbed. You're several rung above me I'm quite sure. When you die, what deciding entity says, 'Okay. Grasshopper time for you' or 'Get to the bottom of the pack so you're a Futures Trader this time around'.'

'It is more about the different states a person can be in during their journey; or samsara.' He smiled benignly. 'Of course it is a wheel shape rather than a ladder shape. The less desirable realms being

Hell Realm and The Realm of the Hungry Ghost.'

'And where would you place me. Now that you know me so well.'

'You are in the Human Realm.' He laughed. 'Poised for ascension into Nirvana.' The Bhante was having the same experience as thousands before him. Helen was beyond special. He would cast away his life's work of devotion if she would only ask him to join her on her journey.

'Wow. What do I need to do to get into that club.'

The Bhante wanted to say. *'Nothing. Keep being yourself.'* Which he would never say to anyone. He went with. 'Only you can ascertain that.' Which they both considered lame.

'So Buddhism isn't a philosophy as some say. It's a religion with and organising force to arrive at an afterlife. Or a bit of a mixed bag of afterlives.'

In her earpiece Helen heard. *Do you have any idea how many complaints this interview is going to generate. Our fact checkers are going to be busy for weeks and then I'll have to be the one writing out the slew of corrections and apologies.'* Helen sometimes laughed on apparently random occasions during her interviews. This was one of them. It was one of the things her partnerships with Artie delivered. A slightly unexplained sense of randomness that would cause Helen to divert off script because laughing made her think of something else.

'Do Buddhists rely on the wealthy so that they can subsist in poverty. The charity Buddhists receive to maintain themselves in a monastery might have been directed to the desperately poor. To those suffering. Are the monks concerned to relieve themselves of their suffering while other suffer around them. Charity is, in any location ultimately finite.'

He paused for quite a while here. 'People come to me, and I see their suffering relieved. Some are in this community, some in the wider community. All are welcome here because we are sustained to be welcoming. There are many kinds of suffering. Buddha's heart was broken by the suffering he observed in the world, and he found a pathway to relieve it. We try to hold on to his enlightenment and welcome any to show them the path he found. And I have lost count of those who have exchanged sorrow and pain for delight in taking that path.'

Helen was happy to take a belt across the head when she deserved it. But they bounced off her quickly. 'Do you think I could cut it as a nun. Meditate all the time.' Helen paused. Looking for something else to add to that list. 'That's about all from what I understand. Meditate all the time. Lose a bit of weight maybe.'

The Bhante laughed. 'There are a range of practices, but what you describe is at the core. Weight loss being optional.'

'Are there different classes of nun. You know. Could I be the kind of nun who still enjoys occasional casual sex, alcohol binges, TV streaming, overwork.' She nodded to herself as if in revelation. 'I guess I'm describing my life. Is there a part-time nun program?'

'No Helen. But you don't need to be a nun. You're already over-flowing with life. You could go on some retreats or you could enjoy and engage in Buddhist practices in company or as a sole pilgrim pursuing the path He lit. We don't try to convert people so much as welcome all on the path of enlightenment. How they tread that path is up to them.'

Before she could migrate this into a heartfelt thanks and wrap up the interview which was less boring than she'd feared he said. 'There is one question you ask of all those you interview. Why not me?'

She heard in her headpiece *Because he might break in half on national television.* 'Do you want to boogie with me?' It may not have been an original closing trademark, but Helen took it on the road.

'Our entire monastery and I have been looking forward to this part of the interview most of all. It will sooth some of the many bruises of instruction you have left upon me.' He stood up and took her hand. The music started to play. She always chose it. He'd given her a good closing line. And they were all up and dancing. Some who had come to the monastery later in life were jiving and shimmying from whatever era it was they left behind. Those who'd been monks from childhood found it a bit more difficult but looked around for guidance.

'She always gets them to dance. Junta leaders, congressman, bag ladies, drug smugglers.' Artie shook his head saying this to the Assistant Producer who heard this comment from time to time, but with a different list.

'No one wants to be the global party pooper and say no. And who wouldn't want to dance with Helen Hunter.' Said Rhonda. Who was secretly in love with Helen. And she was straight with two kids.

They saw the old Monk had locked eyes with her in the dance. He was smiling. Artie had seen this phenomenon with many of the people she interviewed. It wasn't a stare. He contacted a few of the interviewees he had been the one to line up and asked them about it. Many said the experience was, for some unfathomable reason, the most liberating few moments of their lives. Irrespective of their background, their station or creed. They lost everything except their own, simple, pure selves for a few moments. And most were surprised, relieved and grateful. That whoever they were, what they saw in those few moments, could be a good person. It was one reason Artie didn't spend a lot of time looking into those eyes. What they had as a team was amazing, as long as he kept a specific part of his brain shut tight and locked down and buried; it worked. So far.

Any angst or discomfort from her interview evaporated during these moments. The interviewees set their child soldier or ex spy master to one side to get up and dance with someone who would be a much better child soldier, mountain climber, guru, tech titan or orca trainer then they could dream of being. You name it. Helen would run rings around them all. Without a hint of hubris.

That evening Helen got *the* call from her boyfriend Raegan of nearly a year. A record for her. The next longest record was not having a man in her life. 'Hey. Saw the interview. Great. Poor old guy was no match for you of course.'

'I hate orange. It makes me mad. I don't know why.' She knew what was coming and what she planned to do about it. It was time.

'Yeah...the 'casual sex' thing. Just a joke I know but the people I work with...you know.' Raegan would never usually respond in this way about something like this. He'd laugh it off with his friends and with Helen. It was a throw away comment in an interviewed and would be treated as such. However a process had begun for him. 'It's all over the internet. People think that I'm a...'

'Passing phase.'

He could hear in her voice the next phase had already started. He could suddenly see how stupid he'd been. Stupid. Stupid. Stupid. Why didn't he follow his own mantra to never call or e-mail someone about something controversial for at least a day. *Especially* Helen. 'Helen. Helen. Listen I didn't mean…I mean I shouldn't have…' Their assignations had been occurring at greater intervals due to 'work commitments' and, contrary to his usual approach to relationships he felt himself getting needy and jealous.

'Oh look. A red circle with a while phone shape in it. It's been fun Raegan.'

The line went dead. He knew the next thing she would do is block his number. He had thrown away the relationship with the person he loved most in the world. From her perspective she had been given an excuse to cut the ties with someone who had become clingy. *They all get so damn clingy.* She thought. *Time for a man free phase. Maybe break the record. By a lot.* But she wasn't so cold to feel nothing for Raegan purely because he felt too much for her. And it had been fun until it wasn't any more. And sometimes it had even been more than fun. *But they all get so damn clingy.*

She hadn't gone on a bender in a while. This would be a good night for it.

Join Them

Paul closed his laptop once the vision faded of Helen capering about with a bunch of monks in the morning program she had a permanent slot in. It was the only media he watched other than what he cued up on the progress of the latest wars. He knew a lot of people only watched Helen. He didn't mind admitted it to himself, along with millions of other he was sure, that he was secretly in love her. She challenged people's paradigm and then got them dancing. But there was something more.

He looked up at the bookshelf crowded with military histories and biographies, and in one place behind locked cupboard doors, he knew the science fiction novels waited to be read in his office when being a Professor in Modern History, specialising in Military History, became dull for a while. No one would dream he felt that way. A highly regarded Professor by forty, three books; for their genre a success. Which meant they were highly regarded by the critics, made a small amount of money, and gave the publishers a claim to have breadth.

But he had decided he was going change right along with the world. As far as his profession went at least. He encountered young people who, although apparently awash with leisure were pressurised because studies now had to compete with so many distractions which, no matter how much an older generation may not like it, were the cultural norm his student's lived in. And those without support had to work hard to keep themselves in a society in which their dollar bought less than his had at their age. And there was so much more they were expected to buy if they wanted to be 'normal'.

So he made his subject easy to pass. The only stipulation that they attend all the lectures either in person or on the big screen, with camera and microphones on. Excuses where followed up on and having a string of poor ones did spell failure. Other than that, exams were easy and for the truly dim, as long as they had tried, even a little, they did a make-up test. An oral multiple-choice session during which Paul filled the test out based either on their answer or the answer they should have given to get them through. Assignments consisted of coming up with a question about modern history they found interesting or pick one from a long list he provided. If they got some Chatbot to write it, he didn't care as long as they could convince him they'd at least read what the chatbot had written. Some were honest enough to admit they found little interesting about Modern History, but they knew they could get good grades with little effort and focus on what was going to pay the bills later in life. Others prepared great assignment and enjoyed presenting them and leading a conversation. Four periods following the same conversational thread started by a student was the record. It was all fine by Paul. A+ for the enthusiastic. C for those too wasted in class to learn anything and the occasional D for the intractable asshole.

It was during the contact time he tried to get them to engage with a subject that was fascinating if it was allowed to be. It might be a student sharing a reminiscence of a father or grandmother who had lived through interesting times. This might lead to relatives of another student contributing to the topic because it was raised over the dinner table. Maybe the storytellers themselves came in because there was an open invitation for 'older people who'd been there' to come and give their perspective on the slice of Modern History they'd seen for themselves. If all else failed, Paul provided a story from his prodigious grasp of Modern History wrapped in a tale about people, intrigue, technological development with a dose of gore, salacious scandal and blood drenched statistics. Students could ask a question at any time. People also knew they were welcome to openly voice political or moral opinions if they wanted to. Even stridently so. For a maximum of two minutes a semester.

Some days they would watch a twenty-minute edit of one of the high-quality documentaries which were emerging with fascinating insights into wars, the towering personalities of an era or the plight of the common people. Then he'd ask if they thought whether it had any bearing on how things ended up today. Or whether it helped them understand previous generations any better. Or simply how did it make them feel. Sometimes one or more students would come up with the response he was hoping to hear. That seeing it had made them feel grateful and fortunate.

His classes always finished strictly five minutes ahead of time so people could catch up on social media before the next class rather than during his or they could go and 'vape yourself senseless'.

He would point out to his class once per year, that he would rather live in the modern world with all its anxieties and problems, than in a world with seventy million killed, countless more wounded, raped and displaced from their homes forever. And each one of those statistics was a personal tragedy that affected more than the one suffering. However, the last major war on the planet was eighty years ago. And the later crop of wars from the Vietnam, Korea, Syria and Ukraine were partly proxy wars. There had been no multilateral wars engaging the Great Powers directly. There was too much trade at stake. It's didn't make the regional wars less nasty.

From an academic perspective, the problem was that all of the major conflicts had been done to death. New works were sifting through cold ashes or putting a new spin on what had previously been a new spin but was now an old spin. His fifth book, which hadn't been sent to a publisher yet, had simply analysed this phenomenon in some detail and the final chapter was a carefully justified reading list. Some of his professional relationships evaporated when their books didn't find a place on it.

He looked again at all the books lining his office wall. They could fit on a thumb drive now. They were more accessible to everyone than ever before. Yet probably read less. Like the advent of cameras on phones. Most users take many more pictures than back in the mists of ancient history when they had to be sent away to be developed. But they usually weren't composed and curated as they once were. The memories often aren't captured in a physical album or even a 'best of' folder in many cases. The more recent ephemera cast atop a growing mountain of 'the rest' to sift through.

He saw his books, sitting there. Arranged with subtle placement to be mixed within the great works, yet somehow prominent. Now he didn't care. Travelling to a conference in North Africa he realised it didn't matter how many people read his books. What really mattered was the number who *wouldn't*. And the latter swamped the former like a huge wave breaking on an amoeba. Followed by aeons of waves. Poor little amoeba. Of those that did read one of his books, most of the details would be forgotten in a day or two. The main thrust might last a month. If they were good books, the conclusions might adjust the reader's world view a little. Worrying about the average student's world view concerning modern history was a waste of time based on Paul's mildly cynical perspective on life. The rise of the Millennials was the beginning of modern history to them. And why not. The changes in the present happened so fast that except for some fundamental principles, and enduring values and truths, modern history had less to teach because it was so crowded out now, often with novel problems.

Still critically relevant to those who had to respond to geopolitics in a meaningful way including in politics, diplomacy and journalism. Like their predecessors, those in these fields may or may not take note of the learning from the past. Now those that did often made their observations through a lens of ideology or ambition. Not unique to any time, however it seemed to him excessive partisanship could skew any piece of information until it was nigh on worthless. All he wanted was to try to help young people where the teachings of history lay if they ever needed or wanted them. And keep alive his aspiration that the subject could be taught so his students caught glimpses of what it was; fascinating.

Contact

Slater and Peabody saw it at the same time. They were sitting on a log in front of a fire out in the National Park miles from any road or trail. They'd been hiking in the mountains since they were kids and kept it up as ritual every year. It survived partly because they took turns in designing more and more difficult and remote places to get to and it took them both out of a world that had become more and more difficult for them to understand compared to their simple origins. They lived six states apart, so their relationship hadn't suffered from the hallmarks of familiarity. Their wives were pleased that their husbands had such a wholesome pastime compared to what many of their friends were confronted with.

Sometimes they had a lot to talk about. Other times; nothing. And they were relaxed in either mode. Ten days in the wilderness was a long time to spend with anyone. They'd sat up later than usual. Savouring the daily ration of scotch and marvelling, yet again, at how much brighter the stars were. And so many more. Each one lit in their eyes by unfathomably old rays of light.

The ship didn't come in from somewhere and stop over the valley. It appeared. Out of nowhere. And it was huge. It was hard to estimate its size because it took up so much of the landscape. It might have been twenty stories tall or more. A soft rose glow emanated from the entire surface. It was strange. As if a giant ball was supposed to be pressed into the front of it. But the ball was missing.

Slater looked across at his friend with eyebrows raised as high as they would go. 'You don't see that every day.' They were a pair who had always tried to be unfazed with each other by life's developments and Slater was pleased to be the one to get in first on this.

Peabody wouldn't be out done. And some observations had to be made. 'I bet these Aliens are going to dress up like creepy green men, do a bunch of anal probing, or create a memory in us they did. And I'm hoping it's the latter. They'll set us free, and we end up on the front of those magazines you and I usually shake our heads at when we see them in the supermarket. They'll have a good laugh. It's hilarious when a pair of yokels try to make people believe they were abducted.'

Slater nodded. 'Otherwise in a few hours the government is going to announce another weather balloon has gone AWOL. And we're never heard from again.'

Peabody was intent on avoiding both scenarios if possible. 'Not this time Slater. Not this time. *If* I can get her number.' Slater was filming the ship with his phone and started making a commentary to settle his nerves but also leave the impression, for posterity, that

Theodore L. Slater and his friend didn't unravel when a shitload of alien spaceship landed in front of them. In the background he heard Peabody speaking rapidly on a phone that they carried which used the hundreds of satellites Elon Musk had put up there to keep in contact even in places no phone company dreamed of providing a signal for. The first was a friend who had a friend at a Network. Then an Assistant Producer of the show Helen was in. Rhonda reluctantly gave him a number because he convinced her it was a story they would be interested in. She made him swear never to reveal she'd given it out. She wasn't even supposed to have it. Only Artie did.

He called. The call rang out. He called it again. It rang out so he called again. A very annoyed, loud and familiar voice came on the line. She didn't look at the number. So few people had her number none would be so foolhardy to call it more than once. Except for Artie. 'What! For fuck's sake Artie. Didn't you read the text. I've been on a massive bender.' Artie always called three times if it was important. She'd sent him a text. *You'll need to run a pre-recorded segment and get that National Rifle Association guy to reschedule unless you want to see me puke all over him coast to coast.'*

Peabody knew he had a very small window. His voice came out in a rush. 'Helen I'm not Artie but please don't hang up we have the biggest story…ever. Please call me back on the app I'm going to send you a link to. I'm not going to say anything else. *Trust me.'*

Helen's best stories as a journalist, which she most certainly was even if she didn't always make it seem that way, always came to her from people with something amazing to reveal. There were also those that mistakenly thought their story was amazing. She's learned how to let the latter down gently and get the former to reveal what they knew and parts of themselves no one else would ever be given access to. It was one reason she didn't keep boyfriends for long. For a story she dropped everything. *Everything.* Friend's wedding. Sorry. Taxi on the way. Long planned romantic evening. Raincheck. She downloaded the App. 'This better be good. I get *mean* when I'm hungover.'

'Look at this Helen. The camera was on a middle-aged man with a five-day growth and heavy flannel jacket. He had the camera on himself intentionally so she could watch the scenery pan past the forest and understand the scale of the ship. She had only begun to grasp this as a shape which shimmered and pulsed when Slater switched to voice only. He wanted to get this out there before it was shut down by the government...or worse.

'That's one low probability outcome. Two semitrailers carrying beer crashing into each other after midnight. Right up my journalistic alley. We don't want a bunch of drunks on the road if they find out where it is.' At both ends of the call the parties were concerned that end to end encryption wasn't what it used to be. Her voice took on a compelling note. 'You're not playing some elaborate prank on me I hope.'

They laughed. They were both secretly in love Helen. And even given the closeness of their friendship, it was something they'd never broached. Getting her involved was almost as exciting as standing in front of a huge spaceship. 'You don't have to worry about that. We're you're biggest fans.' She heard that a lot, but it never went to her head.

'So what's the play?' Slater asked.

'You guys are no doubt weighting up the risks. Probing…questions about how this beer truck incident happened or maybe a government clean-up crew. One approach is I get what vision you can send me, then people will claim AI made it and you guys probably end up broke and divorced while my career is over.'

'Helen is there a play with a upside?' Peabody had been hoping for an in person Helen experience.

'I get there, and we're going to teach what are probably a bunch of *illegal aliens* in a beer truck to *fucking dance* after a penetrating interview. Gentlemen, it all depends on where *you are* relative to *where I am*.' Peabody said a single word. 'Co-ordinates when you're within three hundred miles.'

There was a long pause 'Life wasn't made to be easy boys. Get some vision and go as close as you dare. If you drown in the suds, it was nice talking to you.'

She called a number. It rang out twice as she was stealing the camera from her cameraman who had gone on his own bender knowing there was no chance of an interview tomorrow. He was secretly in love with Helen. So was his wife and their two teenage sons. Because he worked with her it all came spilling out one evening at dinner. His wife said she would understand…if… something happened. To this she added. 'You could see if she wants to come to dinner.' She changed cameramen every six months of so. They got so *clingy*. She called the number again. She knew he always looked at his phone. The answer when it was picked up was a simple. 'No.'

'C'mon Tim this is big. You'll never need to advertise your joy rides again. Believe me.'

'They are Military Jet *Experiences* Helen.'

'It's a MIG jet experience Tim and since Ukraine less people want to fly in a Russian jet. Tim this is big. And...it's Top Secret. I'll mortgage my house on this one.'

'You don't have a house Helen.'

'God *damn* the internet. You can't lie about anything anymore. I hate it. I'll buy a house to mortgage. Is that how those things work? The Network will pay the full costs this time without arguing.' At this juncture Helen got him to call back on the encrypted App.

'Why me? You don't know anyone with an *American* Jet Helen?' Even if he did secretly love her, he was going to force her to say it.

'No.' She wondered what she would do if she did have a jet option conundrum. 'Shit Tim why would I want one...Yankee pieces of overpriced crap. And...and why would I want any other pilot. The MIG it's...a classic. Isn't it?'

'As long as I get put on the list. Not because I'm angling for any-thing, but for the prestige.'

'What list.'

'The list of who might be next in line to date the most...eligible woman in the world.' He couldn't stop that coming out so added quickly. 'That's what the internet site said. You know.' He knew it was a common ailment. Tim's wife guessed it. She was secret-ly in love with Helen also. But Helen had nearly sent the family broke the last time.

'I broke up with my boyfriend seven hours ago and there's a list. And you're married Tim.'

'Yes. There's a list. It came through on one of my wife's social media feeds. Since we *did* have to argue with the Network to pay full costs the last time, she follows what you're up to. She got the news before going to sleep, which is what I was doing before you called me. I want to be up on the list to make her realise what a great catch she has.' There was a mumbled conversation. He had thought his wife was sleeping and was briefly embarrassed. Then he could advise Helen. 'She wants to be on the list too. One place above me. Bragging rights only.'

'Jesus Fuck Tim. A *list*. Okay.' She tried to pick something meaningful but not too meaningful. 'Would number seven work. And sorry, Gillian is a solid three. Now are you going to able to take me to the biggest story in the *history mankind* in your old Russian airplane of not.'

'Hmmm. I was getting in the car and about to start driving towards the airport based on the resolution of the list issue. Now I miiiiight go for a coffee instead if you're going to disrespect my aircraft.' He would do whatever Helen wanted. He didn't have to make it look that way though.

'I'm in a taxi with a stolen camera. I'll be arriving at the airport with a fulsome apology for casting aspersions on your jet. It will be delivered in person once I have enough time to generate a suitable air of sincerity. Meanwhile I need to try to wake up some people I've never met. Hopefully they own the fastest helicopter in the world. And it's sitting at Denver airport. Because I need to find some way for me to be allowed to step out of you magnificent testament to aeronautical engineering, Russian or otherwise, and step into said helicopter to take me to the destination which I cannot yet reveal.'

'I'll save you endless dead end calls Helen. I've got some contacts to see what can be done to get you something fast. Fast means *expensive* you know. Might be someone who wants to be better than number seven. Which I would want also for arranging said fast helicopters etcetera. Bragging rights only.'

'What the fuck is wrong with the world. Sure. As long as they know that based on what I learned from an old Buddhist Monk, I fully intend to become a nun. Ish. I think from this point forward, after some drinks and a nice meal I'm in nun mode. Unless I'm not.'

'Details I need not pass on Helen. I'll call Gillian and ask her to make the arrangements. Meet me in front of the hangar at General Aviation. I'll call another contact to prepare a flight plan and get us a slot to take off, which shouldn't be hard at one in the morning.'

Soon Helen's taxi was being driven to a jet being warmed up in a hangar. She brought out some extra cash and asked if the driver could keep the whole jet thing on the down low. He said that she could trust him and he didn't need the cash. It had been 'a privilege' to meet her. He was secretly in love with Helen, but also a realist at nearly eighty.

She was laughing with Tim about their previous excursion, the state of politics, the social decay caused by new technologies, their family issues, and notables Tim had provided Fighter Jet Experiences for. With Helen, you always spent a good slice of your time staring down the barrel of the funny side of life. While conducting a meaningful analysis of it at the same time.

She had a brief exchange with Slater. Letting him know she was on the way and expressing her fond hope she was not flying toward

'Hollywood' by mistake.

'No Ma'am. It's still here. The improbable wreck between two beer trucks is even more fascinating when you get to *see what's inside*. We are *really* looking forward to catching up with you Helen. *Soon.*' Moments before she had called Slater, hundreds of doors had opened in the hull of the space ship and ramps came out at what they now thought was thirty levels. The craft started to disgorge aliens. They were humanoid in form to the extent the pair could see from a distance. The ramps were like escalators and once the aliens were on the ground, they were shuffling forward because they were pushed along by those coming behind. There were a lot of them. They were green. Though only light green.

Helen was in Denver in a little over two hours with Tim hitting Mach Two over the less populated areas. She paced on the tarmac for the nearly an hour until a helicopter appeared out of the gloom. When she saw it, she said. 'I guess it's dumb to ask why big helicopters are faster.'

'Yep. Sliding scale for cost also. He wants number three on the list and it's not purely for gravitas, so you'll have to fend off dinner requests.'

'*Fend* and *Off* are my middle names. Actually they're *Fuck* and *Off* now that I think of it. I can do dinner for a big fast helicopter. He'll be a bit surprised when *Gillian* turns up for the after dinner part of the date, but that's the way life goes. Even if this turns out to be a hoax. I'm taking Gillian to a Sushi Bar.'

'Did I hear the word *hoax* somehow get introduced into this narrative Helen.'

'I meant to say *not quite as newsworthy as expected.* Anyway, it will be a great story about how Helen Hunter got fooled into hiring one of the most iconic fighter jets ever made and calling in the fastest chopper for two hundred miles around to arrive at an empty valley where two smashed up beer trucks should be. And then use her ineffable investigative journalistic abilities to track down and *kill,* I or at least shame, those responsible.'

'Any press is good press for a Russian Jet Fighter Experience business in this market. And I'm coming on the chopper.'

'No you're not.'

'I'm your cameraman. The pilot has to fly the chopper, and you need to have your *truly* iconic features beamed to a grateful nation. You might take some footage of me while I look out at whatever it is we're going to look at as I project an air of studied confidence. And you'll focus in on my MIG Jetfighter Experience badge very briefly of course.'

'You're hired. It's a trainee role with no remuneration.'

'I'll take my cue from you as to how to respond to triumph or embarrassment.'

'The latter won't go out live but will be crafted into a little filler story. Some time in the coming months.'

'Which the network will pay for.'

'Yeeeees. Though we might end up in payment *plan* territory. If it's left on me, I'd estimate, seven years. Two percent down and I'll accept one percent interest on the principal. That's one percent over the entire seven years. Did I say seven? Let's call that the optimistic case.'

Helen was calling Artie on an open line. 'Artie. Don't talk just listen. Be prepared to break into whatever tedious pap those two are dishing up live as infotainment.' She used a specific word that let Artie know someone was listening and everything she was about to say was bullshit. She told him about a dying cult leader she was racing towards as he lingered on his deathbed ready to spill the beans.

It had taken so long, Helen thought it was likely by the time she got to what she hoped was a spaceship, they'd be shut out by the military who have faster jets and helicopters. But there would be a story in the tiny video clip and the fact the area was shut down. It would lend some support to it as might the disappearance of Slater and Peabody. The jet and the helicopter had to be getting some attention for such high-speed pre-dawn flights and she wanted to generate a slightly plausible red herring.

The large, and high cost per hour helicopter had to fuel up because it had travelled two hundred miles. The pilot explained that he was often hired as a backup for wildfires and military training. 'Three hundred miles an hour but she's a thirsty girl.'

'Couple of hours?'

'I'll be pushing the limit on fuel there and back, wherever that is, so we may not be able circle around too much at whatever…Gillian… Tim's wife, said we were going to look at. About which she knew nothing. She promised two things. She said we could exchange places on this list if she got to keep her house. And she said this was nothing I could get in any trouble for.'

'Sounds like we're set for a nice brunch somewhere within two hundred miles of where we're going. Oh. And I don't know where that is either by the way. Plus I'm a Buddhist nun now, but I'm not giving away bacon.'

She texted Slater on the app. 'Leaving Denver, heading for Boozewagon.'

Slater sent the name of a town to head for and then wrote 'Put me onto the pilot when you're fifty mines south of there and I'll give him a bearing.'

The fact that a MIG jet had flown six hundred miles approaching its maximum speed and met a the fastest civilian helicopter within a three-hundred-mile radius gradually filtered through the channels that monitor such things. Enquiries revealed it was Helen Hunter who had engaged the aircraft. Her producer was contacted and, reluctantly, advised that Helen was streaking across the country to interview a cult leader who was on his death bed and, remorseful at the end, was willing to reveal all. Bigamy, sex with minors, brain washing techniques, getting acolytes to sell everything for the good of the cult. Most people in the Joint Forces Operations centre were secretly in love with Helen. It sounded like the kind of thing she would do to get a story and those monitoring the strange activities continued to keep abreast of the situation and wait for the interview. One monitor commented to a fellow monitor. 'Deathbed. I'd like to see her try to get this guy to dance.'

They also heard chatter about a crash between two beer trucks. 'There's some Helen distraction for you. Likes to surprise the audience. Who'd get taken in by that beer truck malarky.' It was another good reason for them not to get too concerned about what might usually cause them to scramble a few planes to look more closely.

Or at least a drone.

The helicopter was on a heading for a town which, had the monitors bothered to check, was populated by ninety nine percent God fearing Baptists except for the family who ran an Indian Restaurant and kept their Hinduism on the downlow. When the chopper turned north however it was analysed more closely. It was moving fast for a civilian chopper. Monitors started searching around in its direction of travel. Expecting to find nothing. Because if there was something in there, they would have picked it up on its way in. However when high resolution satellite imagery was focused on a valley in the middle of nowhere, half a dozen people knew their prospects of promotion had taken a dive. By then the helicopter was circling and would soon attempt a landing. All hell broke loose in the military. At that time the best intelligence they had was coming straight from Helen.

She and the two men with her had begun reporting on the biggest news story in the history of news stories. Helen hadn't chanced another call to Slater so she hadn't anticipated there would be aliens pouring out of the ship from ramps on thirty levels. There were thousands, tens of thousands maybe. The Aliens continued to pour out, however the ship had become invisible in an instant soon after they arrived. 'Are you getting this Artie.'

'This is going live Helen. Are you ready for audio?'

'I sure am.'

The entire valley was starting to fill with humanoids who were either bathed in a green glow or had a green hue to them. Green like an iceberg lettuce. Towards the stalk. After flying around and getting a sense of the scale of what was happening, they'd dropped down to get some close-up footage. Helen had started describing what she was seeing and asking the same questions everyone else was. However Helen had a unique mind. She thought about the impact this story was likely to have on people and the upheaval it might create out of simple uncertainty and the fear that comes along with it. And this reenforced the reason she needed to treat it like any another day.

She asked Phil to land in amongst the throng of Aliens so she could give them the opportunity to share some first impressions of earth. Artie had the show's Executive Producer next to him. He was as disoriented as anyone, however he quickly determined that landing among thousands of Aliens for interviews was not a good call. It was dangerous. His love for Helen was deeply repressed, along with nearly everything else in his life, beneath a concern about how something might look to his boss.

Especially what the Network would be put through if they allowed a reporter to land in a situation where she might literally be torn to pieces. The News and Current Affairs Executive Manager had arrived and gave those instructions into the headset. She gave him the famous Helen look which was a simple, and compelling. *'C'mon guys. Let's have some fun with this'*. However her announcement they were going to land among the Aliens was premature, because the mass of bodies below looked up but apparently did not register what they saw. They wouldn't move out of the way of the chopper and if it went any lower, they would be landing on top of a tightly packed sea of Aliens. Shuffling away from the now an invisible ship as more came down. The invisible ramps making the scene spooky.

The Helen that most people loved emerged as the First Contact reporter. After those monumental first few moments of describing a throng of green aliens and after trying to land she advised her audience. 'It looks like we might be dealing with a very large number of rather stupid Aliens ladies and gentlemen. Our special department at the Network whose only role is to calculate the number in people packed tightly in football field increments based on high level helicopter footage will be coming back soon with an estimate of their number. They sit around drinking coffee and let AI do this kind of work whenever it comes in. However our Network is not joining the heartless throng of organisation laying people off willy nilly because of AI. My guess is twenty thousand, Phil is going for forty while Tim is sticking with a conservative fifteen. There's a serious aspect to these estimates as we've decided there's a weekend at a luxury spa riding on it. They would be with their wives if they win. And I…would also be with their wives if I win. Anyway, back to our story. These Aliens are too dumb to move out of the way so we're going to find a space at the edge which will give me chance to ask a few questions.'

Artie was in her earpiece. *Helen. The Network says this is too dangerous. And this time I agree. This is off the charts in terms of risk. And we're live. Around the world. Sorry Helen. You'll need to climb down somehow.'*

Phil was good at what he did. So by then Helen was preparing to jump out of the chopper and Tim was making the world seasick as he bounced around with the camera on his shoulder with the eyepiece hitting him in the eye. She went up to the nearest alien. 'Morning sir. My name's Helen and I'd like to welcome you to earth. What are your first impressions of our beautiful blue and white planet.'

'Moe.'

They stood vacantly looking at her. 'I see.' She nodded with interest and turned to another. 'And sir, have you travelled far to come here.'

'Moe.'

'Okay.' Helen started to give away those familiar signals that she was trying not to laugh in a serious interview, especially when serious people believed she should be taking it seriously. And this was an occasion for momentous seriousness. Or perhaps, for good reason, not.

'Are you excited by the fact that most people on earth are going to remember where they were at the moment they first heard about your arrival.'

'Moe.' Said another

She frowned and nodded as if at an insightful comment. She came at him with a followed-up question. 'Would you like to see more of less of our beautiful planet.' Helen couldn't help herself.

'Moe.'

'How much time do you think you'll be staying. Less time or…'

'Moe.'

Helen started losing it. She found green tinged monosyllabic and apparently idiotic aliens great material to have fun interviewing. Back where she worked the Network Senior Executive Manager was also losing it. In a different way. 'For fuck's sake. The most significant news story in the history of…ever and she's turning it into a puff piece.' Those of the Management team who could get there were sitting around a table with a monitor and gave him a 'shut up and let me watch this' look. One even ventured forth with a 'shhh'.

She turned from the Alien to the shaky camera held by a MIG Jet Pilot who was rather more in awe of the moment, and a little scared by what he was experiencing. Helen spoke to the camera. 'I think we've got a clear picture of our First Contact with an Alien species. They are fairly laid back, but when it comes to earth they would like to know and experience moe. And I think it's fair to say we are looking forward to finding out moe about them. Based on my early interactions there is undoubtedly going to be some rich cultural exchange between our two, hopefully peaceful peoples.'

She appreciated the fact that even in this extremity Tim had been holding the camera up to film them from the chest up. Helen went from holding back a laugh to morph into a *very* serious reporting persona. 'To you Ladies and Gentlemen viewing this momentous occasion, I might as well point something out now, because it's going to end up in the tabloids or on the more salacious television stations. I think it important you hear it first on a reputable Network so that you know about an important angle on this story and understand how it fits within overall First Contact narrative. These aliens…they're…they're not wearing any pants. From what I have seen they are all what we once, very naively called; male in gender. And…I mean…damn. These aliens are *seriously* male.' She shook her head into the camera as she said this. 'What is immediately apparent is that as a good host species we need to help them understand our cultural norms and mores. But sensitively. We need get these guys some pants, so they can start their visit without being embarrassed because whoever planned the trip didn't do some fundamental research. And we're going to need *a lot* of pants. The Network is going to hastily set up a web site called www. giveanalienapairofpants.com so that we can get this situation under control as quickly as possible.'

The Senior Executive Manager almost tore the earpiece microphone from Artie's ear. *'Will you start to take this situation fucking seriously.'*

Helen looked into the camera and the manager in question knew she was looking directly at him. Helen was complaint. In her own way. 'Viewers I've now been informed that I need to take this situation fucking seriously. I apologise to those who may have misunderstood this reporter until now. Let's recap for those who've only now joined us. A large number, yet to be accurately estimated, of humanoid, all male aliens have arrived in a valley in a remote area the location of which…I'm not going to tell you. They all look much the same and from the brief interactions I've shared with them, it's possible that the only sound they make is 'moe'. At this time, we don't know where they're from, how long they plan to stay nor what they want. Oh. And they don't have any clothes on. That's about it from me. Oh yes, and they're green in colour. Light green. Well. That about wraps it from here. Back to you Bridget and Liam in the studio. How are the weather conditions in the major centres at the moe…ment?'

No one told Helen to take her job seriously. She already did that. She was much more than an almost otherworldly pretty face. She had decided as they circled this vast sea of aliens, panic could ensue right across the world. She had intentionally decided to lessen the probability of that by normalising the First Contact via doing it in a way, by coincidence, she would like to do it.

The voice in her headpiece returned and said reluctantly. *'Do it your way Helen.'*

As this happened there was a development. 'Viewers we're going have to push back the story we had planned about a Labrador that can recover a rock from water ten feet deep. And yes, the gorgeous K9 does wear a dive mask. He doesn't have those air tanks though. That would be silly. We'll bring you that later because the US military is arriving in force at the scene of this moe…mentus event. This means it will be a good time for us to leave, confident our alien friends are in good hands. With people who are going to look out for the best interests of these well hung space alien tourists who I'm almost of certain are going to be our very good friends.' She smiled seriously at the viewers. Helen had interviewed a lot of military people. She didn't trust them. 'However it could be that what the US military is planning *for us* would be far more *intrusive.'* Tim panned towards the incoming military aircraft. The viewers could hear her calling. 'Brunch time Phil.'

The Senior Executive Manager in her headpiece was now saying. *'For Christ sake Helen get what footage you can from the military and then do whatever they want.'*

Phil had already heard an anonymous but authoritative voice in his headphones *'Get those idiots airborne'.* This instruction was for a similar reason to that which Helen shared with the viewers once she was back in the chopper.

'Viewers it's absolutely essential that there is no chance of a contamination risk arising from our contact with these aliens, including avoiding any interaction with our fine women and men in the Services. That's why we're in our helicopter, and we're going to get one last piece of spectacular vision and then be escorted to the location of the military's choosing while our *Network* negotiates with them. This intrepid band of investigators, who have been reporting on the biggest story in history, will be guests of the US government in an environment that is one hundred percent transparent. I'm talking Jersey Shore transparent.'

The view from above was even more spectacular than when they arrived. It was a massive spreading crowd of tens of thousands of Aliens. Below; dozens of military aircraft were flying over the area. Some on the ground deploying troops and vehicles. A Blackhawk gunship emerged from nowhere. 'We are now complying with the US governments request that we land, *at the very nice place we're going to live* while we're decontaminated and only have people with white suits visit to bring us wholesome food. We'll be asked questions about everything you all know as much about as we do.'

Over the radio they heard. 'Proceed to the landing locations immediately. Follow my aircraft.'

She knew they should land. It was the appropriate thing to do. She'd pushed what was a very sensitive situation far enough. It would be spectacular to get a view from a great height. And for some reasons she followed that little rebellious piece of her that didn't like being ordered to do things. 'But first let's get one last perspective of his momentous event. Let's go as high as this bird will take us Phil.'

And somehow, for Phil, even more than she might usually be, Helen was more compelling than the menacing gun ship. Phil lifted the large machine straight up at full speed. The Airforce pilot was caught flat footed because no ordinary pilot would ignore a gunship in their face. And this pilot had a military background. 'This is what it looks like from way up high viewers.' Artie gave her the estimate of ninety thousand aliens and suggested she do whatever the military wanted. 'I believe this is what nearly a hundred thousand men would look like if they all got naked, painted themselves light green and packed in really tight. This reporter is predicting copycat events all around the world now that this band of fun loving aliens have pioneered this kind of get together in the wilderness.'

The gunship reached their altitude. Flying so close to their rotor blades any other pilot would be terrified. Phil was pissed off at the game of chicken, but he would usually take the hint from a military pilot. He'd been one of them once. The Blackhawk pilot was being aggressive but ultimately, he simply wanting them to land so they didn't spread anything they may have picked up. However instead of complying, Phil nudged his machine a little closer, and then a little closer and then a tiny little bit closer. The military pilot was worried their blades were about to mesh like gears. He backed away. A more senior voice that had only known authority since early manhood came on the line.

'Ms Hunter your feed has been cut. Time to quit your grandstanding and land.' It was a voice that conveyed his intentions clearly. He would shoot her helicopter down to contain what he believed was clear and present danger to his country. No matter how much he secretly loved her.

She was barely listening because of what Tim said as he was speaking. He said it in his best Tom Hanks impersonation. 'Helen, we have a problem.'

She looked behind the seat into a cargo bay. The problem was looking up at her.

'Moe.'

Basilica

Unprecedented occurrence after unprecedent occurrence seemed to be coming her way. An Envoy never accompanied Deliveries. An odious process for those who oversaw them. To accompany the first was going to be a task she imposed on herself. Chrona appreciated Basilica showed initiative before she was told she would have to. When Basilica was told *what* she was going to oversee; odious had been brought to a new level. The ship had a weapon no Sororibus had ever been made aware of. The Ageless One had imparted the instructions at the same time as expressing satisfaction the retired Princip had taken her Peace. 'A proud mind deceived. I should empathise perhaps.'

Receiving her instructions, Basilica realised how serious a problem Chrona was presented with. She grasped the risk across time and space if the ship, or intimate knowledge of it persisted in the hands of the Author. The unintended consequences of doing what she was instructed to would lead to a tragic loss of a kind close to the young Envoy's heart. The Ageless One had caught the young woman's eye. 'That's right Basilica. There will be no Helen in this Renewal and its new Timeline.' The reason Basilica would find that tragic was obvious by the colour of her epaulette. Yet the Envoy sensed the loss of Helen was something even more deeply affecting to The Ageless One.

Basilica sat in the command chair as the Virides were unloaded.

Her crew were hand-picked from the pool of Renewal Bearers who, based on what they went through to be chosen for that honour, could be trusted with the execution of the unsavoury instructions. She'd provided instructions to the Pilot as to how to execute the Pulse function. She had not releveled its consequence. Abbey, a friend since her youth had gladly submitted to the close examination Basilica had required of all her crew.

The Sororibus were sitting in what was only the massive transport section of a ship made up of two parts. The main command section was the sphere of monumental proportions where the Ageless One resided. It was set on massive carved stone pillars overlooking the Capital. The transport ship didn't need a crew with knowledge beyond of some basic commands if required. Basilica soon wished she'd piloted the ship herself however she had reasoned her place was to maintain an objective and strategic overview. The ship was unloading at the first of hundreds of pre-set locations ordained over the next five years delivering Virides. The Pre-Sets were developed by the Ageless One. They were supposed to aligned with the needs of the Renewal designed by the Authoring Envoy, although the Ageless One might amend or completely ignore this. However the first was always the same. Two men in the wilderness called their journalistic idol and object of secret love and so the Timeline entirely unexpected and new to human history began. The Ageless One was closely focused on this delivery. Helen was always there to report on it. Chrona had selected this moment for this intervention all those aeons ago. It had to be after Kirby had left earth for the second time after her flying visit with husband, son and daughter. And a passenger who was picked up at the behest of someone called the 'Hope of the East'.

Chrona always scheduled the Delivery of the Virides for a fraction of a second earlier than the last Renewal. *Behind* the existing Time Bubble she had to set in place. That was the Timeline the current incarnation of the Sororibus lived in. The Deliveries arrived back in the unaltered earthlings Timeline. So for the next handful of years two Timelines existed. One of the earth's, continuing on its new trajectory, the other, now the ancient history of the existing Sororibus. If they did not arrive a little early, they would arrive after they had already arrived the last time. Chrona suspected that would create a hell of a mess with time.

Now in this latest Bubble, the fifteen-hundred-year-old Timeline marched closer to an Event Horizon. Those who made lavish preparations to cross the Threshold to Oblivion, waiting to be torn to shreds of time and space would have been disappointed to know, that the Ageless One removed the Bubble to start a new Timeline once the Virides had done the job they were sent for and all the Renewers were in place. This would be a new and unique Timeline. Different to that which the earth would have experienced *and* different to the last Timeline experienced by the Sororibus. So those preparing for the final Threshold were not disappointed because Chrona had left in her reconnected ship, to land on some new pillars. In a new capital. Fifteen hundred years in the past. Once again. Those 'left behind' ceased to exist. And after a fashion, never had, when she withdrew the Bubble and started a new Timeline.

She didn't tell the Sororibus about that part. She knew more about time than anyone, except perhaps Elouise who must surely be dead because Kirby never spoke of her. And it was still weird and difficult to comprehend sometimes. Basilica knew more than any Envoy, or any Sororibus ever had. Even the vain Authoring Envoy. Or so the very ancient example of her species thought.

In the chopper cockpit Helen got the strangest feeling. That Moe *wasn't supposed to be there*; first in the simplistic sense that he hadn't been invited. But there was another, stranger sensation. He was *really* not supposed to be there. It was only much later she'd find out what that meant.

Basilica looked at screens depicted the unloading of the Virides. She'd never crossed paths with the creatures. Only an essential few of the Sororibus did. The Virides where she dwelled were self-managed. With supervisors and bureaucrats of their own kind. Producing all the needs for the Sisterhood. And leading full and satisfying lives to do so. As far as the Sororibus knew. And the Adules were reared ignorant of their fate. Or they were supposed to be. There were so many on the screens. But these were different to the Virides who served the Sororibus. These were in a holding pattern in their minds. And she alone of the Sisterhood knew what for. And this was only the first of so many Deliveries.

She watched the small drama play out with the original Helen before any new Timeline was set in place. She'd been shown versions of it by the Ageless One. They always ended the same way. Basilica had laughed along with so many others when she saw the interview and was amazed that Helen could be so calm and light-hearted surrounded by tens of thousands of aliens. Helen was the sole human who was always brought into the new Timeline. The sole human to survive. However the Authoring Envoy had anticipated the Ageless One's dramatic plan for this first Delivery. He knew more about the ship than even Chrona had feared. Basilica sensed there was something wrong. And the script which had been followed so many times was being changed. She had been waiting until all Virides had been unloaded. A mistake both she and Chrona would both realise belatedly. The Author, now a Viride, had positioned himself carefully.

'The machine ascends.' Said Basilica.

'She always acquiesced to the request to land it.' Said Abbey who had been briefed in more detail. They were both of the same lineage. 'The pilot always lands the contraption and her challenge to the military man subsides.' Helen knew her prestige alone would ensure a very brief and transparent quarantine period. She wanted to ask Phil if he'll go high because the journalist in her knew it would be a spectacular closing shot. However her tangle with the military was to be little more than theatre. She liked to disarm the powerful. If only briefly. However this time when the gunship came to escort their helicopter the pilot responded aggressively. Basilica had waited because she wanted all to ensure all Virides would be subject to what she was tasked to do to them. However the Ageless One had told her what to do if *any* unusual departures occurred any time from the commencement of the Delivery. This was the trigger.

'Abbey. Pulse the ship. Now.'

The word 'Pulse' seemed to trigger a change in the tone of voice and posture in the Sororibus she knew so well. 'She is the start of *my* line. As she is yours.'

'What! I don't care. Pulse it. Do it now.'

'I won't.'

'You what!'

'This goes against everything we've been taught. This 'Pulse' is unprecedented in any Timeline. To kill so many…' Only Basilica knew the truth of what the Virides were being delivered for and that it didn't really matter. It was sooner or later.

Basilica saw the chopper leave its position at around the maximum elevation the machine could get to and then streak out of the area. She strode the half dozen steps to see Abbey covering the console with her body, gripping its edges. Basilica suspected both what had happened to her friend and also what was at stake in those seconds she was delaying things. She tore the person she'd known since they were Aspirant Renewers years before from the console and pushed her own hands down on the reader. Both were required for this command.

She initiated the Pulse

She looked at the screen showing a one-hundred-and-eighty-degree view of the scene outside. She'd been told what would happen, but it was disturbing to see it. Every living thing fell over. Dead. Virides, humans, trees and no doubt all the fauna that inhabited that part of the earth. She wasn't sure what the radius was. Certainly, beyond where Slater and Peabody were. They fell dead in an instant. Every machine in the air right up to the troposphere dropped to the ground and every machine on the ground, including weapons systems were fried. But the one thing she wanted to see fall from the sky didn't, at least not immediately.

The Nudge

Helen's strange feeling, as if it was coming from outside her, translated to a clear course of action. She knew when it was time to comply with a General. She had what she wanted, the military learned what so many had. Helen would do the right thing, but not be pushed around along the way. She tended to fly in the face of misused authority. But she knew this wasn't misused. Merely poorly communicated.

However this time, from a mile up, she said. 'Pedal to the metal Phil. With this cargo, let's land out in the open where all the satellites can see us.' *They* could come to where *she* was. Landed, cameras rolling. An interview. Some part of her would not be cowed by a mere General. However this was not the trait she would usually allow to make decisions.

Phil was going to land it. Of course he was. Playing chicken with a Gunship was unusual. He did have trouble with aggression sometimes. It was a trait he'd had to work on. Ignoring a General and going up to maximum height was an extreme example of this tendency. And now to fly off. It was Helen Hunter who asked him to do it. How could anyone deny her? Or was that the excuse he gave himself. He'd still be in the military if the brass hadn't held him back.

Added to all this he heard. 'Phil. Your number one on the list. Now get us the fuck out of here.' Helen had a strange and very powerful premonition of doom. And it was urgent. Phil turned and fled at top speed from a General that he knew was fully intending to shoot them down. The voice gave them one more warning, which Helen was surprised she did not comply with immediately. He was about to order the gunship to fire on the chopper now several miles away when there was an incredible Pulse. A silent, but massive release of energy. Helen looked back and saw the gun ship some distance behind them, fall from the sky like a stone. They had been at some threshold where the pulse didn't bring them down, but it was pushing them forward at unbelievable speed which was likely to have the same result. Phil's machine was travelling four times faster than it was built to go. Twice as fast as any helicopter had ever flown.

However he felt a very refined sensitivity to the motion of the machine as they hurtled forward. In the split second that he felt the pulse weaken he knew it would be his turn to drop like a stone. Not because his machine was fried. But because his airspeed would be too fast for the chopper to sustain without the Pulse. That's if it didn't fall to bits because it simply wasn't built to move so fast. He took the only risk worth taking and spun the helicopter around into the dying Pulse while redlining the engine. He expected the rotor blades to be torn off by the Pulse's force. This was now pushing against them, though waning rapidly. He was flying a helicopter pushed backwards but it was ready to fly at three hundred and fifty miles an hour and the Pulse diminished to that speed over the space of half a minute. What happened next though wasn't a helicopter in flight, it was a rolling spinning tin can in the wind that was slowly brought under control. No doubt partly by considerable skill, yet there was a huge dose of what he *thought* must have been luck. It wasn't a landing. It was Phil getting his pride and joy as low as possible in a semi-controlled spin, letting it bounce and then it lay over. He knew the rotors would disintegrate and go flying in all directions, including through the fuselage. He wasn't left conscious to find out. His passengers were all knocked out. Except for one.

'Moe.' The voice was ironic. Triumphant. Oh how he wished *she* could hear it.

Basilica called up the next in command. She assumed now there was a trigger, hidden by the Author, in all the Renewers. Except one. The Authoring Envoy had entered into the Sharing with every Renewer. And had left a number of reactions to the probabilities which might transpire. All except Basilica. Whom she would convince the Princip and the Suffragaito to appoint as Renewing Envoy. And so he kept her clean of any hint of his malfeasance as she stood before the Ageless One. He had misjudged Basilica but survived.

'Do you even know or care about how many you murdered.' Abbey was coming at Basilica clearly ready to savage her. Basilica had some important analysis to make but she couldn't break the machine out of the Pre-Set. At least at that time.

She turned to her erstwhile friend bitterly. The Ageless One had given her Envoy abilities she'd had no conception could be developed within the Sharing. 'You've killed far more Abbey. Go. Find your Peace.' She said sadly. Even if her friend recovered herself the end would be the same. The Sororibus had an easy relationship with the end of life. Perhaps an echo of the horrific treatment they'd suffered at the hands of the males of their species. The small kiosks in which a Sororibus could draw a close on life were common. In shopping districts and municipal buildings. And on the ship. The foreign sense of aggression in the Renewer seemed to flow away like a broken dam and ebb to nothing. She would never be a Bearer now and never be able to live with the shame of failing the Sisterhood. Albeit under a species of duress. She looked across at her the woman with same colour on the highlight of her flight suit. 'Good luck Basilica.' She turned and left.

'Farewell my friend.'

Looking at the devastation of the Pulse was bleak viewing. But her mind was focused on one specific outcome of the massive force. She'd seen the machine Helen was in pushed at incredible speeds like a swallow before a hurricane. But somehow stabilise briefly, execute a series of crazy, barely controlled manoeuvres to crash land. The vital signs on her screen show three humans alive but unconscious. She felt a sense of relief Helen had survived. However there was also a Viride, barely discernible as a heat signature. Their photosynthetic genes creating oxygen from carbon dioxide in their cool blood. He disappeared into the forest. Lost among his distant relatives.

A tree wandering in the woods.

What Would You Do?

It had been a good friendship. He'd known both Lissa and Jerry before they met each other so it was two, now combined friendships from his University days. Thanks to him. He was studying Modern History, Jerry Genetics and Lissa Anthropology. They'd had a circle of friends and the kind of fun you can only get at university. Back then at least. They were older. Now they had dinner together. And played cards, which Jerry had always had a passion for. Poker then. Gin Rummy or Canasta now.

Any one of them might have been agnostic, lapsed Catholic, or grown-up Uniting Church. Paul didn't know or care. Everyone knew he was an atheist. He didn't push his beliefs onto anybody, and they left him alone with his. Then Lissa got propositioned on the street one day about what a wonderful thing was on offer provided she accrued a substantial burden of guilt, an opportunity to have that taken away, and accept she needed to demonstrate an array of virtues unattainable for any normal human, and, though not attaining them, still not feel like a hypocrite. Jerry went along for the ride in a more muted way because he loved is life and he loved Lissa even more. He didn't want to see his marriage fracture. He hoped it was a phase she was going through, even if only in terms of the intensity.

Paul let them know he wanted to catch up as friends as they always did a few times a year now. They were great conversationalists about politics, technology, the directions of their professional fields. Which were diverse, as were their points of view. So it was interesting. He didn't want to be converted and he didn't like talking about religion with someone who was religious. The exception was the Jehovah's Witnesses who he liked having conversations with, but he was never too rough on them. They had the courage to come to his door and offer, if the person opening it wanted to, some engagement in a discussion about what they believed and cared about. They gave him a magazine he would never read, and he made a few points he thought might be of interest. Usually about how the secular world gave them the vast majority of the good things they took for granted. He didn't hit them with his real atheistic firepower because he didn't take the same view as those proselytising at him. He didn't see it as his job to change their beliefs.

Now he'd had enough of being told what to believe to live a good, meaningful life, and if not, careen towards eternal misery and suffering. For two meals, one at his house and one at a restaurant, Lissa had more than hinted that she spent time worrying about his situation of Paul's soul and she was obligated to at least try to show him what he could do to avoid eternal suffering. She prayed for him.

Jerry looked at whatever tablecloth he was sitting in front of while this process ran its course.

Paul gave her more than a hint that he had listened to the sales pitch, and he wasn't in the market for a soul upgrade. But what he considered a moderate to severe case of brainwashing meant she wouldn't let him alone. He knew many people with faith found purpose in the community and led as happy a life as anyone might. And he was pleased for them. But Lissa wouldn't take no for an answer. He decided to give only one of the pieces of the reasoning behind his atheism. He had plenty more. Although he knew it was going to bring out the very worst attribute of his nature. A belief in his own intellectual superiority coupled with the ruthlessness of the military leader. A trait essential to win a war.

'Okay Lissa. I've listened to your carrot and stick bullshit. The brainwashing you're experiencing is a psychological *parasite*. It's a mind parasite that has *evolved* after many dead ends like physical parasites. The most fit. The most effective mind parasites survive because they fit into the wiring of our brains like the glycan mimicry of a bacteria. They feed off people, grow and propagate. They're an *irrationality* worm that you can't pull out of someones head once they've got their hooks into the brain Lissa. Here's some proselytising back in your direction. Is it fair Lissa, that you listen to my perspective. I've had to put up with yours.'

Lissa knew Paul well enough to know she was in for rough time of it. She thought it was going to be a good thing. It would test her faith and make it stronger. It was a little rougher than expected.

'Sure Paul.'

'Do you still have an imagination left Lissa. And independent imagination that would allow you to conceptualise something that isn't a pre-cooked meal you're obliged to eat.'

Insulted, and seeing no conflict between her faith her own strong intellectual capacity she said. 'You know I do Paul.'

'No I don't Lissa, because I don't know how much that worm...that parasite has burrowed into your mind. But let's see how we go. I want you to imagine...and fully accept that you are *God*. That's what I want you to imagine. One hundred percent God. Omnipotent. All powerful. Gave up your Son for us. Whatever the DNA your species of the parasitic worm has. In your imagination I want you to follow me around. I am going next door. You know the accountant's daughter right? I am going to brutally rape her Lissa. It's going to be viscous. And once I've done that, I'm going to mutilate her with molten solder wire. You're going to stand there and watch me and listen to her screaming and do sweet *fuck all* about it Lissa. She is going to be begging you to help her Lissa. Crying. Pleading. And I'm going to laugh and tell her that you *could* make me stop. No problem. But you *don't*. You stand there. Watching me torture her and then murder her.'

'Then I might wander through the town until I find someone with a newborn baby. I'm going to strangle that baby Lissa, but I'm going to work things out so it looks like the father did it. He's going to go to jail for life. His life is over. A hated man. And a broken man. And you're going to stand quietly by and watch me. Doing nothing. Then I might go and cut a dog's paws off. Only the paws. And stitch the stumps up and see how it gets along. After that I might tie Jerry to the back of my car and drive slowly. He's going to walk behind until he's exhausted and falls over and then I'm going to slow way down Lissa. Way way down. So he tries to get up and walk but he goes down. I'm driving so slow he can crawl. But not forever. It takes hours while his bones grind slowly against the bitumen until he loses enough blood to die. You love him Lissa. So much. And you tell everyone how much you love him. You want the world to know, make sure they know, how much you love him. You're in the car with me Lissa. Watching.'

'This is only one day. I do this with millions of people on millions of their days in millions of places. All of the meanest, nastiest things. Or the petty things. The hurtfulness. Game playing, humiliation, lying, cheating. You watch it all. Every rape. Every murder. Every drowning and tragic accidental death of a child. Maybe the people who say you rescued them are telling the truth. They did something and you intervened. Maybe. But for everybody else, it must be okay, because you tolerate it.'

'And you are complicit in every one of those things. Purely by standing by and watching such crimes you're complicity Lissa. Of course you are Lissa, I mean God. Any court would convict you. But it's worse than that. Because you're not a passive observer in some free will experiment. Not only are you an accomplice Lissa; You set up *the board*. You *made the game*.'

'However you have given people something called faith to cover over your misdeeds. The first precondition to experience faith is to create a story that can neither be proven nor disproven. Like; there is a God. The suckers stuck with the faith *you* demand of them are sometimes required to accept and believe the exact opposite of the scientific process. The flock is told they need to be faithful in order to avoid something unimaginably terrible and get something indescribably wonderful. But the narrative says it won't be easy. You need to *believe things that are ridiculous* and the more ridiculous the things you believe are, the more assured you are of getting that blissful outcome. And in case you need it, there is also a narrative of a great deceiver who tries to make things that are false look like truth. You must disregard his lies. And also, your flock can blame that Evil One for doing all those bad things. Even though they know *you made him*. Who is the greatest deceiver Lissa? You are.'

'Lissa, as God, you can somehow, in some bizarre and twisted process, stand by as I committed those atrocities. And yet, one reason your cult worships the hell out of you, is because you're so fucking merciful and kind. So good. So loving. So forgiving. And they should be like your Son, who's *also* God. In addition to a third entity that made Mary pregnant. Who's the Father and who's the Son Lissa? Three but only One. That would be called *delusional* in normal world. Only delusional people would believe in you. The greatest con artist in the universe. I'm glad I'm not God Lissa. I would find it tough to stand passively by and watch torture all day. Rape, mutilation, meanness, lies, cruelty, and not only towards people. But so many innocent creatures. For millennia.'

'Now we've both shared our perspective. And now I am *never* going to be able to relax and sit with you guys and have a pleasant meal ever again.'

He was at his car when Jerry caught his arm but gently. 'Paul. That was pretty fucked up man. But don't walk out on us. Let's give it a few...' He shrugged. '...years if we need it. And even if it's me and you. We can keep in touch. I love her Paul. That not going to change. I'm standing beside her the best way I can. She's a good person. She's still Lissa. If it's a parasite like you say it is Paul, she's kind of stuck with it. For now at least. She's smart. And that means she'll stick with it, but gradually be more like the smart lady she is, or she'll get past it like the smart lady she is.'

Paul was quiet for a time. Jerry didn't know which way it would go. 'What I did in there was wrong Jerry. Really wrong. I had promised myself I would get up and walk out if she started on it, and I could have. I most certainly *could have* Jerry. I used it as an opportunity to have a big rant about something I say *supposedly* doesn't get under my skin. And when I get like that on a subject, and not only this one; It's a big intellectual superiority trip. I don't like it. And I'm hurtful. Even to friends having dinner in the suburbs. I don't like that part of my personality Jerry. I should go home, and you should be in there giving her a hug. I'd tell her I was sorry if I didn't think it might make things worse.' He sighed.

'She'd appreciate an apology if only to reset things.' He squeezed his friends arm. 'It was the delivery Paul, not the message, which you were more than welcome to share' He knew his wife. And both intellectually and spiritually she would take the content on the chin.

'I'll send her a card.' The lame weakness came through in his voice.

A voice came through the open door behind them. 'Goodnight Paul.'

'Goodnight Lissa.'

Basilica

'I've failed you. I've failed the Sororibus.'

The Ageless One wasn't one to sympathise. But her analysis was fair. 'You came closer to thwarting the Author than he will have anticipated. Now that I've had the opportunity to study the Timeline he created he is truly a genius. He will have left many of his lieutenants of various stripes for later Deliveries. He knew the Pulse existed, which deeply concerns me, and he anticipated I might use it. He had somehow broken into the ships records to study the episode regarding the First Contact with Helen carefully. His powers are such that by his proximity he will have learned all he needed from those like your compatriot whom he misused. I grieve with you at her loss.' Basilica appreciated the gesture of understanding. She found sending Abbey to take her Peace harder than slaughtering tens of thousands of Virides and hundreds of humans.

Chrona continued. 'The helicopter was his one hope. He could only have come to know of its existence with detailed study of the ships files, which I perhaps unwisely made available to the most Senior of the Sororibus tasked with its maintenance with firewalls I thought robust.'

Basilica was becoming aware of a significant detail as Chrona continued.

'He could only have learned of the plan once aboard or he would have delayed his journey. Which he would have been wise to do in any event. Hubris. The undoing of so many. I must go carefully.' She laughed. She had been talking to herself for a moment and now returned to her young protégé, a relationship she was quite enjoying.

'He no doubt lost Virides he had cultivated and has now revealed the capacity to leave an encrypted response within a Renewer.'

'How did we come to have an *Author*, Ageless One?' Basilica had pondered this for a long time and finally thought it appropriate to ask.

'It happens occasionally. A mother will have a child with whom she finds it hard to make the parting.' There was an inordinately long pause which grew uncomfortably long as Basilica kept her eyes downcast. 'But it must be done. Those 'blessed' with boys are usually content to have them brought up in the creche's of the collaborating Sisterhood. Their identities as the child of any one Sororibus dissolve except for the markers that keep genes at a healthy distance. Those few unrevealed coming to the attention of the leadership of the Suffragaito are compelled to find their Peace. It's not widely reported. The Sororibus make and abide by their laws. One is that Adules masquerading as Sororibus are unwelcome. It's a tenant of the Sympathetics that this *should* be permissible.' The Ageless One spoke even more informally. 'Basilica…' It was the first time the Ageless One had called her by name, or any Envoy as far as she could recalled. Her powers of recall were however becoming a capability which was becoming less than it was. '…some Sororibus would like to see males re integrated, to a degree that I find mysterious. These females want all of the benefits our unusual matriarchy has delivered. But pay no price for them. Nothing is stopping a Sympathetic from disrobing and walking out into the wilderness with as many Adules as she can convince or command to come with her. Our society owes her nothing and should give her nothing. She can live as her Adules mature into men. Something that has never

71

happened here. She can enjoy their ministrations based on the instructions she gives them. I don't know of a Sororibus Sympathetic doing that. Nor have I ever been approached via an Envoy by some of the Sisterhood desiring to be returned to the place I rescued them from. Rescue being an entirely inadequate description of the hundred thousand who crammed into my hold.'

The Ageless One was reflective. 'The Sororibus's existence became complicated via my…tinkering to provide genetic diversity and develop a labour source comprised of a modified species. This has allowed the intellectual and creative flourishing their society has enjoyed magnified through the millennia, the number of which I have lost count.'

'However in this case I think the mother of this child was not Sympathetic at heart. She was simply one who found surrendering her child…intolerable.' The Ageless one spoke that word with a strange sincerity. 'And based on what I have now been told about the behaviours of those in the helicopter it would not surprise me that this individual, even as a newborn, has some capacity to magnify an existing predilection to make a decision contrary to what might ordinarily have been taken. She realised he was quickly adept at presenting himself as a child Sororibus. She was surprised at how brilliant her son was. She treated and came to think of him as a daughter, and her son was so good at being one she became less concerned about the child's true gender. And so he was treated as a daughter even to the point of participating in the Sharing. Unprecedented for a male. Half human.' Basilica was appraised of another revelation. The Virides were half human and half of the species from which her forebearers had been rescued from. 'She introduced her son fully into the Shared mind before he was even ten. Then his genius began to reveal itself even if his gender did not. Without needing to position himself he was soon celebrated as the genius of 'her' age. However, eschewing so many other lofty opportunities, he was admired universally for making himself available for the slow and exacting decades long task of Authorship. A task recognised as almost pure altruism. The influential Sororibus he cultivated, including the Princep, supported his desire to commence this in advance of the traditional time. The Suffragaito were convinced that 'she' would prepare an Infallible which the Renewed Sisterhood would praise for the full complement of their Timeline. The Sororibus, and you are a good example of this Basilica, are altruistic by nature.' Again the young woman kept her eyes downcast, grateful for such a warm compliment.

'And while he appeared to be Authoring something both Infallible and exceptional, he was mastering a skill unknown within the Sharing. Another example of genius which I hope I have enough humility to acknowledge. He used the Sharing to transfer his consciousness.' This brought the Envoy's eyes to the Ageless One's.

'He kept many Adules, whom he taught a Sharing more advance of the limited sharing they and Virides were thought to be able to manage to conduct and administer their tasks. And yes. *More* advanced than that of the Sororibus.' Again Basilica looked up surprised. 'This was how he taught, by the thousands I suspect, deep and abiding lessons, and how to conceal anything within their mind. And as we have seen he achieved this with a number of Renewers I can only guess at.'

'I'm certain many Virides know nothing of what they carry. Maybe a template developed with one of his familiars to be turned on at his command. His lieutenants and technical personnel will be conscious of his plans. Once activated. He appeared to take his Peace however he disappeared among the Virides. Of whom he continued to gather lieutenants and cast his will into Adules and Virides providing specific skills which, in spite of my...adjustments, the Adules maintained through the dormitories and corridor and after the transition. I've ascertained some of this by scrutinising information on his mother and the Adules I asked you to arrange to be made available. I needed to interrogate their minds in a way no human or Sororibus could withstand. And so via the details, his strategy became clear. Fortunately he could not convey any abilities beyond a one-on-one Sharing, and they could take them no further. However this would change if he could develop a beacon such as we use to extend the Sharing. Extraordinarily complex to build though they are.'

'That Helen urged the pilot to flee and that he complied are examples of the ability to push the consciousness of other beings. Enough to sway a decision already being considered or strengthen tendencies. He may even be able to amplify this ability when he can do so in concert with other Virides.'

Chrona blamed herself. This had all come about due to complacency. Or had she let it come about through a kind of convenient incuriosity. Had her incuriosity been the outcome of a sub conscious looking for a reason. An excuse to send no more Deliveries and so protect the ship and it's dangerous potential. Would she advise the Sororibus, including the two hundred thousand Renewers who had struggled so valiantly to be the few who crossed from one Timeline

74

to the next, that they were all going to go pass into oblivion this time. Except her. She'd be out of there. Maybe take Basilica with her for some company. A strange thing to consider for her species.

She laughed at her musings while Basilica waited patiently. Her mind began to embrace the depth of the risk. If he had learned of the Pulse, what else had he learned of the ship. He could not make a Bubble in time. Nor could she. Elouise, perhaps alone in the universe had such genius. However the ships capacity to move through time was something that the technology existed on earth to recreate. She was certain he had made a very close study of the ship. It would be fiendishly difficult. However even if there was a chance such a one as he could travel across time the damage could be incalculable. The ship had built in protections, but not so a replica. And once loose in time he need only arrive somewhere she had been. In the past, she wouldn't expect him, and he would take his prize. She had to draw him out. And so Deliveries would continue as always, though with some new Pre-Sets. She'd tell the huge number of Sororibus engaged in the Project these were a 'Preliminary Infallible'. She laughed again. It was not stupidity but devotion that made this race susceptible to her ludicrous initiatives to provide Rituals. Which she believed served a purpose in a healthy society. Basilica continued to wait until she'd finished her musings. She had a final ace to play the Author certainly didn't know about. Because in every cycle, right before the Renewal no Viride, Sororibus or human on *earth* ever survived to tell the tale. By that time Helen was always already with them.

She still wasn't going to give the Envoy an entirely easy ride though. 'So yes Basilica. You failed. But any among your peers would have done so. We're stuck with each other Envoy. The Timeline we thought we had now lies in ruins and the earth Timeline proceeds, now on a changed trajectory. And humans will take a very different posture to our usual Delivery program due to the Pulse, which has created a novel earth Timeline. I will not extend a new Bubble over an unforecast reality. You will need to recruit the best Sororibus who never met the Author and whom I will need to vet their Sharing. They need to start to plot probability trajectories based on this now novel starting point and try to anticipate the moves of the humans and the Author. So that I can eliminate him. *We* can eliminate him. A few thousand you'll require, if you can find so many uncontaminated. Possibly from the far flung regions. And they'll live in seclusion, communicating with no one other than you who will guide them and provide reports.'

Her Envoy was processing all of this. She wasn't putting together a team which had needed to build an Infallible because Basilica now knew there was no such thing. The human future had changed from the one that Chrona already knew intimately. They needed to take the new realities and project the new probabilities. The Envoy didn't know that the ship automatically did this, however it was a huge task and what the Sororibus assembled would be helping it by looking closely at key areas. The biological mind was still capable of intuitive leaps no machine could replicate. Reflecting on the circumstances she said. 'Basilica usually it's big occurrences that create large changes to a Timeline. Not so here. The decisions of a handful may turn the sequence of events which unfold. And may create a Timeline unfavourable to all.'

Jarhead

Helen regained consciousness at the sound of another helicopter landing. Phil was up and shaking her. She got up and looked around as a group of soldiers leapt from the gunship which arrived after the Pulse. They were training guns on them. 'Put your hands behind your head and get down on your knees.'

It didn't take long for Helen to recover her wits. 'Typical male. On my knees? How about – fuck you.'

The soldier repeated his command and men complied with it. Seeing nothing wrong with agreeing to a simple request if it might save their lives. Helen walked closer. Towards the man in front. 'Why not round off this memorable day by splattering a bunch of Helen brains all over the place.'

'Please step away Ma'am.'

'It's Helen.' Her brows furrowed. 'And don't I know you?'

'This is your last warning.'

Helen pushed the gun aside leaned in and gave the soldier a kiss on the cheek and pointed at him 'You're Jarhead from the Graceland Challenges. You've never given an interview. You might feel like it now because you're going into isolation with me. I just gave you Space Alien coodies.'

The man sighed. 'Kirby called me Jarhead even though I'm not a Marine. There was no point arguing with her about some things. Thanks for putting me into isolation. My wife's going to be very unhappy.' Though he knew his wife had a bit of a 'thing' for Helen and would want to know everything about the journalist

Jarhead had to relate.

'That's if the Alien bugs I gave you don't get you first.' The men around him had taken a few steps back.

The Absence of Mercy

Usually Paul gave some suggestions about what to do with the fifty-minute lecture. Sometimes people had other ideas that he agreed were better than his. This time he got to the lectern and said. 'You wake up in the morning, get ready for work, kiss your family goodbye for the day, and start killing people. As many as you can with the best weapons you've got. You work for a big corporation. The boss gives a little talk to your work group about how to kill people better, gives you some better weapons and tells you to go and kill as many people as you can. His boss figures out a way to blow up their houses, wreck their cars, stop them from getting to the train station, cuts off power and water and keep them away from hospitals and schools. Depending on the company you work for he might turn a blind eye if you rape some of them, mutilate them or shoot them when they ask if they can come and work for your company.'

'The only problem is another corporation is trying to do the same thing to you. About half the people who work there are trying to wipe you from the face of the earth. The other half, like in your corporation, do normal bookwork. Forms, Procurement, Human Resources. The Head of the Corporation you work for shows you a bunch of data and some narratives that convince you *their* lives are expendable. If you keep at it you are going to have killed so many of them, they will have to give up. You believe the head of you Corporation. You believe the company cares about the people who work for them.'

'Turns out you lose because *they* killed more people, burned more houses, train stations and factories. Your corporation is the victim of a hostile takeover. They gobble you up. The company you've worked for all your life…they disown you. Assets stripped it's left to limp along with the pieces the winner doesn't want. Most of the people you worked with are dead or have no homes and become refugees. Places you lived and grew up are in ruins. Also those around you heard about terrible things that were done to other ordinary people from the other corporation. Many disown you. Think you're a monster. Even if it wasn't you. It's called a war.'

'Over the last few hundred years there have been leaps and bounds in the killing process which means the people doing the killing can be a long way away. Firing a cannon or a missile. Dropping a bomb from a plane or piloting a drone. Shooting targets from a ship or a submarine thousands of miles away. Soon, no doubt, from satellites.'

'However be they Presidents, Prime Ministers or Generals they still need soldiers. Ideally with the latest weapons, good leadership and intelligence. And specialists among the ranks. But that all counts for nothing if they don't have an important trait. Aggression. And lots of it. Aggression and an absence of mercy will make the soldiers kill as quickly as they can get it done. All that training and leadership will make sure that aggression is targeted and efficient. Soldiers that are passive are dead soldiers. The best killers are intelligent and don't waste time with any other interactions with the enemy. Simply kill, kill, kill. Taking calculated risks. Or rather they take the risks their leaders teach them to calculate.'

'However that aggression may not come naturally. You've lived in a society where public displays of aggression are frowned upon. Its place is in sport and entertainment. Your aggression is tempered by centuries of a civilising influence. And the natural and normal reaction of many is to be afraid of and seek safety from the aggressiveness of someone around you. Get an authority figure to control it. But aggression in most males can be stimulated by xenophobia, nationalism, desire for recognition, fear of been seen to be weak, concern for comrades, the promise of booty…an unfortunate double entendre I know.'

A girl raised her hand. 'Is this why women aren't in combat roles. They don't have enough aggression. Too reasonable.'

'It's one of them.'

'Would there be wars if women ran everything.' She said. There was some laughter from across the gender spectrum.

Paul thought about this for a while. 'You know, I don't think there would be. There would probably be some nasty snits every now and then. You'd have to figure out a way to deal with all that male aggression. That would be your problem. And as you know from experience most males aren't physically aggressive unless they're in a context where it's predominant. Wars. Gangs. Prisons. Many sports. And, sadly, in the family home in some cases. But physical aggression is only one type of aggression.' He looked up at her. Almost apologetic. 'It's mainly due to the *other* manifestations of male aggression that it's still a man's world.' He smiled. 'Only *barely* though. The enlightenment of civilisation is outstripping evolutionary aggression. In some places at least.'

Basilica

Basilica had her first report on the probability assessment. 'Our rec-ommendation is to continue with the program of Deliveries. Partly he will need a critical mass to trigger his next move and hence reveal himself. Partly because the ship is also the vehicles for the Renewers and for the more mundane reason that as with each Timeline cycle the Virides population is brought to an unsustainable peak to pro-vide the largesse the population enjoys for the final decade. In ad-dition to fulfilling their…role on earth. If they are not Delivered as close as we can get to a million per week, the Sororibus's excess will be drained. Unless the Virides are…'

'Senesced.'

No Sororibus knew the full purpose of having the Virides trans-ported to the original Timeline. They understood and not a few disagreed with the build-up of a population to build a magnificent store for ten years of celebrations. Which was a convenient excuse the Ageless one used as cover for the build-up. They argued the Sororibus should be sustainable, indeed frugal, until the bitter end, as was their way at all other times. Probably a great many more Sororibus would have been displeased, and likely incensed, to learn the Virides were docilated as they boarded the ship, and that earth became a giant parking bay until their true purpose was triggered.

'Even those far from Sympathetics in orientation would be uncom-fortable with the senescence of a quarter of a billion Virides on their doorstep.' Observed Basilica, providing Chrona with more and more confidence she was strategic in nature.

Chrona got a sense that Basilica would not be greatly troubled by it.

A kindred spirit to that extent. 'Unloading may take longer as some of the new Pre-Sets so we may not reach the numbers which are the…usual target. We'll make Deliveries into more remote areas, so that it will be more difficult for the Author to muster his lieutenants and specialists, and we can track the migration of such minorities among their heedless brethren.'

Chrona did indeed feel she had the Envoy she needed at this juncture. There had been another time she'd needed a very different kind of Envoy and she had been fortunate then also. 'Very well. Aim for the Delivery of at least two hundred million prior to the Renewal Arrivals. We'll use some new Pre-Sets not far from human habitation initially as there may be some attrition at the Delivery sites until those receiving them are convinced there will be no more Pulses. I might look into some lifespan adjustments at this end to make the equation work.' The Envoy said nothing. However it was a silence hoping for some justifications. 'Basilica.'

'Yes Chrona.'

'Never forget the human world in which the Sororibus find Renewal would end. And always end the same. I did try to fix it for them before I decided to use their planet though I need not have done so. I might have accepted their demise as fate. The human world is torn to pieces. I have *mitigated* the worst of that part of their true Timeline. Ironically it would be much worse for *them* had we not arrived.'

The Panel

Paul was there as the representative of the views of the far right even though he wasn't one of them. He had always been broadly a progressive, though he didn't care much anymore. His position aligned to some extent with some strident 'Protectors'. However his predated it. Yet as an academic he was a tame panellist who could represent their views because this Network didn't want to give a seat nor a voice to a 'Protector'. They could be so noisy and confrontational and the Network, by their mere presence, might be seen to accept their radical positions.

Paul had come to prominence due to a paper he had written for a Modern Warfare journal, likening the Virides very much to a soldier in a war but led by an exceptionally clever leader. If Hitler, he posited, had taken a different approach rather than atrocity, he may have cultivated German Jewry into feel nothing more than patriotic love of the Fatherland and to feel grateful to live good and productive lives appreciated by the leadership of the society they lived in. The same with all the other categories of people he visited such unimaginable suffering and horrors upon. If he took these people and more, from all of the territories he held. As many as he could muster who were not productive or took up the land he coveted for his master race he could use them rather than spend resources visiting unprecedented horrors upon them. If he put the men and boys in poorly made uniforms and walked them over the line along with all their woman, children and the very old, those infirm in mind and body as well as those expressing views contrary to his Nazi Party, his war might have been different. Tens of millions. Walking west from originating all countries, languages and background he controlled or took prisoners from. And his lines snapping tight behind them as they filtered through. There would have been no holocaust. However his enemies would be dealing with a humanitarian crisis of unprecedented proportions causing their war effort to suffer.

So many resources would need to be spent moving and caring for the for a huge diversity of refugees to even a minimal degree. The populations of the host countries may find their generosity tested at the presence of twenty million or more people flooding across their borders. With nothing. Other than the clothes they arrived in. Intentionally unsuited to cold weather. This might stir prejudices in some, driving a wedge into the communities hosting these refugees, and demands that other countries start to take their share. His enemies army might swell, but with the intentionally untrained. All this would sow discord among the allies.

Meanwhile he would keep the most able bodied and capable as slaves and if he was strategic would treat them well and use every method the best of psychology could muster to turn them, partly by giving them some of the now abundant accommodations and resources. In addition to lying to them. Overall his production of war matériel would raise and the draw on his resources would fall.

The Virides were even better than walking the unwanted across the line. The care they required was an order or magnitude greater. And they insinuated themselves into the earth communities not as any surrendered soldiers would ever be allowed to. While no one knew if or when they, unlike refugees, might be switched on and become soldiers. In this case at a second's notice.

On the Panel Paul had been working hard to reign in his habit of tearing down people's ideas simply because, from his perspective, he was right. It made him feel superior and he reminded himself that most of the egregious behaviours of humanity were often associated with a need to experience superiority or at least influence. Magnified to extremes in the megalomanic. Achieved sometimes by a range of egregious behaviours. And when he conducted any analysis now, he reminded himself it didn't really matter. He'd even written it down on a pad in front of him. *'This doesn't matter'* to try to avoid in engaging with people. *'Why am I allowing myself to be triggered into caring about this'*. He wrote. He did this while looking at a speaker as if listening, caring and wanting to capture the essence of their position. It made him smile sometimes because they looked at him appreciatively as possibly the only one who 'got' what they were saying. He tried to reflect on the fact if he did not control this weakness, his only achievement would be to hurt someone who didn't need to be hurt because their ideas mattered as much to them as his did to him. And theirs would have the same impact. *Which was none.* As a historian he'd concluded that usually it was big things that had lasting influences on the future. And some heartfelt view expressed on a TV panel show was about as consequential as a house fly dropping disappearing into the carpet of life. He should have said no when he was asked to attend. He came because Helen Hunter was on the panel. He admired her. And along with a few billion others now that she'd been, albeit briefly, exposed to a world audience reporting on the First Contact, were secretly in love with her. He in a plutonic way. Or so he convinced himself. Having turned up he decided to engage only by giving a synopsis of his paper, which none of the panellists, audience members or viewers will have read. Why would they.

It was hard to keep quiet when some of what he classified as ideologues trotted out such tiresomely predictable views but also some things he was outraged by as a moral being and also a taxpayer. Virides were estimated to be around fifty million in number at the rate of a hundred and fifty thousand a day now. Basilica had introduced a number of efficiencies which had improved on the loading and unloading processes in addition other administrative requirements and shaved hours off the turn around so that they did better than one cycle per twenty four hours. Chrona had assumed the Deliveries had been fine turned over millennia. The young Envoy did not make such assumptions.

The facilitator of the program came to Paul who provided his opinion that the 'Moes' only appeared to be refugees, however they had the potential to become soldiers. Though they achieved a large part of an enemies war aims as high maintenance malingerers.

'The aliens appear to be an abundant resource for those dumping them here. Are they bred for the sole purpose of draining our resources? Will they all be turned on at some point as soldiers? Are they intelligence gathering organisms. Or merely a huge logistical pain in ass. Maybe all of the above. But there is no question that there is another alien power at war with us. And we're stupid enough to buy into their strategy and not go onto a war footing.'

'I think you'll find in the United States we are taking this threat seriously and preparing accordingly.'

In Paul's extensive review of the military literature, General's like the one who had spoken at length and said very little were a dime a dozen. 'I think you'll find General, that as with every perceived threat or the wars in our recent past, all but a few completely unwarranted, it's an excuse for the military industrial complex to get paid for research and product development in addition to churning out vast quantities of what they already have. Which in many cases are the appropriate weapons for the conflict being fought at that time. However the weapon's the US is buying or having developed now respond to neither the potential for a Moe uprising nor an Alien race with the capacity to deliver those devastating energy releases. One of the greatest Generals of the twentieth Century warned of this. But there are too many military men wanting new toys and too many ex-military men and Secretaries of Defence in the pay of corporations lobbying the government to get them.'

The General spent some time being affronted and detailing the many ways in which Paul was both wrong and unpatriotic. In his hubris, Paul decided not to even listen. A capacity he had cultivated in the last few years as cynicism crept into his core. He found it amusing. He didn't care if he looked weak, disinterested or foolish when they expected him to show some kind of reaction. He was usually thinking of what a plot for an original war novel might look like and how he might fit into it. He found that mental challenge quite a conundrum so sometimes he completely lost any recollection of where he was as he wrote what appeared to be notes but was in fact a plot line. He did it during boring conference papers and staff meetings. The result was always disregarded as hopelessly flawed in the historical context he was so well-versed in.

In this case he ignored the General by imagining a clock running down a hill. It was laughing and singing. Which he found amusing. This agony was almost over. He came out of his trance and looked at his watch. The bright spot had been listening to Helen. However she'd said little. He'd assumed not wanting to get mistaken for some someone who agreed with the rest of the panellists. The worst disappointment, though he refused to admit it to himself, was that she was seated at the far end of the long, curved desk.

He heard the facilitator repeat a question directed at him looking for a response to the general's indignant monologue. He should have taken note at that point they were not going out live and recognised the trap that lay before his ego. 'Pretty much the same ideological self-serving crap we've heard from most of the panel.' He looked at his watch again. Which was rude and arrogant. He wouldn't stay and chat. He'd lie and say he was late for an appointment. To do nothing. Which he decided was better than this. Unless *she* wanted to say hello.

'Perhaps you'd like to expand on that.'

'Time is running short and there are others who would like to repackage what they've already said and put their cases to us with even greater passion and vehemence I expect.' Any of his students watching this would be surprised at the dismissive and patronising way he was behaving. He was nothing like this in a lecture. That was that environment people who wanted to moralise or dictate only had a couple of minutes. And a couple of minutes of that sort of thing was interesting and offered its own kind of enlightenment. However they weren't spreading their ideological shit though a whole population on television, which in spite of himself he found annoying. But most importantly, in his classes it was an environment where everyone could have a laugh about the subject matter and often did. Entrenched ideologues never laughed. One of the reasons he disliked them so. The absence of a capacity to ridicule the self was a sure sign of the autocrat, the zealot or the plain tiresome. The was the harbinger of the death of free speech when the self-righteous gained power.

'Not really Paul. Everyone on the Panel has had a good opportunity to provide a point of view. We'd be interest in yours, perhaps you had additional perspectives beyond the suggestion that we're being invaded by an army.' Had he at that moment looked at Helen, he might have seen in those prescient eyes where this was going to land him.

There were no half measures for Paul. 'Okay.' He looked towards a woman who had been representing someone in a court case who had been associated with the Viride sex trade and presented and argument that legitimising it was better than what happened in the 'unregulated sector'.

'First of all, we have our friend Tanya whose client was fined two hundred thousand dollars for running a 'Moe brothel', for the well-heeled. Many lower rent establishments exist underground. Because that's where they should be until they are swiftly closed by a justice system that should be tasked to do so. Does legitimising something abhorrent make it any less wrong Tanya. Madam, your client should be in jail. If you set up an establishment for clientele to come in and have sex with dogs, horses, cows, pigs or whatever else. It means jail. It's called bestiality. But really they were running the equivalent of a paedophile supply service. A girl of thirteen may have sex with a man over eighteen and enjoy it because sex can be a pleasurable experience. However in the legal system generated by the democratic society we partake in, it *cannot* be considered consensual. We have laws that say that girl is not able to make a mature, informed decisions to consent to sexual activity until whatever jurisdiction she lives in has decided she can. Horses also lack that capacity by the way Tanya. These aliens have an intellectual age of seven, and they can only utter one word…so far. Do they become aroused and appear to enjoy sex. I'm told that they do this *without fail*. Can they give consent. No. And is it useful to an enemy for their soldiers to have lots of sex with local women or men. It helps drive a wedge between the sexes or existing relationships of those in a community who agree and disagree. Relationships *are* our civilisation Tanya. We have no civilisation without relationships. All kinds of them. And in a society that was already struggling with the impact of porn on males, and crazy social media expectations on females and vice versa we now have a serious problem with how these enemy soldiers are being used and mistreated. We would never conceive of any of this for a prisoner of war. Or a chimp.'

Before anyone could raise an objection Paul rolled on. 'And we have the young lady from the audience expressing outrage at how these creatures are being maintained in the 'communities' provided for them by governments. Young lady how much do you pay in tax each year? Working for an NGO probably I would guess seven to eight thousand dollars? If that.' She looked grimly and nodded. 'And I have no doubt you're aware the aliens cost forty-five thousand dollars each to sustain for a year. So you and about six of your co-workers are paying for one. If people care about the environment, more food has to be generated, more fresh water used and more fossil fuels, yes fossil fuels which still dominate our power supplies, have to be burned. And the pie feeding the system does not magically grow. So every mouthful of food one of these creatures eats is one third of a mouthful of food the poor person *you used to care about* no longer gets. Society will hand out only so much largesse to the poor who are often poor because of disadvantage and misfortune. They suffer while you sermonise. There is a program where these creatures can be taken into people's homes to undertake light domestic duties, give them a better environment than the 'communities' and take the pressure off government coffers. Do you participate in this program?'

She tried to answer with an explanation as to why not, but he had moved across to a neighbour in the panel. 'And we have the statistician gentleman who suggests delivery of these creatures are falling. Certainly it looks that way in the US. Looking at a *short-term trend line*. However if you look at the longer-term trends, we get a trend line that bounces around. Deliveries to any one country are sporadic in time and space. This is because if we got consistent deliveries, it would be more likely to cause a reaction in our population. Many counties don't provide accurate assessments to inform your statistics because they may not want the number known depending on what they decide to do with the poor creatures. While more than a few of those dumped by the Second Enemy are not captured in statistics because they are being dumped over *our* borders to avoid the very resource consumption issues being ignored by this panel. And we're foolish enough to accept them.' There was a crowd voices responding to this last statement. But one voice cut though. As it always could. And would always get answered first.

'So why that energy surge at the first delivery.' Said Helen. Who had been chastening, for a time, internally and by the public for her bon homie prior to such a tragic conclusion to the First Contact. Internally and from the public's perspective Helen bounced back. That was Helen. Publicly and privately her mischief, mistimed after the fact, was forgiven.

It wasn't hard to pick up that his tone changed. He shrugged. 'Let us know not to mess with them maybe?' She caught his eye and he was gone. 'Or it meant that during the deliveries that followed,

when authorities were too gun-shy to go and…give them pants…'
He smiled. '…the world saw tens of thousands starving to death
on the Networks and internet and everybody felt bad about themselves. Which is a normal reaction. Eventually remote-controlled
equipment brings them out in groups. Now we're assuming it was a
one off and we're hooked.'

'Why not use the weapon all the time though. If it's a war?'

Paul had thought a great deal about this. 'I think they don't want
to drive us into hiding. They want a war of attrition that doesn't
look like one. Because they want our stuff. So many governments,
including our own, have tried all kinds of methods to clear out a
population, but not damage any assets. If every soldier and civilian
is dead in enemy territory, the victor can walk in like Goldilocks and
take over the *Lebensraum*.'

The inevitable question followed that he, and thousands of others
had danced around and those that offered solution were vilified
for. 'So what do we do Paul? Let them die on our doorstep when a
neighbour drops them off?'

Unfortunately for Paul he got the order wrong for what he said
next. 'In a war you have to be merciless. Or you lose the war.' He
and the general shared a nod on that point. 'I would humanely
dispatch every last one of these creatures and every new arrival,
process them into fertiliser and plough them into the earth.' Mass
slaughter wasn't a new concept. Using them as fertiliser was novel.
But it was the fact that the position was being put forward so blunt-
ly by a respected Professor. Someone with credibility. Someone who
might have been seen as an authority figure. On a credible Network.
The audience was silent for an instant and before the vilification

started, he held up his hand. 'Don't worry. It will never happen. This recommendation is *only* if it were to be undertaken at a governmental scale. Country by a country. And our country will never do it because our people are too stupid to see what's really going on and would be too timid to respond to it if they did. I think I'll forgo the ugly jeering you all thought you were *incapable of*.' He got up and walked out. Indeed to a raucous departure.

Basilica

'That doesn't usually happen of course.' Basilica had been shown most of the program. The two were becoming relaxed together, Basilica given occasional reminders when to snap back into Envoy status.

'No. Helen isn't there, nor Paul. Panels like this occur but they are as inconsequential as they all usually are. There was no Pulse. Helen went to a few Deliveries and got bored although to her credit she was diligent in the exposing mistreatment of the Virides. The only kind of interviews she did with no dancing.'

'Is there a chance anyone would take him seriously?'

'He's correct in his assessment that no democracy could take such a drastic step. And those that do 'despatch' the Virides as he puts it, do not do it in large numbers. And those places are the focus of accelerated deliveries on our part. So they get the message. He was correct in nearly every particular he described. Except the most important one. Their function responds to a future reality he could never predict. He's a man who has decided that his actions have no bearing on big events. Keep a watch on him. In his case he's wrong. And try not to sympathise. It's the same in the end. For all of them.'

The Envoy's eyebrows rose.

'All but one.' Chrona, corrected herself.

Jailbird

'Paul, what have you learned from this?' Helen knew Paul would be neither a martyr nor defensive. She did her research including talking to some of his students and faculty.

'I think it's something to do with not trusting anyone in the television industry.'

She smiled. She was the only one who he would agree to an interview with. She was used to that although she found it a bit mystifying on some occasions. 'That's a little broad. It's the Networks that don't like your message you need to watch out for. I've been edited myself. Maybe not with such serious ramifications.'

'My whole social media, email and snail mail is so polarised.' Paul mused. 'I don't open any of it anyway. If anyone has the blood of sixty thousand Moe's turned to fertiliser on their hands, it's the Network. I notice the cell next to me is bare of their CEO.'

'Yes. Omitting your statement that your plan would be unconscionable without a seal of Government was cut out and I quote. She pretended it was written in her pad *'because the program was running over time because Professor Emmerson spent so much of it castigating panellists and audience members'*.'

'I have a superiority complex that is immediately followed by a 'why do I have to be such an ass' complex and then it all devolves into a 'what does it really matter' complex.'

'Sounds complex.'

'You should see it from my side.'

'A lot of people want to know if you would personally slaughter all of the Moes or get some evil henchmen to do it.'

'I think my arm would get tired.'

'You really do like to court hate mail Paul.'

'Yes. It's wrong to trivialise it. Which is what I do too often. I'd press the button Helen to painlessly euthanise every last one. They are the army of an Alien enemy. It's only that they don't look like the armies we're used to. They've come here to fight a war of attrition. And they're winning. It doesn't look that way because they're passive. Imagine if they were even the slightest bit aggressive, our approach might be different. But looked at in a certain way you could say they're raping our women, destroying our resource base, creating discord among the people and their Government, creating international tension and maybe doing a great job of espionage because they are used everywhere as a low paid labour source if someone will take them off the governments hands. And one day Helen, they'll wake up. And that's when the real war will start. But it'll be too late.'

'So there's no hope.'

'Build yourself a bunker. I wish people would imagine the most unpleasant war conceivable. Even if there's a tiny risk, we should counter it now at seventy million. Wars are won by intelligent aggression. The best applied resources to execute relentless aggression which is both a willingness to kill and a willingness to take calculated risks and losses to do so. Civilisation, cradle of everything sacred to me as it is, ironically built on war, has left humanity unable respond to passivity with aggression in an organised way. Partly because some of the greatest travesties in human history have involved aggression against the passive and defenceless. Though I have gone off the fertiliser idea.'

'Oh. Is that a good thing?' Helen didn't have to work very hard to interview Paul to get good television.

'Yes. Although I'm neither an agronomist nor a geneticist, there must be a potential risk from putting a huge volume of Alien genes into the soil and have the possibility of genetic transfer into crops or pastures which may impact the food chain. The most appropriate approach I believe, is to euthanise them humanely, slurry up the remains and pump them into a deep ocean trench where the genetic material will be kept permanently separate from our civilisation.'

'A new take on segregation. What do you say to people who say you're a heartless monster.'

'I say I care about *humans* Helen. Do they? People who say that about me are the *real* heartless monsters. Because that's what they're being toward the poorest humans or those who would take any work they can get because they want the basic dignity of working for what they have if it's possible to do so. If we had a hundred million chimpanzees too many in the world, we would reluctantly cull them. Chimpanzees are closer to us genetically and have an intelligence comparable to these creatures, although I believe that expands where they are given routine tasks. When the first one awakens, whatever their disposition, it will be another chance, a diminishing chance, for us to act.'

'A good line to finish on.' She looked up at the crew. 'Guys could you give me a minute.' That was unusual. Helen often had some observations or possibly ridiculous patter to the camera of her own devising which she might use, only with Paul's permission, and based on what Artie thought. An opinion she had never had a reason to doubt.

No one realised that the reality of being Helen Hunter was gradually wearing her down. The reality of being so admired. Loved. The object of this inevitable clinginess she'd grown to hate. The subject of a list that included millionaires and Emirs and astronauts, lining up to go on a date with her. She'd watched him during the panel. She thought he'd give an objective perspective on a question she'd never asked. When they were alone, she said. 'Why do you look at me like that.'

'Like what?'

'You know.'

'No I don't'

'A lot of people look at me like you do?'

'Ask them.'

'I'm asking you.'

He paused. Awkward. 'I'm not going to tell you.'

'You're not going to…what is this a guessing game for me Paul.'

'People hate me enough Helen. I'm not going to have some negative impact on whatever it is you…have.'

'I have…?'

'Helen, your obviously not fully aware of your…magical powers.'

The look he gave her shifted slightly. 'Ask someone else Helen. If you don't mind, I have some rather important tasks to attend to. I'm very busy writing a book no one, or a vanishingly small number of people, will read. And those who do will have forgotten most of it before they finish it. But I enjoy writing it.'

Helen realised only then both how much this had been eating away at her and that she had developed a belief, having observed his reaction to the challenges the whole world faced, Paul was a man who might help her explain it. 'If you know *anything* about me, I'm persistent Paul. This isn't over.' She tried to sound a little light-hearted. She was so tired of the list and becoming more and more confused by the strange effect she had on people. It had benefits. But it was like the whole world as getting clingy.

It was over for Paul. He'd come too close to the fire. No more Helen for him. It wasn't an uncommon outcome. It was another thing that troubled her. Some disengaged with her well before the clinginess phase. On a variety of pretexts they became unavailable. So that desired and admired as she was, she had few enduring friendships.

Basilica

'*Slurried-up* and pumped into deep ocean. Is that new.'

'That detail is new. This is the first time he's been put in a position to think on it, and he's accorded more credibility now he's been brought to prominence because of his moderate origins and now pathological attempts at detachment. Movements try to make him their leader, even as a figurehead and he simply doesn't respond anyone. About anything. Even to her now.' The Ageless One was grim. 'On this occasion he may be proven right, but not, ironically because of us. The Sororibus would be the Second Enemy *if* we were to persist in humanity's Timeline. Short though their tenure would be. However soon, for the first time, we may have a common enemy.'

'I've been thinking on this a great deal and the analysis of those you have set to that task has been valuable. The ship generates probabilities which become more and more likely as it has time to make the analysis, however it is slow, and it lacks the kind of intellectual leaps a biological mind can make. The Delivery schedule might change, drastically. The Author will have read our designs in this process. When he sees we are adjusting to disadvantage him to a much greater degree, he will be caught within increasingly sub optimal circumstances and may choose to move sooner if he thinks he can execute a plan which will have more options if he launches now.'

'The ship must be filled and turned around constantly in accord with his Infallible which will serve my ends. We'll send some Sororibus with the appearance of covertly visiting some of the planned loci of his Renewal. He will believe this is a common feature of the Renewal because its processes are known to none but me.' She smiled. "And now you. He will surmise we accelerate our schedule for the Renewal. He will wager if he can truncate the deliveries even though it might disadvantage him, it will leave the Sororibus with too many Virides at home, and too few in their destination to complete the task set for them. However his great goal is to take the ship. He will risk all for that. We must look for a drift. A movement of Virides from many places converging towards one.'

Basilica was given some abilities via the Sharing. She felt the presence in her mind that had visited her a few times now. A revelation. How everything worked. And why. Along with this realisation came a capability she would not have believed one could wield with a mind alone.

Barrion

'You're not allowed to do that.'

The two late teenage boys were pushing a Viride around. They'd found him a half an hour before on the outskirts of a town known for the rough treatment of 'Green Fuckers'. This one didn't have a tattoo, and hence no chip which is what the US gave all 'Arrivals' and as many 'Dumplings' as they could find. The technology to keep up with them all was always improving but not perfect given the huge numbers they were dealing with. Thousands of Moe's died every week, the victims of misadventure, jealous rages, torture fetishes, overwork, drug overdoses for those who liked to watch the effects, and being the victim of illegal dog baiting or 'boxing' matches. 'Clean' Moe's were much sought after as they had no tracker and no tattoo, obvious even when effaced unless by an expert. Though a tattooed Moe, or 'Tat' could still end up dead anywhere with few consequences in many locations. Some police departments were not always subtle in suggesting they had better things to do. The police prioritised and worked at solving the more blatant acts of cruelty or violence. When it came to court, precedents were still being created. There were well funded organisations on both sides of the divide lobbying and providing legal counsel for those representing Moes and those caught in some way mistreating or taking advantage of them. Many of the latter wanting to 'claim' Paul as a figurehead. He was beyond caring and provided a clarifying statement to that effect.

When one of the teenage boys had come across a 'Clean' wandering in a large parkland near town, he had called in his friend to bring a gun and some drugs. They weren't going to kill the thing, but it was funny to get them tripping on acid and then shoot at them or tie a bag around their head or maybe get them to start masturbating, which they would only do when they were 'fucked up on drugs' or being stimulated during sex. All of this was prime viewing on the scores of web pages which ranged from torture sites to those devoted to hidden cameras or walking in on girlfriends, boyfriends, sisters, brothers or mothers getting some 'Green'. The suicide rate among the victims of this callous voyeurism was eight times the national average.

The boys looked up to see a 'Moe lover' who'd told them to stop. The oldest boy said. 'You're not allowed to be a self-righteous little prick, but you seem to get away with it. Fuck off.'

'I'm *in charge* of the local Chapter of the Defenders.' The sixteen-year-old had started one in a town known to be 'tough' on Moes. He was holding up a phone. 'This is streaming straight to a web page about people being assholes. Assholes who always want to blur *their faces* in their videos. Because their a*shamed*. Guess what *asshole*. We don't blur yours out.'

Coming from a younger, smaller and not well-liked teenager switched on the older boys abundant supply of aggression. 'Now that we're on video, we might as well beat the fuck out of you. There are lots of web pages devoted to giving Moe lovers the kicking they deserve.'

For all his bravado he got a strange feeling from this sixteen-year-old. This was a boy who thrived on the long game. He might take a beating. Because he liked to orchestrate the payback.

The Moe baiter was coming at him with a gun, purely to scare the 'Defender', and then he planned to laugh and walk away. However he appeared intent. He would usually give some cues he wasn't serious. His companion was worried he might get himself in trouble. Rather than simply call out as he would usually have done, he followed his friend and pulled him around saying it wasn't worth it. The older boy had grown up with guns. He was as surprised as his friend when it discharged, barely missing the one turning him around, and hitting the Moe, who had taken a few steps towards them and to the left. The bullet scoring a little a trench across the side of his head. He blinked and spoke in a strange halting accent. The three other players in the little drama stopped to look. The youngest still filming. The Moe's voice was plaintive. 'Don't hurt him. It's me you hate. It's me you want to kill. Kill me. Put me out of my misery. Kill all of us.'

This was a little like the moment Helen made First Contact with the Aliens. A Moe was speaking, English, on camera. And it was beaming out first to a small group of 'Defenders' monitoring abuse and then it hit the airwaves. The teenager came over and held the gun stretched theatrically towards the creature. The Moe, visibly self-aware, leaned into the muzzle. The young man with the gun laughed. 'How does it go? *Make my fucking day punk*. If I weren't being filmed, I *wouldn't* waste a bullet you green piece of shit. You'd still be dead though.'

Barrion grabbed the gun and ran before the young man holding it could react. Which was strange for him. The Moe ran through the park and then into the main part of town. Looking all around he started finding Moes. He would run to them and shoot. There were a lot of people with phones fleeing but stopping to film once they thought they were safe. They saw him move away always only to find more Moes. The gun clicked. He passed by several others to come to a specific man. 'Where can I get more of these.' Barren pointed to the gun. They were one back from the main street and it was only a few hundred yards to the gun store. The man smiled while he shook his head in wonder. He'd watched with interest as a Moe, all of whom he despised, emptied a handgun into his kind. He pointed to the gun store a few hundred yards away. 'Please help me to get more of these things. We all need to die.'

'I like the sound of that. Follow me.' The man was having some fun in front of the mobile phones that were following him. Which was out of character no matter how much he might have liked to kill the wretch. He'd been a Deputy in his younger years. He opened the door and held out his hand in an 'after you' motion that the creature didn't appear to understand at the threshold of the store. So he held both hands out and made a pushing. 'Move that way.' An instruction which the Viride followed. The man followed him in. Which he knew was unwise but did it anyway. He needed to explain to the owner why a 'fucking Moe' was coming into his store. The man behind the counter wasn't as startled by the situation as he later thought he should have been.

'Barn; this green fucker has been blasting away at his own kind. Maybe he'll start a trend and these pricks will annihilate each other. Sounds pretty good to me.' No one had followed him into the store.

'Where's your licence little green man.' Laughed the owner. He'd been upset that anyone would think of ushering one of those 'abominations' into his store. Initially he'd been angry, then nervous and now strangely calm.

The two men laughed. The Moe said. 'Licence?' He slid the empty handgun across the counter.

'How many's he going to kill with his bare hands Barn. Give the guy some ammo. I'm carrying. He gets out of line I'll give him what he wants.'

'What the hell. I'll take the heat if he can let those mother loving 'Defender' assholes *see* these things don't want to be here anymore than we want them here.' He went to the cabinet behind the counter and pulled out five boxes of bullets. 'This is how you put them in the magazine you ugly fuck. Make every bullet count. Now get your green ass out of my store.'

As they were walking out, the store owner began feel like a curtain was drawn back open. A real concern about what he'd done emerged. Sure, he'd like to see this creature go on a rampage killing his own and proving the point he had made time and again. But giving him the ammunition to do it was a long way beyond what he'd normally consider doing. And the consequences he'd causally accepted started to loom large in his mind. As they would normally. Barn called to his long-time friend and customer at the door. 'Let's stop and think this though a bit more. What if it kills a human Godfrey.'

'Even better.' Said Godfrey as the door closed. Now Barney Elliot was truly worried, and indeed found out what 'the heat' was like.

But it was too late. And his defence of 'mind tampering' was disregarded when investigations found a relative was part of a clandestine dog baiting group. When Barney found that out himself he was as disgusted. Barney Elliot didn't like what the advent of the Moes had done to his town. He was more compassionate to their plight than he revealed and had no shortage of character witnesses to speak on his behalf. Being a martyr to the cause of the Protectors was cold comfort from a jail cell.

'I want to end their misery.' Said the Moe to Godfrey. All the Viride knew him as Barrion. Only an inner circle knew him as the one-time Authoress. The Virides could not pass on his 'downloads' beyond direct Sharing with him, but all knew who he was before they walked through the corridor that made them docile. He could reach out to any in the same proximity as the Sororibus might. Hailing distance. And transmit a simple message to be passed along. His capacity to bend a being to his will was much stronger with his own kind. They were compelled. However his powers with the humans were growing rapidly. He stared to walk along street shooting every Moe he came across. Humans running in fright or taking cover to watch.

Meanwhile Helen was driving at a speed which her new cameraman began to object to, no matter how much he secretly loved her. The woman who had been Helen's sound recordist for six months, and was now getting clingy, was calling directions based on the landmarks she could see from the live feed. Helen had the advantage of already being in the middle of interviewing some of the 'Protectors'. She had plans to interview the young head of 'Defenders' Chapter later in day. The Protectors agreed to be interviewed with their identities hidden and voices altered. They had killed Moe's and intended to kill more. They hated them. They were Protecting not only loved ones and country. They were Protecting the civilisation the 'Defenders took for granted'. Helen had been doing a four-part series on the impact of the Moe's on communities. One story in another town had been about several families living contentedly with Moe 'helpers'. Interviews planned in this town were with the families of teenage girls and boys, mothers and schoolteachers who had committed suicide after being filmed having sex with a Moe. Sometimes they had been drugged or manipulated into situation they would never contrive for themselves by low life internet web entrepreneurs who called it a genre.

She was in a town believed to be one of the most polarised in America. Horrific abuses of all kinds were reported, sometimes the remains of Moe's were found bearing this out. A lethargic police force made perfunctory investigation. No one had yet been charged and it was accurately alleged that some policemen were active Protectors. However a very vocal Chapter or the 'Defenders' was also active in the town. Some encouraged to visit there by the young Head of the Chapter to draw attention to the 'enormity of the abuses'. This had led to violence during Defender protests. People were open about what they believed about a town that had once been an unremarkable, but generally good example of a town wanting to be a city in middle America. Both sides referring to how the divisions had ripped through churches, families, schools and businesses leaving anger and in some cases hatreds even deeper than the Protector's hatred for the Moes themselves. 'At least they've got the excuse of being an ignorant fucking animal.' Was the last morsel she got in her a truncated interview with a Protector before the news came in from Artie.

Helen saw a Moe doing what had never been seen before. Walking around and doing something in very a focused and deliberate way. He was shooting while moving quicky through a street one back from the main street. He had killed a few dozen, awkwardly reloading the gun from the boxes carried in the other hand, and then walking and running in short bursts to find more. She saw one man shadowing him and a lawman in a crowd of spectators standing by watching. The man said later he was completely certain the Moe would only kill his own kind. The reasoning for such certainty he found very hard to explain.

The creature stopped, unable to find new targets. Helen ran right up to Barrion and asked the simple question. 'Why are you doing this.'

His answer was one with a poor grasp of language. 'There is only suffering for us. A prison our minds have been locked in. What they…do to us to make us all like this. It was…incomplete for me. The pain broke through into my…mind. We want only to return home to our families.' He lifted the gun and put it in his mouth. 'But they will never allow that.' After a pause he fell forward and shot himself.

Now the polarisation of the people of earth widened. *They want to die. Let's help them do it.'* To be countered by. *'There are beings as sentient as any human locked inside a tortured mind. The same as an intellectually disabled person who can't communicate yet there's nothing wrong with their mind.'*

Paul

He heard a familiar voice speaking to a guard. He had hoped she wouldn't come. He'd let the guard know that she wasn't welcome. It wouldn't have mattered. The guard was secretly in love with Helen.

From her perspective no one had ever refused when she asked for an interview. And to have a stringer for a regional newspaper get in front of her was something she was unaccustomed to. It was times like this she wanted to say. 'Does she have a list?' It would be a sour joke now. She hadn't gone out to dinner except with the production crew since the whole list thing had started. She was brought a chair to sit by the cell. She smiled. 'I thought I was your go to journalist.'

'I thought I'd give someone early in their career a chance. I spent a few minutes pointing out what was already analysed to death in the media. Because it was coming from me, she thought she'd got some new insight. I was happy it made her happy.'

'Because nothing really matters.'

'Because it's not worth the energy to get emotionally or even intellectually stimulated about something humans will be too collectively weak to resolve. In other words. That's right.' He sighed heavily. And was then annoyed he'd done that. '*However*, I have prepared some perspectives and some investigative opportunities for you. Only because you're good at what you do and the most likely to lever out some objective facts. I was going to send them off today but you're visiting so here you are.' It was a slim A4 manilla envelope with her name on it. 'A few ideas you might want to pursue.'

Paul gave the impression the meeting was over. She was a little surprised by the tone of his approach. 'You don't want to hear what it was like talking to the 'Sentient Moe' Paul. From me. Maybe speculate on his motivations. Why he killed himself.'

'He probably didn't want to have to go through the awkward process of having to boogie with you Helen. I have to…'

'Get back to a book no one's going to read.' He was surprised to see she was hurt. 'That's a mean thing to say Paul.' She was stung more than one might ordinarily be, because virtually no one had ever been mean to her. It distracted her for a moment while she contemplated that revelation. Then her focus returned. 'I always thought it was a bit of fun. Humanised people. There goes that justification out the window. You're all mysterious and now you don't want to know me.'

He smiled and shook his head. 'Never experienced this before?' He sighed and stood up. 'I'm embarrassed. It's like I'm a school-boy. It's...pathetic and I could do without it Helen. So take the envelope and go.'

'Oh.' This simple interjection carried with it everything he needed to know. Strangely it made him feel better. He needed to get over her and that simple acknowledgement his hope was vain at best helped. He all of a sudden knew he could stop feeling the way he did, perhaps never quite completely. It was not uncommon to those who were left behind to feel better. They still loved her. But they didn't have to hope any more. Except perhaps a tiny little bit which they could cope with. She offered up a solution which was com-bined with a half-smile, half wince. 'I guess...ah...an esteemed only slightly older brother would be out of the question.'

He was thoughtful for a while. It was a strange moment. 'I could try that. You might need to accept periodic brief lapses of a tiresome pathos.'

'Intermittent pathos? I can work with that.' She thought about it. 'That may have not been very sensitive of me...you know. I am flattered Paul.'

'I'm sorry I was rude. Let's strike out together on our journey as siblings shall we. Some things deserve to be forgotten.' He changed tone to the geniality he was known for with staff and students alike in the University. 'Many people have noted, with justifiable concern, that the creature knew how to operate a gun with no experience shooting or reloading. While trying to conceal this with some pathetic attempts to suggest he was a clumsy amateur. He pulled it off pretty well, killing what; twenty-three of his kind. Sometimes taking a few bullets to do so. But there was always a kill shot in there. Forgetting all the predictable responses to date, I'm surprised to find that no one's provided any analysis of what what's in there - yet.' He pointed to the envelope. 'The military have probably done it, but don't want to talk about it. It would make them look even more pathetic for sitting around doing nothing.'

'They do have the whole Commander in Chief thing to deal with don't they?'

'A fair comment. Usually that's a good thing.'

'So what's in here?'

He smiled. 'Go and be the exceptional journalist you are and do the analysis first and we'll see if we come to the same conclusions. That green sack of manipulation has only so many options available to him to keep us stupid earthlings divided and paralysed for as long as possible.'

'Three hundred thousand killed worldwide so far is perhaps not the response he was hoping for?'

'It means nothing to him. It's a few days of deliveries.'

'Don't you mean that it would mean nothing to him if he

was still alive.'

'You could be busy investigating that right now. Your professional talents dwarf whatever else it is you have going on.' He lied.

She smiled. There would be time to have the 'whatever else I have going on' discussion later. It was a nice compliment. 'Chow.'

He got on with a much-needed session of Helen pathos which he knew would now reduce in frequency and intensity. She was back at seven the next morning. 'Big news this morning is that the Network boss fell on his sword. *Protectors'* have a civil action pending and more than a few are saying if you're in here there are a few producers and editors and corporate enablers who should be here with you. The *'Defenders'* all think you're in the right place, except you are not being given hard labour, which is what you deserve, if not worse. Yet no one casts aspersions on the charming reporter who asked you the question that caused all the trouble.'

'Unsurprising.' He was feeling relaxed now, which was good. 'Anyway, there can be no wrong questions. Only wrong answers.'

'Who said that.'

'Me. Just then. I'm sure there's a few thousand others before me. I've made a lifestyle of not caring or I'd Google it.'

'You cared enough to uncover something interesting for which I would very much like to interview you about.'

'I don't have any better ideas than to slurry them up and pump them into the deep ocean as a dramatic conclusion. I've been working on it, but you can't beat it for genetic separation at scale.'

'What we have on that will be fine.'

Interviewing Paul again in jail allowed her to introduce some of the travails a rival network was experiencing as gratuitous competition bashing dressed up as context. Then she moved on to the substantive matters. 'You've come up with some observations about the recent 'Awakening' I believe Paul.'

'Yes. The first is the movements of the Moes in the town even before the 'Awakened One' moved off with the young man's gun in his hand. Analysis of the satellite image acquired at great cost to the Network no doubt, and the various phone videos and some questions asked of the people in the area before and during the 'Release from Suffering' revealed some interesting facts. When they first arrive, as you know, Moes are almost helpless creatures, however set within a relationship framework such as a workplace or family they can develop into beings that perform some basic functions. A nice trait to get humans to feel good about integrating them from a low base. The Moe's in this town, like a lot of places where they have been ill advisedly normalised into our society, might be carrying home groceries, in the parks with children, washing cars, walking dogs or doing a few tasks that would otherwise be a low paid job for a human. But the 'Awakening' happened in that town for a reason. It's because *you* were there Helen. While he was still being pushed around, several Moes started to move towards the middle of town. Some left the homes where they were 'guests' without being told to, which was unusual, or they changed their route on some errand or walking a dog, which were let go of as the gunman approached. There was never more than two in any location, and their movements were a drift rather than an intentional gathering.'

Helen continued the story. 'We're looking at an animated map of the town, the green dots being the Moes and the red dot the…you called the Moe a 'gunman' Paul. That should have been a 'gunalien'.' She smiled at him. 'You can see the drift but what else is interesting on the animation on the satellite map?'

Paul continued. 'The Awakened One follows a route towards where Moes are and doesn't go to places where they aren't. He's not moving randomly in a search one might expect. He shoots at them missing or wounding. However there is always a kill shot to the brain or heart. None survive.' Paul turns off the video on the tablet he was looking at, as the audience watched the same animation on their screens. 'Retired Servicemen, and active soldiers who are not supposed to speculate, say it would be tough for a handgun user with no experience to achieve what appeared to be lousy shooting on the run. These aren't very accurate weapons in spite of what Hollywood would have you believe. And he *convinces* a gun store owner, now in jail, to get more ammunition followed by an embarrassment of poor acting as he struggles to reload. He's smart but that doesn't automatically make him a great actor.'

'All of this occurs when one of the most accomplished and trusted journalists of her *age* happens to be a few miles across town. There's a coincidence for you. Investigating what are vile and sickening abuses visited upon the Moe's. And one happens to 'Awaken', nearby, filmed being about to receive his dose of abuse. The creature spouts a load of crap about wanting to die, kills some of his own kind and provides you with a few choice words of propaganda about being in a torture chamber inside his own head.'

She didn't usually do this. But she gave Paul the set up. 'And then he kills himself.'

'No Helen.' He gazed at her. Letting his superiority daemon out in lighthearted recrimination for his status of being unloved. 'One of the very few times your journalistic instincts have failed you.' While the camera was on him, she gave him a *'that wasn't in the script Paul, but it's refreshing to be disrespected'* smile. 'He killed a body. A body of a Moe. It doesn't matter. There are seventy million of them now. That we know of. If you scrutinise the footage carefully, he pauses before shooting the gun. This isn't for dramatic effect. He's moving house. Look at his eyes and then watch him falling forward as he shoots himself. He probably didn't expect such fine camerawork to catch this so perfectly.' Helen was glad Craig would see this. Wherever he was now. He got clingy so quickly. 'These are a hive animal. And the ultra-low and ultra-high frequencies which emanate from them are part of Shared mind.'

'Worker bees are expendable. A half a million dead means nothing to these creatures. There's a leadership and there is a consciousness. Perhaps each unique or only some have elevated intellects as leaders and technicians. It may be that there are many, like him, part of a group that were always 'Awakened' and are biding their time and making preparations. The rest may have only the same degree of diversity and autonomy as soldier ants, it doesn't matter. What you witnessed is the violent and merciless capability of every single one of them. The leader is desperately trying to hold on to the status of the sufferer. Trying to maintain a narrative to solicit pity from some and at least doubt or ambiguity in others. And so maintain the fiction aggression towards humans by the creatures would be unthinkable.'

Paul gave the impression he wasn't even that interested himself in what he was saying because it was pointless. 'He says they are perpetually in pain and wishes to end their suffering. Some believe that. Others say it's now obvious there is an enemy in our midst that needs to be exterminated. He's laughing at us. We're even more divided now. Soon we'll be fighting between ourselves with real and organised partisan violence. Fighting about them rather than fighting them. They can afford to lose a million, ten million in a nasty extrajudicial killing spree. That drives government further away from making hard choices or multinational collaboration because they would be condoning what I have always said is wrong. I would love to see what would happen if all governments announced a unilateral policy of extermination. That would cause the Moe's to bring their schedule forward. Until then, they want their numbers to build. I'm not sure any more if this is the plan of the Enemy behind the Moe's. This latest development suggests maybe this is a personality who has broken out of their narrative for his own designs.'

'You're always such a bundle of fun to interview Paul. Are you encouraged that the military has been tasked to prepare scenario's for a massive 'intervention' if there is an Awakening on a large scale and violence turns towards humans.'

'It's what they should do. They should conduct a variety of modelling exercises. One model should be that the Moe take a stance of being only aggressive to defend themselves from abuse. In that model, the military will need to deal with humans who will rush to the defence of the Moes. That would lead to a complex conflict between humans aligned with the authorities and human allies of the Moes. They might act as human shields or become partisan to the degree they start to exhibit aggression and violence towards their own species. Human against human is the best outcome he could hope for. The leadership of countries would then need to start to consider if they are willing to kill humans in large numbers.'

'But there's another kind of violence. Another kind of massive damage they can inflict. That would be an emergence of the passive sentient. Sentient Moes would need to be given rights. More than the confused version they've been provided with so far in a docile state. Moes with a pathetic tale and an IQ not so different to the average human would be expected to be more self-sustaining and less of a drain on the host nations. They would be competing for low paid jobs, and accommodation, of which there is little enough already and there is more than enough downward wage pressure in our benighted country to keep the working poor; poor. This is a form of violence against the most vulnerable in our society. Many middle and upper class people in America hardly take any notice of that class of the population. Which is quite large. Fully sentient Moe's will be like a huge influx of unskilled or maybe semi-skilled migrants. In another year of deliveries the equivalent of a sixth of our entire population would be competing for jobs, services and accommodation. A race to the bottom on wages will be one more strategy to weaken humanity and integrate an enemy. Demonstrations and riots might arise among those that are truly suffering because of the sentient Moes. Including human migrants already marginalised. And so humans trying to protect the meagre things they need to survive will be law breakers. If they are violent towards the Moe's they'll become criminals. Our society will protect our enemy and criminalise it's citizens for only wanting to hold onto the level of poverty they had before the Moe arrived.'

'And what of his statement they are victims of a master race, and they only want to go home.' Said Helen.

'I'd love to see the logistics involved in that. Is their home further than where these creatures are dumped here from? They'd need to take control of ships to get home. That would mean they'd control ships that that can also destroy a small city of ours. Maybe some of them may come to believe our blue and white ball is better than where they come from. And they won't want to go home even if they could.'

Helen gave that famous winning smile that didn't matter who you were. You fell in 'like' at the very least with her. 'You know Paul, being *the reporter of my age* and all, and thank for that by the way, I try to background people a little. I've spoken to a few dozen past students of yours and some of the faculty you work with. They almost all say you're a sweet guy who somehow gets a tech generation to enjoy modern history. A little. Now however, half the time you'd find your name in an internet search, a technology you don't interact with anymore… choose your adjective meaning 'monster' or the alternative captured in a phrase like 'the man who would save planet'. Is there some reason for the Paul Paradox as some call it.'

'I'm a war historian. That's all. They say that truth is the first casualty of war. That's bullshit. If you want to win a war, mercy *has* to be the first casualty. If there's a threat, whatever it is, you destroy it. Fast. First. And if you're good at war, you don't waste energy on atrocity, because you are too busy destroying your enemy. Destroying them as swiftly and completely as you can, using every weapon or tool or technology your best and brightest can muster. To win, there can never be mercy until there is an unconditional surrender.' He laughed. 'All of my students have heard this before. But we're not in a fair fight. Because our very *mercy* has been *weaponised*, and we've permitted our enemy to surrender, and integrate among us. Compromising out ability to join battle when it happens. The best general is the general that wins the war, yet never joins a battle. He needs a political context to do that in however. Hence a great Statesman and her or his diplomats might realise their war aims without a war. But when diplomats fail, warriors come into their own.'

'Ha. That's the nub of my books probably. If you want to truly waste your time and hence understand the utter pointlessness of everything you should read one. Not for the content. I *guarantee* you will have forgotten most of it by the time you finish. I know I did.'

Helen nodded seriously. 'I don't allow commercial content in interviews Paul. Except for the shameless product placement I continually try to contrive so people send me free stuff. And free military history books aren't really on my wish list, so I can fully support your advice to people that they should not read your books, and I can vouch for that approach, having not read them myself.' Businesses large and small sent Helen things, product placement or not. She had to hand it all over to the Network who found someone to donate it to. Royalties were starting to flow in for Paul now, no matter how irrelevant he believed his books to be.

Basilica

She looked up from the screen. 'He moves freely. Spreading lies and misrepresenting who he is and how he came to be. And now we know there is no death for him.'

'And there will be others. The Professor's comparison to a hive is a good one. Except that the various roles in this hive can be interchanged. There will be more depth than a leader and a few subordinates. The Author's life and habits involved huge numbers of Adules as our investigations go on. And those are what we know of. And I'm sure he could pass across the basis of an acolyte in seconds and an information source and instructions to pursue a specialty beyond what he could supply from his prodigious genius. He will have a leadership. Each one gaining specialist knowledge now on earth. Echelons beyond what was lost in the Pulse. Possibly he can duplicate them as Virides one on one as he moves through them. From my interrogations he will chance all to get the great prize he covets. Dominion over all Sororibus, Adules and Virides after humanity has met its ordained fate. But his genius and hubris want dominion over *time* and his ambitions may be greater than one planet. It's for this reason, beyond and above my beloved Sororibus, that my responses will be drastic.'

Basilica could not help but notice 'beloved Sororibus' carried a hint of insincerity the weary Ageless One struggled to conceal.

'The Deliveries will continue as planned. However I will amend the preparation protocols on the third delivery from now.' Basilica in recent times had been one of the few in a very long time, to experience some of the Ageless One's considerable capacity for warmth. However the long lived 'Shepardess' had another side. Expedient and ruthless. 'The Virides from that delivery on, unless or until this threat is neutralised, will have their consciousnesses permanently degraded to an infantile state and configured such that no greater consciousness will be able to recover into their minds.

119

What he thinks is an army continuing to build will become a liability which must at least dent his ambitions and harden the hearts of the humans who will find the impost unbearable. For our purposes, once he is dealt with, the Renewal will be very focused. The new Timeline will need to be launched from a smaller base.'

'You will travel on the ship on that delivery. We can assume that he has the knowledge to build a program to predict the ships Pre-Set locations. On the next two Deliveries select a trusted Sororibus whom I will vet and instruct her to acquire those odious things we have eschewed all these long millennia.' Basilica blinked hard a few times as the capacity to use those odious devices, designed for killing, was transferred to her. 'On your visit you will need to contact those two in the interview you saw. They are the most likely to understand what's at stake and you can give proofs to them of what they already suspect. You cannot reveal our ultimate objective. They must come before me, and I will provide them with all the revelations they need. Particularly what the rather prescient military historian will demand.' Her proofs might also come with a delivery into their minds far more powerful and subtle than her newly arisen Adversary. However she was dealing with a species irrevocably doomed. They would return to earth with a compelling story and various proofs. Helen's sojourn there would be brief. This much more expedient Ageless One looked her Envoy in the eye. 'Basilica, it might appear that every tenant and value we have will be cast aside. However no Sororibus knows, or ever has known, what occurs on earth in advance of the Renewal other than those who manage it, and they take their Peace before the Renewal begins.'

'I'll be giving you skills and two essential tasks which only you can know of or perform. You'll need to contact *him* and present a bargain. He is very unlikely to accept it, but I want to begin to make a more accurate assay of his mind via such an exchange, which I will make a study of after your return. He is my Adversary and there is nothing more important than defeating or at the least disempowering him.' This was beyond the expected duties as the Renewing Envoy. The Princep and the Author had chosen poorly in terms of their aims. Basilica was determined to rise to any challenge. And was untroubled by the expediencies that might be required to achieve the tasks she was assigned.

Cracking the Code

Paul was finally allowed out of prison. In no small part because his prediction had come true to some extent and the full transcript of his statements during the Panel program became a clarion call for free speech. He turned up for work the next day. Hoping his doomsday celebrity status would not follow him there. As with his decision not to care about anything anymore, he continued with his habit of not looking at any kind of mail, texts or any other communications or media. He blocked all the callers on his phone except Helen and his boss, the latter, although understanding of the communications embargo, had to field a lot of requests and make many refusals on Paul's behalf. Two people not enrolled in his class decided to turn up to a lecture and see if they could engage him at the end of it. He anticipated this ploy and people had to sign a roll on the way in. They paid a couple of students quite a bit of money to sign in so they could take their places.

Towards the end of the lecture, the older of the two, sitting at the front trying not to say it too loudly said. 'We've cracked an important code Professor. We're not affiliated with anyone or any organisation. We're a couple of people with something of interest in the current situation with the Moes.' Paul had a good enough bullshit detector to know they were genuine.

'Come to my office in ten minutes. Walk right in.'

'They went there and found a note directing them to another place. This happened twice more, Paul watching their migration, until they were in the storeroom off the basketball court. He gave them a pleasant greeting. It was hard for him to conceal though, that he believed they would have nothing of interest. He appreciated the trouble they'd gone to. However he knew who they were really after.

'We've cracked it.' The older of the two, Cody, eighteen, believed he was able to come up with an accurate prediction of the deliveries. He'd been right for the past nine. 'All over the world. We're amazed we could crack the code for such a huge range of probabilities.' His brother JD, a year younger said. 'And I've developed a program that can allow us to see the ship. It's blurry, but it works. Might be clearer in closer proximity. I downloaded the vision of the live feed of the first delivery, and I was able to play with all kinds of weird parameters.'

Paul found it interesting but had truly disappeared into an *I don't care about anything* state of mind. 'You've achieved something remarkable. Why bring it to me?'

They were a little uncomfortable. 'We agree with your stance. Sort of. We know it's right but it's hard for us to want to kill all of them.'

He knew that was bullshit. 'Helen.' He said. After a moment they nodded sheepishly.

Paul had another question. 'I'm not intending to patronise you, but have you ever demonstrated this kind of capability before. Some of the greatest minds on the planet are trying to figure these things out. Although there are examples of young people with clear vision and maybe a dash of genius doing remarkable things in a garage or basement or whatever, is this one of those instances.'

'It is sort of…out there.' The younger brother laughed. 'Given the grades we come home with. Good, but not stellar.'

'Do you have a Moe in the house?'

There was a pause conveying a little distaste. 'Yeah. My parents said we should 'do our part' in taking the strain off the economy. We're never mean to it like some people are. I find him creepy and yeah, like you've been saying. We can't trust them.'

'Think carefully. Has his behaviour changed. And did you start to take an interest in this kind of thing in a fairly short space of time. Both of you. Have web pages been left open that you assumed your bother left. Maybe a series of tiny revelations in your mind, which felt strange because it's not usually how you analyse things or come to conclusions.'

They sat still for a while and looked at each other. Frowning. They'd had quite a few strange things going on in their minds but hadn't mentioned it to each other.

'This thing's helped us out?'

'Their leader wants to know the answers more than you do and you have some of the tech to do it. Not in a high-profile location though. It's the same Moe that appeared to shoot himself, or maybe his technical lead, which I believe there will be one among many other specialists. An entire leadership. A hierarchy perhaps with multiple layers down to the soldiery and shitkickers who are completely expendable to him. Like any army when it comes down to it if there are enough men to spend.' Paul knew he was drawing a long bow in response to the information he had. He didn't care what anyone thought. And was certain nothing he did mattered. He thought for a moment. 'It may even suit his purposes for you to come and see me.'

'What do you think we should do Professor.'

'Thanks for calling me that. It's Paul to you two. It would be good to get eyeballs on this thing to prove up both propositions. And interesting right? He'll probably be turning up. You see, he wants a ship. I suspect he also wants to be interviewed or he would have kept the revelation to himself.'

'So let's see how good your collaboration with the Green One was. I still don't understand why the enemy behind this enemy would be allowing your Moe to do what he's doing. I suspect there's some element in their sleeper army that don't like the part they've been cast to play by their masters. Could make it interesting, but ultimately our interest will never align with either species. Unlike most allies, these creatures have no territory to return to. Whatever the case, if the majority have the kind of skills we saw that bullshit artist display, it's going to be a nasty war and it will be the first in advance of the one their slave master's prosecute. However I'm the one to give you what you really came to see me for. A link to Helen.'

The looked at each other and nodded. 'We're both on the list. I doubt she looks that far down.' He said this light heartedly. Almost. 'She's one of a kind that lady. But it's more than that. We want to see if she's interested because she's pretty good…at what she does and we thought she might want to be involved, without the network. We knew you had a…closer relationship with her.'

'You might say that. I'm not on the list by the way.' He was out of the loop now because he only looked at computers disconnected from the internet. 'So where are you two. On the list.'

The older brother smiled. 'One point two Mil.'

The younger less enthusiastic. 'Five.'

'Five million. It changes that much depending on when you sign up?'

They laughed. 'No way. The list is way more complex now. The geeks who started it developed an advanced AI which is continually improving and updates itself. It has every single detail about Helen's life and preferences, previous boyfriends, books she's read, you name it. Who she's been talking to, and about what to the extent anyone can know, and what her work schedule is. To get on the 'official' list you have to answer a three hundred question survey and allow the algorithm to go searching through all of your social media. You can feed your personal records in if you're willing to hand them over and it may or may not improve your ranking.'

'Hence the five million.' Said the more conservative younger brother.

'I suggest you don't mention the list to Helen. I think if we approach her with something that needs to be kept off the books, Network wise, she'll accept that. Until she doesn't. Where's the next Delivery?'

'Today it's in the Andes. A few hundred miles from Ecuador.'

'What's the schedule over the next few days from now.'

'Siberia and then in the middle of nowhere in Canada. Poplar Reserve or something north of…' He pulled out a notepad. 'Lake Winnipeg. Probably going to be one of the cases where half the poor bastards die before a scanner picks them up.'

'To make us feel bad.' Said Cody. Attuned to Paul's pronouncements.

'Yeah.' His brother continued. 'We don't have what you might call pinpoint accuracy. JD's always been within a hundred square miles or so. I find them after some searching around but they're gone by then and I get the blurry vision of the ship in an earlier satellite pass. Way in front of the government types though.'

'What you said about him wanting an interview makes me think of something.' Said Cody. 'I'm not getting anything hitting the same probability numbers after Canada.'

Paul nodded. 'Has his behaviour changed at all?'

The pair looked at each other. JD shook his head and smiled at the realisation. 'We sort of…haven't noticed until you said it just now.'

Paul simply nodded.

Do you think you could line up a meeting with….' Somewhat embarrassingly, they said Helen nearly in unison.

'A good chance. And gentlemen my advice is enjoy any contact you have with her. Hope is your enemy.'

'I guess having over a million guys in front of you does make a plutonic thing the best I could ever hope for.'

He laughed. 'It might as well be a billion Cody. The Helen I know could not give a…I'll say it how she might…a flying fuck about a list and who's on top of it. Number one the list would probably be the last person she'd go out and have a drink with. These AI programs are worthless.' He laughed. 'I'd bet even *they've* become infatuated with her. They're probably trying to build an artificial Helen they can settle down with.'

He called her. Gave her the boundaries within which the two wanted to operate within which she had no problem with. 'Like every other human I have a vested interest in this. It doesn't need to be about my job. To hell with the Network.' He told her where the next deliveries were scheduled for and she agreed Canada would be a good option.

'Sounds like a job for a MIG jet fighter and the fastest commercial helicopter in the sky. Brand spanking new.'

'Would that not ring a few alarm bells.'

'You and I will be 'live' broadcasting an interview while we're out there. It will be about your mind numbingly boring early life.'

'My early life was boring?'

'I do my research Paul. Anyway, we can snoop around Canada because Tim has a high roller client list now and I'm sure one has suddenly decided he wants to fly in a MIG over Canada before he dies. Phil has to visit some relative he never knew he had up there. That's off the cuff. I'll do a little better with some time to think about it. And maybe a beer.'

'If you make it happen, hard as that's going to be, I'll wager you might meet an old friend up there.'

'I have so many. Which one.'

'You have about twenty-five million people wanting to be your *friend*. This one is of the green variety and wants to rule your world.'

'Why tip his hand?'

'I believe he wants a ship now because he has only so much time to operate without the 'Second Enemy' responding to the news you and your sidekick, who is the military genius part of our duo, have generated.'

'Genius I'm not so sure about.'

'Also I think he's starting to see that humans have their limits. I don't know how many of those creatures are supposed to end up here. But he's starting to sense the tipping point when people will start to listen to people like me, who are growing in number, may not be far away. If he could take over a ship, he'd be ready to chance it all. But he'll try for an 'us against them' alliance first. That's why he convinced the two young sleuths he both used and helped. To find out what he needed and to line up an interview. Most importantly, he missed out on the dance segment of the last interview and wants another go around.'

'My strange and more and more inconvenient magnetism, *which we haven't talked about yet*, no doubt has no boundaries across species.' She stopped and was silent in thought for a minute. 'I've only realised now a dog has never barked at me.'

'My heart goes out to you.'

'Shut up. I'll make the arrangements.'

'Could be quite a bill to pick up if we've misplaced out faith in a couple of kids.'

'These guys owe me. They get others to fly their aircraft except when they get five times the rate to do it. All they need to do is talk about their First Contact experience and show them some intentionally grainy 'classified' phone footage the media never got hold of.' She pretended to be pensive. 'The government didn't get it either now that I think of it. Poor old Peabody and Slater. And naturally they want to hear a little about the intrepid newshound they were with. I give them permission to tell them they're top twenty on the list. Which people are apparently impressed by.'

'Ha. The list doesn't work that way Helen. You're way out of touch. They have to complete a big questionnaire and then take what they're assigned to by the generative AI. No queue jumping.'

'An algorithm?'

'Ask your acolytes.'

'Fucking list.'

Paul got his passport without any problem from someone who behaved like his acolyte. He and Helen conducted an 'in depth' interview which was billed as a sharing of two of the more influential commentators on the subject of the Moes. Even though there was no new content, it was an interesting and complete narrative of the journey and Paul spent some time preparing analysis in the frame of War History.

Meanwhile they were in a helicopter flying to the middle of the reserve north of Lake Winnipeg to be ready with JD to try out the visualisation program. Cody arrived and used the scanner in the MIG fighter jet, which he thought was very cool. Though not as cool as his brother flying in a helicopter with Helen. Everyone had individually and collectively studied a map of the Park and used science or intuition to guess a location. They came up with their top three. Tim had a limited window he could fly considering both fuel and a good enough excuse to take a high paying customer around what a was beautiful place, among many which were more beautiful.

Tailored

Paul knew they needn't bother looking any more when the call sign came over from a pontoon plane. They were told it had some passengers aboard who would like to meet them. They were guided to the shoreline of a very remote lake, landed, and watched the plane come in. It was a Cessna Caravan so Paul estimated there could be ten or more aboard. Basilica observed all this from the Bridge of her ship which had landed. Four men and five Moes came out of the plane and walked along the jetty used to bring stores to some summer hunting camps in the region.

It was a curious assembly. The Moes were well dressed in clothing that had been tailored to suit their species rather than human clothing and it was strangely affecting to see them dressed so. Jessop had organised this. He was now State Head of the Defenders. Partly because of his involvement in the momentous events in his hometown. But also due to some of the approaches he took to influence. The Virides created a presence of a People who had recaptured their dignity. *Or perhaps well turned-out Nazis.* Thought Paul. The young man was familiar but even Helen's sharp mind couldn't quite place him. He had been behind his phone filming the mistreatment of a Moe in a Park. She had been scheduled to interview him, but it never taken place because of the 'Awakening''. He had organised the tailor to provide the clothing in secret after he'd been contacted. Three more humans came with him, one with the bearing of the quintessential ex-serviceman, another a hunter dressed as such and the young man's father in suburban clothes with a fishing vest over the top. The best he could come up with for a trip to the wilderness.

Paul now recognised the young man was the 'Defender' who had intervened during of the abuse of the Moe who had gone on a killing spree. The hunter was a friend of his father. And the ex-serviceman a distant cousin. Or so the son was told.

'This'll be interesting.' Said Helen.

'Better than that lame interview you're dragging me through at the moment on the Network.'

'Journalist can only do so much with the subject matter. And you wouldn't dance.'

Helen got in slightly before the young man's introductions of his alien companions. 'We meet again.' She said to one of the Moes. Who looked no different to the others and whose clothes were equally well cut for his species. By his bearing it was immediately apparent however. He was the leader.

He smiled and shook her hand. 'I'm Barrion. We haven't met.' He moved on, introducing his 'brothers' and taking it upon himself to introduce the humans as the host of the group. 'Jessop, as you may recall, took some footage on the day my brother took many Virides to their Peace and then followed them. He cared for our interests, so I reached out to him to enquire if he wanted to meet with us. I advised him what we planned, and he said he would ask some people of the same mind if they would be interested in being involved as witnesses for humanity.' He'd said all were 'Defenders'. However they were unable to hide the fact they were not as enthusiastic about that cause. Which was the very the reason Barrion accepted Jessop's choices. He wanted people to see what kind of people were willing to support him. And they *would* support him when the time came.

'This is our third encounter now that I think about it.' Said Helen. 'I also saw you hiding in the back of a helicopter during that memorable first Delivery.'

Barrion smiled. 'Yes. On that occasion it was me. Our lives are governed by probability. My journey has had a very low probability of advancing thus far. Possibly lower going forward. Yet I'm intent that our slavery should be ended.' He turned to Phil. 'This will sound like flattery, but it is not. Surely only one among thousands of pilots would have apprehended the risk of the Pulse so quickly and have the courage to make such a drastic response when you felt it recede.'

'You have a magnificent grasp of language and idiom.' Said Paul.

'Paul.' He smiled. 'The man with the most perspicacity of all. I spend time listening a great deal and have gained some grasp our your…idiom. Many of your observations have merit. Except those concerning our motivations. But I would be no more trusting than you are. And no more easily satisfied. We continue to learn about the risks you see in us. Your perspectives as a Military Historian takes time for us to grasp as we have no such history.'

'Must have been boring.'

'We did not appreciate the merits of boredom until we were en-slaved by an alien race. A risk which you also are confronted with.' He smiled again. He was confident. 'But not from us.' The Alien looked down, somewhat incongruously at a watch. 'The ship alights. We will meet with them as the Representatives of the Virides who have been brought to your planet. We will remonstrate with them to return us to our planet and alter their designs upon yours.'

'A very tidy proposition Barrion if it could be achieved. What will be their motivation. They have the hardware after all.'

'They have only one weapon apart from our debasement and slav-ery. The Pulse function on the ships.' It suited Barrion to maintain the fiction there was more than one ship. 'It had never been used before that first Delivery to your planet to our knowledge. They used it to try to eliminate me because I was given the knowledge by one of their own, disgusted with the way their species enslaves those they conquer. That individual developed the technology to return the Virides to their true nature, rather than the embedded warrior nature you have so accurately warned of Paul. And having been so readjusted, their army is gone. Replaced by a people peace-ful for long millennia. These aliens have no other troops than those they co-opt in slavery. As would be your fate in time. To Pulse so much of your world would be contrary to their objective of pre-serving it. In any event, between your military's analysis of what would be required to destroy such a ship, and the intelligence we can provide with respect to their technologies, they will realise an attempt at invasion will be futile as their ships would eventually be destroyed. We are aware they have options elsewhere. Which we need not impede.'

'Sounds great. Good luck Barrion.' Paul seemed relaxed however he followed them down the short jetty within sight of a fishing cabin by the remote stretch of lake. The first Moe had reached the float plane when Paul asked. 'Oh. One question. What's going to be their motivation to take you all back to your home planet. Might be further away. Might take an awfully long time to move that many…Virides is it? Why not cut their losses and leave. If you get repatriated, how long will it take and who will get taken first. Until then we would have over seventy million awakened Virides in our population. Many may not want to go home. Especially to such a boring planet.'

'All will be explained if we survive the coming hour Paul. You are outside of the Pulse zone here if they try to kill us. If that happens, my suggestion is you go into hiding with as large a supply of the necessities of life you can amass and try to get people to listen to you.' He was half in the plane when Paul had another question. 'Barrion, in a few words what are the key differences between our planet and yours. You know, two moons, purple oceans, mountains made of crystal. Do Virides eat giant centipedes. If you don't make it back it would be so interesting for people to have a few snippets of what the differences are.'

'I'm in haste Paul. If our endeavour goes well, I can answer all your questions. Perhaps while you tour the ship and meet those who might have been your masters.'

As he sat in the float plane while it took off Barrion had an unexpected caller via the Sharing. Her message delivered directly into his mind. From so far away. The capacity she had been given channelled him in. An amazing adaptation of the Sharing. It was more for him to learn. He would master this new talent. A gift from the one he loathed. She was foolish to assume his limitations.

Basilica

'We know you're coming. The Ageless One has made some alterations to my mind so that I could greet you appropriately. Can we bargain before you make your attempt to take the ship.' The Ageless One had made several adjustments to her consciousness. To be able to exchange with Barrion was a major advance on what those with the Sharing had in terms of clarity and distance. The Sharing itself was a phenomenon which the Sororibus had spontaneously developed on the century long journey from their own planet. The Ageless One had honed it into something remarkable. Now she reconfigured it further into something unmatched for only her Envoy to experience.

'An Envoy so young. And so accomplished. That old Princep got more than *she* bargained for.'

'I would return the compliment. However I dislike you so. I would be disingenuous to deny your genius though. I suspect my station is due to you however. Not the Princep. I can only hope I disappoint you.'

'We met as Sororibus Basilica. You were in awe of the Authoress's achievements. And you provided me with the kind of subtle but sincere compliments only the mature can craft. And I was appreciative of them. And yet you concealed a ruthlessness that ancient devil has been able to cultivate and manipulate as is her way.'

Basilica knew she would be drawn into time wasting as he flew closer if she allowed it. 'The Ageless One sees a bad end for both our Species without an alliance.'

'You're bargain?'

'You've come to try to take the ship which we have anticipated. If you can awaken all of your…brothers…and make a plea to your hosts that results in you forming an alliance against us with them, that is something to Bargain. We on our part can achieve our ends by Pulsing every square foot of this planet where any of your brothers might be. It would still leave a great deal untouched because we can trace your whereabout now. Thanks to the humans.'

'We both have much to lose Envoy.' He said. 'You have something to offer?'

'Asia.'

There was genuine surprise in Barrion's voice though he didn't believe it. 'I had not expected that Envoy. I will admit it approaches our aspirations.'

'That's five thousand generations of your kind and this gesture is enshrined in the future Timelines. Our…' She laughed. '…Ineradicable Sympathetics will see this as a positive step towards integration. We will fly them to your lands at no charge and they can take whatever they want to bring to be with you.'

It was Barrion's turn to laugh in kind. 'An enlightened few. Very few I suspect Envoy. And they would be treated with honour. However we'd need diversity. As do you. A hundred ship loads of human females from all regions and locations on the planet. We would prepare bunkers underground where we can see out the inevitable carnage of the race of the humans until the toxin dies away. The old viper you hold in such high esteem, with such youthful allure, would need to remove our block on reproduction.'

She was surprised he did not know of the intervention Chrona had contrived at the start of the Renewal to avoid that carnage. He also did not know some vital information about the toxin. 'We assumed that's a given.' Though she didn't. 'And I am certain that at this moment your prodigious mind will be calculating on how you would broaden your domain.'

'It would be.' He laughed. 'If I were so stupid to believe such a ridiculous proposition purely contrived to draw me close to the ship to be pulsed. I will have *everything* Basilica.'

Miscalculations

Basilica's mind snapped shut. Though he might have learned the great talent she had been given. He could not direct a Sharing over may miles as she had. But his immense genius had learned enough to sustain the pathways she had created. At that moment Barrion sought to harness the collective consciousness of the Virides on the huge ship and burn her, not only her mind, but her body by harnessing the powers of more than a hundred thousand of his kind. But he was discomfited to find their consciousnesses had been stripped bare, with no latent mind left. They were infantile things, even less capable and self-aware than all those usually Delivered with their true nature behind a block in their mind.

He spoke to her again. 'I thought that brooding Witch had plumbed the depth of callousness. To give brothers their peace would show some decency rather that to turn them into these pathetic creatures, most bound for death by simple incapacity to care for themselves in even the most basic fashion. A greater excuse for humans to commit the casual violence and humiliation they wreak upon us *if* these are rescued at all.' Basilica could hear Barrion clearly. She realised at this proximity harnessing even his ruined brothers would be enough to pierce the minds of those on the ship. Her mind had been made impervious. And the minds of her crew had been scrutinised to ensure they were free of any latent triggers put there by the Authoress. But they were susceptible to an attack the Ageless One believed she had countered. 'Prepare Envoy. That Evil Creature you revere, heartless through ages, has badly miscalculated. These my Brothers will be *sufficient* for my purposes.'

She tried to Pulse the ship. But minds around her, her own Sisterhood, were suddenly boring into hers and taking control of her every thought and action even as she sat at the controls. The Ageless One had indeed miscalculated. Basilica realised, vetted as they were, all the Sororibus around her were enemies now. Harnessed. She retreated into a place in her mind Chrona had made, took the Control Key from its holder and ran. All the ship could do now was follow the Pre-Sets. Endlessly. Unless she chose otherwise from the small freighter used as transports for the Renewers. Any one of which could beckon the ship with the key, but only when the Envoy was signed on as the Pilot.

Suddenly those who had been some of her most trusted Sisters and long-time friends were now in front and behind her attacking her violently with fists and fingernails trying to push and trip her. She could see in their eyes they would like nothing more than to kick and beat her to death. In an instant *they* all lay dead on the deck. They'd had to submit their whole mind to the Ageless One to take this voyage and she had set in place a pathway Basilica could trigger via the Sharing none could block. They had been given their Peace together in an instant The young Envoy was running from her next enemy. Broken hearted. So many she loved and respected gone via an exercise of her will.

Trembling now, she neared the Renewer craft which had been prepared and kept in readiness for this eventuality. Barrion needed to insert an imperative into only one of the ruined Virides and they shared it and they became focused on one thing. Using what small capabilities they had. A swarm of Virides were crawling and staggering towards her. Coming from all directions to overwhelm the small craft before she could get to safety behind its doors. Again Barrion was discomfited. She had left a cache of weapons along her way and at other locations in the ship with more in the small freighter. The Ageless One had studied the probabilities and this had been a very unlikely one. While in this swirl of activity Basilica wondered if this was the outcome the Ageless One might find most satisfactory. She had to focus now. Contrary to hundreds of millenia of Sororibus social mores, she began to slaughter the Virides en mass. She had picked up machine pistols and knew how to use them, casting the emptied weapons down to take more on her way as mounds of dead made the passage of the simpletons difficult. In her small freighter more weapons were stored, put there by a Renewer appalled by the task she'd been given. Basilica brought down any coming near the craft, leaving hundreds dead, and was able to close the doors and launch unmolested. Her mind impervious to Barrion.

Basilica had four machine pistols, several different kinds of rifles and handguns and even knives. She streaked away from the ship to a Pre-Set hidden in the wilderness randomly selected. She sat for a long time after landing. The Ageless One had confidence in her. But her confidence in herself was being sorely tested. She was pitted against an enemy in her experience only second to Chrona herself. She began to treat the many scratches, cuts and bruises. Such wounding by another Sororibus was unheard of but for those few who could not adjust to the Sharing and went insane, a few becoming violent. Barrion had the ship. But the victory was muted, held in Pre-sets and no capacity to Pulse it. He wasn't defeated however. He had brought Virides with him, their minds with a great depth of knowledge of the Sororibus technologies and this ship in particular. He had packages of knowledge that he had shared thousands of times within what Paul called the hive. And his knowledge of the ship was intimate. He had also studied the Beacons used to enslave his kind on Sororibus. He would study the ships Time capabilities in great detail when he had leisure to do so.

He reached the command deck and had his specialists commenced work. He stood in silence looking at the dead Sororibus. Shocked again at the novelties his great enemy was willing to chance. 'Your monumental hubris will be the undoing you old despoiler.' He said quietly. Looking at the dead he had come to a realisation. He saw an opportunity which would accelerate his plans immeasurably. He told his companions their priority was altered. These Virides, cultivated since before even Adules in age, the brightest children in one of the many male creches, would do his bidding. They did express concerned however, because what was being asked of them would impact what they had believed was the singular priority of the journey. He was untroubled. He must try to utilise the potential the old Witch had inadvertently brought his attention to. When he returned with a hundred thousand of his elite soldiers in harness, there would be nowhere for the Envoy to hide. She would come to him and give him all he asked. And then he would burn her mind out. As he would do with every world leader, every general, and any and every inconvenient individual on earth. Such as Paul. Unless it suited him better to have them proselytize his message or masquerade as them until it suited him to cast them aside. While Helen, reserved for himself, along with millions of other females would be brought to places safe from the coming catastrophe to start a new race. The old yet youthful hag would be a prisoner in a cage of her own making, unable to re-join the ship and only able to await the great waterfall of the cosmos.

He started to off load the infantile Virides via compulsion built from their own energies. They were useless to him, and they could die in the wasteland for all he cared. He had them cooperate to the very limit of what they could achieve to clean their dead away while he had his least talented Viride technician drag the Sororibus away to a compartment he could lock. There was more than a billion Virides to collect from Sororibus and the ship would work constantly to bring them all to his domain. A civilisation for fifteen hundred years, until he also would recommence from an earlier time. Perhaps much earlier. He didn't intend to follow the Ageless One's strictures about arriving after some unimportant human's visit. He would be the Ageless One. And he would rule a planet which would one day be too small to play host the possibilities of his mind.

Losing full control of the ship was a setback. However it was not essential to his first objective which was to use the technology they'd brought to awaken all the Virides. He had grown in capacity so that he could awaken them himself at any number, but only in close proximity. So he was able to have only some of his leadership and key technologists around him who had travelled to where he waited. Others were awakened and ready. Some had already been coached and configured to be unaltered even by passage through the Ageless Ones docilation corridor. They had trained over his lifetime as the Authoress. Adules with unfettered access to every technology and process having taken the Sharing to a new level. And they had continued their studies secretly as Virides among the humans in positions as slightly higher functioning 'Moes' who came into contact with human technologies. Others he had templates loaded into their personalities for half a dozen roles but mainly as foot soldiers.

At the beginning, moving from the creches as the brightest minds he assayed, his core adherents appeared to be tending a botanic garden in their youth and beyond, an initiative set up by a wealthy Sororibus the Authoress had cultivated a friendship with, and 'convinced' to make the contribution to the public good. A slightly unusual initiative so late in the fifteen hundred year cycle. The Authoress settled down next to it, and the hundreds of Virides working there easily exchanged places from one day to the next to work in the Authoresses private garden. The methods Chrona used to turn the Adules into Virides, rather than naturally matured men, had been reconfigured by Barrion. The technologies of the Ageless One meant the Adules had to lay unconscious in large dormitories for a week to mutate into Virides, forgetting their former lives. They walked through corridors to bring them fit for various roles in the hierarchy of Virides as slaves to the 'Sisterhood'. They were controlled via a connection from a beacon to the Sharing of the small number of Sororibus needed to guide and supervise them to maintain them as fully grown men but beings that were complaint, diligent, passive and low maintenance. They had low food and water needs because they photosynthesised. An initiative Chrona was very proud of. They made slightly more oxygen than they consumed. Nearing the end of the fifteen-hundred-year cycle, a larger population was allowed to grow, partly to create a surplus of all the things the Sororibus could enjoy prior to the end, and then be gradually loaded into the giant freighter component of the Ageless One's massive ship. They passed through a corridor converting them to a monosyllabic being who could mature to the intelligence of a seven-year-olds when being useful to the humans. They were autonomous in this phase and didn't need to amplify the limited Sharing the Ageless One had given them. She awakened and managed them for their tasks on earth via a Beacon. Barrion needed a Beacon of his own. Which would awaken his Brothers to a different purpose than the odious task they were being brought back in time for.

He would awaken all his kind on both planets, take over both and strip everything from Sororibus before it disappeared over the Event Horizon. His beacon would install a part of the Virides mind to his design to make them ruthless soldiers, loyal to him or whoever he commanded them to follow. But soldiers able to share every single learning they experienced one to the other within the range of Sharing or via his Beacon when he would use it occasionally without allowing the humans to lock onto it. They would pass any details about any locality, capabilities with weapons or vehicles, field craft and intelligence to a Shared Mind.

Once his technicians were at work, he had to deal with the people by the lake shore who could make the next twenty-four hours much more difficult if he allowed them to. Or they could sow the seeds of enough uncertainty and hope to convince some humans of his tale of the wretched fate of his kinsman. And his announcement of a successful bargain with the masters of the great ships to return the Virides to their home. He would need to deal with Paul. Whom he could only both despise and admire for his clarity of vision. However he knew Paul's weakness. And it was though this method he could keep him silent, or maybe, depending on how much power he could harness from his Bothers, he could possibly suborn grudging support from the Historian. He would jam their technology until it had recorded a message in his interests. Only then would he transmit it.

The spoiled cargo had now absorbed the compulsion to continue independently to clear and get off his ship and exerted a shared will to do so. He didn't lower the escalators; they were instructed to throw themselves from the hatches. He wanted all the space free for soldiers on his return journey. He knew he was stuck with the pre-set pattern of locations and durations for at least this cycle. Breaking that was the third most important task for his Technicians. His mind cast about for the Envoy who had delivered a few surprises to a situation he thought he'd have mastery over and so have a crew of Sororibus under his control. He took the float plane to pick up the people waiting. *All* of them. His powers of compulsion growing. He believed he could harness humans in the same concert one day. Soon. When he had the time to perfect it.

Relentless Negativity

While he'd been away Paul had lost no time coming to his own conclusions and anticipating Barrion's need to contain them for the next twenty-four hours. While Helen engaged Jessop in a conversation about whatever he wanted to talk about, Paul spoke with his companions. He said. 'I'm hoping you guys aren't really Defenders.'

They looked over to see that Jessop was fully occupied. His father said. 'I've always taken a low key approach to things. I kept quiet when he and his mother became 'Defenders'. Decided I'd prefer a happy household. This whole issue has ripped some families apart; whole community to pieces. This Moe contacted him and said he wanted someone to come along and 'witness' that his intentions were 'benevolent'. I was a little surprised when Jessop came to ask me if I was interested and if there was anyone I could recommend. He and I have not always had…an easy relationship. He's…navigated his way to being in charge of the Defenders in the whole State now and could have had all sorts of prominent people involved. He asked me to keep the whole thing quiet. He didn't want any of the people he engaged with involved. My cynical interpretation of that is…it will leave him the sole Defender in the spotlight and we'd be the also rans. So I contacted some friends to see if they would come along and 'Witness' with me.'

Kurt, an ex-Marine as it turned out said. 'We've never been too vocal either way. For the same reasons as Malcolm. We're hoping that if there's something that needs to be known, we can get back and get it out there. We know it's all bullshit and…probably there's a slim chance of us getting home.'

'Got any weapons.'

They looked at each other. 'Handgun and a knife each. I feel naked really.' Said Linus, the man in hunting garb.

Paul looked to check Helen was still engaging Jessop. 'A couple of observations. You can shoot Barrion, and he'll simply turn up in another Moe. But it might give you some time. Never give him *any* warning. Just do it. Be ready to observe closely what's going on in your minds. He can exert some control of your thoughts and actions. I plan to test that out if he comes back. I suspect he's desperate to get one more day of inaction out of humanity while he gets the technology he needs to turn…the Virides…all on at once. I don't know how it works with the ship in terms of when you'll get a signal, but I'd keep your phones hidden, have a big list of contacts and keep sending the texts about what you've learned. I'll try to get the military and others to listen. When he comes to pick you up, you should come out very hard against *me* while I try to antagonise him. Use the anger from bad memories if you need to but he needs to be convinced you're at least pliable.'

Helen cast a look of relief Paul's way when he nodded advising she could disengage with Jessop who went back to be with his 'Witnesses' and Helen went off with Paul to the extent they could not see her pronounced slow headshake. 'If being naive was an Olympic sport that kid would scoop the pool every year. Christ. And what is it with these people. They all want to tell me what place they're at on this fucking list.'

'It's a condition called the *Love is Blind* syndrome. When it's on a normal scale the antidote is that once people get to know you it becomes the *That's been a Real Eye Opener* syndrome. With you however the syndrome is at such a scale it's like a pandemic. So comparatively few people get to know you and hence experience the cure.'

'That kind of callous and needlessly carefully constructed rudeness is what I need. It's like a breath of fresh air. I'm really starting to appreciate your *Habitual casual disregard for people's feelings spiced up with rampant superiority* Syndrome. But I can't take much more of this. I'm going to get an ugly and stupid makeover when we get back. I want a normal, simple life being the journalist of my age. Not all this other shit. Is that so much to ask.'

'Moving right along.' Said Paul. He motioned toward Jessop. 'There's something about that boy. I wouldn't be surprised if he's playing his own game. Maybe he's already scoping out his reward but he's a curiosity to be sure.'

Paul was now able to relax with Helen knowing he was permanently off the list. 'If Barrion comes back, he may tell us he's 'remonstrated' with an enemy who kept his people enslaved for who knows how long and they've capitulated based on the fact there is potential for an alliance between our Peoples even though our interests are not strongly aligned beyond defeating the second enemy. If he's taken the ship, he will have a capacity to Pulse wherever he wants. He can move from one…Viride I think he said…to another and so he can't be killed and can turn up anywhere anytime. We know he has a capacity to influence a human mind which would be another weapon which our leadership, asleep at the wheel as they are, would be susceptible to, particularly if he learns to *inhabit them.*'

'Me not being a military historian, what does this all boil down to.'

'I'll set my mind in a way that is relentlessly combative, and I'll aggravate him as much as possible.'

'So…you're going to be yourself.'

Paul ignored that. 'He wants *all* of us on that ship so that I, inconsequential as I've been certain my life is, will be kept quiet until you've got yet another story of the century by inspecting a very cool spaceship. Maybe even transmit a story about how it's all going to be great now that Barrion has these evil aliens at heel. I assume you'll follow your esteemed older brother's advice and not go there.'

'Did I come up with that relationship arrangement.'

'Yes you did. Esteemed was certainly in the mix. To avoid the pathos as you'll recall. Which you come across all over the place but have only recently begun to see it for what it is. Since the list.'

'The esteemed part I don't recall signing on to. How about esteemed within a narrow range of topics and situations. You have studied war, battles, military leadership and geopolitical strategy. I dance with Monks. Ergo we complement each other, and I'll go with your advice on this as long as you show me the esteem I deserve when Monk Dancing becomes a strategic focus. I assume we start beaming the story from here.'

'Yep. On two platforms. One obvious, the other using this satphone and those little satellites I hope will work for us out here.' Paul held up what he'd acquired for the trip which might have been used in a number of situations. Including a crashed helicopter. 'He's going to dissemble and say all will be revealed on the ship. He's expecting you to keep me on the leash. If you're interested, see what it feels like to let him push your mind down the pathway that suits *him* if you create a position favourable or at least open in that direction. Which in this case will be getting me to shut me up.

'Is that even possible.'

Paul ignored this also. 'We've got to get as much of his reactions out as possible before he either has some nameless henchmen kill me or Pulses the ship once his consciousness is out of harm's way. I think as soon as we have what we want we'll have Phil cued up to get us out of here. He can stay in the chopper while JD runs the camera, and I have the pocket cam connected to the satellite phone. I'm certain he'll be turning the former to white noise unless it's the message he wants. I can only hope I irritate him enough so he can't find and jam the satphone signal. Jessop doesn't know about it and the other three are cued to fill their minds with being angry at me.'

As they were speaking, they saw something streak across the sky. Where it came from and where it landed was difficult to gauge. They waited over an hour before the float plane again came into view. During that time Paul had asked Phil if he had any weapons. Reluctantly he handed over a handgun. 'This has great sentimental value.' Paul replied it might go into space and would have even more cache. Phil said. 'I'd rather get it back when we leave.'

Helen was surprised what a good guess Paul had made. He should have some sort of list she thought. Military history buff intellectual groupies list. Ranked by algorithm. It dawned on her that she now possessed real power. She could say that whoever built the best military history algorithm to generate an intellectual groupie list for Paul would jump straight to twenty on her list. She could imagine a geek bloodbath to get it done. She was excited, and afraid. To think about what the world had unleashed. If her dark side came out. She laughed inwardly. She didn't have one.

Paul had to nudge her back to the present. Barrion walked towards them. JD had the camera rolling but the suave Moe was indeed scrambling the transmission but recording the footage until he knew he had control. Starting an interview and having to abandon it was as bad as having his message contradicted. His mind had limits though and did not detect the satellite phone. Which had not yet been turned on. Paul wanted him very distracted first.

There were two other Virides in the float plane. Barrion would have preferred to bring only one and leave a larger team working on the revised Beacon. However he had to balance that need with his desire to use them to augment his power. Barrion came out projecting the persona of one bearing monumental news. Helen, as instructed, had her defences down and tried to be attuned to a foreign influence in her mind. Paul believed that Barrion was at his most powerful when he was pushing the target mind in a direction it might be inherently open to. In this case starting an interview right then but acquiescing to come to the ship for an interview and either convincing Paul to come or leaving him with the helicopter. Had she not been aware of what Barrion could do she would indeed have soon been arguing the point with Paul. Staunchly. Knowing that ultimately, she would win any argument she had with him. No matter how wrong she was. A fact he knew might be fateful.

'Those who have enslaved us can see their circumstances have changed. They aimed to deliver half a billion of us to your planet and then activate us. Tens of millions lost is of no concern to them, as they have another half a billion to strategically deploy later in a slow process of attrition. They could never conceive an alliance between us, with humans having such an array of weapons, likely to destroy their ships with the aid of our intelligence.' He looked to JD.

'And of course thanks to the discoveries of this young man and his brother. We have no weapons to defend ourselves against humans and so can be a subservient race until we transport ourselves home in the ships one of which we now control. They're only condition is that their planet is left unmolested, and their technologies preserved known only to themselves. They don't want to be visited by humans arrayed against them with replicas of their ships. They are wise enough to know when the tide of fortune flows against them. There are hundreds of millions of my Bothers on their planet who, as a gesture of our goodwill, shall remain enslaved until all on earth have been repatriated to our home planets. And Paul, my Brothers on your planet will remain similarly enslaved with the blocks on their minds to assuage at least some of your concerns.' Paul turned and pretended to cough and turned on the satphone. He didn't want to transmit that part in case it was edited by Defenders. He had edited Barrion. The alien continued. 'I am eager to show you the ship and introduce you to our former enemy. Paul you will …'

'…Never trust you. Of course I'll never trust you Barrion. Every single thing you said. All of it. Every word was a *lie*.' Helen could feel herself getting angry. She was the interviewer, and it was she who decided how it would be conducted. And where. She tried to speak but Paul talked over her. 'You cut a deal with a *bus driver* on a ship? Did you consult with the leadership of their *Planet*?' He didn't wait for an answer. 'No. And you want me to believe you're on our team now? With another billion soldiers you can land in this fleet of ships anywhere in the world at more than a hundred thousand a day for each ship? And they can pulse any strategic location you want to. You don't even know basic details about the planet you come from Barrion. You're either not answering because it's total shit or you've been enslaved so long you don't know anything about it. In which case why would you go back there? Staying as 'Moes' is bullshit Barrion. Even if your planet exists, there are tens of millions of your Virides that might tell you to go fuck yourself. They like it here. And they'll want their piece of it. Any way that they can get it. And this bullshit that an Alien power with ships like this would scurry off with their tail between their legs because they met with you for half an hour. That kind of thing *never* happens Barrion. It takes weeks, months or years of negotiation to come to a deal of this magnitude. The only way you could get that ship is to either to have killed or taken the bus driver hostage.'

Helen knew she was being compelled. Though she still said the things she knew she'd been warned about. But Paul kept talking over her. Loudly. The Defenders were also getting angry, and would be genuinely so had they not also been warned to watch for the signs. They started to try to talk over Paul and said he was not speaking for anyone but himself. Unfortunately for them Paul had given free rein to what he saw as was one of his worst attributes. Unbridled superiority when he believed he was right and a complete disregarded for the feelings of others. Intellectual callousness. In this mode he was unassailable. 'You look me in the eye and tell me those Aliens are sitting quietly in their ship waiting for you to return. Are they dead or tied up Barrion.'

Barrion's discomfort was manifest, but he continued to drill into Helen's mind knowing she could master Paul if she chose to. 'Come to the ship and satisfy yourself Paul.'

'What, you won't look me in the eye. They're dead. You cut a deal with dead people. It isn't worth shit. But something didn't work out quite the way you wanted it to. What was it Barrion.' Paul was thinking about that streak that travelled through the sky soon after Barrion would have arrived.

Helen felt the compulsion in her mind relax. It was now brought to bear on Paul magnified to the greatest extent possible via his two associates on the plane. Barrion didn't realise however what a big problem Paul had with intellectual superiority. If he let himself embrace it. He was the worst kind of human for Barrion to try to dominate because any attempt from anyone to better Paul only magnified his trait to slaughter people in conversation, or a diatribe, when he believed he was right. Behaviour he would, even during such a rant, accuse inflexible ignorant ideologues of displaying. And yet never see the hypocrisy. 'You're trying to crack my mind. Was he doing that to you Helen. Breaking into your mind to try to influence you.'

'Yep.'

'He's trying it with me now. But I knew it was coming and I decided to be relentlessly negative. Which is the only thing I'm really good at.'

The witnesses were now shouting that they wanted their opportunity to look at all of this firsthand before the ship took off. They were shouting at Paul to shut up and let them go. Everyone has some anger in their lives. So they'd tapped into theirs and let it flow out as Paul had suggested. He wanted Barrion to relax with them and believe that they believed him. They went to the plane and climbed in.

Paul went to the plane and said. 'Hey you 'witnesses'. I expect you'll be able to send sweet little video commentaries before the ship takes off. Don't do it with one person in shot at a time. All of you. Agreeing what a great guy Barrion is.' Kurt got out of the plane shouting and pushed Paul around. Barrion looked at his watch. His dislike for humans escalating by the minute.

'The ship is on a Pre-Set for the first journey so I must return. Helen. In spite of all of this ill will, I had expected your journalistic instincts may have been piqued by the opportunity to tour a spaceship. You need not join us in the journey. The offer extends to you Paul. I can set aside your rancour and your many erroneous observations.'

It was hard for Helen to say but she waved her hand dismissively. 'Spaceships. Dime a dozen.'

'Barrion, why don't you at least tell us about your females. Longing for your return. Your rich culture when you're at home. Tell me about your mom and dad. Did you have parents. Is the ocean purple on your planet. Is the gravity the same. Is the ratio of gasses in the atmosphere different? Do you have the equivalent of Christmas? The Easter Bunny. Does the shit also float to the top in your society? Oh yeah…and why would the people you negotiated with bother *taking you home*. If they can't use you, and you're as irritatingly peaceful as you say you are. They'd simply leave you here and use those billion Virides *where they are* for some other target. You are completely *full of shit.*' Paul knew it wasn't a where, it was a *when*.

'I will give all these answers on the ship Paul. As I said I must leave now.' Of all the Professor's accusations what struck a chord most for those within hearing was that Barrion couldn't grasp the depth of Paul's sarcasm.

'No time for even a tiny second rate lie Barrion. I guess it would reveal what a second-rate *liar* you are.' Barrion turned away, anticipating the day this particular human would pay for his disregard for a genius he could never hope to understand. 'We're not coming Barrion, but I do have one thing to say to you that you will find *very* useful.' Barrion turned back. Paul stepped forward as if to share something a little more intimate. He pulled out the gun Phil had given him and shot the Viride though the head. 'Hasta la Vista Baby.' Paul didn't know how far Barrion could relocate when his body was killed, he was hoping he would need to consign one of his lieutenants to nothingness. And that's what happened. And only by a fraction of a second. Jumping as he saw the gun rather than risk a failed defence.

The propellers had already started turning as a Viride, now Barrion, closed the door. 'I didn't see that coming.' Helen made a thoughtful face and was nodding to herself. 'I feel like I get all of the great stories from you Paul when I *should* be helping a younger generation of female journalists along.'

'They'd all just end up wanting to get into your... good graces Helen. And on the list.'

'Will you shut up about the list Paul.'

Kill them All

'Let's finish the interview on something *really* momentous Helen. You ready.' Paul handed the satphone to JD. He looked at it at nodded. It had been sending.

'Okay. I must say I'm a little dubious about what might be more momentous than what JD has confirms we transmitted Paul.'

'Keep the camera on my face JD. Don't move it until I'm finished. Ready?' Paul was initially Professorial, but not superior. 'To everyone out there. *Kill them all.* Forget the government. Forget the 'Defenders'. Please, Please. Please. Do it humanely. That's who we want to be as a species. Humane. But kill them all *now*. You have twenty hours. Bombard your governments to sanction it and get them to initiate the protocols they all have. If you weren't able to read between the lines, I mean the *lies*, of that creature, you're all a bunch of fucking morons and suckers. Every Moe you kill now will be human lives saved. I'll be shut down or in jail soon. If not, I'll be as good as my word as you saw. Everybody who cares about our planet will need to get their hands dirty. Please. Humanely. Take the time to think about a way achieve that. But do it.'

Helen called for JD to point the collar camera towards her and looked into it. 'The views expressed by Professor Emerson, do not represent the view of the Network I work for. And, quite sincerely, as an unbiased journalist, I have no opinion to express. In fact, I feel fortunate on this occasion that it would not be appropriate for me to form an opinion on this very vexed topic. Thank you all for watching. I'll forgo the boogie on this occasion as we are probably about to get Pulsed.' The phone camera was turned off.

As they climbed in the chopper Helen said. 'I really thought you'd peaked with the 'slurry them up and put them in some deep ocean trench'. But you're the story *machine* that keeps on giving Paul. And now we'll get Pulsed because of the bad blood you've created with someone who only wished he had an actual olive branch to hold out. He was such a nice guy.'

'We've got a pilot showered in compliments by an alien with a Rolex. Who else can lay claim to that. We'll be fine.' Phil was redlining the machine away from the Pulse that never came. Because Basilica had the Control Key.

Paul and Helen didn't want the military reception Tim and Cody had received so Phil dropped them in the carpark of a large mall of the first decent sized town he could fly to across the border. It had a small airport where he was hoping to refuel and fly to his brother's farm while the 'world got weird'. He and JD had struck up a friendship, and the teenager said he'd like to come along while Phil's family drove there at high speed. 'I suspect my brother and mom and dad are being interviewed by government people around now'. Phil forgot to ask for his gun back.

It was like a war zone in the city centre with Virides being run down and killed. Unfortunately there were Defenders and Protectors facing off and they knew that in some places it would be a life and death battle. Paul was watching the results of what catalysed.

'The man of no consequence strikes again.'

He gave her a look of a university professor who might have swum a little too far into the deep water. 'How about a coffee. Then maybe a beer. Or three.' He followed Helen as she confidently strode into a department store and went to the costume section. Soon they were wearing wigs of Halloween quality and hats and glasses bought from the stores fashion departments. They looked at each other and laughed, skipped the coffee and went straight to a bar over the road from the Mall. It was wall to wall news of Paul's interview and Virides being exterminated around the world. In the US the message was they were assessing their options but not yet convinced wholesale euthanasia should be triggered. However all Virides were to be brought into 'containment'. A surprising proportion of the population were ignoring this. There was quite a bit of analysis of the conversation between Barrion and Paul. Some countries, including Russia, China and surprisingly Norway, initiated their euthanasia protocols.

Helen's phone had been either ringing or had a text coming in every thirty seconds. She'd put it on silent and said. 'Let someone else be the journalist of her age for a while.' They would have liked to go home but they wondered if home for them would ever be the same. So they set on the idea of getting a hotel room and simply going into hiding for a while.

In the cab Helen said. 'What happens when Barrion comes back and he is a nice guy. And takes this Jesus 'turn the other cheek' approach. Awkward right?'

Paul tried to rein in his superior tendencies. 'There is an enemy that stands behind even a 'Jesus like' Viride.'

Helen remarked to the driver things were quiet where they were. 'All the green folk are dead or have bolted. Human's started to feel stupid fighting each other when there were no live ones around to either defend or protect anybody from. I try to keep out of the whole thing. I'm old. Caring about things is a young person's game as far as I'm concerned.'

'I like your style.' Helen gave him a hundred dollars. In case money wasn't going to be worth anything anymore she might as well give it away to people she liked.

Fortunately credit cards still worked. After fifteen minutes in a line to get to the reception a harried young woman said. 'Half the staff are out killing 'em and the other half are trying to protect 'em so don't expect a meal in the restaurant or your rooms to get serviced.'

'No problem. We want to get some rest. It's been hectic.'

'Sure. Don't I know you from somewhere?'

'Yeah. I look a bit like that Helen Hunter woman from the TV. It can be a real pain.'

Two men came up behind them. 'Paul Emerson. We'd like you to come with us please.'

'Sure. Can I see some identification to support the authority you have to say that. I'd also like to speak with your boss.'

A man for whom conscience had never been a strong driver in life said. 'My boss told me to incapacitate you to the degree required achieve compliance.' He shrugged. 'Hence no need for the call.'

Paul nodded. 'That's all the identification I need.' He leaned in and told Helen to be ready, even if she didn't know for what. He stepped back quickly, pulling Helens wig and hat off and yelled out. 'These men are trying to abduct *Helen Hunter*'. Helen liked the idea, and she was no slouch when it came to getting physical. She'd reported in some of the most dangerous places in the world where there was no list. She spun around and gave the person who she'd found tiresomely overconfident a savage knee to the groin. Paul was hitting the other man in the head much less effectively giving him time to pull out a high end taser.

'Help me. Help me. I'm Helen Hunter and these people are trying to abduct me.' Those waiting in line, several of whom were on the list, immediately attack the two men who had been convinced of their unassailable power. They were intent on doing their job no matter how they felt about Helen. Government agents weren't allowed to be on the list which helped.

'Come on.' Helen turned and ran into the hotel restaurant where some guests waited truculently at tables for servers that weren't at work while those more pragmatic would-be diners helped themselves to the bar.

She went down a corridor and opening some doors and found a conference room and a little further along a smaller meeting room. 'As good a place as any to hide while we call in whatever cavalry I can…' She groaned. 'From the list.' She had locked the door and had turned to Paul remarking on her bad judgement because of the lack of beer in this hiding place when the door handle was shot through. 'Also the fact they could track us down using the phone you started Armageddon with.'

Two men in suits with handguns and five in black and grey military camouflage with machine rifles crowded into the small room so that even those holding the weapons thought it was overkill to have so many guns pointed at two unarmed people in a corner.

'Anyone for a list upgrade.' She said. Which did send a strange ripple of conflicted disquiet among the gun pointers.

Basilica

At that moment a Sororibus walked in behind them. 'Go away and don't come back.' She said. Amidst the heartbreak of lost friends and the concerns for the destruction Barrion was causing to the next Timeline, she did find the mental powers the Ageless One had given her rather cool. For all of her maturity, she was still in her late-twenties and caught up in a huge adventure.

The men nodded a goodbye to those in the room and left. Basilica was badly scratched and bruised. However she was business like. She was determined the Ageless One could be confident that there was *no* Envoy through all the Timelines that would do better. She intended to sweep the pair with a commanding glance, however could not help but catch Helen's eye with a strange look. 'It would be prudent to leave here as soon as we can.' She turned. 'And no Paul, I'm not compelling you to come with me. I thought you might be interested to meet your 'Second Enemy'.'

Helen got in first. 'Paul. You can do whatever the hell you want. I'm going with her.'

They were looking at a woman. Not quite human, but very close. Difficult to pin down what wasn't. 'Things are all getting a bit dull so I'm in.' He said.

In the car park, after walking through a crowd that might have mobbed Helen but didn't, Basilica motioned to a car and for Helen to drive. 'I haven't mastered these.'

'Sure.' Said Helen. 'Key?'

'Foolish of me. We don't use keys where I come from. No crime.' She got out and approached a man putting his luggage back in his car. Having poked an exploratory head into the reception area and decided better of it. 'We'll need to borrow your vehicle. It will be at the large grass covered field where you give instruction to older children.'

They were about to drive off when Paul said, having taken the back seat. 'Perhaps we could give that chap a lift to where his car's going to be. Might be hard to get a taxi.'

'And here I thought we were the civilised ones. Of course Paul.' Once he was in and they were driving Basilica apologised for her thoughtlessness and thanked him for the use of his car. The man, in a crisp business suit, appeared stoned and simply smiled. Basilica would risk nothing.

They pulled up in front of an empty oval. Basilica answered before they asked. 'It sits a few hundred feet above. If you can get over your trust issues Paul, you'll avoid certain death. With some of your kind you are…unpopular.'

Helen nodded to Basilica in a familiar way. 'Lead the way girlfriend.' The alien laughed. A pleasant, slightly ironic laugh.

Paul vacillated only momentarily. 'I'll not be much vexed at your fate Paul. It's Helen I'm concerned about.' The car they came in drove off as others, of several kinds, began to arrive. Many people had begun to track the phone from the 'Call that changed the world'.'

'You're on her list I suppose.' Was all he could think in response.

Helen was annoyed. 'Fuck Paul. Alien species *number two* in the *history of the world* giving us a ride in a *spaceship* and you're still obsessing about the list. It's grown up time. Your superiority buttons got pushed by *not being much vexed about*. Now come; man who thinks nothing matters.'

The Alien laughed as she and Helen stepped forward, vanishing from view. He joined them quickly after a glance behind. 'Paul you cannot appreciate the irony. It is *Helen* who is on is on *my* list. Or the start of it.'

They were in an elevator. It was very high end. But still an elevator. Before anyone could make any kind of observation the doors were opening, and they stepped out.

They followed Basilica to the 'bridge' which was very simple and functional. It was small so all that space was, Paul assumed, for some kind of freight.

The alien introduced herself. 'I'm Basilica. Envoy of the Ageless One. A Sister of the Sororibus and representative on the Suffragaito.'

Helen couldn't help herself. 'Are we talking Marvel or DC Comics.'

'This is straight from George Lucas.' Sometimes she and Paul were very much in tune with each other. 'I'm itching for the sequel, and I haven't even seen Part One yet.'

Basilica was tolerant. Pleased even. 'Exotic aren't we. A Spaceship. And here I've picked up the heroin with her comic side kick.' She had watched some elder earth movies as a girl. They were frowned upon by some for their violence and overt or covert chauvinism. She found them fun. Perhaps that's why she was doing what she was now. 'And here you are meeting a mysterious Alien woman.'

'Who's planning to take over our planet.' Said Paul. 'Spoiler alert.'

'We'll get to that Paul.' Said Basilica. 'If you had let me *finish*, we also have a villain. A very powerful villain.'

He was about to respond but Helen squeezed into the conversational spaces he barely left for anyone when this mood was upon him. 'Shut up Paul. It's my turn. Basilica. Let's compare notes. Barrion;

Gets in your head. Lies about almost everything.'

Paul would not be quelled. 'Unlike the rest of his people, who are captives of evil slave keepers?'

Basilica was an Envoy and endeavoured to retain the dignity of the position. But being in proximity of Helen was intoxicating. 'Mysterious and alluring slave keeper I had hoped for Paul.'

'I can support that.' Said Paul. There was something familiar about her. Helen nodded in agreement.

Helen led off. 'How about an interview. You're word limit is zero Paul. This will be yet another monumental event in the history of humanity.' She struck a pose and smiled as only she could. 'And I'm…'

'The journalist of your age.'

'Thank you Paul. Zero word budget remember. Anyway the audience already knows that.' She turned on the phone already the cause of so much upheaval and in journalist mode said. 'I'm interviewing Basilica from the planet Sororibus. She's just been attacked by the leader of the Moe's who should now correctly be known as the Virides. They stole her spaceship, and she escaped in a transporter. Sounds a bit like a space movie. Basilica, how can we convince an audience you're not an actress in a studio. A very alluring and mysterious actress that would be.'

'It's not my concern to convince anyone of anything. That's your problem. I'll tell you things. People can believe all or some of it. I can't make people believe anything other than the spaceship we're in is real. Because we can go to various destinations at high speed. I can demonstrate that later if it would help with the credibility issue.'

'You have a good grasp of English for an Alien race.' Said Paul. Smiling and shrugging at the glare from Helen.

'We follow the doings of a target planet in intimate detail. That's why we know so much about you both. Unlike what you choose to believe Paul, your life, and a handful of others, have had significant consequences. The people of Earth, the Sororibus and the Virides have all been powerfully impacted by you.'

'The dynamic about which we are not fully appraised of.' Hinted Paul.

'Unfortunately, some of this is for the Ageless One alone to explain. I would love to impart this information Paul. But's it's not my place to do so.' She laughed again. 'Now you will be vexed by both suspicion and curiosity. An interesting conundrum for you. I can say, as Paul largely adduced, Barrion will endeavour to take over Sororibus first. There are nearly a billion Virides whom he will try to take control of to bring progressively to earth. He can bear losses in the tens of millions every year. As you suggested, they have developed a hive mind so that any useful intelligence or capability as a soldier can be shared outwards roughly in the proximity of a loud call. Barrion can pose as anyone, and he has demonstrated a capacity to harness tens of thousands of minds and focus them on one point. Like a huge magnifying glass in the bright sun. He can burn a piece of paper in a place of his choosing. He tried this on me, and he turned my Sisters against me and then left them incapacitated. Sisters I'd known since childhood and trusted completely…attacked me.'

'And he's coming back.'

'Yes. He was discomfited because the Ageless One has the capability to change the state of the Virides. Their mental age is preserved at eighteen on our planet. They have pleasant lives both in the orientation of their mind and they do gratifying work, for which they partake many of the benefits, as do the Sororibus.'

'Slavery.' Said Paul.

'Yes Paul. I hope you're not about to embark on one of the superiority drenched soliloquies you're so…adequate at. And then you lie to yourself by saying you can't seem to avoid this 'bad habit' you have. And later express regret and apologise. Then you deride people who behave the same way.'

'Nailed it.' Said Helen.

'It can be very tiresome Paul.' Basilica was talking as she placed her hand on a pad of that shape glowing amber which turned green. If they were moving neither felt it. 'In ancient Rome slavery was integral to their society and that Empire's achievements are widely admired and left many a positive legacy. Your own country had slavery only an eyeblink ago in time. On your planet there are still millions of slaves. More than ever in its history. Kept for the purposes of abuses any moral person would find repugnant. We do not practice the kind of slavery humans are permissive of Paul. Sexual abuse of women and children. Some of your slaves are on ships they never disembark from. You also have huge numbers of debt slaves. Their wages don't pay the costs of work or living. Their debt and incapacity to leave becomes greater by the year. And millions of child slaves working tirelessly so you can enjoy coffee and chocolate.'

'The various forms of slavery, in your world right now, would be an anathema to us. But what I find most irksome about your world, is the massive inequity between rich and poor. As a university professor of average means, you receive more than two hundred dollars per day. The majority your population subsists on around six dollars a day and a tenth, the poorest on your planet, on a dollar a day. While some earn the or a hundred times more than you. The gap between rich and poor is very narrow in our society Paul. Of course the divide between wealth and opportunity also cuts deeply between genders here. At least a third of your women experience some form of abuse There are no weapons in our society, and we've never had a war.' She smiled. 'Although there is the occasional nasty snit. So there you have it Paul. You've finally met someone who has the same conditions as you do. Someone who makes themselves feel superior when it doesn't really matter. Because we are such inconsequential things. Are we not?'

Paul smiled and nodded amiably to Basilica. 'I have no rebuttal to any of that.' He looked at her as one who couldn't help himself. 'Oh. Except the gender equity thing. Perhaps you should have left that observation alone.'

Basilica had the laugh of one who had worked so hard, given up so much, hence it didn't happen often. Those who heard it felt fortunate. 'A point *very* well made.'

'Let's creates a space we can put feeling bad about being human to one side for a moment.' Said Helen. 'What are your intentions Basilica?'

'Naturally I'd like to recover control of the ship. This is in both of our interests. It would cut off Barrion's capacity to feed an army and Pulse strategic locations. He would retain the capacity to masquerade as any Viride or probably human and project enormous power through harnessing the minds of his kind, and who knows perhaps he'll be able to use humans for this purpose also.'

Helen looked directly into the camera clipped on Paul's pocket. 'Monumental as these developments are ladies and gentlemen, and contrary to what might be suggested by the strange workings of an even stranger algorithm, this reporter is a mere humble female human. Who needs to wee. I'll be back with an update on this heart-warming story of two Alien races battling it out for control of mother earth.'

Basilica pointed the way to Helen. Paul was on this occasion more interested in what someone was about to say than crafting his own conversational input. 'It might sound like flattery Paul, but we're alike enough to have studied conflicts on earth, much more the-oretical in my case. To their credit I think humans have Barrion's measure. Although, you know better than anyone, there have been many 'regrettable' wars on earth. This is the first time all earthlings have a common enemy. There will be much, though not universal co-operation, and humans are capable of fantastic leaps of innova-tion and production as has been seen before. Those great dictators and autocrats, some, but not all, were brought down by their own hubris. Which Barrion has in plentiful supply.'

The Play

Helen arrived back to a comradely silence. She motioned to Paul the transmission was over. Paul thought Basilica's last observation fit-ting and pursuing her on her species intentions was going nowhere. 'So what's the play Alluring One.'

'As to the 'play', an attack to recover the ship might be made by stealth. The three of us. The Ageless One configured my mind in such a way that I would have some protections and defences against Barrion's powers. However at the time we had no conception of how advanced those were, and I think they are expanding in a way which is a surprise even to him. The ship is set on Pre-Sets for destinations he can now predict and hence could have a small army in place to focus his energies. However I have one advantage. I took with me a Control Key from the ship.' She brought out a short rod similar to a large cigar in size and shaped in a way that looked like a crystal but cut like a metal. The facets ranged from large to minute and had fine grooves filled with a variety of metals so it could only fit into one place, in one way and needed to connect to a complex interface inside the carrier. 'We made adjustments preparing for this Delivery and he is unaware that using this Renewal Freighter I can countermand the pre-set and cause the ship to land at a place very remote so that if we can find protection from him, there will be nowhere for him to go. This may give your species a few more precious hours to fully accept the advice you gave Paul. Now. You may now point out the many potential falsehoods I have been including in my narrative.'

'You're an intelligent woman…or alien female Basilica if you prefer that. So I'll curb my truly tiresome need to couch everything in a mantle of superiority…'

'Helloooo.' Said Helen. 'Superiority alert. *Mantle couching*…I mean please? Who talks like that?' This was easily the most interesting day of Helen's life. A life with so many to choose from and she felt great.

Paul continued. 'From my perspective, my species must come first.

To what degree can we have a shared objective? A species who is overtly in the process of taking over my planet wants the ship back that was facilitating that. I think I am correct in now deducing there is only *one* ship.'

'To resolve this situation you would need you to do something contrary to your conception of war. You would need to trust an enemy. Remember I could have pulsed the ship in Washington DC. At any time.'

'I've met a few Americans who might have been in support of that.' Contributed Helen. 'But do we have time?'

'More than a few Russians feel that way to name but a few.' Replied Paul. 'So why didn't you pulse the Capital.' Said Paul.

Basilica smiled. 'You'll have to ask our Guide of long ages for your answer.' She continued. 'Barrion might recover this Key and Pulse the ship in any number of places, and then disappear into any of the Heads of State. Our opportunity as a Second Enemy has vanished Paul. We conquer planets by stealth using strategies you saw the early phases of. Hard to believe as it may be, where I live there is not one single weapon. I hope you are not going to give me a lesson the evils of conquest Paul.'

'It did cross my mind.'

'There is barely a nation on your earth that has not either been conqueror or conquered. Often both. Need I point out New Mexico, California, Texas and the Philippines after a fashion. What of the colonial and war conquests undertaken by most of the nations you call allies. Tens of millions killed, huge numbers wounded, raped or unhomed. A vast number dispossessed. Would you say, as the conquering species, our approach is foolish or intelligent. We are at arm's length from violence, our species is safe and doesn't need to become martial in nature. *And…*prepare to be incredulous Paul. We select planets based on their imminent demise.'

'I admit. It's a pretty good model as far as conquest goes. Simultaneously drain the enemies energies relying on their good nature whilst at the same time bringing out the worst in some and creating perfect conditions for intraspecies conflict. Preserve the infrastructure as much as possible.'

'Hence the reluctance to Pulse.' Said the Alien.

'I'm not conflicted on this.' Said Helen. 'If the Sororibus win, I'll have a new place to call home. Paul will be turned lettuce leaf green but hopefully he'll be able hang around while you show me your planet. *Still* platonic Paul.'

Basilica could bear only so much in the way of banter. 'As Paul achieved by being a relentless contrarian, there are techniques I can provide to you which will be effective defences against our common enemy. But to make these work as he gains power you would need to let me ah…'tinker' somewhat in your mind. A capability the one I so greatly admire has provided me with.' Paul looked at her. Suggesting he need not say it. 'And who knows what kind of latent capacity I might leave in there to take control of you at a whim.'

'You can rummage away in mine. You'll find less going on than everyone seems to think'. Said Helen.

'Not to be disrespectful Basilica. I'll risk Barrion so we have a spread of outcomes and I have a reasonable chance to tell the truth if I'm allowed to survive.'

Helen turned the full force of her personality on her companion. 'I'd rather get taken over by a *Basilica* that a *Barrion* and I'd rather not have Barrion standing next to me because he's occupying *you* Paul. Sooooo…you are fucking well doing this because I am *telling* you to.'

Both were a little surprised to see Paul shrug meekly. It was tinged with a sadness his two companions were too distracted to fully appreciate. Basilica approached the role of investing Helen's mind with safeguards with what looked like reverence. For Paul it was more workmanlike. In both cases it was done quickly, and their minds felt nothing. 'What's your favourite colour Paul.'

He frowned. 'Lime green. Though…I'd always been partial to sky blue. That's the colour of my car.'

'Ha. You'll have to buy a lime green one now. But it's the only thing I've changed. And I can tell you that truthfully; as your mysterious enemy.' She'd wished later she could have taken control of Paul. However her mistress had not given her more than she'd promised them.

'I've always been a cerise kind of girl.' said Helen. Basilica laughed. She nodded to the highlights on her smart flight uniform. 'A few billion of my Sisters already knew that Helen.' Basilica found being in proximity to her original mother, as with the Ageless One, who loved Helen for different reasons, a kind of intoxication. And she had a natural affinity to Paul. Like it or not they had their similarities. She had been revealing more than the bare necessities jousting with him. Which was a mistake.

'We'll go to the new landing site. Barrion won't know he's off the Pre-Set until shortly before they land. However depending on how good his technical people are, he may be able to hover the ship, and if he's able to build the beacon device I'm certain he's been designing for decades, that's when he'll awaken his army. Which based on your announcements Paul, one hopes is diminishing as a force. And if we gain the ship he will not be resupplied.'

'Why would he not Pulse us when they land.'

'The same reason he had to spare you as you fled him. He can't. Such a drastic function, only ever used *once* by the way, requires this, and both my hands on the sensors. The protections I've provided you are essential for the self-preservation of earthlings. To inhabit you would be a great benefit to him. You might communicate a change of heart based on what you would claim you'd seen. And to inhabit Helen and use her journalistic credibility to send messages of peace and a false description of the real threat. The Sororibus. Aligning with his message that salvation from us requires the two species to join forces. This would be disastrous to both our interests. Which are more aligned than one might think.'

'Success for him would be to take the control key and any useful contents of my mind then a swift death. I would imagine he would begin a process of destroying strategic locations of all nations and move through the bodies of key leaders in politics, the military and those highly regarded in religion, entertainment, science and maybe the internet and youth influencers. Sending instructions contrary to the best interests of earthlings and sowing false hope, confusion and doubt. His objective will be to subdue the population in weeks, not months.'

'I didn't really have a choice about the little brain surgery thing did I Basilica.'

'It's so much more pleasant as a voluntary process. You benefited from Helen facilitating your cooperation. The lime green thing was mischief. I too am a lover of sky blue as it happens.'

A Boon Unlooked For

He returned to the bridge in a foul humour stimulated by Paul and enraged partly at himself because he'd spent decades preparing for all eventualities and counter moves for each. Now he reflected on what he had not anticipated. He had made the mistake of believing, that although some expediency might be tolerated, no Sororibus would completely cast aside the moral norms that had been entrenched for millennia. And yet the Envoy had killed her Sisters, all long standing colleagues, whom he had hoped to use for his purposes in convincing the humans of his resolution of the threats. She had left a wall of his ruined brothers four feet high dead and dying, not all of which had been removed. Those compelled to move them, dying themselves. Basilica had weapons none of her kind had ever touched, though they lay everywhere on earth each time during a new cycle of Renewal. Or so he mistakenly thought. Some truths only the Ageless One, and now her Envoy were aware of. He was mistaken if he thought he could access her mind. The Ageless Once made sure of that in one of her 'upgrades'. Basilica had asked for such a failsafe after it had already been installed. She was indeed the Envoy Chrona needed.

Barrion would never have guessed the Ageless One could insert such a powerful thrust into the mind of an Envoy that it would leave her companions dead, strewn around the bridge. However that all meant little now due to the insight into this capability of the

Sharing which was a monumental miscalculation on her part. It had alerted him to a possibility that would alter the entire balance of power permanently. If his technicians could make the Beacon to do it he could use his unique capacity to Share as one of the Sororibus. After which he could take what he pleased from the planet unhindered during the years left until it was compressed to nothing. He'd told them they still must deliver the function of the Beacon to awaken their Brothers ready for their return. But they must have the new project completed also. In less than eight hours.

He needed to load the ship with a force of Virides to use them as magnifiers to find and capture the Envoy. That was his first mission on his return. He had to be able to Pulse the ship and break out of the pre-sets. Every resource he had, including his prodigious genius, would be focused on this outcome.

Initially he was briefly the charming host to the 'Witnesses'. They felt a presence in their minds. Only because Paul had suggested they be alert to it. They were incurious about the 'Second Enemy' who he said had retired to their quarters but would come out as a delegation to meet them before arrival on their planet. They felt the soft sensation of departure and he bade them to tour the ship. Sections of the ship inconvenient to his narrative were locked. Jessop remained on the Bridge while the other 'Witnesses' went to look around. But also discuss strategy, however as allusions and reminiscing about hunting trips or actions during battles Kurt had been in. They had seen enough. The majority of the ship was utilised for transporting Virides, and in a few places they saw the suffering of the remnant of the ruined Brothers. Their condition never explained. The pathetic sight triggered compassion in these men that had seen them as a dire threat to planet earth. Yet they appeared not to be a consideration that Barrion gave not the slightest thought to. They hatched a plan. They were curious about the ship because it clearly wasn't built for moving around a vast population for a war of stealth. This was a trading vessel. Converted to this purpose. Chrona had forgotten more than she knew. Even though what remained to her was breathtaking by the standards of any ordinary citizen of the universe.

When the ship made that soft sense of touching down, Barrion was shocked. And felt like a fool to have thought there was any limit to this creatures disregard for life. Like Paul he could not see the irony of this point of view. He would never have believed even the immortal manipulator would do such a thing. One ship full of his brothers made into imbeciles perhaps. A ruthless strategy. But *all* his brothers. His great army and it's hierarchy of officers and strategists spread in secret via the Sharing. The powers they would be awakened to. All gone. And yet how could he expect her to stand by and watch him take what he pleased. He hadn't anticipated she had this kind of power. They had not needed to walk through the corridors. She had achieved this travesty via the beacon. The very machine he was building. The one that was used to enslave them had been used to reduced them to helpless things. Incurable. It was a disturbing scene. Those Virides who had been preparing for loading when the ship returned standing and swaying or on hands and knees. Crawling. The senior marshalling Virides who managed the loading were calm. Maintaining order. There were no Sororibus to be seen in the marshalling areas. She concealed so much of her brutality from them.

However Chrona and her Envoy still needed the labour of the Virides. So it was for only the mustering area where every Viride had been reduced to the permanent infantile state. The rest moved out of his reach by many miles. The Suffragaito would be outraged were they aware, but they were contained within their precinct for now. As always, the vast majority of the Virides worked on the huge farms and manufacturing centres and continued to be supervised by their own. He discovered that the Ageless One had suspended the powers of democratic rule and established the young Envoy as a virtual autocrat. The Author had wanted a young and inexperienced Sororibus to falter at the challenges he presented. He had misjudged her entirely.

He called the 'Witnesses' to the control room. Jessop already with him. Beside him in companionable silence. Leaking anticipation of what the life as a familiar to Barrion might involve. They looked out at the Virides who had been mustering by the tens of thousands for the ship's arrival 'You see. The heatless cruelty of our slave masters.' The trio, a little separate from Jessop, who appeared ready to believe anything he was told by the alien, tried to share his compassion and soon after outrage. Their actual perspective was that this amounted to less enemies for humanity to deal with.

Barrion wielded such a powerful ego and ambition it was difficult to conceal himself behind the facade of meek reasonableness with an expectation for a harmonious alliance against a common foe. They had seen him dissemble before Paul's questions. They felt another intrusion into their minds. Their arrival was not consistent with his tale of a capitulation of the Sororibus. As he endeavoured to contrive an unlikely narrative for them to assimilate as a belief, he was endeavouring to instal ideas that would propagate rather than transient nudges. He had done this with the ruined Virides for the first time. Barrion's experience of duplicity was only that of himself and the Ageless One. A planet full of habitual deceivers was something he still struggled to fully grasp. The Witnesses had agreed with Paul's advice. 'No warnings'. They turned as one while they believed they still could towards Barrion and opened fire.

He was hit in several places. In a split second he turned the full weight of compulsion upon them such that Leon, the Hunter turned and shot Kurt and Malcolm shot the hunter, however in the dying throes of compulsion, Jessops's father fought back and shot his friend in the leg instead of the chest as he had been compelled to.

Barrion had to move quickly out of the dying body they had riddled with bullets in the split second they'd had to attack. He displaced the most junior of his technicians in a room nearby. Jessop's father picked up the military man's fallen handgun and pulled Leon along limping. He shared a glance with his son who stood calmly by. *He was always a strange one.* Thought the father. Not for the first time. The two men decided to retreat to a place deep in the holds they'd found while they had investigated the ship during the journey. They immediately joined hands and recited the Lord's Prayer to try to keep him out. And it soothed them.

Barrion had no dispensable bodies in cargo to occupy and so lost his least talented technician, which was still a heavy blow. His anger simmered. The two could delude themselves that they were safe. Make their strange invocations to a god he had never conceived could exist, so pragmatic were the Sororibus. They would be making a fulsome call for everyone to seek an alliance based on what they'd seen. Barrion knew politics. It took only a small measure of doubt to create enough uncertainty to drive action or inaction depending on the manipulators objectives.

The Pre-Set would have them leave the planet in an hour and a half, the time it took to load, with scores of ramps deployed on many levels and the large ramps on the lower decks of the ship. He tried to compel at least a few to crawl towards the ship. However they perished due to in a further block installed by the Ageless One.

Then he was given the news by his Lead Technician. And he smiled. Everything which had been a disappointment was swept away. The Ageless One had been a victim of her pride and failure to conceive his genius by demonstrating that the Sharing could be used to neutralise the crew of Sororibus. She'd made a desperate move to deny him the ship, or at least the Control Key if all her plans went awry. She would not have suspected he had trained technicians for decades as the Authoress to master every aspect of the Sharing. Beyond the simplified version the Virides were permitted. And then beyond the Sharing of the Sororibus. Its weakness was that pieces of information could be Shared with a close friend, or a family member, a whole work group. On rare occasions, information needed to be disseminated to all the Sororibus. The barrier against misuse had always been assumed to be impossible to crack. But she had shown him it could be done and where to look. All he needed was a Beacon to spread the signal to all Sororibus across the vast wildernesses between the cities and towns via their Beacons as they were too distant for the Sharing to be transferred by proximity.

The technician nodded once the Beacon ready and the Authoress calibrated it to the intimate Sharing. The entity masquerading as a Sororibus had been an honoured guest to so many minds in their most intimate mode that he could transmit an incredibly powerful signal and insinuate an urgent message, a need to respond to a threat as a Species. A threat to the Renewal. It needed to be shared immediately. This message carried a plague. A curse and it only needed a few to take hold in each far-flung location to re transmit it.

They stood watching. Hacking into cameras in public places was a trivial task for Barrion's mind. It allowed him to watch as they started to fall. It propagated itself. Thirteen billion Sororibus fell in any position they landed in. Vehicles collided; those swimming drowned. Mothers simply dropped their babies and collapsed. All still alive. Other than those unfortunates who fell to their death, drowned or died on operating tables. All older than fourteen, before which their lack of discipline created a discordance in the whole. The youth Shared only among themselves. It was seen as a mark of maturity and a Rite of Passage to join the Whole. And hence created an incentive for the young to mature and be responsible. All above this age were unconscious. And only he could rouse them.

He timed this event to occur minutes before the ship departed on its Pre-Set. His Beacon, originally only to awaken his Brothers, had performed an unlooked for mighty purpose. Now his technical team could focus on the next task. The Beacon to awaken his army. The Ageless One came onto the screen.

'I hope you haven't come to bargain.' Barrion laughed.

She looked across at him. Sad. 'If there was anything I could offer I would. So many who suffer will be babies. Girls, boys and young men.'

'You know you have nothing to give. I'll pick and choose what I want of those that remain. And don't bother offering to save some of the Virides beyond my reach today. Turn all their minds to mush if you would do so out of spite. A painless end compared to what your arrogant and privileged Envoy will suffer.' Barrion had a thought. 'Unless you would give me the Orb to make the ship complete rather than a mere bus.' He smiled. 'I'll restore your slumbering slave masters at once for you.'

The Ageless One sighed. 'My mind has changed.' She was dealing with a being that had known nothing but lies since his mother concealed his true nature. 'We have ten years until the end. My heart breaks at the suffering to come. But I will give you *nothing*. And if you believe you can return here with impunity, I'll take what small pleasure left to me to repay you for your efforts.' The screen went blank.

An Army Awakes

He turned to the technicians remaining. Only three now. 'We celebrate a miracle. An unlooked-for victory you have brought to fruition. But you need to meet this next challenge, establish the Beacon to awaken my army. I will now need each and every one of them. Husband carefully your focus. I'll work on breaking the ship out of the need for a Key and countermand the Pre-Sets and give us the capacity to initiate a Pulse.' He was talking to himself now. 'Once I can disappear into the population my efforts alone could win a war.'

His kinsman had been a little uncomfortable to have Jessop stand at his side through all this. However Barrion had skated across the surface of the boys mind. He knew the motivations of such a one.

181

He cast his mind over to the 'witnesses' who were still praying. He let them believe they were locking him out.

He asked Jessop, as a comrade might, if he could prepare a meal for his bothers and if he would join them. The technicians were pleased to see him gone. He was fascinated by the Beacon, and they were afraid he would break something.

Barrion had to unlock a part of the ship to allow Jessop to do this. Jessop's talent had long been to find and use secrets. He was surprised to find still a few of the dead and dying Virides. This led to more investigations which led to the discovery of the Sororibus no longer behind a locked door. The Enemy Barrion described as such heartless slave masters. He was disturbed to find they were all female and had been thrown and heaped together. He needed to conceal his response to this. Even from himself.

He returned with food and while they ate, the technicians doing so quickly, he asked if he could take some food to his father and his friend and Barrion was understanding but demurred. 'They would have killed me Jessop. You are our friend. I would not chance that some harm should come to you. They may still adjust their views with time to reflect on developments.'

Barrion was focusing intently to a part of the bridge control with two hand marks and a slot for the Control Key. He didn't need to take anything apart; he was simply following the complex circuity with his mind which terminated into a solid piece of crystalline stone which revealed nothing of its inner workings. He was demoralised, however his powers, which had grown to be an adept at the Sharing, were expanding to a mental emanation unparalleled among any for a thousand galaxies distant, except those of Elouise and The

Hope of the East whose mental capacity none could measure. In their case though, this was now an augmentation via a technology they routed their minds through. Barrion believed as his capabilities grew, they must be unmatched. With intense concentrations he could see the wires of all kinds of metals weaving into millions of filaments. Again he was demoralised. However he sensed if didn't try to use an analytical state of mind, but rather let his genius float through untellable complexity his intuition would make leaps of insight which analysis never could. He began to see, very slowly, how at least this remarkable feat of space and time manipulation might work. It was disquieting to realise another genius. Whom he had spoken to only shortly before, had woven this. He could see it was a bespoke work because where dead ends of possibility were reached, they were left. The entire conception did not appear manufactured but inspired. There was only one of these anywhere. And he had the good fortune to control it. He did not realise that the 'Bubble' by which Chrona created a new Timeline was an entirely separate part of the Renewal process. An unintended gift from Elouise. It didn't matter. He would take everything he wanted from her, when he turned up unannounced in her past.

He lost hours examining the instrument and thinking of what he must acquire if he was unable to break out of the Pre-Set, even only to delay the ships departure by introducing a reversible fault. He would take out every freighter and anything useful and return at a time suitable to him with the powerful human weaponry he would by then control. Returning to a future stripped of any individual or structure which was useful to his aims. And he would burn her out of that Orb and recover it in the past. He was unaware of the heartbeat stricture.

His opening move was going to be to get as many of his soldiers on earth to safety as possible and then occupy the leaders of the Great Powers to recommend a truce and initiate talks regarding an Alliance. With a thousand brothers in harness Helen would support it. And even Paul. He would strangle humanity slowly via their own leadership rather than take them head on. And once he'd figured these instruments out, he would simply reset the game. There would be no Sororibus and there would be no Virides. He will have taken the entire ship from that ancient space farer and there will be only him. In complete control of humanity. From whatever era it pleased him to start from.

Two men rushed into the lab. Still saying the Lord's Prayer. They each got a shot off as he drew his mind from the intricate workings of the ship and his machinations. One hit his arm. The other though the fleshy part of his ear. A second later, the Hunter changed his aim and swung across and shot Jessop's fathers then turned the gun on himself. They had managed to shoot him at a time he couldn't afford to interfere with his remaining technicians capacity to work. He would need to bear the injuries for hours. Barrion was able to nullify the pian as Jessop went to his father's body and sat on the floor and held the old man's hand.

'I'm so sorry Jessop. Could they have only waited they would see that although I might posture, and in spite of what others might think, my aim is for an alliance with humanity and a future that is bright for them.'

The young man, only halfway to seventeen, dragged the tears from his cheeks with his fingertips. He appeared to recover himself. 'They're minds. All of them…these sort of people…their minds are so closed off.' He looked up and appeared concerned. 'You're bleeding.' He said nothing more and went to get some of the cloth he'd seen in the kitchens for bandages.

Barrion was appreciative but amused by this. He could sense an expectation in the boy's mind that he would fare very well in the new world. He had championed Barrion's well-being on the day they first encountered each other against bullies and stood against his own family to be a true 'Defender'.

Virides did not make emotional displays because their emotions had been muted. Barrion disliked the creatures almost as much the young Envoy did whom he could not help but admire. They; like the humans, were a means to an end. However when one of his technicians clasped his arm and smiled and said. 'It is done.' His 'Brothers' were bathed in admiration and an assurance they personally would be remembered as the architects, with him, of a lasting glory for their kind.

Barrion looked up smiling. 'You triumph for the Brotherhood. You three will be remembered. Our quest would have come to little without you.' There was mutual smiling and arm squeezing. He would allow them that and then insinuate himself into their minds and mute the entire episode while the least proficient would provide an uninjured body while his message was delivered.

He believed he could bring the ship, with concentration, to a brief hover while he spoke to all the Brothers via the Beacon as it freed them. He expected to be met by a substantial gathering of leaders and foot soldiers he had awakened thought his sojourn. However he was now confronted with another setback. The Envoy was able override the Pre-Sets. Something he'd understood to be unachievable without the Control Key in the main Ship's carrier with hands placed on the pads to change it. He realised though that the probability of him taking the ship was not unforeseen by that alluring hag. The new Pre-Sets made his preparations on the ground useless. His anger partly assuaged at the bitter price the immortal one was paying for her failure to see all ends. But he was a long way from anywhere. Two large islands in the far South Pacific. New Zealand. Far from the location he'd bade his Brothers gather and be ready to take orders. And then he would take a freighter to acquire a powerful weapon to be carried back to her realm and shatter the Orb to shards if he could not hold the ship.

A Viride came to the Bridge. 'All is in readiness.' The creatures mind died, and the wounded body Barrion had occupied fell dead.

Barrion caused the disappointments and challenges to disperse from his mind. The message must be one of certainty and unshakable confidence. This was the moment he had dreamed of since he was a boy and saw how his gender was treated. A screen lit up. Every surface of the ship could become a screen. This took up the entire one-hundred-and-eighty-degree viewport on the bridge and a huge number of surfaces on the ship used for major announcement. On this occasion beamed to the Viride world. Beamed on the high and low frequency the humans knew was a 'Moe Communication Capability' but could not block. 'Brothers. The moment has arrived.' Tens of millions of Virides stood still, many which had escaped in hiding in the most remote and difficult country nearby to where they had been. The Ageless One had left this within them as a setting at the first evidence of organised violence against them. They were an asset she wanted to protect. The setting was that they needed to preserve their lives at all costs and kill any that impeded them. Some that stopped to obey the beacon were being pursued and killed. However Barrion was confident now. He needed soldiers.

Yet when he surveyed the news signals Barrion was again discomfited. He thought he had blocked the transmission of the camera the young man had been using as he disputed with Paul. This took concentration. For all of his genius he had not anticipated a second camera. He realised more and more that the people that he had grown up among, apart from their mysterious benefactor who was never seen and rarely discussed, were honest, trustworthy beings. Albeit he hated them for what they did to his species and gender, in their daily dealings there was no duplicity and very little rancour let alone violence. Hence, he was finding to his chagrin, in spite of his Machiavellian manoeuvring, he was unprepared for the devilry humans could adopt on a whim.

Paul's interactions with Barrion and final message had set off an orgy of violence directed towards Virides and between humans. The intense, relentless negatively Paul had bombarded him with had caused him to split his attention to try to create a cogent argument in return, jam the camera with the open transmission signal, beguile the minds of Helen, and block the thoughts of the Witnesses and the pilots to the impact of Paul's narrative. Now he learned the interview had been transmitted. The unavoidable weakness of his arguments had been spread throughout the earth. Thanks to Paul, Virides had been slaughtered by the hundreds of thousands before escaping. Some, in the compounds they lived, died when 'Protectors' with rocket launchers, destroyed Virides en masse. Government efforts to follow established protocols were sometimes held up in the courts and sometimes by human shields. Anything from a handful to thousands of 'Defenders' mixed among them or formed around them. However he quickly regained his confidence. His approach would adjust to self-preservation tactics until he had navigated his way through some of the Heads of State. In the guise of the one he chose as the most fit for his purpose he would create tensions between two nations or blocs of allies. The nation he took control would send a barrage of their deadliest weapons against another. These creatures, little better than beasts, would never restrain their reactions, which would be to retaliate in kind. They would destroy themselves.

Barrion's voice was clear and grim. The Beacon allowed them the natural response of anger, fed with a calculated message of the need for absolute obedience to achieve their ends. He gave them a taste what being the masters of this world could hold for them. Every piece of useful information about war, weapons and strategy every one of their Brother had ever learned was being pooled into an available Shared Mind. This would take time to analyse and redistribute in the most effective subset for each Viride according to their rank and location. 'My Brothers, you have been humiliated and misused by two races. Maintained in a state of subservience and consigned to the tasks fit only for drudgery and misery. You are free now.' He lied. 'Free to be part of an army that that will take possession of the jewel in the crown of both of our enemies. Yes Brothers. Our Slave Masters have been defeated.' This came across as a glorious mind shout as they saw the images of the Sisterhood who, all but the young, seemed to lay dead. 'And now it is the turn of the abusers. You are now feeling your bodies and minds fill with skills, knowledge, operational plans and arrangements which will be provided to you more individually by this Sharing and the Brothers who will lead this army. You have only one objective now. Follow my instructions. Spare none who obstruct you from doing this. An expert on war from this place has told us how to win. We must banish mercy from our hearts. In freedom we may live differently. So break any bond to escape. Sacrifice some so that most can find freedom. Take what you need to live and find safety and survive. Trust no one and leave none to tell of your passage or whereabouts. This transmission has made the trackers various governments put in you worthless. You will hear further messages from me, via this great Sharing device your own Bothers devised. Your leaders will begin to emerge and find you. Our days of being misused are at an end. Break free.'

Jessop had never left Barrion's side. Barrion's message came from his mind, not as a narrative inside the ship. He had not invited the boy into his thoughts as it would reveal the truth in everything his father and his friends had believed. Barrion was pleased he had at least one human who would be compliant for the next broadcast. A plea for a ceasefire. Curated images of the Sororibus before their disastrous Sharing. Doctored images Barrion had prepared for years. A message that the Virides had details of the technologies they could join together and use to create effective weapons. But the Virides needed assurances to enter an Alliance to destroy the Sororibus and return to occupy their world. The humans must leave them in peace, and the Virides would disarm as a token of good faith, though they would disperse to safety until they could return to Sororibus. Trust having its limits he would quite reasonably suggest given the circumstances.

While Barrion's full focus was on crafting a message trying to respond to the new complexities which had arisen due to Paul's transmission, Jessop was sending the messages his father and Leon had prepared while saying the Lord's Prayer. He sent the texts initially and then the short videos. Had Barrion known this he would have been surprised. Not Paul though. Nor his father who knew he had a son who could be sneaky and as a child and had played his mother off against father on many occasions. And the same for many others. Friends, teachers or other relatives. Jessop was inclined be a Defender initially. But the stronger motivation was that he was immediately in charge of the local Chapter because it was a location so dominated by Protectors no Chapter had been established. This gave him an authority he could never have gained by talent or effort. He had heard that Helen Hunter was interviewing people about the abuses being visited on Virides and he had contacted the Network describing, indeed exaggerating, the state of his community and the almost open abuse of the Virides. She was to be interviewing him later that day when Barrion, from a distance, had nudged his mind with a suggestion he go for a walk to where the Author knew another young man was going to the outskirts of town smoking marijuana. That young man's father was a dog baiter. The friend he called had a father who was a policeman who openly refused to investigate cases of abuse. It was not Jessop's habit to go for walks in a local park.

Barrion's message was complete. It had been taxing to hover the ship and project power into the minds of tens of millions of his brothers.

Jessop was relieved. All his texts and videos had sent because the hunter had acquired a phone with satellite capabilities as had Paul expecting they may alight somewhere where communication using standard services was not possible. He did this while the Alien was fully immersed in his message. Barrion turned to him. It was so easy to manipulate this boy he thought. Barrion again, disingenuous as he was, had very little experience with someone who was sneaky and such that everything on the surface was a duplicitous pretence. It was unknown among the Sororibus. He was accustomed the petty vanities of those such as the Princep. Though even these were not without some basis. 'I would be happy to make an announcement suggesting there should be a ceasefire and that if the leaders were willing, you would meet with them and discuss the peace you have only ever advocated.'

Barrion smiled. Having this boy come on the screen first. A human. Before he took up the narrative would play well. 'That is the posture I have described to my brothers. We need only an assurance there can be a pause, even a brief one, such that I can provide proofs to all earthlings of my good will.'

'I believe if I could say some…things to help avoid…' Jessop looked at his father's body and appeared distressed. 'A lot of people from both our species could be saved…it's all…unnecessary.'

'Your message is a good one. I will leave it to you to present what you know in any way you choose.' He lied.

Jessop's eyes were downcast when he said. 'Barrion. For those that have…helped you in your cause.' The boy shrugged. 'Will there be a good life.'

Barrion smiled, looking at the young man and thought. *These humans would sell their world for a life of pleasure.* He answered with what appeared to be complete sincerity. 'You Jessop. Will live like a king. And be ever by my side as my indispensable advisor.'

Basilica had been watching all of this with interest, all tempered with despair and a sense of urgency concerning what she had learned of the condition of the Sisterhood. Any surface of her ship could be used as a screen, and transmitted to her because she had the Key. She admired the men who gave their lives even to cause some injury to their enemy. And the son who could deceive such a master deceiver. She could easily turn on Barrion's message to make it audible in their freighter as it was the Ageless One who had invented the Beacons and inculcated into the Virides their form of Sharing. She transmitted the message. Helen suggested they end the transmission after Barrion's call to arms. She said Jessop's words were hardly something they should relay. Paul and Basilica exchanged a look. 'Barrion will send it in any event. We'll record it all and we shall see.' Said the Sororibus. However she grew impatient. Minutes were precious now.

Jessop saw his face on the screen. Transmitted to an entire world full of screens. A vast number had paused in what they did to learn anything of their dire circumstances. Jessop would speak and then Barrion with his faked newsreel of imagery. The alien learned too late the outcome of the reaction Jessop had when he watched the interview between Paul and Helen. That proved Barrion's killings of the Virides had been orchestrated and he had come to the same conclusion they had. He was not as invested as a Defender as many believed. Ultimately everything was a means to an end for him. So when Protectors called him a dupe and fool, he knew it to be true. Jessop the opportunist was replaced by the Jessop who would repay any slight let alone a humiliation with orchestrated machinations to punish his target. When Barrion reached out to him to be a Witness, he had no idea Jessop, a sensitive and not a very athletic boy, was one to make people pay, and often out of proportion for their crimes. Jessop, an individual who further believed himself to be under appreciated, would now have an opportunity to be a player on the world stage, albeit at great cost.

So this was a double victory for Jessop. He repaid a villain in kind and would have a place in history as the one exposing that villainy. He looked out as if over a crowd. From what Barrion could see his mind full to the brim with what living like a king might entail. And it was tawdry. The instant the technician nodded to him he knew he had only seconds. 'Kill them all. They're planning to take over and they will do it unless we stop them now.'

In his disbelief and rage Barrion turned upon the young man's mind. Jessop had turned, running and was shouting the Lord's Prayer and he filled his mind with negative, combative hate. Pushing hard through Barrion's mental grasp with one objective. He clumsily elbow charging it like the football player he had never been. Smashing into the beacon, falling on top of it and being cut in many places. He got up and ran. All at once the ship settled to earth. Jessops heroism in the ship was transmitted. Basilica's mind reached out, magnified by two others, both powerful for humans. They'd agreed quickly. Paul knowing he would be 'told' if he tried to argue or set limits. The trio endeavoured catch Barrion in a vice. It was pointless once he was aware of them and could retaliate, though he could not break through and destroy them from this distance. It had been enough of a distraction for Jessop to escape. He might be useful to her. And to make Barrion realise his only option was to flee. Before the feed was shut down people saw a Barrion surprised, and momentarily indecisive.

She controlled the ship to the extent she could send it anywhere though not Pulse it. The Beacon had been receiving and retransmitting the latest learnings about human technologies and the most successful strategies being utilised by the Brotherhood. It had intended this would be propagated resulting in a vast trove of knowledge being transmitted over hours every day. All were now constrained to local learning with a Sharing only within hailing distance. Still formidable, but much less so.

'Seventy three percent.' He heard in his mind. 'That's how many of your Brothers remain. The humans are hunting them down as we speak, even with the trackers disabled. Your army shrinks and weakens. Your minions must cover a great distance to rescue you. They have many skills now I will admit. But you'll be gone.' Barrion could see the ship entering a departure sequence. It had protocols however. There were a lot of moving pieces in a ship like this and it would not take off without ensuring it was entirely capable of getting back to when it came from.

The Bargain

He spoke into the screen. 'I can damage this ship irreparably. It is the only means to deliver the remedy you seek. If it leaves now without you, it leaves your entire Sisterhood dead where they fell. My bargain Envoy; is that I leave you this ship. My ambitions will become more modest, and I might appear to parlay with the humans as to a place for us. But it will be with you whom the real bargain is made. Decide.'

'As if anyone would believe that. Touch and take nothing and flee with your henchmen. I would have a word in private as you pass.'

'I'll must have the freighter.'

'That's impossible.'

'Then your Sisterhood be Damned. You are more that I bargained for Envoy, but my mind calculates probabilities to a nicety and mine are negligible left here without shelter and transport. My heart turns bitter from the unwelcome developments in these last few moments. It's not beyond me to cast away *every* dream I had to see your miserable race, the project of a being of unspeakable cruelty, snuffed out with you stuck here forever more while that witch watches them die.'

Basilica knew she had no options. 'One ship for another. Nothing more is agreed or believed. We both have capabilities we are not fully aware of. We despise each other. Can our trust stretch that far?'

'It must. We meet between the ships.' Barrion believed he was powerful enough in close proximity. He could still take it all.

Basilica turned to Helen. 'We leave now.' And Paul with them after what was only a short pause of silence to them. She was impervious to questions and took the Control Key.

'You made some kind of deal with…'

She talked as she walked to the elevator. Paul could only follow. 'A bargain has been struck Paul. Stay and take on Barrion if you want to chance it. He will use you well. Flee if you believe you can into the wilderness and return to your quest for irrelevance and an end to your imperious nature. He will catch you. To you Helen I can only say that I am convinced that if you accompany me, you will believe your decision was a good one.' She was in the elevator. It took barely a glance from Helen and Paul was following. He had decided to anyway. For his own reasons.

Basilica was then left seething standing in sleet between two ships for nearly ten minutes. Three figures emerged from the ship. It had come down over a vast plain of button grass in New Zealand and so had a ramp lowered which was a simple walkway unlike the escalators for the Deliveries. Two Virides ran to the freighter.

It had taken a few moments, because this was the first time. Barrion had found the boy and broken through the pathetic recital of a prayer. And so it was Jessop's body that strode to stand before them. 'Envoy.' He smiled. 'This pathetic human will recant his judgement, for the small impact it will have before I move on.' He turned to Paul. 'Your famous insight fails you if you choose the Sororibus for Allies Paul. They are led by...'

Basilica brought her hand up so quickly swiping her nails across Jessop's face Barrion had no time to react. 'That's for my Sisters. The one's you corrupted.'

His eyes flashed. Another precedent from a Sororibus. 'Fool of a girl! I am not the Corruptor. And your compensation for what you and your kind have done to my Brothers will be paid in full. Stay and cross the Horizon to oblivion or return and see what the earthlings weapons will do to your ship. The present is *mine*. And more.'

She could see it coming in the boy's eyes. Basilica threw up a screen using every erg of energy she could draw from the three of them and barely held back a killing blow directed at their minds. She flashed it back at him with hers, now combined with two more and he staggered back. Jessop's face revealed shock. She'd nearly killed him. He turned and ran. He'd had power. She'd had fury. What would have surprised him even more was that she had to govern that fury. She *could have killed him*. But didn't. She was following instructions.

Basilica had signed on to the ship with her mind as soon as it was in proximity of the Control Key. She was amazed at the powers she'd been given by Ageless One and aware that such a power might stimulate a creeping desire. For more. She turned to run as soon as she'd given Barrion the measured but stinging blow as he reached the freighter. It took Helen and Paul a moment to reorient after being drained by her harness.

Paul started asking Helen questions. What it had felt like for her. He kept glancing towards where the freighter was parked. Helen's mind cleared. 'We need to go. Come on.'

Paul caught her by the shoulder as the freighter disappeared. 'Helen, I think you should stay. The last part of this…adventure…hasn't been transmitted to humanity and having someone who has been up close to both of these species could be essential to saving ours.'

'Paul…' She gave him a confused look. 'No. That's bullshit. You stay if you want. I'm getting on the ship.' She turned and ran; the ramp was starting to lift. Paul was beside her as she neared the arched entranceway. The ramp lifting above their feet.

'Helen stop.' He said it in a commanding voice. As if he had identified some immediate danger. She stopped at look at him however he turned, and with as much force as he could muster grabbed her in a tackling embrace and pushed her back and sideways the ten feet to the edge of the ramp, pushing her off. She fell eight feet into the button grass and there was no way she could jump back up on any portion of the closing ramp. A satellite phone landed next to her.

It took Paul a few moments to find the bridge.

'Where's Helen.' Said Basilica.

'Weak bladder. She'll be with us soon.'

Basilica opened a menu next to two hand prints and paused the departure protocols, lowering the ramp. 'You cannot understand it Paul, but Helen is more important to our society than any other human. I'll watch with interest while you go to greet her and invite her aboard.'

It was not a warm greeting. Paul allowed Helen to pour invectives over him. While pushing him backwards. He said the world deserved to know what they knew. He lamely followed up saying it was dangerous and he...shouldn't need to explain his desire to see her safe. This started a fresh round of abuse about her being patronised as if she was unable to decide what risks she wanted to take and what it had to do with him. Paul all at once retreated into a sadness she could get no purchase on, so she left.

On the Bridge Basilica was overriding any protocols she could. Paul decided he should say something on behalf of his species. 'Now he can go anywhere. Unobserved. Move troops around. Take over leaders.'

'I feel no obligation to craft some apology to you Paul. It was the first time he occupied a human. The capacity I was given have held him at bay and that would have been the eventual outcome if I was to chance regaining the ship. And no. There is no time to communicate anything to your people.'

'It's a thirty second message about what he's capable of now. What he's planning.'

They felt a slight lift. 'You're people are warned of what he can do, they are capable and aggression Paul. You chose to cast away your communication device partly because of an evolved predilection to what you perceive to be a weaker gender. My race lies stricken and will begin dying on mass within hours. A fate neither of us believe in Paul has ordained me to wield the singular opportunity to resurrect my species from its demise. You could have remained behind with the communications device, but you threw it from the ship instead.' She put on the footage of the thousands of Sororibus, as a sample only of billions of female aliens, human in appearance, lying everywhere. Screaming babies and toddlers crying and confused early teens trying to wake their mother's others forming groups together in confusion.

She excused herself and went to the room the Virides had used for the Beacon. Jessop had done extensive damage The ships library automatically made detailed plans of anything that came aboard. When the others arrived, she said. 'We have the information, tools and parts to fix this. The ship has generated a list, and these tablets will guide you. I'll appreciate any help you're able to provide.'

'Don't you need to pilot the ship?' Said Paul.

She was a little dismissive. 'It will make the journey and land itself. I've restored my control. It will have been seventeen hours since Barrion departed by the time we arrive. If I've not repaired it, my hope is Adule technicians can be summoned and be able to do so before too many my Sisters begin to perish.'

Hard Choices

Paul pulled out the control key, walked over and shot Basilica in the thigh and shoulder. He had seen how she invaded his mind, and it was not so different to the tactics Barrion used. She needed a modicum of acceptance. A mind aware, relentlessly negative, and merciless could hold her at bay, especially when she was experiencing intense pain and now a deep-seated anxiety. 'Time to hear the real story.'

'Jesus Paul. What the fuck…' Helen absorbed the glance from Paul and her voice trailed off.

'I'm going to shift the focus onto *my* species for a moment Helen. There are three sides here. I'm on the human side of that equation. Billions of them. We need to know the truth. And not from some very old person in six or eight hours. I already know we're not going some*where* Basilica. We're going some*when*. Even Elouise, the *'genius of our age'* wouldn't suggest we could get very far in six hours in space.'

With a gun on her, Basilica didn't feel at liberty to do anything about the bleeding wounds. Helen started tearing up the clothing of the ill-fated 'witnesses' still lying dead in the Bridge. 'Yes. The Sororibus live on earth. A millennium and a half into your future. We've dwelt peacefully all that time.'

'No small achievement. So why come back and take over our future now?'

'Humanity is on the crest of a cataclysm of their own making. As I told you. We take over a planet deserted of its master race. And not though our doing.'

'Convenient. That doesn't explain why you'd come back. It does my head in trying to think about it, but if you return to colonise the earth…again…wouldn't you crash into the existence you've already had.'

'It's not like that. We start a new Timeline. There is no future involving the Sororibus in the original earth Timeline. We return prior to our last Renewal and reside in the original earth Timeline initially. After the Renewal the Bubble, which is being drawn forward in front of us, is withdrawn when…certain conditions have been met. Only a small proportion of our population is transported. Those reside briefly in the Original Timeline. While those who's end approaches have ample past to sustain their present. And then that Sororibus Timeline is withdrawn and encircles the Renewers who now have fifteen hundred years of untrammelled future. Because the previous fifteen hundred years of Sororibus existence…never occurred. It disappears completely. A new Timeline is cast forward.'

'Why not live on. Why come back to repeat the process.'

'The process is never repeated. The learnings, culture and civilisation continue to evolve, peacefully, but from a nucleus again. The planet is, once more, a blank canvas.' She hoped he wouldn't pursue the line of questioning he was intent on.

But this was Paul. 'That's hardly a reason to cancel the existence of, what was it, thirteen billion of your people. Why are you so concerned about them now if only a handful are going to survive.' Paul would remember that point long into the future though take only a little solace from it.

Basilica knew she was revealing something to Paul which would have incalculable consequences, but it could not be concealed. 'The Planet is unfortunate to be in the proximity of a Black Hole which, contrary to our best science, arrived unannounced and unwanted in a location which pulls Earth inexorably towards a Horizon from which there is no return. Our society was established and has been guided by the Ageless One. She would have moved on after rescuing us from being the brutalised chattels of the male of our species. Abused and used for pleasure, procreation and drudgery. I think this is the kind of work her species are tasked with.' Basilica could not imagine the Sororibus had become the project of a benevolent and unusually gifted example of a species of trader. 'However she could see the place she brought us to had only a brief interval for us to survive. She used her genius and the capabilities of her ship to return us to the end of your civilisation. And it became an ongoing practice.'

Paul nodded. 'And now you have the Virides to deal with. Fighting against you for once rather than for you. You usually walk in and clean up the mess, now you have an enemy digging in against you. While you need to transfer a whole population on a schedule in front of extinction. With one ship and a sixteen hour turn around.'

Basilica began to sound fatalistic. 'Of the thirteen billion adult Sororibus on our planet Paul, only two hundred million Renew. Most of those have conceived children from your present-day population, such that our diversity is maintained.' His eyebrows raised at that. 'A combination of the old-fashioned fertilisation method and utilisation of sperm banks. The Sororibus can be very alluring and make the one they are assigned forgetful. This is an honour for those chosen, and while some see it as a fleeting pleasure, others dislike men other than the Adules they are accustomed to and find it odious. Via this process we generate a new Diversity and a new and unique Timeline.'

'You can mate with humans?'

'The Ageless one has made an insert. It strips the male gametes of their species but maintains their contributions to our diversity. Once we conceive Adules, these are the male form of our species.' This is what Basilica and the Sororibus believed about what was in fact a half human male progeny. The girl children, with two X chromosomes, were pure Sororibus who take diversity from their fathers. The pure male of the Sororibus genes matured too much like those Chrona had rescued some of their females from. Violent and aggressively dominant even in childhood. Human genes moderated this somewhat and some genes from plants, pacified them in adulthood reconfigured mind and body.

'And where does all this leave us now Basilica. Although they are a credible threat, the Virides will be utterly destroyed by my species. Barrion doesn't account for the fact that he has not grown in an environment of violence. Brutal, relentless warfare and with technologies he will be unable to control to a sufficient degree to master the billions who are against him. Unlike many conventional wars, on this occasion humans have only one clear enemy. And apart from their leader, they cannot conceal themselves as members of another population. The Defenders will see the Virides for what they are. Unfortunately humans have a tendency in war to convince armies and populations their adversaries are sub human. Like it or not, this will be easily achieved against the Virides further eroding the countervailing impacts of mercy. The Virides will be a target for any civilian. Man, woman or child with a knife, a gun, a baseball bat or a rock. Barrion's tricks will lead to some early gains, but I suspect he needs to stay in one place to harness his 'superpowers' in focusing his bothers. This has to create a readable signal. They, and any humans foolish enough to harbour them will be shown no mercy. Every leader, every soldier and every kid who played a video game and always wanted an enemy they can kill with absolute impunity will be doing just that. That's what the Virides are up against.' She realised how little capacity she had to have an impact on a fully grown, unpacified male. Paul's mind, surprising when it revealed this side to her, was so far outside of her experience she realised she probably shared more in common with Barrion. An unexpected naiveté and vulnerability of the relentlessly civilised. 'What does an alliance with the Sororibus look like.'

Helen was occasionally glaring at Paul. Who appeared for once disinterested in her mood. She was interested in what was being said and very grudgingly knew it was the only way to get Basilica to say it. The shoulder wound was difficult to work on and it was a competency Helen had never developed any skill at. 'You tell me Paul.' Basilica said quietly. 'It's your specialty.'

He sighed. 'Present day earth makes room in the less salubrious part of the planet for the Sororibus. They can't expand. They continue a culture of embarrassing sustainability while mating with nubile males and emasculating older males to be their slaves. Reducing the drain in resourcing the slaves they photosynthesise. All of which is better than what we men deserve of course. Though this element of their culture might be curtailed. But what do they do with the mature males Basilica? Some nations and 'movements' look on with interest. And as in your own accurate words, the Sororibus are rather alluring. Some human populations have a not insignificant minority of misogynists who place very low value on the females of their race and even less on other races. This will be even more diminished for those of another species. However you have destructive capability which, if people can't get the original, they'll want a copy of, and a time travel capability. That means eventually some strong man or trillionaire will figure out a way to take or replicate what you have and will create carnage throughout human history, irrespective of people saying it can't effect the future.' He paused.

She smiled up at him. Sadly. 'You're not going to believe my 'convenient' observation that humanity is destined to perish.' Before he could answer she turned to look at the Beacon. 'It's repairable. I'm sure of that. And without it, every beautiful thing I've ever known will be gone. Art, friendship, music, home and the peace of the Sharing.'

'I have no doubt that it is a magnificent society if you're any example of it Basilica.'

'Yet this isn't a Superhero tale. With a happy ending? Even if a little obtuse.'

Pauls voice took on a note of desolation and he repeated her words back to her. 'A fate neither of us believed in Basilica has ordained me to wield the singular opportunity to protect my species.' She looked up at Paul as he raised his gun. 'I'm so sorry Basilica.'

'I know you are Paul. Mercy truly is the first casualty of war. How could it not be?'

He took one step forward and shot her cleanly through the forehead. Helen jumped in surprise. She had not understood Paul was merely sharing a rationale with Basilica before he killed her. She stood up and shouted at him. 'Have you gone fucking crazy.'

'They're going to take over *our* planet Helen if their society is restored. No matter what they look like or sound like they will stop at nothing. Their planet…our planet is about to be destroyed.'

Helen couldn't believe what he'd done. There was a reason he was such good news fodder though. 'This isn't some lecture topic Paul. This is billions of women and children. They're not soldiers. They're not killers. We need to take some time to look at the angles here for Christ's sake. There's probably someone, when we get there, who could fix that thing. Or replace it.'

His voice became very quiet. 'There's no going back to our time now Helen. We can't take a chance that Barrion or anyone else ever gets this ship…and…' His voice dropped to a whisper. 'I won't be able deny you once we get there. Or even if you agree that we have to look after our species interests. What we have to do…or not do. I couldn't bear to see what it would do to you.' He brought the gun up.

She looked on. Incredulous. 'Paul.' They stared at each other. 'Paul…what…what is this. It's me. Helen. You…' The shot blasted through her cheek. He had shot Barrion and Basilica cleanly and assumed it would always go that way. Helen had dropped to her knees screaming. One hand covering the wound, she reached out and waving to grab his trouser leg as he stepped forward and screamed his name. He took a fraction of a second to aim, deliberately on the same side of the head as the wound, down from the hairline above the forehead and out of the base of her neck. She slumped down. He stood for a long time looking at nothing.

He took her under the arms and dragged her to the wall and slid down with his back and took some time arranging her so that her head was lying on his chest, the uninjured side out. He ignored the seeping moisture. He drew her legs up, bent at the knees, and arranged her arms as if she was lying against him asleep. Then he started to cry quietly. He had an arm around her shoulder. His hand occasionally caressed her hair with the tips of his fingers.

How much later he didn't know, but he felt a very light settling of the ship.

The face of a woman appeared on a blank wall inside the control room. He would learn that any surface could become a high-definition screen. She was one of the most striking people he had ever seen. But he didn't know why. She was yet another alien race he knew that much. Though she was somehow familiar. He didn't much care though in that moment and had nothing to say. He kept a protective arm around Helen, the irony of this not lost on neither. Chrona spent some time absorbing the scene.

'This was always a *possibility* Paul. I thought it would be too difficult for you. I should have taken more note of your lectures. Your teachings were not purely about the theory of the demise of Mercy and birth of Expediency. Now that the ship has returned, I can see my Envoy has already made her pleas for the babies who lay crying in their cribs or those older children screaming with fear and confusion as they try to rouse their mothers.' There was a very long pause. 'I could guide you to repair the beacon. Is there any possibility for...'

'Mercy.' Paul went back to saying nothing and the Ageless One did not intrude on it. Eventually he said. 'If I would not show it for *her*, there is no other that could sway me.'

'Of course.'

Reluctant Genocide

There was a long pause, suggesting neither of them had any more to contribute. A thought came to him. 'If you show me how to Pulse the ship I can travel through the larger centres and put an end to some of the suffering.'

'Our cities are large. With urban areas of all sizes spread throughout the planet, it would take a long time to Pulse all of the populated areas.'

'We could relieve some if not all.'

After a pause Chrona said. 'You're right of course. I can prepare pre-sets which will be the most efficient pattern and the ship can Pulse automatically as each is reached.'

'No. I pilot the ship to the locations you guide me to. I deliver the Pulse. You must demonstrate you have no power over the ship.'

'What you suggest would be far from efficient and require continuous co-ordination. The process will take many days. And piloting the ship is not as simple as you might think.'

'This isn't negotiation. I'll sleep a few hours a day and you can teach me to pilot the ship. Decide or turn off the screen and leave me.'

The screen went blank however the woman, early thirties in appearance returned within a minute. 'It's worth what can be achieved. But you would have vision of what's occurring on the ground as you travel so you can understand the consequences of the decision you've made.'

Paul snorted. 'And here I thought your objective was to achieve whatever mercies we can contrive from our circumstances. That's only secondary to making me suffer for the consequences of deciding to save my species. It's not a decision that sits easily believe me. Go away. Mind games with an Alien aren't high on my list of things to do.' Yet it was with a strange reluctance that Paul said this. While Chrona was stung to be spoken to in such a way. It has only happened once, a few hours before from the one she despised. It made her recall something Helen had said. *I only realised now I've never even had a dog bark at me.*

Chrona disappeared but again came back soon after. 'My proviso was ill advised and it did, I hope you will believe, misrepresent my priorities. I will guide you through the process of taking control of the ship.' Her voice became grim. 'The…hands of the Envoy will need to be placed on the control panel imprints. Her hands will need to be…body temperature.'

He went to Basilica's body and moved it carefully from the adjoining room so he could lift her up as one sleeping. Sitting her in the command chair and holding her two hands to his chest. It was awkward. Her head could loll back or fall forward and he could not help but feel it was wrong to have her head falling back in such an obvious posture of death. So he arranged her forehead on his shoulder. Tears were flowing again. He had immediately liked and respected her. Hence he chose to have her head on the shoulder, awkward as that was. He was now drenched in both Helen's and Basilica's blood. All this time the stranger watched on.

'You have one opportunity Paul.'

When he was ready, he gave Chrona instructions. 'Take five steps back from where you're standing.'

'Paul this isn't neccess…'

'I'll decide what's necessary.' She did as she was asked.

'Now thread your fingers tightly together and put them behind your head.' A displeased Ageless One would no doubt be very intimidating if she didn't have the need for the collaboration she was obliged to. She had saved the downtrodden and with help become the master of time. To be treated so. 'Now turn away from me.' Another glare and she did as she was asked.

One of the reasons he asked her to turn away was that he was not going to be able to give any consideration for the dignified treatment of Basilica's remains. In a motion he'd gone through in his mind a few times he put the control key in the slot which he had removed after he'd fired the fateful shots. He clasped a wrist in each hand and slapped her hands hard on the panel, sliding them up such that the fingers splayed out into the recessed shape. In doing this the Envoy's head was thrown forward and cracked against the control panel. There was a list of commands in a screen that appeared on the blank console one of which was to 'Add Controller'. He let go of Basilica's wrists, tapped that line on the menu and slapped his hands in the outlined area, glad his were not bigger than the places for them and hence might be rejected as too large. 'Controller Added'. He pulled the Control Key from the slot. Chrona had just arrived back in front of her controls.

Paul was looking up at someone petulant at being outsmarted, then caught. Or so he thought at the time. 'I'm surprised you can't control the ship.' He said.

'There is a reason both Control Keys need to be in place. It's a failsafe so no one can take control from one end, given the havoc a ship like this could wreak. I risked an augmentation for my Envoy. But it was for her alone. At this time I only wanted to take over the pre-sets. And Pulse in the fastest and most efficient way.'

'We're stuck with what we have. My trust issues aren't going away. I want to Pulse right here first. I assume this is near the middle of the Capital.' There was a long pause. 'And I assume your Orb is immune.'

'Yes...'

'This is the only place the technology and possibly the...Adules... are they, exist that might repair the Beacon. This is where what mercy we can contrive is going to start.' Paul had been all business like and assertive. Chrona had played at being haughty as she did with Envoy's she didn't like. But then he heard her voice and could not but appreciate what a monumental moment this was for her.

'Do you know Paul. I've forgotten. How many times. The new Timelines...' She said sadly.

'There is no way I could understand what it is you've achieved, and now what it is you're losing. I can only give my species a chance.'

211

This was beyond anything he imagined in terms of a difficult decision to make and stick to. And it was about to get much worse.

'I understand. Paul; Basilica wasn't lying about the virus. Your species is doomed. Come what may.'

'She may not have been. Unfortunately, in the human world at least, you lie about one thing and people tend not trust anything you say. That's where things have landed.'

'Move to the other control station. The one on the left. A suite of options comes up with your left hand on the pad. One reads Pulse. Press it. It will ask for your right hand, then press it again.' Before he hit the button, the control room he was in was surrounded by a three-hundred-and-sixty-degree view of the surrounds of the ship as if it was glass. He had known nothing of the location of the ship in relation to populated areas. He saw now that in the time they'd been talking thousands and gathered around the ship. Girls younger than their mid-teens and boys and young men of all ages under about eighteen. And thousands of Virides crawling around the docking apparatus surrounding the ship. They were all thrown back like trees in a meteor strike as a thin electric blue line ran out over every surface leaving everything dead and inoperable.

Paul looked up to see a sight no one had seen. Tears were sliding down the Ageless One's cheeks. She had cried on two other occasions. Then she had cried alone. She smiled. Embarrassed. She spoke quietly. 'Bring up the same menu to get a map to appear on the front screen.' The map that came up was of the earth he was familiar with. 'Hit change map and it will take you to our time. Usually it responds to voice commands but there is a manual system. If you would allow me to give the commands the ship will pick up my voice it will allow you to watch and familiarise yourself with the process as we…work through the Capital. Then you can take over manually.'

'Okay.'

It was arduous to witness. In the streets, and piazzas which were a common feature as were a plethora of canals and gardens and all kinds and eras of housing. While some were completely foreign, some were unsettlingly familiar. As Basilica had said, small children were kneeling or lying next to their mothers whimpering in confusion or crying. Young men similarly confused trying to wake up what he imagined were lovers or their slaveowners or however it worked. Chrona was working her way methodically through a city crafted and preserved with love and pride. A city never touched by war or rebellion. He looked up to see Chrona, on the far wall. She had her eyes closed and was calling out the pulse centres from an intimate knowledge of the city. A city she had never set foot in. Paul began to see the movements on the map as a pair of sighting lines like cross hairs. He could take over the location in the cross hairs as a touch screen. 'Shall I take over. I think I have some idea of the centres.'

'As you wish. I'll advise you if there's too much overlap or gaps are being left.' He felt like he was bombing Dresden again and again. Pointlessly to demoralise a population. But this was to euthanise an entire species. Genocide at the greatest scale ever imaged. He came to a sector out of the city exclusively comprised of skyscrapers. He initially thought they were housing, perhaps for the Sororibus who couldn't afford a house on land. But they were huge agricultural complexes reaching into the sky. Hundreds of short levels in buildings with a floorspace the size of a small field and a system of mirrors which created light regimes for whatever crop they wanted to grow. They were vegetarians. And from what Paul had seen all slightly built. He could imagine greenhouse gasses reverted rapidly to a more natural setting soon after the arrival of only two hundred million new tenants. All around the city, and every other of the dozens he visited, was an extensive and heavily treed parkland with lakes and holiday resorts, each set within the distinctive landscape of the region, beyond this only untrammelled wilderness of the type that had originally been there before being 'tamed' by man. The cities were largest in North America and Western Europe, and these took weeks, long after the Sororibus had perished, in addition to the small children who had no older children or Adules to care for them. And there was the Virides by the hundreds of millions. These were no longer the clever weapon of an unseen enemy. They were beings now. As innocent and harmless as any slave. Emasculated though they might be. Sentient. Killing on this scale caused him to refelct his recommendation to 'slurry them up and pump them into an ocean trench'.

After four weeks they started to see the signs of violence. The older Adules, without the constraints of a Sororibus civilisation around them and the conversion to Virides began to kill and soon after rape. Evidence of small gangs forming and looting in a more organised way. Attacking the defenceless with their hands only, there being no conception of weapons in the society. Other groups developed an equality between the genders and were violent as aggressors together or primarily in defence.

'So it is with males. When civilising constraints are removed.'

'I have no argument with that.' Paul was broken. Yet resolved. Even if his mind were to change, it meant nothing now.

It was the first time they had spoken in nearly a week. She had suggested that the continuous view he absorbed eighteen hours a day of the terrible process could be turned off. Its purpose having been served. He said. 'I will drink this bitter cup until the end.'

A few days later they were working on smaller centre. Places that a single Pulse had ten times the diameter of the population centre. Chrona said. 'Were it not so horrific, Lissa would see some irony in this. Do you think?'

Paul didn't immediately get the reference and was caught out by the fact that Chrona could know such intimate details. She continued. 'You might recall your riposte to her proposition there was a god not so long ago now. You questioned her contention that he could be a merciful god. You asked her to accompany you while you committed all kinds of atrocities. And she was to stand by. A spectator only. And here you are. Doing something you thought inexplicable.'

'I could argue about motivations, but the reality is inescapable. I wish I could see her again. Tell her I was being arrogant which I often am. I conceal it behind what I pretend is intellect. I didn't realise what else was concealed there.' A self-loathing was settling upon Paul he was certain he would never eradicate.

'The greater irony being your contention to all who would listen to you that your life was entirely inconsequential. Our core beliefs are so often wrong Paul.'

The Ageless One sidestepped any inquiry into her miscalculation in life and said. 'These few centres will be the end of this purge as far as I'm concerned. We're seeing that the Adules are dispersing now. The Sororibus loved the natural world that makes up vast majority of the planet and most would prefer to leave the plants and animals unmolested and to their fate.'

'I can see the sense in that.' They both knew the reality was they were emotionally exhausted. 'I may make a survey from time to time to see if there are Adules forming groups and committing...abuses.'

'Males regress so quickly. Do they not.'

'If they live in a context of a healthy civilization or even a stable culture of the hunter gatherer, their worse nature is mitigated. There are reasons why they regress. To a degree it's not regression its survival in a situation they evolved for. But the reasons don't justify the outcomes.'

'Our collaboration is at an end Paul. This is goodbye.'

He hadn't been quite ready for that. Their relationship has always been cool and only ever procedural. To end it so sharply was a reminder of her distain for what he'd done. He got a 'Goodbye' in before the screen when blank. He sat quietly, apart from the necessary functions of his body, for two days his mind generated no meaningful thoughts not having anything to do or plan.

Helen, Basilica, Jessop's father and friends were in a larger chiller room. The Sororibus who had been on the ship when Barrion took it over and three of his 'brothers' and those poor creatures who had been slaughtered by Basilica and simply been unable to fulfill Barrion's call to get them and themselves off the ship had all been taken out and laid in a large, pleasant meadow two days into the pulsing journey before they began to rot.

Now that he was alone, he roamed all around the ship getting to know it intimately. It gave him something to do. Then he decided to fly around and get to know this future earth on more intimate terms. He found many opportunities to Pulse the ship and distracted himself, macabrely, for a month. He thought he would get on with being depressed and lonely and end it all. Yet the Event Horizon would be interesting, and he'd be the only human to ever get dragged over one. He might fly right into it. Helen would like that. He thought about her a lot. He believed he'd made a mistake. He'd judged how she would decide and treated her like a child. Maybe she would have led him to choose differently. It plagued him when he failed to distract himself with further killing and then beginning a project which gave him the undeniable pleasure of being the greatest and most successful treasure hunter in history. The Sororibus had no money, a tally was made and kept in their Sharing. They only used precious metals and gems selected for beauty on the pillars supporting the orb. The place which housed the entity who saved them and their daughters from a misery barely made worse in the retelling. The Sororibus had adorned themselves with things from nature that any could access and craft according to their skill. Paul was a human. Raiding all of the biggest and some of the most famous storehouses of gold and precious stones on earth and loading them into the ship didn't qualify as greed because he couldn't spend it. It was a pleasant diversion. He had become the greatest killer in history and so he thought he'd style himself as a pirate. A robber. Soon storehouses of cash which had been kept underground in cool, low humidity environments and great works of art and sculpture and objects from antiquity once the prize exhibits in great museums were being sorted through. It kept him very fit lifting it all and carrying it to the ship. Many a tragic remnant of a masterpiece once hard to appreciate for the crowds standing in front of it were the victim of mould or the simple dissolution of the materials that made it. He decided to make some into quirky collages of the great masters.

Ultimately his thoughts returned to the Timeline he was from, and whether some intervention, pulsing a Moe stronghold, might tip the balance in an ongoing war against Barrion and his compatriots. He had mastered the piloting and deadly power of the ship certainly better than any Sororibus had ever needed or would be allowed to be and he believed this could give him sufficient protection from Barrion for a brief visit to make an assessment at least. Or was the war over. He started to spend hours trying to understand the time functions of the craft. He believed he understood the space aspects from interrogating the Menu. He was certain that the ship could only return to space with the great orb attached into the massive half-moon indent in the front of the freighter section. But he knew it could travel through time. And he believed he could achieve that from his control room with the Key. As he did this, he considered methods to make the ship immune to being taken. Though reluctant to admit it, there was one thing he would like to recover from what was now elder earth and it was a strong motivator for the trip.

Chrona watched as he examined the time adjustment mechanisms. Eventually she couldn't master her determination to have no communications with him.

Thawing

'You're going to break that. It's a very fragile and delicate piece of

218

equipment. There is nothing like it nor will there ever be again.' A note of guilt crept into her voice. Which was not so harsh now. 'I wasn't supposed to make those upgrades. They're very dangerous.'

It was as if he'd been waiting for her to appear on the wall. He didn't look up. 'Yes. But I'm a history professor.'

'To our enduring misfortune.' Chrona was trying to be cold as she pretended to be with an Envoy she didn't like. 'I should imagine that professing history and tinkering with time machines, although not necessarily mutually exclusive are neither noteworthy for their common denominators.' The Ageless One had been experiencing some unexpected changes of perspective. She was feeling her age. Not in her looks, but in the forgetfulness she had been so good at hiding with the stern persona and the predictable rhythms of her life, long though they were. They were gone now. It felt strange. And liberating.

'Why don't you help me? Anyway. If I break it hardly matters. We're bound for the greatest, blackest waterfall in the universe.'

'Succeed and you could give my ship to Barrion. Make futile efforts to warn the people of your era about their impending doom while they take the ship and eventually give it the capacity for space travel and create havoc not only on earth but all over the universe.'

He stood up from bending over for some time, pushing his back in and his stomach out. 'As someone who has spent nearly a lifetime studying human conflict and conquest. I can tell you that your analysis is entirely correct.'

'As I said. This ship is special. Dangerous. That's why it self-destructs if it's away from me too long or my heart stops beating.' She shrugged. 'All our ships had that feature.'

'There are more like you.'

'I didn't appear from nowhere Paul. However as to where I came from…'

'You're not going to tell me.'

'It's more a case of…I can't remember.' Chrona seemed all at once to have thrown off her imperious nature to that of a simple conversationalist. She realised how much she had enjoyed this when circumstances led to it with Basilica. Whom she missed. Which was also strange. Basilica had been added to a very short list.

Paul didn't want to diminish the gesture yet didn't quite know how to respond. 'Rather a long time ago I imagine.'

'Yes. I don't think we were really intended to cycle through one and a half millennia again and again. The whole 'starting all over again thing' was something I developed using, ironically enough, the time and space bubble which your genius Elouise created. Which was the very same thing that led to such an unfortunate outcome for your species.' Paul knew it would wrong to assume she could or should have avoided humanities doom.

'Believe it or not I couldn't have avoided that fate Paul. The biotoxin had emerged from the thing years before the door was left open by people coming out intent on killing anyone they could find. People came out of the bubble barely a split second after they in. Impossible to trace. I could find it only because the door was left open. I knew a little about Time, so I brought it on board. These ships are not supposed to go back in time other than to observe. That's what I did when I first came here. I saw the fate of humanity, awful as it was. I decided this would be a good place, guilt free as it were, to migrate at least some of the Sororibus from their benight-ed existence. I had been observing their misery for centuries in my travels and resolved to find at least some of them a new home. I recovered them and scheduled our arrival some years after the cat-aclysm after the remains were less confronting. A lot of your tech-nology and infrastructure was a mess. Still, we muddled through and set up a beautiful existence in North America. That's why we speak English. They had your era's television until they largely gave it up as an unhealthy influence on the population. Except for some movies. They were free of the brutal shackles of their males and able to build a civilisation using your species technology as a start-ing point. Science, literature, art and agriculture flourished, and the population grew. How we did that with an all-female population would be a discussion for another time. Should we ever have one.' She added quickly.

'Because of that, and the fact I was quite enjoying watching the whole thing develop they built these huge pillars to hold the Orb while I began to tinker with the bubble. We were in the original Timeline so I only needed to surround the ship in it, and I could go back to any time. So…I enjoyed, vicariously, pre apocalypse eras of earth's culture which were fascinating, edifying, instructive and of course in many cases, left a lot to be desired.'

'All because of the male of the species.'

'Stating the obvious. Though it turned out males were good for some things later in our evolution as a civilisation. Until then I ge-netically engineered diversity. Then I started to use the bubble to become more than an observer. I met some people, drank some

221

wine, ate some meat. Living among billions of Vegans was one of the hardest things about my situation. I was thinking it was time for me to leave the Sororibus as their civilisation was well established. I was going to give them some generic diversity technologies I'd almost finished developing. And then…they discovered the damn Black Hole. Who would have predicted these things simply turn up. We had a few centuries left and I spend most of them figuring out a way to significantly extend Elouise's Bubble. Eventually; to planet size.'

'It was complicated as time always is. I'd bring Renewals here right before we'd arrived. Otherwise we'd already be here. During the time before the reset, we would move a large amount of technology, much more advanced than humans had developed. Tools, equipment, agricultural implements and grains and trees. We settled at new combinations of places, so our Timelines were always different. It was fun. Back then. When the time came to end one Timeline, there was a big ceremony. The orb re-joined the ship, we said our goodbyes. I took the bubble which had been receding in front of the Renewers. All the things we did, the children, the art and music, dance everything – gone. They had never existed. Including those waiting for the Horizon, who never got to be ripped apart by it. They weren't there to be disappointed and a little annoyed with me.'

'I've heard people say that things that changing things in the past can't effect the future.' Paul didn't believe it but would be interested to hear the views of someone who knew more than any expert he could have met.

'I'd like to see them say that after I let ten nuclear bombs off in their backyard yesterday.' This last sentence, supposed to be light-hearted grew a harder edge as the Ageless One realised they were becoming too familiar.

'So back to the matter in at hand, are you going to help me visit earth or am I going to destroy your labour of love, unique in the … cosmos…because I'm a simple war history professor.'

'Hmmmmm…' It sounded to Paul like she was going to pretend to give it some of thought and then say. 'No.' Instead she said 'One hour. If there are two heartbeats in the ship it will automatically vent the oxygen. If *your* heartbeat isn't back on the ship after an hour, you're on your own. I'll send you somewhere you can make the assessments you want to achieve and…get the other thing. But you would have to give me temporary control of the ship to make those two provisos a setting. So the whole proposition is…*academic*…Paul. Excuse the pun.

'Hmmmmm…' Paul's choice was to be torn to pieces on an Event Horizon without satisfying his curiosity because he was never going to figure this ship out. Or for his genocide to become something that never happened but dooming his species. 'Okay.'

'You're sure.'

'I trust you.' He said this with a trace of sarcasm and another of a strange fatalism.

'Hands on the pads and rod in the holder and I will give you a one hour pre-set. I know where you want to go Paul so don't bother asking.'

He put the rod in the slot and immediately he had put his hand on the pad a flashing sign came up beside them saying 'Access Authorisation Terminated'.

He stood there while Chrona laughed and laughed. 'Paul. You never trust *anybody*. How could you fall for that. How could you *think*, that after murdering billions of the beings I guided and loved for millennia I would leave you in charge of the ship and risk having it taken back to your time.'

'Maybe truth *is* the first casualty in war.'

She laughed again. 'I only wanted to see how sad and stupid you would feel. Put your hands back on.' He read 'Access Granted.'

He laughed. 'Got me a good one…'

'It's Chrona Paul.' He didn't make anything of what to him at least, was a very significant moment. The impact Chrona on him had started the moment she flashed up on the screen so many months before. Deeply buried in his confused determination as it might have been.

'For me to do the Pre-Set you'll need to web your fingers together and put them behind your head. And take, what was it, five steps back and turn and face away.'

He did this saying. 'I know I don't need to do this Chrona.'

'But isn't it fun. You see, I can vent the oxygen out of the ship now and lock all the doors from my control panel since you've left the rod in. Then I'll go back to your time, kill you when you're a child, make a bubble with the Timeline from before the first Delivery of Virides with Barrion aboard, kill all of them on the ship and get back for a nice meal and some wine I liberate from the nineteen seventies. And tell Basilica what happened while she was dead.'

Paul was strangely okay with that. And curious that she didn't ultimately do it. He'd assumed the stand she'd commanded but turned his upper body and neck to say. 'Do you really have to kill me as a child. My mother and father are…were good people and they'd be devastated…I think. How about kill me in my twenties once they'd gotten to know me and won't really care.'

'Okay. Might be simpler if I kill them when they're babies.'

Paul sighed. Fatalistic. He didn't really care so much about his species anymore. He was tired of the whole thing. 'You know Chrona…whatever.'

'You're all sullen and jaded now Paul. It's worse than the superiority thing. I must say for all my prescience I didn't see that coming.' Then her voice took on a strange, distant tone. 'I didn't like what happened Paul, and I'm conflicted. But…' It was her turn to sigh. 'The whole Sororibus thing…' She was silent for a long time and changed the subject. 'When you get there, you might need something in locker…' She tapped at a screen a little irritably. 'My memory really has turned to shit. LVL 22R. Your Pre-Set is for *one* hour.' He saw the ship running through the take-off protocols. 'Or maybe ten minutes. I'm becoming so forgetful…it is Paul isn't it?' She had never been so familiar with another being in…Millenia, and now with the one who had killed everyone she'd laboured over.

Paul broke in to help move past a sudden rush of bonhomie she was embarrassed by. 'In case I don't see you again Chrona. Is that your real name.' It sounded like an earth antiquity name to him. As with many of the names they'd taken for the species, some of its organisations and people.

Her face became sombre. 'I don't remember.' After on a short pause she said. 'Goodbye Paul.'

Way Back When

It was a seven-hour trip. He looked in the locker and thought he better put one on. He was supposed to be arriving after the same amount of time had elapsed during which he'd spent in the Sororibus future. Or maybe she was going to drop him into the middle of an orgy of human aggression caused by the Toxin to make a point. He also thought a contingency would be good. For an unwelcome visitor. It was not a pleasant task to prepare it.

He'd had the second suit and contents running on hot for three hours when he felt the gentle landing while in his suit he was shivering on the coldest setting he could bear. A recording of Chrona came up on the wall. 'What you're looking for is on the third story of the building on your left. Third office off the stairwell on your right. Left hand drawer. Second from the top.' He absorbed this enough to remember it though was sure she could have no inkling of one reason he'd come. What immediately captured his attention on the screens projecting the landing site was a scene that was in some ways familiar. Every human and Viride he saw was dead. They were rotting. For most there were no signs of violence. Neither of war nor the results of a toxin causing uncontrollable aggression. They fell where they were standing. Chrona was on the screen again. A Recording. 'He knows you're there so go and get it.'

Paul quickly set up the decoy he felt a little foolish about now and ran into the building and straight to where Chrona had guided him. He opened the drawer and saw a hard drive that said. 'Highlights.' He knew lots of people would have a reel of their favourite parts of interviews or ad libs. But Artie would have everything. Uncut. He was running back to the ship when he got the alarm that the freighter was flying at great speed towards him. It wasn't easy to run in the suit.

Barrion landed not far from the main ship. He was wearing a suit. At the first sign of sickness, which manifested twenty four hours after Basilica had delivered that scratch to the face, he had jumped from one host to another and on and on until he got within proximity of a suit and put it on. He tracked down a few of the best Brothers in hiding and got them protected. It was a special toxin designed to kill humans *and* Virides, leaving the Sororibus unaffected.

Barrion saw a figure in a much superior suit with a rifle pointed at him. 'I want that ship back Paul.' Barrion's probing mind came up against the thawed-out brain of Basilica tied in place with ropes, so it looked like she was sheltering behind a car with a rifle pointing out. Not directly at Barrion though although Paul made a reasonable guess where he was likely to land. Barrion was about the harness the collective minds of the three Viride left alive. A pulse hit and killed him, his companions and fried their freighter. 'That from Basilica you asshole.' He said this through the speakers he'd learned about having spent weeks playing with the ship's menus. Paul couldn't be sure, but he suspected he was the only human left on the planet.

Chrona turned up again. 'I know what you want to do Paul. Believe it or not, there are all kinds of USB inputs, HDMI cables, CD ROM and even a floppy disc player. I've had millennia and I find some interesting material, sometimes on old media after a Renewal. Plug it the hard drive, put your hands in the Pads and I've pre-set the transmission.'

Helen's voice and then vision came on the screen. It was a long string of some of the parts of the best interviews, ad libs, outtakes and dance sessions with the most unlikely cast of characters. He wanted hers to be the very last human words and sounds on earth. If there were radios or televisions run from solar panels and batteries or even having it blaring from the ship, he wanted the world itself to remember what it had produced. In his mind and many others, she was the best of humanity. It seemed only a few minutes and the doors were closing, and he felt the slight movement of 'take off.' He thought of Helen. Still in the freezer.

As soon as he arrived Chrona was on the screen. 'Get what you went for? Part of which was to rid the world of Barrion it seems. And all within an hour. For the other thing you could have asked me. I have one just like it over here.'

He let that pass. 'I also had time to notice that every human and I assume Viride on the planet, as far as I could tell, was dead.'

'Yeah…' She smiled. She was obviously relieved by the news. 'I didn't know for sure though, because you *killed* Basilica, my mysterious and alluring Final Envoy, before I could make sure she'd completed that part of her mission. When she was there, she was to create an opportunity to deliver a tiny amount of toxin. Simply grasping someone by the shoulder, and they wouldn't feel even a little pin prick.'

'And it kills a planet. You would be gratified to know it was delivered by a slash of the nails to her arch enemies face.'

'That was my girl. I'd hate to see that one in a nasty snit. There were two toxins of course. The Virides need a bit of herbicide in theirs. Ha. They're twenty percent plant.' She laughed unashamedly at her own humour. It had been so long. 'But it's all delivered in one mixture.'

'And the difference between you and I is?'

'The absence of mercy thing. On your part that is. You see I observed the process of the aggression stimulated by the biotoxin several times. I did some non-interventionist viewing of the past and figured out where it came from. Elouise's Bubble. And the Bubble door is left open *before* Kirby's second visit. So I couldn't do anything about it.'

'Kirby?'

'Yes Paul. Another human who thought they were inconsequential.'

'I meant to ask why you had to wait for her to leave.'

'I'd had conversation with one of my…species before I went to rescue some Sororibus. She said she'd travelled through a galaxy that looked like whirlpool. Kirby called it a Nautilus I was to find out later. She'd heard this earth woman who somehow propagated a war that broke the grip of a civilisation bent only on destruction. Several billion killed I believe. *You humans!* She said that Kirby came back to earth with a husband and a son from one species, and a daughter from another. I was told when they returned to the planet she'd settled on her husband reconciled with his father and he became one of the most wealthy and influential Li; as they are called, on the planet. Her son rose to the Presidency. Their ambition, after visiting earth, imperfect as the gender equity was here, was to give the females of their species choices as to who to mate with, whether they wanted to study or go to work and maintain a relationship with their sons which they hitherto could not.'

'They are a very deliberate people, so this task was planned and executed in stages. A male from the other side of the planet, the most celebrated genius of his and any age in that galaxy, lent his influence to the project and his mate, a powerhouse of energy, worked closely with the males and females alike to make the changes; slowly so they were lasting. Kirby was simply a catalyst for all of this. Her main contribution to the planet, and her primary occupation while she lived there, was raising a very diverse family, surfing and drinking a type of alcohol known as rum.'

'She led a rich life.' Paul had no background as to what Chrona was taking about.

'So you can see, if I went back and say...killed Elouise, the biotoxin carnage would not occur however the Graceland Project would never happen. And the inconsequential life of someone from... Australia...we had a colony there once...would never have changed the fortunes of a galaxy.'

'So it meant every time went back we preferred it was before you people had given free rein to shall we say, your baser instincts. Those Renewals weren't much fun to clean up believe me.' She shook her head disparagingly. 'You people. What happened on earth was horrible beyond words. Small toddlers trying to kill their mothers, *and sometimes succeeding* if they weren't killed first by the ones who adored them a moment before. It drives people to kill violently. No mercy. However they still have clear heads. If they're good snipers, they start sniping people. If they're good at boxing. They box them around. If they're simply nasty, it's no holds barred street fighting. So I developed something...*humane* I think you would call it. Ergo…my multibillion killing spree; merciful. Yours on the other hand; Let's not go there.'

Paul had many questions. 'Why would Elouise create a toxin like that?'

'She created a *carrier* for antidotes that somehow had a time-based trigger. Her rationale was a vaccine sent with the carrier would circulate until nearly all of the population had it and then switch on during the course of a single day so that the malign virus was all destroyed at once and could neither build immunity to the cure nor mutate to escape it. Being Elouise, no one would have any choice if they wanted it or not. The problem was when someone got into her bubble, they must have been people who had been to one of *your* lectures. The one about soldiers needing to be aggressive.' She tried to moderate her tone. Beating up on the only other being left alive could become a bad habit. 'I assume someone built a genetic trigger for aggression. It was impossible for me to tell because they went into the bubble a split second before they came out so it could be anytime and anyplace.'

His other question was. 'So why not do that for the Adules and the young Sororibus here which we…'

He saw a sombre look in her eyes again and she said. 'I don't remember how to do any of those things Paul. Adules and Sororibus would need a…bespoke toxin. I prepared those toxins for humans and Virides many many cycles ago. I would never foresee a need to cause a mass euthanasia of Sororibus and Adules simply because a merciless history professor decides to kill a whole planet load of peace-loving females. My forecasts of probabilities don't extent so far into the improbable. An interesting detail Paul is that when you arrived here, or should I say arrived *now*, you didn't go crazy with violence. That's when I realised the carrier was time sensitive to the extent it was triggered on a specific date only. You jumped right over it so it didn't turn on.'

'Time's weird.'

'Yep. I came and took some of your blood when you were sleeping, rather heavily because of the gases I had released into the ship. You have the toxin alright.'

'Oh.'

I made an antidote. For both of us. Didn't want us going nuts on some random day and trying to kill each other. Last ones on the planet and all.

The Wednesday Thing

'Yeah. Anyhoo. Would you like to come over for dinner. I could show you some of the highlights of the culture you destroyed, and the highlights of the human culture you're the only one to survive.'

Paul was caught off guard. Not long before she'd loathed him. Now she was looking for a friend. He supposed that everything she knew now was history and they were all that was left so they might as well be on friendly terms. 'I'd like that.'

'You'll need to do some shopping before you come over. The ship's in a bubble now to keep you from going nuts. However the biotoxin wouldn't have hit earth for quite a while anyway.'

She sent him on a Pre-Set. To one of the locations where a large group of paranoid people, who turned out to be right, kept huge underground food stores with systems maintained on thermal power.

For the meal, he took a freighter to the Orb so he didn't need to walk across the drying remains of thousands of the dead around the ship. Walking into the huge transparent ball was a strange sensation. The level he visited on the hemisphere facing the city was very pleasant. The décor was varied and interesting.

He stood talking with her while she cooked two steaks with salad and shared the first of a few bottles of red wine. 'The Sororibus were vegans and didn't believe alcohol had a healthy effect on society. My species however enjoyed the equivalent of a steak or a lamb roast wherever we were so as their spiritual guide I had to get this smuggled in when I had an Envoy I could trust.' Once all was prepared, she said. 'You're not afraid of heights I hope.' She didn't wait for an answer 'Wonderful. Let's eat it with a view.'

She took him to some doors opening to reveal the hemisphere facing away from the city which was a twenty-story globe of a crystal clear glass like material. It was what fit into the other part of the ship, this part facing out. They walked out on a platform which appeared to hang with no supports. It was wide enough so that they were a long way from the edge. The end of the platform had a small Command Bridge with a table for dining and some couches on a level in front a few steps down. Chrona didn't take her meals or meet the Envoys here so the dining table hadn't been used in hundreds of thousands of years. She did come here and sit in stasis. For years at a time sometimes. Once seated, Chrona held up her glass and they made a toast to being the last of their species, as far as they knew. It was the start of a pleasant meal. Paul was relieved that the steak and wine were excellent. 'This is amazing.' He said. 'I have only a narrow repertoire of meals, but I think I make a good spaghetti bolognaise.' He was suddenly worried he had assumed they would dine again, and he might be showered in dismissive ridicule. Which he could now ill afford.

'Sounds delightful.' When they finished the meal, she said. 'I'll clean up tomorrow. I'd like to show you something.' They navigated their way around a huge ship and took several elevators. There were curved widows enclosing many rooms full of art. Paintings and sculptures of all kinds of material. There were rooms full of the most exquisite examples of taxidermy and sacred, beautiful and some macabre objects from many histories. The art was strange and varied from appealing to confusing. 'I throw away what I don't like every Renewal when I can no longer hurt anyone's feelings after they give me the stuff. It *was* part of the theatre is for me to let the Envoy know how much I love it all.' She took him to a room that was filled with art from earth. There were painting and sculptures that could only be the work of the old masters. 'I would have gone and met them all if it wasn't for the Kirby thing. Ironic lots of people blamed our Viride 'Invasion' on Graceland.'

Paul wanted to be certain he didn't outstay his welcome. He expressed what was easy to see was his sincere gratitude for being asked over and being allowed to see such amazing art from two cultures. She said. 'Spaghetti at your place. A week from now. We'll make it a Wednesday thing.'

He smiled. 'I'd really like a Wednesday thing involving something for carnivores and…those that like a drink.'

'Surprise me with the wine. Maybe some cheese.' He was looking forward to Wednesday. And so was she. There wasn't much else to do. Though Paul continued to fly a freighter all over the planet taking in the most beautiful places on earth and looting them. Most landscapes had returned to close to their original nature and it was quite a hunt to find things. When he went shopping, he made it a monthly journey, bringing back a range of the makings for meat dishes, cheese and everything else one might have on a platter, all kinds of wine and varieties of beer.

They were both avid conversationalists and did some study through the week to have topics of interest to mention. A hint would be introduced the Wednesday before for the other party to spend some time on. Sometimes Chrona was reflective. 'Here we are, the last two individuals of different species on what was home to diverse eras of two creative and amazing peoples.' She smiled thoughtfully. 'And we killed them all. You killed all the Sororibus, ignoring remanent Adules, and I killed all the humans and Virides on earth. You nineteen billion and me nine.'

Paul had been drinking as much as he did on Wednesdays. Which was the only day he did. 'Yes but you killed that many every few millennia. Again and again. That adds up. I killed mine only once.'

'Doesn't really count because they were the *same* people each time. Still piles of dead bodies. It was one of the reasons I had the Adules morph into Virides in the first place. You and all the other humans thought the Virides were an army to get turned into soldiers. Nope. They were the clean-up crew in waiting. After the release of the toxin I made, the human one, there was a quarter of a billion Virides to clean up the mess. And then…they got the herbicide version. Of course there was always one human who was saved before the carnage.' Chrona paused as one wishing she hadn't said that and hoped Paul didn't ask.

'One human?' He'd heard Basilica say who but wondered why.

'Another glass of wine perhaps. Later on I want to show you something that's been a project close to my heart for more millennia than I can remember.'

'One?' Paul poured them both another glass of wine. 'Human?'

The Tiny Sliver

What the hell. Thought Chrona. *There's no one to hide it from anymore. And if anyone would understand Paul would.* 'It was an infatuation. Pathos. You know how it is.' Paul wondered if she knew everything about him. 'I used to love to watch some musicians, all sorts. And there was one I started to watch rather a lot of. I did this vicariously from recordings I made in the bubble. Became quite a fan. Had all his albums, or perfect facsimiles of them. And one day I thought. I'd like to see him in person. Go and watch a concert and get out of this glass ball for a while. Strangely, I don't feel that way often. Our species must like living in giant fishbowls. Anyway I took the ship, no one knew because I was back a fraction of a second after I left. And I broke my rule about not doing anything predating Kirby's final visit. I went to a rock concert. Maybe more middle of the road. Hard to say. He played across genres really. Anyway I was looking up at him, embarrassingly like an adoring fan. I was. And he looked at me. Only for a moment. The concert finished and I started on my way to the little freighter. I'd come across in from the desert where I'd parked the ship. He turned up beside me. Asked me if I liked the show. It was nice. He asked if I wanted to come to dinner. He followed up with. 'Only dinner'.'

'I was going to give the Ageless One's reply. Leaving him feeling like a minnow in time and space. Or at least a polite no. He said I could invite anyone I liked. He could organise for some minor celebrity to turn up. Less minor than him, in case I was worried he thought I was a groupie. We had a meal in a little Italian restaurant. Yes it's a classic tale. We were both intoxicated. By being together. We both knew neither of us had ever felt that way before. And one thing led to another, and it turns out I was a groupie. Except after; we stayed together talking till the middle of the next day and then had a lunch I'll never forget at a restaurant with a beautiful vista of the sea and the coastline. Some people turned up and said he'd missed the plane to that night's 'gig' which was in another state. They'd organised a private jet, even though he wasn't really in that league.'

'He told them calmy they would have to tell the audience he was sick. He had plans to have dinner with me and that was more important. They said there was thirty thousand people coming through the gates waiting for the opening act who were going to have to do two sets and there would be a riot if he didn't show. An exaggeration and we all knew it.'

'He looked at me and smiled. 'Private jet?'.'

'I shook my head and said that, like him, I was supposed to be somewhere. Did I tell you about the heartbeat thing. The ship has to detect the beating heart of whoever's in charge of it within forty-eight hours or it de oxygenates, packs up and goes home.'

'He said he was going to cancel the tour. Do this one show because people were arriving already, but he was going to spend time with me. Even if I could only spare a little. I was surprised. Especially having been so infatuated with *him*. I thought I'd be another fan in the crowd. I told him not to cancel the shows. We could work something out. He didn't care who was watching. He gave me the most beautiful sincere embrace of my life. I guess…that's not saying a lot really. But I knew it was special. He walked away with the minders but then he turned around and came back and said. 'I'm not supposed to say this yet. But I love you.'

She was speaking more quietly now. No Envoy would recognise this Ageless One. 'He didn't expect me to reply. I stood there as he left. The greatest regret of my long life is that I didn't say it back. And don't tell me I could have wound time back and said it. It had to be then. I was indecisive. Okay, only for a few seconds, but I toyed with the idea of letting the ship leave me there, stranded, with my musical idol. Anyway our assignation had been a little more consequential then either of us knew. Being sick in the mornings simply doesn't occur for my species. Must have been because half the child was human. I thought it was some illness I'd picked up during my visit.

But my Envoy of the time, discreet fortunately, told me that I was 'showing'. I asked her to say nothing, and she kept my secret, which I'm sure wasn't easy. I didn't want my child to be brought up by a Sororibus, and I wasn't going to bring up a child here. It had to be a human family. The criteria were that they were people who were going to unexpectedly lose their child and that they looked general-ly like what a child myself and my 'idol' might have. I finally found some people that fit the requirements. It was going to be nice to save them the anguish of losing their child and they were good people. Intellectuals, but loved a laugh and a drink and were a little bit hippy. My Envoy helped with the baby swap. Looking into the original Timeline their poor sickly daughter lasted only a week. I brought her here, against the recommendations of my Envoy, but I wanted to be able to love a child…for a while.' Her voice had gone quiet, and she was as close to shedding those very rare tears. 'She lived for three years. I've never felt anything like that. It made me realise how detached from real life I was.' Paul knew instinctively any words would be the wrong words and he reached across and took her hand.

Her voice retuned to someone telling an amusing story. 'But I got to watch my own child grow up. Only ever once. They called her Helen. I liked the name. And no matter how much I tried to simply put it down to maternal pride, she was exceptional. Not at school. Not at sport. None of that. She was simply exceptional at being lively and fun and insightful and irreverent yet never hurtful or full of herself. I loved her along with lots of people.'

Paul was digesting this but could contribute. 'Including Military History Professors.'

'I was like everyone else. Her interviews were the only media I watched, but I also got to see a bit of her life. You'll be pleased to know that the magic box I made, when it focuses in on one person, screens out anything intimate or…you know…the bodily functions.' She laughed. 'So I would get the Sororibus introduced to her, via her interviews and her lifestyle. Only I got to see how she responded to the arrival of the Virides. I would always change the one word they could say purely to see what Helen would do with it in the interview. She always had that interview with them. I convinced the Sororibus she was a child of some benevolent visitor from the stars. I said she would always be the one human who join the Renewal from among us from the entire population of earth. They saw it as a symbolism. A gesture to the species whose place we took.'

'How did she respond to that.'

'In lots of ways. Fascinated as a journalist. Angry that we didn't save more. Grieving for her friends. Secretly grateful she'd survived. And most foreign to her; a little anxious about the future. She, nor anyone Sororibus ever knew I was her mother, and I never…met her. It would be a…hint you know.' She was glad Paul was astute enough not to suggest things perhaps could have been different. Then there was the glance, right as the second Paul realised it himself. The irony. But then he realised another layer of sorrow for the Ageless One. She had killed her daughter. Over and over again. There could not be two Ageless Ones. Or there would be two, fifty, a hundred Helens. Chrona's voice didn't miss a beat. 'She became a much-loved journalist and author among the Sororibus. And she only ever had one Adule.' The Ageless One smiled with a cheeky grin. *At a time.*' Then she laughed. 'She would never have dreamed she'd have many children and yet she was a devoted mother, though never choosing a Sororibus partner, which is the usual way. And she had a remarkably long lifespan for a human which led to quite tribe. However…like all, she found her peace at great age. Her body wasting around a mind still razor sharp. A painless affliction it was assumed to be the pedigree of her alien ancestry. She Passed surrounded by intimates of family and friends who shared a love with her beyond words. She was mourned on a planetary scale so beloved she was by the Sisterhood.' Paul knew Chrona had watched this process only once. And she described it as if it had only happened once. Paul imagined that the narrative would need to change and perhaps there was perhaps some misadventure. He could not imagine this echo of a love lost. In its brightness and darkness. Again and again.

This was the Ageless One. She shrugged off the fleeting mood. 'Her decedents, even if in a humble station, were proud and thought themselves lucky to have descended from Helen. This time around of course you shot both her and one of her descendants in the head. Then killed all the Sororibus so it put the…what do you say…put the kybosh on the whole thing.'

'You had to finish the story with that.' She noticed Paul found it hard to respond in kind to the piece humour Chrona was trying to inject into the moment. She became more conciliatory. 'Even though I struggled with your decision Paul. I'm not sure I'd like her to have seen what we saw, and then be stuck with us. A prowling lioness with nothing to kill.'

Paul regretted raising it as soon as he started speaking. It was the superiority thing. He wanted to show off what he could deduce. 'And I imagine her father, though never knowing it, found his brief association with you somewhat life changing.'

'Do tell.'

Paul cleared his throat and shrugged. 'Finished the tour. Lukewarm reviews. Never toured again. Didn't record again but maybe had a contract so they released some also rans from his studio time and he didn't care because he was gone. It started out as a journey looking for you. Eventually he probably convinced himself it was a journey to find himself and meandered through a few spiritual pathways to enlightenment. Buddhism, Daoism maybe. Old time religion. It doesn't matter. None of them were satisfying because they didn't answer the simple questions he had. Which was 'Where did she go?' And the other one. 'Why didn't she stay?' And so he settles down. In the city you met maybe. Takes up some creative endeavour. Writing. Art maybe. It doesn't matter. He's treading water.'

Paul had gone into the mode which came naturally to him. As with Lissa. Analysis in spite of the pain caused by deconstructing something to those who deeply cared about it. He looked up and saw Chrona was crying. Silent. Paul made no effort to be comforting because he was too angry with himself. The next stop in the pattern of behaviour was self-loathing. 'I'm so sorry Chrona. I'll leave. It seems being callous is the only consistent personality trait I have.'

As he got up to leave, she reached out her hand and nodded for him to stay. 'Why the inaccuracies?'

Self-Loathing and Adulation

Paul knew he would be close to the mark with his analysis, and he knew why. 'I have no idea who Helen's father is Chrona. The outcome's not that hard to predict if you're a…'

She was digesting the fact that Paul didn't know, yet he'd guessed so closely. 'A what?'

'I should go. Maybe this Wednesday thing doesn't really work for either of us.'

She knew he didn't believe that. 'If you're a *what* Paul?'

'A person Chrona. Any person. You can see the affect Helen had on people. You're the source. Pure.'

'Paul a middle of the road musician is hardly a big sample.'

242

'Who have you associated with Chrona. For millennia. No males. Only Adules were here but they knew nothing of you but a few esoteric descriptions. And your Envoys. What's the one common thread that runs through all of them. No matter how diverse.'

She thought a moment. 'They gave up everything to be my Envoy. All for a fleeting exposure to someone who was only ever rude or aloof or both.'

He tried to develop a strategy to bring the discussion to a close. He would never come back again. This moth had come way too close to the flame. 'And not one would regret their decision.' Again he rose to leave. During all those days and nights he had convinced himself who and what he really was. It had been the only way.

Again she took his hand and nodded for him to sit. 'So why are you immune to this intractable state of adulation.' He simply sat looking at his hands.

'Oh.' She said.

He laughed. It was a big genuine laugh the like of which hadn't burst out since he left earth. 'I've heard that 'Oh' before you know.'

She looked across at him evenly. 'Of course I know. About that 'Oh'.' He tried to get up again and it with considerable irritation she said. 'Will you please stop doing that. I can understand that you might feel the need to…conceal such a thing.' She tried to lighten the tone. 'Our Wednesday's have been pleasant. Uncomplicated. You seem to have managed to find a way with Helen…'

'Yes Chrona. I found a way with Helen. And with you for the six and a half days we're not together I remember what I am, what I've done.' She let him sit in silence for a while. 'As you know I could

243

operate any camera I wanted. Zoom in or zoom out. I agreed with you. I shouldn't do what I was doing without confronting it.' It was time for his cheeks to have tears running down them. 'So I saw the crying children, skeletal trying to wake their mothers. Then lying beside them as bodies, starting to rot in their turn. The Adules so quickly reverting to something brutal…and so the young Sororibus, lining up, cowering around the machine the Sisterhood used to 'Take their Peace'. But the machines had no power. I gave them what they wanted. But for others I was too late. And what of so many others in the tiny places I never came to? They roam even now.' Tears kept gliding down his cheeks. 'I'm sure deep down I knew Basilica was telling the truth. Humanity was finished. I was simply demonstrating what a real military leader would feel compelled to do to protect his species. I was playing at the role of Generalship when ruthlessness was the only option even for the civilised. But perhaps it was the Generalship that I had always wanted, and this was the way to get it. By the time I admitted I was lying to myself all the adult Sororibus were dead, and I could see no way to resurrect the society from the dying or disoriented youth. I was too proud to admit I was wrong and hand the ship back to you.'

He sighed. 'So that's how I manage the 'adulation'. I remember who I am and that I've never been able to constrain my capacity for hurtfulness. On an enormous scale if given the opportunity. You wanted to spend time together on Wednesday and it was the same with Helen. It was a privilege that so many others wished they could have had. I wanted to give her the best I had to offer. The very best I could be. Because I loved her, and yes, eventually only as a friend. I wanted to be a good friend. And then I shot her. With the same superior mindset.'

244

He didn't expect *this* to be an opportunity for Chrona to have a big laugh. But she did. 'Paul you're even superior at self-loathing. Most people do it in a kind of disorganised and confused way. You've turned it into a lifestyle. And it seems I'm the justification for it. At least to the degree that you discipline yourself so as not to give away hints at this…adulation. It's like reverse meditation.' It was Paul's opportunity to be irritable and he got up again and once again she grabbed his hand. 'Will you *stop* doing that.' She looked him in the eye, which she had never done before, and he stopped breathing briefly. 'Paul; I *used* you. That's all. You did things that I was too afraid; too weak to do. I didn't like how it was done, we'll come back to that, but before you castigate yourself any more…' She sighed now, about to embark on something painful and never before revealed. 'How long do you think it was since I had that unforgettable slice of love and then gave birth to this strange girl who was so much adored but didn't know why.'

Paul made the face of one doing a simple calculation. 'She's twenty-eight, or was it twenty nine…even though she looked early twenties. I know why now.'

'That was her age when you killed her…my daughter Paul.'

He pretended to be annoyed. 'Oh yeah, I forgot about that. So say twenty nine years.'

'No Paul. Use that brain you convince people is so much better than theirs.'

He frowned. 'Oh.' He said as the realisation settled upon him.

'That's right. 'Oh'. I stopped counting at fifty Helens. That's seventy-five thousand years ago.'

'That's a lot of Helens.'

'And every one unique after she met the Virides and interacted with different Sororibus. It's somewhere between one and two hundred thousand years since I fell in love. It's that long since I gave up my precious little girl. That long since...' Her voice was breaking. 'The little girl I brought home. She was supposed to die within days...' The ancient trader was silent for a long time. 'she lived till she was *three*. I did everything to save her. I didn't care my species lived alone. I didn't care I'd tampered with a time before Kirby left for good so I could change those babies over. I cared about her. I'd learned to kill billions. And yet I couldn't save *one little girl*. Tens and tens of thousands of years ago Paul I learned one thing. Only one. How to be lonely. My species don't *get* lonely. But I figured out a way.'

Cycling

'I was caught now. The Black Hole made it hard to leave. I knew if I left, I'd never come back. I still cared about them, was pleased and proud and...the ceremony. Pageantry. Ritual. Ha...adulation I'm now advised. Have you looked closely at the pillars this giant ball sits on?'

'I have. Didn't mention it but ...wow. Gold mouldings. Beautiful wood inlay. Amazing carving. So detailed and intricate on something so huge. All set in perfectly joined stone that looks like it's come from all over the place...'

'It does.'

'And there's an overarching theme. A vision. It's remarkable.

Remarkable craftsmanship. I mean craftwomanship.'

'I've had better than these.' She laughed. 'But this is what they do. Or did. How long do you think that took.'

Paul shrugged. 'Ten years. Twenty maybe.'

'Try two hundred. Great granddaughters would be working side by side with their great grandmothers who may have done the same with their mothers in little intervals shared by the best artisans to arise in the culture. Tens of thousands would participate. I'd have plain temporary pillars when I'd arrive. There would be a huge celebration when I'd move the orb to these massive pieces of art. It was the closest to religious fervour these atheistic species got. And in the party after, it's only one of two times they allow themselves some mind-altering drugs. The poor Adules would get worn out from a whole week of celebration. I'd have to tinker with the population in advance so there was a higher ratio than usual. The other festival is the decade before the Horizon. Everyone lived from stores which had been accumulated for a century. A gift from those who got a full span of years to those who would not. A ten-year party. Or so they believed.'

'I hit the play button in the new bubble and all the people here waiting for the last ride would cease to exist. New locations in North America or Europe of South East Asia. We started in Sydney once. Mumbai. Durban. By the time some colonies chose to move other places, the new batch of Virides would be sent out to clean up those places. For the Renewal, when they first get 'switched on' as you almost accurately predicted, they would operate bulldozers and all kinds of earthmoving and demolition equipment. They'd blow up buildings not part of the Renewal plan and take all the bodies to old mine sites and bury them or fill up cruise liners with them to be sunk. As you've suggested, there are a lot of bodies to deal with and the Senior Virides who supervise all this sometimes needed to be creative. Never thought of the whole 'slurry them up and pump them to an ocean trench'. That takes a certain breed of what did you say…callousness.' She was trying to convey he should not be feeling unique or special about that. 'A team of older Sororibus are chosen from volunteers to oversee the first clean up before the Renewers arrive. It's a bit of a ritual when they take their Peace before the first refugees of the last Timelines come back. One of the few times I turn up in person to thank anybody.'

'Hell of a line up to get that dirty job I'd expect.'

'Yes.' She ruminated a moment. This whole adulation thing explained quite a bit. 'As with Basilica, girls born in the window of twenty to thirty years before the Renewal join in a massive competition, though it isn't supposed to be like that. They are chosen to be to be one of the two hundred million Sororibus who bring new diversity into a fifteen-hundred-year-old gene pool. Some go down to the planet to beguile some very specific individuals in the Infallibility plan. Others go to raid sperm banks.'

'There's a big list of men for them to work through. They are picked out over a century of planning. Those developing the Infallible, such as the odious Barrion did posing as Authoress…' Some of this was news to Paul beyond what Basilica had told them, but he knew he would never get the full explanation. '…are not allowed to know who got picked out the last time around. One of my jobs as the Ageless One was to vet their choices. Ha. I get rid of half of them and put a new half in. I'd try to change things up a bit. Focus more on where we were going. Dilute the anglophile leanings we had because of where we first arrived. When it comes down to it though, if you're looking for the best couple of hundred million mates on earth after Kirby's left...' She shrugged. '...a good man's hard to find you know.'

'Initially, I'd forced myself to bring in a new twenty percent every time but as the number of cycles grew I had to simply leave a good gap between cycles and the genes we took. You may have had a visit. I never *watched that side of things closely*, if you know what I mean. It was interesting to know where the Sororibus gene pool came from and then where the civilisation went with an influx of new male genes. And as I think my ill-fated Envoy told you, many Sororibus don't like males. The tales of the terrible plight of the females on their planet are handed down from mother to daughter. After a few generations of this it's not so much 'a good man is hard to find.' More a case of 'a bad man is all you'll ever get'. Some mate with the Adules a few times and then either live alone with their daughters or more typically would settle with a Sororibus partner. Or in some more, 'open minded' households, abide with three to a few dozen Sororibus shacked up together. *Each to her own.* Was a motto here, I mean it was, until you came along. There were no drugs, weapons, geopolitics, religions or meat and a strange mix of prudes living in harmony with 'whatever floats your boat' types.'

'Near the end of the Timeline, there are pregnant Renewal Sororibus all over the place. Girls with not a human gene among them and the most diverse crop of boys which will become Adules our science and the best traits humanity could produce.'

'As the centuries passed, I got more and more irritable and often

249

rude to the Envoys. Which bizarrely only made some overqualified and talented young Sororibus more determined to do what was ultimately a dead-end job. I think my species isn't supposed to get bored and lonely. They might have all died out while I've been cycling around in a time bubble. Though I guess in their reality it's only fifteen hundred years ago. I don't know how long we live, but with a bit of bubble tinkering and trickery I don't age at all inside this ship.'

'I've learned that those who hope for eternal life should try it first. It can get you down ultimately. Fortunately I spend a lot of time eavesdropped on your history and I learned something of particular interest watching what was going on in Kirby's ship when she came back for a visit. It allowed me to learn how the Li generate 'stasis'. I can contrive most things technological or biological. Or I used to before I began forgetting everything. So I was able to replicate what they did.'

'You seem pretty sharp to me.' Paul lied.

'Do I? What was I talking about?'

'Stasis.'

'Oh yes. I would have been in real trouble without that. I would sneak back in time and watch Kirby and her husband, son, plus that very noisy baby girl. They loved her, but her brother and father were in stasis quite a bit.'

'And so when you came along Paul, in the original Timeline, it had a very different trajectory. Due to the Pulse and Barrion, you were thrust into the centre of things for saying what you thought. Most true as it worked out. Don't get all superior about it though. It was the first time we had anyone new in Helen's orbit or having a new impact globally in…ever. Because the run up was always the same. Helen would change because after the first 'Delivery' they would continue in pre-sets adjusted to reflect the 'Infallible'. She would be closer or further away from the action. Eventually it wasn't a new story. She did report in detail on the mistreatment of the Virides. An outcome of my plans that could make me a little…uncomfortable.'

This is the thing Paul. I used you. Shamelessly. I couldn't break the nexus. Amazing daughter, delightful society that depended on me. They could be bitchy sometimes but most of the time good hearted and grateful. To me. All these rituals and observances and traditions. Again, many to do with me. I grew to hate it. Hate everything. Except Helen. I loved Helen. And even like you and all those humans, I did so secretly because no one knew she was my daughter.'

'It's obvious now.'

'Everything is in hindsight Paul. You killed her. Don't misunderstand me mentioning that, and only for the first time I think.' She squinted and looked pensively at nothing. 'You killed her and took one piece *off the board* Paul. *For me*. Because of Barrion and the Timeline he altered, I was flying blind until this big ball started its massive job of predicting probabilities based on what every butterfly gets up to in a rainforest. Which is bullshit by the way. But ultimately it didn't matter Paul. Basilica did what she needed to do and delivered the toxin, except it happened a long way ahead of schedule.' Chrona's voice changed. 'You were one of the few people on earth with an understanding of what an enemy could look like.

Which was anything. You believed that if there was only a one per-cent chance that we were lying to you, you would give your species that chance. The Generalship thing is an overlay by your adulation induced self-loathing.'

'Irrespective of what you might feel now, you believed it was more than one percent.' Tears were slowly rolling down her cheeks again. She shook her head. 'You must realise now I could have stopped you in half a dozen ways Paul. I could have sucked the oxygen out the ship and sent over Adules. Skilled technician of which there were hundreds in the capital. Or there were until you killed them all.' She sighed. 'I try to make it a little joke Paul. I could have had an Adule bring the necessary things to *me* and I could make the beacon *in the grey limbo* while you lay dead. I didn't do that Paul. It's true I begged you not to do what you did, and if you'd agreed I would have accepted that that as 'fate'. Which I don't believe in. But deep down I wanted you to do what I couldn't. Once you started, it was too late to stop.' He knew there would be no more jokes. Tears continued in a slow stream. 'You watched it. Forced yourself to. I saw the camera's light up. Do you know how much I watched Paul?'

'You saw the distance shots like the one on my wall.'

'Nothing. Not *one second*. I turned the screens from my perspective into maps. I admired your willingness to be the god that looked at what he was doing. Took accountability. Then I told you that chasing down Adules and sending handfuls of child Sororibus and Virides to their Peace was not what the Sororibus would want be-cause they loved the nature of elder earth. No Paul. I couldn't keep doing it anymore. And I was grateful, and I admired you that you went back out and kept doing it for those fewer in number but suffering none the less. That's why it's ironic that you castigate your-self to avoid showing me…adulation. After what I did. Who I am.' There was a long pause Paul was supposed to fill it. 'What do you think about all of that Paul?'

He was honest. 'I'm confused.' He smiled. 'My superiority hasn't arrived yet to explain everything.'

'I'm lonely Paul. I'm honest enough with myself to admit that now. We have some time left before we go over the falls…but less for me. My mind has snapped back like an overstretched rubber band now that it's over. And now it's shrinking. *Don't argue.* I could take this ship and go. Back to my wandering ways. But it's too late. It's been too long. I don't want adulation Paul. I don't want self-loath-ing. I want more than dinner on Wednesdays. I'd like cards nights on Thursdays. Movie nights on Saturdays. A Barbeque lunch on Tuesdays and wine and cheese appreciation on Friday afternoons. Sundays off. Do you think that you can do that Paul. No adulation. No self-loathing.'

Paul wasn't going to spoil a simple question with a quali-fied answer. 'Yes.'

'Good. Do you know any card games for tomorrow night.'

'I played cards Lissa and Jerry and I played quite a bit of poker when I was younger.' He felt better. Better than he had since before Barrion. Before coming into Helen's orbit.

Chrona stood up and held out her hand which he had to get up to take. 'Let's not play cat and mouse for days or weeks Paul. I'll take you to a room no one has ever visited.' He followed along. She turned to him and gave him a look. She was breathtaking. *'Limited* adulation will be permitted.'

She awoke to a smell that made her wonder why, in her long years, she had never made it for herself. Bacon and eggs and toast. With a coffee sitting on a tray. It was a coffee that people make with a special machine which she did not have. Why had her species been so adverse to sensual experiences. She knew why. Because they could not endure the years. Thousands of them. With yearnings or appetites. A memory of only that thin slice. That sliver of love. It soothed her so, and then it tormented her. She wanted to make the gesture a pleasant surprise free of complex responses. It wasn't difficult to deceive Paul. He worshipped her. Even though he was now going to do an exceptional job at concealing it. Halfway through savouring the meal she said. 'You're the plan maker. Surprise me.' After a pause she said. 'Every day.'

He couldn't help but reveal how delighted he was, but also a knowing smile that 'every day', for her, might mean every day up until today. And then she'd never see him again. He didn't mind. There were only so many days left, if he was able to enjoy one or a hundred days with her or three hundred it didn't much matter. They'd had one together. She knew now that her mind would be gone long before the great dissolution of the earth. Without the demands to stay a course for the Sororibus it had relaxed. It opened a gate on a dam and the pent-up waters were flowing out.

They went to Hawaii for a few hours for a pleasant swim and then to the top of El Capitan for wine and cheese as the sun set. What had been part of Yosemite National Park was now a rock mountain within thousands upon thousands of square miles which nature had largely healed itself of the scars of human habitation over the previous fifteen hundred years.

Visiting iconic buildings and structures which were faithfully recon-structed, or beautiful ruins became a fascination for a time. As did going to the top the twenty highest peaks in the world. 'Without the bother of climbing them.' Days past. Then weeks. Paul made sure Chrona need never compare him to that 'tiny sliver of love' she'd shared with a 'middle of the road' rock star all those thou-sands of years before. He was able to enjoy the wonder of someone who, powerful and apparently worldly was she was, had not travelled widely out of the Orb physically.

What is the Past

Her forgetfulness was becoming more and more extensive and in-tensive, and it was a frequent frustration. Paul tried to be a salve to the degree she would permit one. Reminding her that it didn't really matter so much anymore, and she could enjoy the moments that were passing by. They were good moments.

One night she said. 'When I'm gone it'll be the same as if they'd never existed. The Sororibus. The dangers of rescuing them and long journeying through time and space to bring them here. And all those civilisations starting and finishing again and again. Billions and billions of individual lives. Good lives mostly. Creative, nurtur-ing and concerned for one another and the place they called home.' They were sitting in the fishbowl looking at the stars. 'Now it's like they never happened. Like some dream I had that I'm finding it hard to recall.'

'It was real for them Chrona. All those billions. All those lives lived. Worthwhile lives. From what I know they, like humans, we're only supposed to span three or four decades. It's all they expected. And all they had to work with for most people. And for many all they really wanted. They felt fortunate if they've had some love in their life and not too much meanness or sorrow or grinding poverty. And you gave them that existence, you gave them those lives. But they *are* forgotten. Yes. Like most earthlings before you arrived. In our long history whether they existed or not doesn't matter. It's the way of things. Those few humans remembered for centuries or Millenia were either outrageous villains or had the traits that generations always looked for, so they created a narrative of a hero or a god that was probably quite inaccurate. And where are they all now. Taking up space in my brain. Nowhere else and that will soon be crushed to a piece of matter unimaginably smaller than a piece of dust.'

Chrona nodded. Unsatisfied with the reality. But acknowledging it.

'That was my superior part coming out for a jaunt around. But here's a story about memories for you. One time I called my aunt. She was my favourite aunt. She was everyone's favourite aunt. She was full of fun and mischief. Telling us things children weren't sup-posed to know or taking up some new spiritual belief, like a de-votion to the Norse Gods. With never a mention of it the next time we saw her. I was doing a short stint as a visiting lecturer in Australia and asked if she'd like to accompany me on a holiday around New Zealand. I made up a story about winning it in a char-ity raffle and it was for two and most people found me to be an insufferable bore. Since she was deaf in one ear, and it was the ear that faced the driver, she could ignore most of what I said. She seemed to hear the things she wanted to perfectly well though.'

'It was a big dent in my saving and the amount of leave I used up. But it was one of the best things I ever did. She wasn't always an easy person to be with. She was old even then and set in her ways and she probably had several secret complaints about me. Not always secret come to think about it. But we had a fun. Had some memorable times doing a lot of things people her age didn't usually do, though I drew the line at letting her go bungee jumping. Fortunately so did the person running it.'

'Twenty years later I visited her. She was ninety but wasn't a dementia patient. I wanted to reminisce about the time we'd had. But she was sure she'd never been to New Zealand and certain that we'd never been on any trips together. When I came home I felt so... sad. I might as well not have gone to the effort if she was going to forget it all. Eventually I thought what would have happened if she had died of a heart attack a week after we got home with all those memories fresh. And then I might have followed a week later due to some accident. And all those memories, that experience, but for a few postcards family members may have kept, were gone. I decided it was worth it. It was still one of the best decisions I'd made because we had a lot of fun in those few weeks. And that was the main thing. The memories are nice. But we did it. And in a few years that trip, with imperfect memories of it still carried around in my brain will *really* be gone. We had a good time in the moment. That's the best anyone can hope for.'

'I hope I'm not your aunt by the time we hit the Horizon.'

'It would be nice if you remember me a little. But having a good time in the moment Chrona. This moment. It's the *best* time of my life. Even if it doesn't come with memories on the side. That's fine with me.'

That conversation resulted in a week-long visit to New Zealand after which they were back in the Orb. Sharing a Caesar salad, with chicken and egg and blue cheese mayonnaise. He could tell when Chrona had had enough adventure for a while. He also made sure he could pick up on cue's that suggested she'd had enough of him for a while. He would say he wanted some time to finish what was going to be, no matter how bad, *the last book ever written*.

Paul loved her bluntness. 'As long as you don't expect it to be the last book ever read, that's fine by me.' He would disappear into the cargo part of the ship until her visage would appear. He always missed her terribly, but never showed it. She'd give him a menu plan and disappear. She was so relieved he wasn't getting clingy. If he did it would not be inconceivable that she would suck all the oxygen out of the ship one night when he was staying over there. She was still the Ageless One.

Nouveau Balinese.

One night she became earnest. 'I want to show you a project very special to my heart. I intended to do this after our first steak dinner, and it's only now floated back into this wandering mind I have now. This project went against the taboos I made up for the Renewals. One was we didn't turn the ship into Noah's Ark and bring back a large breeding population of Pandas so they could jump start a truly a magnificent population around every bamboo infested town. However there was one group of ...you could say mammals...that had the entire population relocated *every* time. They lived out another fifteen hundred years and got picked up and taken to the same island, which was one of the jewels in the crown of Indonesia. Bali.'

She got up and went to the controls which could turn the entire Orb into a very disorienting movie screen until one got used to it. They had introduced each other to their favourite movie genres. Chrona's affections for Paul grew when he read the cues that she would be delighted to never be exposed to some genre or other ever again. 'Primates.' She looked back smiling. 'Maybe two hundred thousand years of evolution. I don't remember the number of cycles of course.' She laughed. 'Now they have a language with quite a bit of clicking and other strange sounds a bit like the Xhosa from Africa. They have little schools and, *without any tinkering from me*, are matriarchal.'

'Matriarchy. That *is* evolution.'

'Correct. Should be late afternoon in their part of the world. She brought up some vision of a curious village. They were both silent. Several bodies lay around public spaces around the buildings with some of the simple but well-conceived and built dwellings burned or vandalised. They had a light fur but were closer to a homo species than any ape. Chrona panned around silently.

'Why didn't I realise the Adules could learn to drive boats and island hop from Singapore to visit new areas. Probably to find young Sororibus or flee those Adules on the cusp of being grown men, more violent and territorial than they. I imagine this is a part of what they would call an adventure. Please don't attempt to comfort me.'

'You know you only have to call.' He stood up. Gave her a comforting embrace whether she wanted it or not. And left without a word.

Her affections for him grew steadily. He appeared to have his adulation under control. Which she was slightly conflicted about. But he devoted his superiority syndrome on understanding someone who had lived virtually alone for hundreds of millennia as if it was an issue he could be insufferably confident about. She went to her room and cried. Which though it had only happened so rarely, was escalating in frequency.

She put herself in stasis for a week When she emerged, she looked at what Paul had been up to.

He knew she would see what he'd been studying. He had been reeling back through the last Millenia of the daily lives of the creatures she called the Nouveau Balinese. Each Renewal she would spread toxins for the existing monkey population on Bali and anywhere in the region. The Nouveau Balinese were settled in an old caldera forming a lake. Once the Virides had done their clean up tasks, they helped relocate the evolving species into the villages identical to what they had left. These became more and more sophisticated as Timeline cycles passed. Chrona had the Virides replace the crops they grew to the same standard they had attained at the end of the preceding Timeline. Including new varietals of grains, vegetables and fruit trees. An increasing number of villages were situated by good-sized streams around the edges of the lake. They could walk to the ocean in a few days and developed ceremonies and rituals and a proto pantheism possibly absorbed from the remnants of the Hindu cultural relics of the island. However the Nouveau Balinese had many unique traits.

Paul packed up a freighter with food, tools and weapons. It was fortunate that he supplied himself liberally because the main ship cargo section soon after he left and didn't reappear in its bay next to the orb for six months. He didn't have access to the Orb without

Chrona's invitation. He went to the Capital to check several times to find the ship still absent, somewhere in time rather than space.

He didn't mind. He found now he liked having a break from adulation, which he still felt, such was her powerful magnetism, but he'd learned to manage it. He was busy. He arrived at the village they'd seen on the viewer to a scene, on a much smaller scale, he was so familiar with. Bodies. Spread around. In this case murdered with violence. It made him angry. There were a dozen villages and to some degree death and destruction had been visited on each. He'd made a close survey of the island in the freighter. He didn't care that he had superior firepower. He came quietly on the three groups of Adules, some with young Sororibus. He killed them all, loaded up their bodies in the boats they'd come in, dragged them out to sea and sank them. He tempered his anger with the recollection of his enormities and everything that was happening, all of it, could be traced back to what he had done less a year before.

As he'd been working on loading the boats, he could hear the strange sounds which were words. Hums, ticks, tocks and sing song phrases. It seemed that those dead at the villages were likely the only ones the Adules had slaughtered. The majority of the population dispersed. His next job was to manage the remains of their relatives.

His research had shown that when a Nouveau Balinese died, they were placed on a platform in a type of forest tree, encased in the bark of a another. He later found this tree species repelled insects. There they would dry, and perhaps years later, be interred in a large cave only visited for the purpose. He didn't want to remove any remains already dried out in bark to the cave. Nor try to relocate the now putrid remains according to the rites they observed. So, given

261

the surplus of dead Nouveau Balinese he started building platforms to as near a replica as those existing as he could manage. This required a good deal of cutting sticks for the platform from specific trees in an exacting way and joining them with reeds and a resin that needed to be chewed into a gum. He completed one after a week, and within two weeks was making one every three days. In three months he had built enough to take all the fallen and had created a pile of the bark from the tree used for the purpose in each village. But there had been none moved by the survivors and no indication they planned to reoccupy the villages. He had broken this up with inveterate treasure hunting. He was going to walk away defeated, unsure when or if Chrona would return. She had possibly forgotten how to operate the ship. He laughed at that, and he laughed that a little-known history professor come mass murderer was the last man on earth chewing resin to make platforms for sentient monkeys slain by half caste aliens. Devolved because of him.

He'd made a few sightings of the beautiful, intelligent and spiritual sentient creatures but none had approached with anything like a welcome.

He roamed the islands in Indonesia in a radius of a few hundred miles around and found several groups of Adules. He studied them. Some appeared to have stopped roaming and begun to live peacefully. However he liked the monkey people more. If he ever got back to the main ship he would come and pulse everything in a radius of five hundred miles. How Lissa would laugh. Maybe.

He was getting low on stores and had been eating fruit from the Gardens of the Balinese. He made a last visit to the villages and was gratified to see some empty spaces where the fallen matriarchs had been. It was they who had defended their villages while the main population escaped. Some bark encased bodies began to populate his platforms. The Capital and every city and town had been flattening with every living thing killed. He had run out of stores and so roamed around finding outlier communities which had focused on production of some staples or luxury items. He visited a large Cacao plantation and associated manufacturing infrastructure with a few confused Virides still in residence. He was able to liberate a huge quantity of a variety of chocolates.

After no contact for six months two words come up on the screen as he flew along the coast of Brazil, having checked on his Balinese charges from time to time as they repopulated the villages.

'Come Hither.'

They were both surprised at how warm their greeting was. It was a long, fond embrace. And it was a mixture of lover and friend that pleased them both.

'I went into the grey nothingness of time for three years. Even if we're all torn to pieces by the relentless workings of physics soon, they can live in peace. The Adules will soon be no more and I've done it also for the remaining Sororibus and added in the toxin for the Virides still wandering about. It took me a long time to do what I used to so in a few weeks. And I had to calibrate it so the toxin wouldn't kill you. That was tough. You're the only human. I had to take the bubble and visit you in the university. You died about fifteen times, but I kept going back a few minutes earlier until you survived. You're way more interesting since you took on the Virides, hooked up with my daughter, killed the best Envoy I ever had and became a mass murder.'

'And my adventures as a lab rat is something I of course, never remembered?'

'Like your aunt.' She said. 'I decided to do what I should have done way back when you wore yourself out with killing. The remaining Sororibus and Adules and Viride will be dead in a few weeks because I turned it into an aerosol. I appreciate what you did for the Nouveau Balinese. I'd assume the Adules had run down the entire population. Once I did a proper survey, I realised most went into hiding. Now they're moving back into their villages.' The breezy, flippant example of her species, passed down to her daughter, changed to a sincere note. 'It means a lot.' These few words were loaded with emotion along with another message he didn't fully appreciate at the time.

Through the powerful telescope on the ship they started to see stars begin to disappear into an empty blackness in the middle of what used to be the Milky Way. 'Planet formerly known as Pluto will be gone in a few years.'

'Tides are already getting weird and gravity's making little temporary shifts now and again.' Paul observed.

Pranks

It was a week later Paul regained consciousness to a grogginess he had never experienced no matter how much he'd had to drink. Chrona was sitting in the command chair with her back to him. He had regained consciousness at a small table for two. Checked red tablecloth and remnants of a much-practiced Linguini in front of him. He would never know she had made and thrown away the meal twelve times until it was, as far as she could remember, like what she had for lunch. During that tiny little sliver of love.

The Orb had been restored to join the ship as it had been every fifteen hundred years. He knew this because the four retractable arms from the ship had, like massive crabs claws, extended forward. Now embracing the Orb from four quarters. This didn't impede the forward view from the outer hemisphere of the magnificent, curved ball hundreds of feet high. The enclosing arms reached only slightly past the diameter.

'Ha. There you were you trying to keep your adulation in check Paul. Thanks for all that by the way. And here I was playing the 'Long Game'. I lulled you into a false sense of security. While having a very pleasant time I won't deny.' She spun around on the chair, gave him a penetrating look and spun back. They were out in space. Facing the blue and white ball of the earth.

'I'm off to restart the whole enterprise with a new batch or Sororibus. That's diversity for you. I'll take them from a different part of the benighted planet. I may spend some time in the grey limbo to figure out how to blow it up on the way out to save the other Sisters. After a fashion. If they don't generate the Sharing which they developed to provide comfort to each other last time I'll help them along. In between 'Stasis' which I didn't know how to do last time.'

She looked at him again. 'Hmmm. Or maybe the Sororibus have had their day. A quarter of a million years ago, or however long it was.' She was at her haughtiest best and turned back to the front. 'Way back when I spoke to one of my species while I journeyed to pick up the Sororibus. I learned about a species called the Böse who's males were as bad a mate as those of the Sororibus. I can't remember all the details, but Kirby somehow killed half of them. Billions so the story goes. As soon as you humans are allowed near an alien species you can't help yourself but start killing them en masse.' She spun her chair around and gave him a piercing look and a little squinty headshake.

Paul was relaxed about the whole thing now. 'It's okay. My point of view has changed. My species had their time.' He shrugged. 'There was only fifteen hundred years left anyhow. And as we've discovered, once the future turns into the past it…ceases to exist. So why worry about it even as the future in the first place.'

'That's deep.'

'Do you think the Böse females will develop a Sharing as the Sororibus did?'

'Doesn't matter. I can load it in. I can also load in the biological process the Li use for statis. They can sit zoned out for years. Need a nappy but we all will in the end.'

'You've got it all planned out. Can I come.'

'Ordinarily I'd say no. I'm rather annoyed that you killed my daughter and the best Envoy I ever…remember having. Oh and there was the genocide you committed. However, since you redeemed yourself with the Nouveau Balinese and you're a passable…cook, I've you decided to take you along. As a male, you'd have to play the part of…a kind of pet. Given whatever females I fill the hold with are going to be a bit leery of males. Especially when they find out what you did to the *last* all female free society I set up.' She faced him with a frown and a headshake and turned back to face the earth again.

'I know all you really need from me is my sperm Chrona. And that's okay. You'll put it through your diversification process. I will have helped impregnate tens of thousands of females. Kind of cool from an evolutionary perspective to be such a successful male, even if my genes do get deidentified.'

She spun the chair around again. 'You know me too well Paul. And yet your eagerness to impregnate a…ship load…of alien females… it does cool my ardour a little.

'The main pleasure would be supporting you on another grand undertaking.'

She'd turned away and sounded a little flustered. 'Yes…Yes and I can tell you something else… listen…listen to this Paul. This will make you really take notice.' There was a very long pause. 'Blast. I can't even remember things like this long enough, even for a God damn prank. You responded in all these unexpected ways that I didn't bother mapping out all of the probabilities for. You threw me off my script Paul. I'm not happy.'

'You had me Ageless One.' She hadn't really.

'Yes. I think it was going well for a while there.' He noticed she was dressed in clothes he had never seen before. They were slightly pira-tesque he thought. He realised that her species were traders, maybe even space pirates. Chrona had a streak of compassion, deny it as she might, which ran deep. Laying alongside her capacity for expe-diency and casual ruthlessness.

'The real reason the ship is joined up and I'm dressed in the slightly silly garb which passes for my species day wear, is that I'm about to, after a gazillion years, leave my beautiful ship forever. You are going to have your heartbeat linked to. If you decide it's time to rid the universe of it's terrible potential and destroy the ship; go and have a few nights out in a row.'

Paul sat absorbing this and had to be called to attention about what she said next.

'I've programmed it to give you one chance Paul. One bubble ride to *before* Kirby's final departure to change the fate of humanity. Then you'll have to wait and see. If it doesn't work the bubble goes back to before your intervention and resets the unaltered Timeline and the whole bubble function gets fried forever. After this *intervention*, you won't visit earth again until Kirby leaves *exactly* as she did the last time…or…again. Time is weird Paul. Well. I'm off. It was nice meeting you. No need to write.'

'And where are you off to.' He was now plunging into despair. He was losing the person, whether she liked it or not, he loved most in the universe, and she was treating it like a fling. A victim of her poor memory.

'I'm going to live out my days with the Nouveau Balinese while you abandon me to try to pull off some hare-brained scheme.' She remained dispassionate.

'I'm coming with you of course to say goodbye.'

'We can do that here Paul.' Her voice started to take on a trace of emotion.

'It's not you I want to say goodbye to Chrona. As if that that would matter. It's Nouveau Balinese. I'd love to see them back living as farmers and villagers.'

'Oh.' The fact that he could even say such a thing created a crack in the façade she found hard to fill. 'Whatever. Oh yes…and…and um. I forgot. We need to get that heart of yours wired into the ship.' It was much riskier than either of them realised. He put his hands on the pads while Chrona navigated through at least ten menus to find a page. These didn't come up in English. Rather it was curved runes. 'I have absolutely no idea how to read these anymore. Wasn't that great at it when I was being taught this stuff. Certainly not top of the class. From memory the right button for this three from the bottom.'

'From *memory* it's third from the bottom?'

'Yes? Paul it's not like it's a big deal. Remember your aunt? You ready?' She'd hit the button while she said this. Her representation of a profound lack of concern shattered when Paul's heart rate rose to two hundred and then plunged to twenty. This cycle went on again and again. However the gap closed. A hundred and eighty down to thirty. Eventually eighty down to sixty and settled at seventy. Chrona restored her disinterest. 'Probably never been done with a different species. Still we squeaked through. It was far worse for me than it was for you Paul. Oh…no I got that the wrong way around. Anyway, I'm off to live with some very civilised and erudite monkeys who won't mind it if I tell them the same stories every day. Polite you see. They'll take turns having to listen to me.'

'They'll count themselves among the most fortunate.' Paul was not going to go all the way with the pretence of disinterest. They rode out on the freighter in silence and arrived at the edge of one of the smaller Nouveau Balinese villages.

Paul swept her up in the embrace he had always wanted to but had never quite thought she was ready for. 'I can't leave like this Chrona, I have to tell you…'

She put a finger to his lips. 'No. I'm not going to make the same mistake twice Paul. I love you. I remember that other time. I'll never forget it. But I also have a beautiful memory of breakfast, swimming in Hawaii and then dancing as the sunset with wine and cheese on, what was the place called.'

'El Capitan.'

'See. I remember most of it. It's one of the two times in my life I know I'll never forget.'

He smiled at her. He knew it was the sincerest smile he'd ever managed. 'I am without a doubt the most fortunate human that ever lived. I love you Chrona, and I'm going to miss you, but you are right in what you've decided. As you were with all you've ever done.'

She smiled back. She reached into her bag and handed him a folder. 'Thank goodness I remembered to give you this. Now you better got lost before I forget why we're here.'

He gave her a last embrace. Said nothing more and went to the freighter. The Balinese had kept their distance, picking up on the social cues. Once Paul was gone, they were all around her. She had visited them often enough to know members from each generation. And she spoke their language fluently. She was happy and relaxed. And she knew, whatever else she forgot, she was going to feel that way until the end.

Approaching the reconnected spaceship was to see a thing of beauty. The giant clear Orb held in the embrace of a massive ship which with four giant claws. Now it was balanced, elegant and its scale seemed suddenly to be fully realised once it was proportioned as it was designed to be.

A Desperate Plea

He opened the envelope and read the contents. It was simple. But could the minutest change to the Timeline be avoided? She'd given him the phone number, the timing and what to say. She'd prepared the Pre-Set and he didn't bother to wait. He'd cleaned elder earth out of treasure and beautiful objects to the extent he was going to. He even had a few terracotta soldiers from China among the vases and other treasures of a twice over antiquity. He pressed the Pre-Set and went back in time to speak with a person no one had ever challenged as being the genius of her age. Many said of her species. But he had to get through to her first.

When the text came through to the man preparing for bed he was surprised to receive it on this number and more so to see it disappeared once he read it. He thought that a was Graceland initiative. 'Please take my call.' The man's phone rang. He opened the line but said nothing. It was Company policy to answer phones that way. The caller had to know who they were speaking to and prove it. Paul was trying to balance urgency with credibility.

'Sir. I'm not from the military, I'm not a journalist and I don't represent any commercial interests. Unlikely as it sounds, I'm calling you about the fate of billions. Ultimately *tens* of billions.'

The last sentence piqued his interest. 'It's Manion. I'm listening.'

'Manion. Forgive me for this but the person who sent me insisted that I convince you beyond any doubt.' Manion said nothing and

Paul ploughed on. Manion could hear the discomfort in the callers voice. 'The night your partner died, of course you were beyond despair. You never imagined you could love someone so much. And yet she asked your forgiveness as she drifted in and out of consciousness.' Paul could feel the listener stiffening at this recounting of such an intimate moment of his life. 'She apologised for not doing what you'd agreed. It was no secret that she was very close to your daughter who can, I think it's fair to say, be…persuasive.' Manion laughed and this relieved some of the tension. 'Although you'd agreed she should go to a school for gifted children, you believed she should experience as close to a normal childhood as possible. But it was revealed that night she'd been given special tutors and had completed the same sets of tests and assignments as any other student. In a short time she advanced though the school grades. However, unless she got a score of a hundred percent in every exam, she would reject the result and ask to sit another. By the time you learned of this your eleven-year-old daughter had one degree in physics, one in chemistry and one in engineering and was writing her PhD on 'Rocket Propulsion and Time' however she destroyed this and prepared another on 'Ultra-Low Friction Synthetics.'

'This meant so little to you in that moment. Not what your daughter had achieved, but that it might cause your wife a moments concern. You wanted the one you loved most in the world to feel peace and deep satisfaction with her achievements. One of which was to be a good, honourable person who loved life and…'

'…all of its secrets.' Manion finished the sentence. He had said these things to her. Manion was going to say he'd heard more than enough and ask what the caller wanted. But Paul rolled into another intimate setting again when only two people shared the room. 'Three weeks later Elouise persuaded her 'governess' to leave her in the lab with you for the day. She said little and looked at one of the A0 size project summary pages you used to capture the essentials of each potential invention or theory. She got a thick red marker and began, after some study, to draw a diagonal red line across the page and move it onto a neat stack that was forming. In the afternoon she took an interest in one of the ideas you'd been working on. She selected a thinner red pen and began to mark it up. Crossing out sections, adding equations and rewriting the project in clear neat text.'

Manion confirmed this by saying. 'It was barely recognisable from what I'd been working on. I knew I was working with a person of unprecedented genius, whatever my relationship to her.'

'The woman who sent me has been my only experience of genius. And it was…magnificent to witness. She insisted I tell you that had you been interested in academia you would have easily been acknowledged as one of a handful of great thinkers the earth ever produced. A polymath. However it was your fate to stand next to someone so incandescently bright it made your own light look ordinary. Many might feel a little cheated. But you spend your life adding pieces and perspectives, and moderation, to the outputs of someone unprecedented in any age.'

'Tell whoever it is that sent you that's a kind sentiment.'

'I wish I could do that Manion.'

'If there's more, I really don't need to hear it. I could provide some conjecture as to how you were able to make these observations, however I'm starting to suspect that…' He laughed. '…you are talking to me as a means to get through to the…incandescent one.'

'Sir from what I understand she's never taken a call in her life. She designs things and assures herself the specification and quality she expects is delivered.' It hadn't happened yet, so he didn't tell Manion David Garret makes this process much easier for her in the future.

'She's never taken a call. In fact the only time she has used a telephone was an occasion when she was dissatisfied with the manner which I was conveying her message.'

'I've told you what's at stake sir. I've tried to convince you with what the person who sent gave me. She wants to assure you there was only very few and very discreet observations of such intimate moments.'

'I suppose you can't tell me your name. I'll meet with my daughter with your evidence, to the extent I will reveal these private experiences to her. I'll try to convince her to take a call.'

Manion could hear the great relief in Paul's voice. The older man thought this response might be premature. 'Manion. My name is Paul and the one who sent me is Chrona. Or that's the only name she could remember. She had a final request. To make anything I've said meaningful. To avoid a disaster here and the loss of a magnificent evolution in other worlds you would need to continue in the morning precisely as you would have done had you not taken this call.'

'I wish I could say I could do that. But the human mind doesn't work that way. I will invariably make adjustments, even if only small.'

'That's why she asked if, once you've spoken to your daughter, you could go to your bedroom, sit at the end of your bed, with your eyes closed and your hands resting on your thighs, and don't do anything until your daughter comes for you.'

'Strange as this conversation is, it has a coherence. Call this number. Thirty minutes. Don't expect it to be easy. You'll be fortunate if it isn't very brief.'

'Thank you Manion. Goodnight.'

The Incandescent One

It was nearly very brief. 'Elouise.' He asked when the line opened to silence.

'My father convinced me I should take this call.'

'It's Paul and…'

'He said you'll want to offer some proofs of your bona fides. You can dispense with that.'

'The one who asked me make this call, and…made use of…your bubble, said I must.' Again he ploughed on. 'When your mother passed away you were distraught, more than anyone could know because, and no one would argue, including yourself, you're not especially demonstrative.'

'Are you saying this in order to preserve my participation in this call.'

He knew he had very little time. He didn't agree with what Chrona had demanded but he trusted her. 'You made a *book*. It recorded…the nights you cried yourself to sleep. Being who you are you felt terrible grief, but you also analyse thing. Somewhat like David

Garret whom you plan to collaborate with. You measured the minutes, each night that you did this. And then as there were gaps between the nights. You converted all of this into graphs. You felt unbearable grief. You loved your mother so much and by mingling this grief with science, a subject you had both loved, it made it easier.'

Paul was afraid there would be the fabled icy edge to her voice. Yet it was flat. 'Go on.'

'You'd created something precious. The only material thing that you would categorise in such a way. Except perhaps the outcome of your truly great undertaking. And you wanted to keep it safe, at the same time, even if was only you that knew about its existence, a fitting monument to the woman you loved and admired so much. So you created a Bubble in time and space. If someone ever wanted to find it when the bubble was sealed, it would be the very last place they looked if they searched through all of time and all of...'

'You *can't* know about that. It's impossible.' He heard a voice that didn't believe in the impossible provided it was within the immutable laws of the physical world, however these changed as they became better understood.

Paul could throw caution to the wind because it would only work if she found a solution to the problem he was soon to lay at her feet. 'You start to keep other things, in addition to the book in there. Inventions and ideas you'd agreed with your father were best destroyed. Things your incredibly creative mind would conceive of in the vein of pure research. However all were vetted in case a sinister use might be applied using them. However you believed your bubble was secure and even though you could recreate these ideas, some very complex, it was more efficient to store them, catalogued so you could simply go and get only the piece that would make something else work, but leave no capacity for the whole to be subverted.'

'You *can not know this!*'

Paul suspected the phone call was about to be terminated. 'I know that every single man, woman and child on earth dies horribly because of something you have stored in that Bubble.' There was a long silence. 'You're the only one that should know that you can disappear into it for less than an eyeblink that could be hours or days experienced inside. Anyone watching you would see you perhaps blinking at the changes of light as you returned. That's why it's impossible to know where and when it's found and opened. Until it's too late. And by then you...you've left the planet.'

Paul guessed correctly, that on one level Elouise was aghast at what she was being told. On another she was exhilarated that someone could know what he knew. And there was only one way to do that. 'I've called to beg you to take everything from the bubble and destroy every trace of what was in it.'

'You've given me much to think about...' She was about to close the line.

'Elouise. Please don't hang up. There is one more thing to the story to avoid a loss of *another* kind. Everything you do from the moment you wake up in the morning is a part of a chain of events that first lead to an upheaval and then to a hugely beneficial outcome in another...*galaxy*. But it won't happen if you remember what we've discussed.'

There was a very long pause. 'I live my life to seek the incredible. Push towards the very improbable which others describe as impossible. Dispassionate as I might seem, this is my passion. With all that you've told me…I can hardly wake up tomorrow without my curiosity not having been…stimulated.'

Paul knew he was one of the very few that had the opportunity for such a frank conversational interlude with Elouise. 'And yet you must. The *slightest* change to what your do, or what your father does, once you arise tomorrow morning, though it would save *humanity* from a terrible fate, would rob hundreds of billions from a peace and prosperity *you will catalyse.*' Before she could provide a protest about the credibility of such a statement he got in first, which was one of his strengths. 'Your genius. You must exercise it on this very difficult problem of obliteration of any memory of this call and what, I hope, it stimulates. Very difficult problems are what you solve. I am urging you to destroy all but one thing in the bubble and place nothing more in it and destroy it. While inside you need to figure out the puzzle. The one who sent me has given us only one chance to achieve this. If it fails, if things deviate to even the tiniest degree, I'm required to return to a time before we have this conversation, and…we will not have it. In the Timeline I have now altered, it must be the same future as the original until an essential event occurs many years into the future. Your father waits for you. Sitting at the end of his bed. Eyes closed.'

'I have much to consider.' The line went dead.

At least from his perspective he had plenty to keep him interested because the ship had created a bubble an hour before his conversation with her. He would reside in it now. He reeled the ship forward to the Graceland Challenges, which he now watched with interest. The ship would halt at tiny diversion from the original Timeline because it would not be the future the ship had traversed so many times. He had only seen the television coverage of the most unusual competition in the history of the earth. Now he could focus in and see close up what he knew now would be the main players. He followed the young woman who had chosen to give herself the name Amazon. She reminded him of Helen. He was able to see the agony she suffered before dying, Kirby by her side. It was never reported by the coverage of the Challenges.

The ships reading provided an exact match between the two Timelines. It reeled forward to the launch of the ship Elouise had built, which he alone, with Manion, was able to witness. Once the ship was gone, it was out of his capability to follow because the Bubble never extended beyond the planet. It had to retreat from the launch site to let Elouise's ship out. Chrona had programmed things carefully Now he had to wait until Kirby returned.

At his point Chrona came on the screen. It was like a blow to see her again. 'Still there. I wasn't sure if you might disappear if Elouise emptied the Bubble and then I didn't come along and take ownership of it. In case you didn't figure it out, as soon as you set up the new Timeline, even briefly, and made those telephone calls, I vanished from here because you created a new future with it. You finally killed me off like you did all my many daughters. And a future I was quite looking forward to. Plus the monkey people Paul. How could I have trusted you. You probably thought it didn't matter because I had a case of the 'Aunt on Holiday' syndrome anyway. If I still existed to have it. Which I *don't*.'

'If you're seeing this, it means your bubble survived because it's a time bubble and it doesn't know where or when it is. If what we tried with Elouise fails and Kirby doesn't leave *exactly* the way she did…does, you'll reel back to before the phone call and the ship won't let you make it again. I wonder if that will mean I'll reappear here with a bunch of erudite monkeys. Time's weird.'

He had the ship reel forward to Kirby's return. It was fun to watch. Broadway Shows, surfing all over the world. He was surprised to see the squirrel people, when they didn't need simulacrums, had taken to with a passion. High stakes gambling with chips liberated from the backroom of the casino. Activities which father and son seemed a little uneasy about. Kirby winning and losing hundreds of thousands of dollars with a complimentary rum and cola at her elbow. When she would win big she would jump up and grab her 'mate' around the neck and Paul would observe the look on his face. He knew that look. Dancing, visiting the locations of the Challenges, including where Amazon had been so gravely injured and died. Her husband and son trying to comfort her as she sobbed uncontrollably.

And they left after the ship got wedged in the Eiffel Tower due to Kirby's failure to tilt it to allow for its atmosphere wings. Not necessary from an aerodynamic perspective. Hope of the East, a genius comparable to Elouise, thought that Kirby would think they were 'Cool'. And he was right until they nearly brought one of the iconic structures of humanity toppling down.

The alluring visage on the wall appeared right as her son, which Kirby had named Manion, finished welding the famous tower and they vanished into space. 'If we got this far it's looking good, and Kirby is gone. *However*, it doesn't mean that Elouise removed the toxin. She'd be difficult to live with that one. Not like other geniuses you're familiar with. She may have decided to put a few more locks on it and decided it was easier to create an outcome to forget you and make her father do the same but keep the Bubble and make it more impossible to crack. To achieve what I asked her to would be fiendishly difficult because the bubble existed in her future.' It had been fiendishly difficult. The only thing that made it possible was that she had never taken anything out of it. Although it gave her a theoretical sense of comfort to have such complex ideas stored, she could never contravene the intent of an Agreement she struck with a man she respected so deeply. Irrespective of their relationship.

Chrona was back. 'I meant to tell you I figured out how it was the bubble found. A man called Ryker. Worked for the Russians who were partnering with the Chinese who wanted to steal Graceland's inventions which had been some of the biggest commercial successes in history. Ryker was a good man. He loved his family. And his work. And would never willingly betray Elouise, whom he worshipped intellectually. However family, those he worked with would all die in grisly circumstances at the hands of blackmailers unless he did as he was told. I observed a fellow in Britain like that once. The nearest I came to meddling ever. Except the rock star of course. Emma came through all right and he got *well tortured*.' She paused. 'What was I talking about? Oh yes. Genius though she was, what she'd created had been identified by a Russian lab as an anomaly. They poured the latest Artificial Intelligence surveillance into Graceland to try to lever out some secrets. It picked up the anomaly they didn't understand but knew was something remarkable. They used Ryker to find out how to crack it. Graceland had AI tools lightyears ahead of anyone else and Ryker gave those to the Russians who gave it one problem to solve. How to get into that bubble. It took years. They achieved it after Elouise had left the planet. She had created a second bubble on her Ship Without a Name and she didn't give up hope she might figure out a way to get home to around the time she'd left. All we can hope is that after your telephone call there was nothing to find in the one she left on earth. You'll know in *fourteen years*. So you can meddle with the Timeline as much as you like now. It doesn't matter; Kirby's gone. That part of the new Timeline you started has gone on unchanged. But did the key part we wanted to change happen or will things end up in the same old bloodbath. And there won't be any humane toxin from me this time. Billions die horribly. *Again*.'

Interventions

She returned. 'I'm sure we don't need to broach the subject of my daughter, given the relationship I think I remember we had. This is really the last Goodbye. I think.'

'So let the meddling begin.' He said to a blank wall.

Fourteen years until he could be sure the toxin is released...or not. The ship was in a new Timeline now. He could look at the original Timeline in detail but it wouldn't let him reel forward. He knew it could, provided it was an exact match with the earlier Timeline. But as soon as he set foot on earth, it wouldn't be the same. And he had a lot of ideas to fill in the next fourteen years.

He had plenty of things he wanted to do. However, just as Chrona had decided not to meddle until Kirby had gone off to do what she did in another galaxy, Paul decided he wouldn't meddle too much with the world until a certain journalist finished dancing with an old Buddhist monk. Because it was her life in her Timeline. Until then.

After that, Chrona turned up to take over the world and eventually started sending Virides to earth the next day, a few seconds in advance each cycle. So from that day on, he decided the world was his oyster. There were a few exceptions.

Lissa was walking from the University to a market area because she and Jerry liked to cook with fresh ingredients every night if they could. There was a man smiling at her as she approached. He had a booklet in his hand. She was in no hurry so thought she would spend some time listening to the man and then, politely deconstruct his arguments. A little. She wasn't going to try to evangelise him. If he was happy and content, she was happy and content to leave him that way. But she would offer him enough to give him pause. In the original Timeline it didn't work out that way.

However a stranger arrived, Paul was in disguise, he engaged the man in an earnest discussion before Lissa reached him, so she walked on. Paul, based on what he'd learned about what a human was capable of, didn't bash god around in his conversation with the man as he might have once done. Paul thanked the man and said he'd given him much to think about. Paul could see he was a good person and understood how he might reel another good person into what Paul continued to believe was a belief system which had evolved. And it succeeded among a few others, because of the combination of successful psychological latching methods.

One of his first tasks was creating a new identity, at great expense, with a multigenerational history completely different to the man who played cards with Jerry and Lissa. He kept away from himself unsure if a Time anomaly might be triggered by proximity. He got to know some people important in Helen's life. He started having fun investing the vast wealth he'd accumulated from the future. He had to manage the circulation carefully with the cash when two notes with the same serial number started to circulate. He spread his investments over thirty portfolio's and paid very expensive lawyers to make it difficult to track them back to him. The ship had gone through this piece of history a number of times and his small footprints on earth were not having an impact on markets initially. He had watched the market in advance enough over the coming years to buy and sell at times near to but not right on the peaks and the troughs to avoid scrutiny. He knew investment on a massive scale would change the markets and would be fascinating to observe. However he would wait until after the monk dancing for that scale of investment. Buying in early in stocks that were going to have phenomenal performance was an easy way to have a limited impact. That and the fact that he had more gold on the ship than the US held in its massive reserves. Moving it around had been a fun fitness regime when not with Chrona. He'd never been driven by wealth. If he had been, being a history professor would not have been the ideal vocation. He had an idea though. It would be, as much as anything could be, a lasting testament to the one he loved.

The next intervention was easy. It occurred while Helen was dancing with a monk. He went to a man's apartment. Modest but in a nice area. Decorated with the mementos from a life of wandering for the past thirty years and a few memorable objects from a fifteen-year career in music before that. When the ex-recording artist arrived home with some shopping he found a note on his kitchen table. Paul had called a former student whom he knew had beautiful, yet also easily readable script. He said he needed someone with nice writing to prepare a personal note and a classmate mentioned her name. She was paid a large sum of money for less than an hour's work, but also for 'discretion' which wasn't necessary because she had no idea who the note was from or to.

My Love

I'm not able to tell you why I was gone when you returned from the concert, nor why you could never find me on your long travels which I know began as a journey to reunite us, however I hope, became a journey through which you found much you came to understand and value.

I have never forgotten that night and day even as almost everything else begins to slip away. Short as it was, that tiny slice of sweet affection was the best I ever knew.

I could fill my mind with regrets if I chose to look through my memories for them. But I have only one true regret. I wish that when you'd told me, after not even a day together, that you loved me, I had told you I felt the same. So I'm telling you now. Nearly thirty years too late, but it blunts my sorrow that I didn't tell you then.

I am old. Far older than your imaginings. My end approaches but I look at your life and I see someone who has so much more to do. To give. I've been fearful you turned your back on music because of me. Perhaps that was a good thing. However if you chose to return to it, it would be with a vast store of experiences and emotions. You have new perspectives, and unlike some that never paused, you might find a new place.

We shared only a tiny sliver of love. But it has sustained me all these long years.

Paul thought Chrona would not be pleased with this but she, thanks to him, had ceased to exist. She must have had some unbelievably complex sensors on the bridge because as soon as he returned, she splashed up on the screen. 'You wrote him a note didn't you.'

'Yes.'

'Don't bother answering me Paul! This is a recording. How stupid are you? You snuffed me out of existence remember. One among billions. It better have been a good note. Chow.'

He wondered how many topics she'd made recordings about that would be trigger presumably by his body language or some sensor in the ship he was unaware of. His life within the bubble was being recorded and analysed. And he didn't mind at all. It was evidence she'd cared.

She reappeared. 'And it's not hard to guess what you did about Lissa. You're so predictable.'

She disappeared.

She came back. 'I appreciate you letting my daughter lead her own life until now. But *our* girl is going to need some guidance. I have faith in you Paul. You'll need to use the little mind tricks I taught you to manage the whole *adulation* problem others have and help her find the person she needs to be with. I've analysed it. There's only one. And by the way, *how* rich do you need to be. Chow.'

He waited for a while in case there was any more evidence to be presented of his predictability.

It was eight years before he would know the outcome of his conversation with Elouise. He'd been following the doings of Helen for the past six, on the ship mostly, sometimes in stasis when the world was boring. She was twenty none, though she looked early twenties. He was relieved when the first time he saw her again any feelings he had for her that weren't platonic had been washed away. He still admired her.

Now, without the arrival of the Virides and the admission to the Sororibus world, he could see she was drifting into a more and more strange state of mind. She could not escape the scrutiny and focus and had no explanation as to why she was somehow different to everyone around her. Paul made an intervention within an hour of the news that Helen had broken up with her boyfriend Raegan.

He turned up with baseball bat that evening when two young men were about the launch the List. He knew the last thing that they wanted was to do Helen any harm. He explained what was going to happen to Helen because of them. He told them. 'I know because I'm from the future'. He believed it made no difference what he did anymore. He put a very large pile of high denomination cash on the desk. I am buying your computers. Now that you know what a terrible effect *any* kind of list would have on the person you are both secretly in love with, I'm *hiring* you to make sure no list ever starts. The baseball bat is only a prop.' He nodded to the two stunned late teens. After he'd closed the door behind himself, he opened it briefly and put his head through and raised his eyebrows. 'Or is it?' When you've killed billions. And you want to. You can somehow convey that.

After the Monk Dancing

There were no Sororibus in this Timeline, so Helen woke up mid-morning. They had used a backup interview for the program. Her cheerfulness was a little dented. But she'd bounce back. She had a question she could not find an answer to though. And it was beginning to gnaw at her. Artie called and said a friend of a friend had a project he wanted to pitch to her. The man happened to know one of her lecturers at university who had been somewhat of a mentor. She met a man named Paul. She'd never heard of the Paul that was a History Professor. His life was, and would always be, inconsequential in the greater scheme of things. He made some efforts to change his appearance. A closely trimmed simple beard, reading glasses and a lighter hair colour was enough. His building wealth allowed him to 'dabble' in any number of things should it suit his purposes. As he waited for that fateful day eight years hence.

She'd come out of University with a degree in journalism. She found life easy. And though she'd needed to learn strategies to move clingily boyfriends and one girlfriend along, she had a pleasant nature and she loved her parents though her mother had died a few years before of cancer. If other people became complex around her, she knew it wasn't her doing.

He had been getting to know friends of Artie's, some of Helen's relatives, some of her lecturers and people who she would trust. He'd made his assessment against a long list of possibilities and decided who she should spend her life with. Her biological mother had appeared once he had decided and revealed she had come to this conclusion also. Neither had qualms as to their interventions. Helen had many of the attributes of her mother. A pathway might be laid, but Helen would never tread it without complete volition.

Paul ensured people she'd known and respected for years were at the dinner when they first met. Again. When he approached them with an idea, they were swayed by their respect and in some cases, secret love for Helen. They may have had a little Barrion-like nudge which Chrona had much improved and Shared with him. He made some adjustments. Such people retained their good opinion of Helen; however all the minds he visited were relieved of the 'allure' problem so her circle became more and more normalised. He'd bought a publishing house which, from a management perspective, he usually took a hand-off approach. He worked the idea up with both an agent and a highly regarded critic, who much improved the concept.

Over dinner Helen was provided with an offer for a book deal about the Graceland intergalactic space travel venture. Especially about the Challenges. There was a list of those who had agreed to be interviewed who no one else had been able to convince to participate in previous treatments. Everyone from Vyra's family in Dublin, Jarhead, Kirby's father, some of Gaspar's old regiment friends and even the girl who'd knocked Kirby over causing the sensational few moments when the young Australian was almost flying across the ridgetop, covered in blood, to confront her.

The culprit had attempted suicide twice, and owed money to the wrong kind of people when Paul tracked her down. Since their 'chance' meeting she had 'chosen' to go into rehabilitation and now worked at his publishing house. She was studying part time to pursue her passion for bronze sculpture. Taking his advice without any mind tampering, she changed her name and appearance after what turned out to be a cathartic interview with Helen. Paul had the benefit of making clandestine assessments of people's lives. He saw a basically good person who had made a stupid and callous decision which was uncharacteristic. It happened because the Challengers vied for a prize unequalled in human history. If he found someone who for good reason deserved his help, he was grateful he was in a position to be able to do so. It made his life better and he knew Kirby would be the first person to want the girl helped out of where one bad decision had landed her.

Like Chrona, he'd noticed Artie was different. He had a unique relationship with Helen. Irrespective of the highlights reel he kept. Paul had spent years examining and assessing the man against many other possible candidates and had made his decision.

All Helen knew was that a fully developed project with everything it needed to be successful was put in front of her. Previous works on the Graceland Challenges had been anaemic purely though a lack of participation of the key people involved or those close to them. And of course the main players left the planet. The project even included never before seen drawings from Vyra of scenes from the Challenges and the people she joined in the final crew training. One of which would go on to be the cover. A beautiful drawing of the crew, however it had the ill-fated Amazon standing in the middle of them. The crew that should have been. If Helen had a fraternal twin, it would have been Amazon. Paul had been able to see it as he watched Vyra drawing it in the days before the launch and had an artist recreate it from the footage he could clip out of the ship. There were other photographs he'd been able to acquire of iconic moments in the Challenges that were superior to anything that had been circulated in the past.

At the dinner Helen was a little suspicious. Paul realised his set up had been too comprehensive

'Why me?'

He had what was both a plausible and accurate answer. 'These people want to be interviewed by you because they have all seen your work and believe you will give them a good hearing and create and outcome that provides a balanced view compared to the earlier works. The other author's conclusions were already drawn before their books were written. And the deal is if they don't like some part of the transcript, it gets pulled.'

'Not exactly journalism is it. If the subjects don't have to commit to what they say.'

Chris Flesser, who lectured in journalism and ethics, joined the conversation with confidence. 'This isn't journalism Helen. It's an analysis of one of the most significant psychological studies of a scale no university could ever attempt. Nor be permitted to. No one has taken this perspective to investigating the Challenges. And before you remind us you aren't a psychologist, you'd have access to professors across the disciplines in the University to support the study, naturally their motivations will partly be to write papers on specific aspects of it. And I call it a Study, because if you decided to write the book, we'd like you to consider completing your master's at the same time. Most of the work would be collected and presented via the book, with the master's prepared as a reconfiguration of it, with some of the associated research that would go into it analysed and referenced.'

Helen was going to point out that she had to do this while holding down her 'day job' however she knew she had the capacity to achieve both. She could sense Artie was hoping she took the opportunity for the simple reason he genuinely believed it would be a good thing for her. One of the many things people liked about Helen was that she was straightforward and decisive. 'When do we start?'

Paul disappeared from Helen's life for a while. He had a few things to take care of. The ship had had the capacity to commence the incredibly data rich task to predict things, accounting for his changes, until 'Toxin-Day', as he believed it would have been called had anyone survived it. There were a few more meetings about the book, which he was to join, but on some pretext or other, being a businessman with a range of interests, could not attend. Chris coordinated the academic side of the project. Interviews were scheduled. Some in France, Dublin, Australia and Japan. One with a retired General, who at the time of Graceland was a Colonel. There were clearly things he could not say, yet he was wistful at an opportunity lost because of 'a domineering personality which I've since tried to tame'. Her meeting with Jarhead gave them both a strange feeling of Deja vu Helen generated new interviewees from those she spoke with. Her exposure to the Morning Show fell from four to three segments a week, more often pre-recorded. Her remuneration stayed the same because the head of the network was aware the advertising dollars more than compensated for it.

The Network got some stories out of the project and said they'd air a documentary if she would get enough participants willing to be on camera.

A Sudden Departure

One evening, Paul initiated a meeting about this, as his Production House would be interested in producing it, however he was called away at short notice. The meeting was at a high-end restaurant.

Ultimately only Artie turned up. He was notified as he arrived Chris and the film maker, had failed to be invited due to an 'oversight' on the part of Paul's assistant. Paul didn't have an assistant to forget to make the invitations. The pair chatted amiably as they always did. They both usually had ideas for interviews for the Morning Show to scope out. These meetings had always been the only place the decisions on interviews came from, no matter what the input from the network was. After several years of the show however, they both begun to quietly wonder if they'd hit the high-water mark for the style of journalism they did.

Artie was upbeat but a little apprehensive. 'I got this offer out of the blue Helen. Assistant Director for one of the big movie studios. The first job is on a big budget fantasy movie. They said they'd been watching me, you know, partly because they were watching you.' He laughed a little nervously at that. 'And they think I have what it takes. I would never believe I could get a chance like this.' Artie was giving way to a real sense of excitement to the extent he wasn't showing much concern that a winning formula and what had always been a great partnership was coming to an end. Or not as much as she felt he should be. There was a reason for that.

She also realised that her interactions with Artie had been reducing as she travelled and often interviews for the Show were set up for the country she was in, and they might not see each other for weeks. This was all contrary to what she'd become accustomed to, which was a gradual migration by the other person in a relationship towards clinginess followed by what had become a skilled disengagement initiated by her. Or the other kind of disengagement which was also troubling. People left her orbit completely. She'd been on her own since disentangling herself from Raegan a year before. The whole fascination people had for her was becoming wearing and disturbing.

Artie was different. However Helen was unaware that without the need for an 'oh' moment Artie had driven his feelings for her to a platonic place hard, so he would simply work with her every day. However he knew it couldn't last. It meant, like many others he might have to get right out of her life so that she was out of his. And she couldn't seem to change it. To turn this bizarre fascination off people simply left town. Hence ironically she had few lasting friendships.

However in Artie's case Paul turned up. He had a conversation with Artie which he was destined to forget. Paul explained everything to him. Chrona, Basilica, Barrion and why people became so fixated on Helen. He told Artie he had a technique which could create a mindset which would allow him to interact with Helen in an ordinary way. And Paul didn't define 'ordinary' because, meddler though he was, he would leave that up Artie and Helen. He would merely take away any obsession so Artie could develop and bring adulation levels down to an abiding and sincere love. Artie 'made his mind available' to Paul who was able to use the techniques Chrona put there in the same fashion she had done with Basilica. However Paul had a wider range of options whilst some, such as the kill function, were not included. She had learned some of these techniques from Barrion whom the ship took a detailed assay of when he was briefly in charge of it. He made the adjustments and caused Artie to forget the episode. Paul wondered what else she'd been up to when *his* mind was available to her. He was now very fond of fluorescent pink as a colour which she no doubt had a chortle at.

The dinner was leaving her Helen little disoriented. Artie was leaving in a week, the Network had been understanding, also thanks to Paul, and they had a back catalogue which meant they only needed a few new stories a month by which time she and Rhonda should be operating at full speed. Helen could see it hadn't occurred to him that she was flying to Ireland the next day as he continued to talk about the remaining set up interview options which he'd been working on recently while she'd been focused on the book. It might be a long time before they crossed paths. He was going to Chile which she had no reason to visit. When the show had been starting to build years before they'd spend hours together planning, justifying and getting in touch with contacts of contacts of high-profile potential interviewees. In recent years they were batting off presidents and tech billionaires, so they didn't need to do so much on that front. They would still spend a lot of time strategizing how to the get the best from an interview. The success wasn't purely the attributes many saw in Helen. It was careful research and investigations of the many options and directions an interview might take.

He looked up and saw the expression on her face. He shook his head. 'You're leaving tomorrow.' He had an idea. 'Before I leave the country how about we invite everyone who helped us in the production to a big party at the Network.' He laughed. 'And maybe another one where we invite all the people you interviewed. Quite a few would need a pass to get out jail though.'

She smiled. 'Maybe. I'm off to Marseille for a week after Dublin.' She knew the Network would want to get Rhonda involved in the process of identifying and working up projects. Helen quite liked

Rhonda. However she was at least one quarter the way to the kind of clinginess that spelled doom for the relationship. In fact Rhonda was three quarters of the way there. Like Artie she tried to fight it as she enjoyed her profession and was good at it. Like so many others it had to be Helen, or nothing. In her case it was causing a tension with what was a healthy professionalism and family life. She was reluctantly planning an exit from the show.

'We can scope things up on video calls as much as we need to. The movie is being filmed in the Pantanal. It's a beautiful part of South America. The Director thinks it's the perfect backdrop for this fantasy world from a book. It's a weird story. All the elves and dwarves and whatever else are mean and the goblins and ogres and really cool easy-going types. It was a very obscure book and quite underwhelming I'm told, and very poorly edited, but the screenwriters have made some adjustments and I think it will turn out okay.'

She could see he was trying to lighten up what they both realised was the last time they'd be together for quite a while and there were a few contact hours away from the end of a partnership that had lasted six years. However she got a feeling from him that he had confidence that she would have a great career and life irrespective of whether he was involved in it. She now realised how it was for a lot of people. She'd always been the one trying to make *them* feel that way. They'd finished desert and she was surprised at how upsetting it was to hear Artie say. 'We need to make sure we keep in touch regularly…you know. After.' Paul had taken a tiny bit of perverse pleasure in helping Artie to that line.

That was her line. Except when she delivered it, she also conveyed the message. 'You're really clingy now and that's it I'm afraid.' They got up and went to the door. It struck Helen that her time as some-one on what appeared to be a puff piece concealing real journalism was over. It had always been a collaboration. His suggestions in the set up and then comments and observations during the interview were what made her laugh or stopped her from making the kind of misjudgements she could be prone to. Always letting her have enough freedom to be relaxed. Half that partnership that had made her a success by her standards, even if others might have still had this strange obsession if it was done less well, was gone. A sudden-ly insecure Helen wondered if Artie was sincere about staying in touch. She was feeling a little hurt. Abandoned even. Completely unfamiliar emotions.

She gave Artie a hug. And he was gone.

It was hard to find a place in their schedule to keep it going. She decided to resign from the Network, and they reduced the slot to one per week which ran out for another three months. She hoped to leave quietly, but the boss asked for what he thought was a reason-able request, that she host an hour long special of what she thought was the best she and Artie, whom she'd always referred to as a col-laborator, had produced. Running through the choices she became upbeat about the project and called Artie hoping he would join her for his first ever on-camera appearance. He laughed and said he was enjoying being behind the camera but would be happy to do a little spot on the show so they could share the details about how their collaboration had worked.

The day before the scheduled filming she got a call advising her that Arti had got as far as Dallas and was told by the Studio that he was being sent to Spain to take over as Director on a project that was 'off track' and he'd be out of the country for a few months. The person who'd called her said 'Mr Yellen said he'd line up a time to join you on a video link for the interview as soon as he's landed and has arrived in the hotel.' She said the change had occurred after midnight her time so he hadn't called but wanted to get Helen the message as soon as he could. She told Helen he was really looking forward to it.

Helen was surprised at the intensity of her reaction to this. She had been looking forward to seeing him in person. She put on the face of the Helen so well loved by her fans to finish the project with Artie only having an hour to join in via video. She found it worse than not having had any contact. Because behind his good-natured enthusiasm, she could see in spite of his best efforts to conceal it, he was distracted. He was taking over a film that was a creative and political disaster area and he didn't know why he was being given such a challenging role. Paul did. He had a controlling stake in the studio.

The interview, her last association with the Network, was the beginning or a period with no career other than being an unusually well-resourced author. She flew to north Africa where she had meetings with some ex-Legionnaire friends of Gaspar, one of those who travelled on Graceland's 'spaceship without a name'. After a few days she contacted Artie, via his assistant, to let him know she was going to 'be in town'. She went to Spain and booked into a hotel. She could write the book anywhere and would wait around until he was available to catch up with her ex-collaborator and she had hoped, good friend. She was relieved when he called personally that afternoon to suggest a dinner that night. 'It might be late though.'

The Anointed One

When they arrived, a little early at the same time, the was a quiet frisson of excitement as they both realised they were hoping the dinner would turn out to be a first date. And yet neither wanted to be seen to be in a hurry. However they dined together every night for a week and were surprised at how little they depended on the relationship of a former time to make conversation. And it was not all about their new occupations. Collaborating on hundreds of interviews had worked so well partly because they were fascinated by the world around them and kept themselves closely informed about it and loved analysing it. It's what made Artie a well-rounded director. There's no question it was helped by the cache that went with working so long with Helen Hunter. It also helped that Paul was friendly with the board. He was able to help them out here and there, sometimes with amazing stock tips. For the two people catching up for dinners, it all came together. Paul had been able to help Artie to a mindset which benefited from the things the history professor learned being with the full-strength version of Helen. Her mother.

Helen and Artie were decisive people. The film was launched, to mild acclaim which was a good outcome for a first-time director taking over a 'lemon' and the book launch followed a month later. That it was an instant 'classic' surprised no one given who had written it. They were in danger of being the kind of couple that were reported on widely and had to experience daily intrusions in their lives by the vicarious or those who populate the bottom feeding niche of journalism. In addition to neither of them courting this, there was a strange dampening effect coming from somewhere. Tabloids bought. Sometimes shut down. Journalists deciding to make a project of some other couple or simply losing their jobs if Paul didn't like them. It was a fascinating game to Paul and yet he could not forget his self-righteous rant at the religious version of Lissa. In this Timeline she'd moved to a University in Scotland on a secondment. With Jerry taking a posting in London. They were making it work, and planned to settle in London for a while when she was free of her commitments.

Artie started pre-production on another film, with Helen doing a limited tour of the book. 'Followed by joblessness.' She would say. Though Artie knew she wasn't looking for anything yet and there had been plenty of offers. Partly because she had better things to do. They were catching up every few nights when Helen gave Arti a penetrating look that was pure Chrona. It was breathtaking in its power and confidence. 'Can we skip the engagement thing.' Artie knew a sensible plan when he saw one. He had a month before he would be engrossed in his first fully directed feature which was being shot in three countries. However what he had heard was the best news of his life, and she could see it in the way his eyes lit up.

Both the families and the friends they trusted thought it a good strategy to have a reception after the pair eloped. They were married on a beautiful island you needed to get to via a boat from Bali. In their case an old pearl lugger Helen's 'Publisher' had put at their disposal. After the ceremony the plan was to have a week with nothing electronic. Only some classic old page books they had always heard were 'must reads' but they'd never had time. They knew they were compatible when halfway through the second day Helen said. 'This blows.'

'I'll ask at reception if they can send over a faster boat. I know Paul won't mind. The great thing about that guy is he only wants what's best for people. However that lands.'

'Quite a guy it seems. I've only had the pleasure of meeting this high rolling friend of yours once you know.'

'As it happens, he wanted to schedule a meeting with you when we got home. Wants to catch you before some other publisher comes and steals you away.'

'I'm the faithful type.' He knew she was. But he'd also had to accept that he was married to someone who was, it seemed, just about everyone's dream girl, and he had prepared the ground in his mind for the occasional lapse in her faithfulness. He knew he would struggle getting through himself with the strange magnetism she had. This wasn't helped by the fact that she was getting towards early thirties and still looked early twenties.

Paul had determined from the beginning he'd always only be in the background in Helen's life. On Toxin-Day it would make it easier to shoot her...again if he had to. He, like the middle of the road rock star, had met something impossible to replace. Although at least Paul had been with her, even for a while. Her mother had been his unforgettable slice of love and he couldn't hide his pleasure when catching up with her daughter in person. For her. Having the alien's perceptiveness, even at half strength, she could sense a strange echo within him. Created by the adventure they had never had and an unforgettable mother who had ceased to exist. He had a daughter now. Though she wasn't so much younger then him. Even if she looked twenty years younger.

He outlined the two-pronged proposition he had in mind for her.

'We'd like to capitalise more of the breadth of your creative and journalistic capacity Helen. People in my business have been analysing your prose and believe you are a natural storyteller. Others have been following your journalism since the outset and are convinced your journalistic capabilities could take a new, and they hope, interesting direction.'

'My journalistic reputation struggles when I try to find out too much about you and your…interests Paul.'

Paul smiled at her in a way that a father might at a much-loved wayward daughter. 'There could not be a more magnificent test for my…management systems.'

'I know when I'm beat.' She lied. She reached across and squeezed the back of Artie's hand. 'My husband says you enjoy making opportunities that might work out for people, yet you're not concerned about how things land.' He had put that into Artie's mind so they would both know it. 'However…I'll be straight with you. I don't think I could write a novel for shit, but I'll try anything once. And depending on the journalism your after…I'm in.'

'You know I *had* something ready to go on the creative writing front. A sister publishing house in London had this great little *'ideas generator'* thing I wanted to buy, which might have been a good start. Last week it got thrown in the Thames River. I still don't know why. Now I think what would suit you the best is to relax, write any story you want; however you want to write it, and if people don't like it…' He laughed. Like someone who knew her well might laugh. 'Do exactly the same thing again and see if that works. People who know prose and creativity believe you have what it takes. Believe them and give it a try.'

'It's the journalism that I believe could be the mainstay of your collaboration with the publishing houses I maintain and interest in. This includes a company with a small stable of magazines. One of the publishers approached me because he was aware I had a role in the Graceland Project research you did.' The publisher had received a simple nudge straight out of the Barrion playbook. 'You would be a reporter at large and work up story ideas to present and then if approved you'd work with the editors of the various magazines to deliver them. There's six so you'll generally be able to find something interesting to pursue. You could do a series based on 'what are they up to now' for all of the most memorable interviews you and Artie collaborated on. It would be interesting for most readers. Including me.'

She didn't need to ask what was in this 'stable' of magazines. That much she had been able to unearth after digging through a few well-constructed barriers. It was a stable full of winning horses. Paul's phone vibrated and he glanced at it. 'I find it unforgivably rude to take calls during a meal; this isn't a business call however, it's a dear old friend who can be…sort of…dramatic. Which I enjoy. I'll be brief.'

Paul moved away from the table but not so far away that they couldn't hear him say. 'No I haven't asked them yet, we've had some other matters to discuss…Of course your needs are more important, that's why I'm leaving them until last, so we'll have no other issues left to follow on…I'm not sure how they'll answer, they're sitting at the table now waiting for me to come back while I'm speaking with you. They may get fed up and leave…Yes I'll call you as soon as I know.'

He came back and smiled, this time a little tentative. 'My good friend has put me in somewhat of an awkward position. She wants to take a break from the 'Los Angeles scene' as she puts it and is going to live in Milan with her daughter. She wants someone to look after her house and asked me if I'd mention it to you as she's heard you're moving there and might be looking for a place to stay.'

Artie's approach was almost always to allow Helen to make the decisions. Unless she didn't in which case the clean air meant he had to. She would rarely make a bad one. 'We'll need a place to rent while we look for somewhere. Not too far from the studio though. It'll need to be an easy commute for Artie. And no cats. I don't do cats. Always wanted a dog though. Sort of a loaner dog for a while would be okay. As long as it's not a Shiatzu. Had a bad experience there once. Come to think of it we'll be travelling quite a bit so no pets. Can't guarantee the survival of house plants or gardens either to be honest. Maybe you should let her know we could turn out to be the house sitters from hell.'

Paul seemed relieved to have a yes from Helen. Albeit heavily qualified. 'It's not far from the studio. And there are people who come and look after the garden. She'll be away for a few years so that will give you plenty of time to get to know LA and look for a place that suits you. I am going to have one very relieved and grateful octogenarian on my hands.' It was also somewhere Paul could develop some land to take a shot from on Toxin Day if he needed to.

Helen already knew who owned the property, so she wasn't even going to bother breaking though the carefully constructed concealments to confirm it was Paul. 'Sounds great. When can we meet…?'

'Lilly. She's in Milan now. Maybe you can come up with a magazine article to give you an excuse to visit.'

His eyes didn't bother trying to conceal who owned the place, so she wasn't about to put him under any pressure to get in touch with *Lilly*. Her logic was if she didn't like the set up, they shouldn't move there. She had nothing against someone who wanted to help them. And there didn't seem to be any strings attached. She expected the house would be nice. What they walked into the next day was tasteful celebrity nice. It had everything anyone could want and people who came and maintained it all. It was in a location and on a piece of land that made it very private. It would allow them both to settle into careers they were excited about and relax or entertain friends and colleagues in pleasant surroundings.

Motherhood

They were having a romantic dinner in the outdoor area surrounded by a carefully maintained garden when Helen broke the news to a man who was so delighted and excited it made her cry. Which usually only happened after she'd returned to the sanctity of her hotel room after conducting an interview with people in truly awful circumstances, which drew out a compassion and sorrow no one saw the depth of. 'Oh. And it's a girl.'

It turned out she could come up with ideas for fiction, again as a collaboration with Artie in long rambling discussions about what some interesting character might get up to or how some circumstance or challenge might be confronted or viewed from a perspective not yet taken. She did articles for some of the less daunting titles but found she didn't need or want to travel much anymore. At least not at that time. She wanted to be with Artie and to be pregnant without having to try to fit her pregnancy into half a dozen other things she also needed to be doing. She wrote a story. Read it. And re wrote it four times. When it came out to very positive reviews, it was unsatisfying because she knew its success was, to some degree, was because of the 'Helen Thing' and it would have sold even if it was total crap. At least her first offering would. She decided the next one would be under a pen name. When she let her publisher know of her intentions there was a week of silence. She knew it was Paul who responded via her publisher that it sounded like a 'good idea'.

Artie was delighted, though sceptical when Helen said she was going to be a full time stay at home mother. When Amanda came along, the baby girl stimulated the changes that often occur in women who had no idea they had such maternal instincts buried in their breast. She was besotted with the baby and was soon bringing her efficiency to the necessary tasks and her humour and good company to the parents group she joined. Though everyone could see there was a prowling lioness within.

She was devoted to her cub. However after a year, deep down, the lioness was finding the cub was growing up too slowly. She began to pace about but couldn't see it. Artie however, had been interacting with this big cat for nearly a decade and had been given a unique clarity from Paul. So he could be direct with Helen when the time was right. She mentioned something about no longer having meal ideas when he said. 'You need to get out more Helen. And I mean seriously out more. You know it but you don't want to admit you're not cut out to stay at home full time. Even though that's what you want. Many people are. Women and men. But you're not.'

She was a little despairing but relieved to have the conversation. 'It's made me realise how hard it is that's for sure. I used to look at people who made this decision as if they were taking an easy option. Hah. But I don't want to leave our girl with someone I don't know.'

Artie had an idea. And he used the tone of voice they both knew gave her permission to be relaxed while she told him she wasn't in-terested. They got on well. 'If you wanted to come to the studio a few days a week there are endless jobs you could do. Might be entry level initially because neither of us would want a sort of nepotism thing happening. They have a creche there and you already know some of the parents. The people who run it are lovely.'

Helen immediately brightened. 'I could be an assistant make up person. Or help out the gaffers if there's a job for that and I could maybe learn to sew and help out in wardrobe.'

'Sure. And sometimes you could work a few hours in the creche. It's what some of the mothers and fathers do.'

He could see she was more relaxed and upbeat than he'd seen her for a while. 'And I could spend more time with you when you're on a break.'

Artie had one of those beautiful moments he felt so fortunate to have in his life, and she could see it in his eyes. *Helen Hunter wanting to spend more time with me.'* He thought. *'Imagine that.'* She smiled. He was the only man she wanted to be adored by.

She started in makeup, then became a person who filled in for lots of things when there was a gap because she learned quickly and for all her celebrity was humble enough to do anything. But she was Helen Hunter. And soon, though never on Arti's projects, she was consulting on scripts, then acting as an extra when there was a no show. When an actress with a minor part was insufferable the Director fired her and asked Helen to take the role. She did, but never pursued what might have been a successful acting career. Helen loved writing and journalism more than what would be a magnifying glass if she had a career in the movies.

Everyone loved Helen. However Paul circulated widely and in the same style as for Artie recalibrated the 'Helen Thing' for the acquaintance, friend or co-worker. He happened to 'walked by' those in proximity of Helen and they become 'normalised'. Which was good them and her. They didn't become clingily or need to move interstate or out of the country to flee the effect. It had taken a long time, but the Ageless One had even developed a very simple little mind nudge so that a dog would bark at Helen. Once each though. Helen was able to develop relationships at work which were less intense and have friendships what were lasting.

Rachael came along two years later, and the process repeated. Devotion. At home mostly, now with two children. She wasn't leaving a baby in a creche. She went to parks, beaches and museums and kept up with two parents groups now. She was surprised how many lasting friends she made there. Once Amanda hit kindergarten there were lots of little kids at their house visiting or Amanda was off with friends in the afternoon or even over weekends at an age many thought a little early. But it was Helen. She was never clingy. She loved her kids but treated them like adults once they went to school. That's what she wanted. Hurry up and be adults damn you. The prowling lioness began to pace. And Artie sensed the Studio was not the answer.

Biography of a Genius

Paul turned up with another project. Speaking with Elouise for only those few moments years before had left him intrigued. So much of what she'd done was behind confidentiality agreements in Patents or was all destroyed before the military moved to try to take over the facility, citing that the organisation constituted a national security risk. Elouise and Manion had foreseen that possibility, and the US government got ashes and the rest of the world lost the benefit of all the ideas and wonders from Elouise's genius as yet unreleased. She had carefully scheduled their release as she forecast humanities capabilities to integrate them. Her ideas would have been coming out for two decades after she left the planet, the timeframe she coolly predicted as being the remaining time her father would enjoy his stay on it.

What Elouise and Manion had not foreseen was that in fact Graceland was a national security risk. The government picked up traces of a Russian groups focus on Graceland and uncovered the existence of a hugely powerful AI capabilities developed to monitor what went on there. The backers of the project, which, behind a screen of business interests were the Russian and Chinses government, knew only a few inventions accessed prior to commercialisation needed to be levered out of the surveillance to pay for the project many times over. The espionage program could not have been so successful without Ryker, their inside man, who could target their probing, yet have no one know of his involvement. Elouise, otherwise so clear headed, suffered the human hubris that no intelligence could be better her own defensive systems. However Ryker provided it to those he was forced to work for and those breaking into it used an unprecedented AI capacity with only one focus, and find an entry point she would never believe could be opened. Not least about the existence of the bubble. Hence the US government had some justification. They knew Graceland didn't release inventions with harmful potential but were unaware they were destroyed. Or supposed to be. Hence their approach was to deny them to their enemies and acquire them for themselves, rather than approach Graceland about the breach. They had a poor relationship with Elouise. The government knew the breach would be corrected with barely a thank you they and the organisation shut tight. Hence blocking their own substantial surveillance efforts.

The youngest general in the US army was thought best placed to plan and execute the raid because he had first-hand knowledge of the organisation and possibly additional motivations. He refused and condemned the plan. Graceland had a surprisingly small team working in a small space with respect to anything associated with ideas, inventions and how information about them was stored. The team ran drills every week. They were all in the bunker reenforced by remarkable polymers within minutes. Elouises rare spitefulness in the creation of this plan won out over the consideration of the fact that those that might attack Graceland were only pawns doing as directed. None survived the attack while those in the bunker survived and speak to no one about anything associated with Graceland. Any legal action taken against them died in the consideration phase below a tidal wave of public backlash. Only one emerged from the bunker with mixed feelings. Ryker. He was free. He had been given the genius of those he admired to those he hated. Paul had a spiteful side also and arranged for Ryker's handlers to be assassinated and then right up the line to the head of the spy agencies. He's spent months on the ship figuring out a way to make it look like the Russians had done it to the Chinese and the Chinese to the Russians. The process gave him an idea which would lead him to return to his old ways years later.

Paul spent a lot of time on the Ship. It was nice not to age. He had his own plans once he found out whether Elouise had destroyed the contents of the Bubble or not.

He was at dinner with Artie and Helen and said he wondered if she would like to write a book on Elouise, and try to get an accurate picture of this genius, probably the greatest humanity had produced up until that time. Elouise had only been the subject of insubstantial treatments until then due to the paucity of material. As always Paul had a surprising list of people willing to participate. A little nudge here and there.

He had bought several of the Patents Graceland had produced at enormous cost, though he left them with the companies using them on favourable terms. This allowed those who had owned them to at least speak about the process they went through with Elouise. She handled all the negotiations. Often her greatest concern was about the capacity of the Patent Holder to deliver the technical outcome which would realise the idea's potential. This was a focus as much as the commercial arrangements. They knew part of her genius was to be able to measure the economic value of an idea, and so she never negotiated on price. Elouise would sometime relent when she became strident, thanks to the moderating influence of her father.

Given both she and her father were gone, many people who had refused to participate in a book out of respect to Manion, stricken as he was both by illness and heartbreak at what the government had done. Now many were prepared to share an anecdote or two because in every case they were proud to have had dealings with Elouise and her father and before that with Elouise's mother in the early years. People were pleased with the way Helen had written the stories of the Challenges, and the usual admiration for her, less intense also now that she was married with children, led many to participate where they would not with others.

Paul somehow got the man who famously never gave interviews, David Garret, of ReOrient, a well-known collaborator of Elouise's to join them for lunch and share a story or two. Paul had engaged ReOrient to give each company he bought, and there were many, though shrouded in commercial and legal mechanisms, the full ReOrient treatment. Which gave him some exposure to David. The maverick died a few years later after some extraordinary adventures in Eastern Europe. What David helped bring to the world's attention before he died profoundly affected Paul. And it resonated with the mission of the one he'd loved most when she rescued as many Sororibus as her ship would hold. Paul would later also smooth the way for Helen to write a biography of David Garret after his death.

Paul met with Ryker and explained to him everything that had transpired. Even if he didn't remember it, he wanted the man who believed he had betrayed Elouise and her father to know that all those involved had paid a price, and what he feared were damaging leaks had resulted in very little of any consequence. Or so Paul hoped but could not be sure of. It didn't matter. If Elouise had not emptied the Bubble Ryker would take part of a brief killing spree like everyone else. He would join others and speak of his relationship with Elouise and her father even if not divulging any details of the project and his manipulation. He already had some notoriety due to the part he'd played in the Challenges. Paul could not leave all the details with him, however, again after much tinkering, Chrona had learned how to leave a sentiment from something resolved like the memory of a dream.

Helen, hearing the details of a biography of Elouise was excited. The imperious genius had been at the centre of the Graceland story; however she was elusive and mysterious. 'Like someone else I know.' She said. Yet she was immediately conflicted. She wanted to catch a plane the next morning and visit the ex-Patent Holders, the girl's nanny, friends of her parents. Everyone on the list while she created a bigger list during the process. But she had…. encumbrances.

Artie stepped into the conversation. 'This is amazing Paul. Once again. To do it properly Helen is going to need to follow this story wherever it goes, and I believe you've given her only a starting point. Now that the game has changed there will be lots of people who want Elouise's story told because she's contributed so much. Maybe even some disaffected ex-military and secret service person-nel will provide some insights after that travesty many in the military were disgusted by.'

'I forgot to mention those.' Said Paul. Paul was enough of a patriot that he would provide the US government some justification for their concerns if not the actions they took. Ironically the Russian and Chinese government had already taken control of their main objective before the attack. They had the bubble, at least in the orig-inal Timeline. And so what the government destroyed was entirely benign. And Paul still didn't know if Elouise had either destroyed it, or at least locked it up effectively before she left in the Timeline he had created.

Marty looked across at his partner. 'Helen and I are going to come up with some ideas to make this work.'

Helen looked at Artie. Rather than being annoyed at having him pre-empt what would be a significant issue to resolve, she looked at him with complete faith in his judgement. Which gave him another Helen moment, as affecting as any of the intimacies they shared.

'Since that's going to be all fixed.' An outcome which Helen would find a huge relief more broadly, even if she didn't know how it was going to be achieved. 'I'm in. You've been so good to us Paul. We'd love it if you started to become more like a family friend rather than someone who turns up now with these ridiculously wonderful opportunities.' She had been doing enough research to know that it was he that got Artie his first stint as an assistant Director and then had him moved into a project that was off track. 'It's strange to ask and not let it happen, you know, organically, but it's what we'd both like.'

She expected a noncommittal and possibly slightly awkward 'Sure.' However the Elouise Biography had been one of the last things on his list. He'd decided early on to keep a low profile in Helen's life because he didn't think it was right to manipulate his way into a close relationship. Only enough to give her what he character-ised as 'options'. So she was surprised when he immediately looked pleased, as if he'd always hoped for such an invite though would never have allowed an organic friendship to grow. 'I'd love that. Tell me to back off if I become a pest.' Artie's and Helen looked at each other, surprised to have what they, and some others rightly suspect-ed to be one of the richest men in the world, categorise himself as a 'pest'. They were right, he had large stakes in the companies that started as tiny start-ups and were now behemoths. He had more gold than any one country. That asset class alone making him the richest person on earth. He wasn't going to bother putting any gold into to play until after T-Day. If there was no T-Day, he had an audacious plan for his wealth. The people who the plan hinged on however, had not done what they did in the Original Timeline. He hoped he hadn't screwed that up with his tinkering. What they did was important to him.

After he'd gone Helen waited to be advised of their new life arrangements. Artie said he had done what he wanted to do as a director and there were a few projects, movies and a TV series that he believed he could turn into successes but also meaningful creative projects. They would need to borrow money as he moved into the role of producer, with some partners but he was confident. Helen knew if Artie was confident, it was a close to a sure thing as one could get. And she already knew who one of the partners would be, at arm's length, even if Artie didn't. 'But I'll only take on what I can do *part time*. I'll work when the girls are at school, and we can work out a loose schedule so you can get away as much as you need to but still be home with us when your writing or not travelling. We might get someone we trust to come in every day and do the stuff, like washing nappies and cooking and cleaning that, we could do without.' Up until that point, liberated woman as she was, Helen had always cooked and cleaned with Artie helping as much as he could. He would rather be relaxing with Helen and their daughters. He was surprised to find his partner crying on his shoulder. 'It's what I've wanted but…I want to be with the girls while they grow up.'

Artie gave her a perspective she hadn't considered. 'It's something I want for myself also Helen. We'll have to share it.'

'I need to get away Artie, but I feel like it's wrong.'

'Well it's not. You've got a lot of things to contribute to the world. I believe I do also. We have the good fortune to be able to do that and live as part of a wonderful family. All we need to do is be grateful for it.' Helen smiled and added nothing more. Artie wasn't sure if he should be grateful or not at the fact that his wife had not aged, in any way he could measure, since he'd first met her. He knew she had to resort to all kinds of artifice to make people think she was getting older. There was another person in their orbit doing the same thing.

She surprised everyone by spending three years on the biography of Elouise. The more she looked into this remarkable person the more she wanted to do her justice as someone unique in history. As an unassailable genius. And as a woman. Her publisher might have hurried her along in ordinary circumstances. But neither Helen, nor the owner of the business were ordinary. When the publisher mentioned that there were others progressing Elouise biographies and although they may be inferior, if someone buys one because it's out first, they don't tend to go and buy the next one irrespective of the reviews. When she raised these concerns with Paul, he said this was a book that was going to be definitive. If it didn't sell strongly in the short term, she shouldn't care. It had to be how Helen wanted it as this was a project that would stand the test of time. If Elouise hadn't destroyed the vaccine carrier in which case there was not long to go until Toxin-Day and the 'time test' would be very short. As it happened, the two other authors working on biographies both had the same experience. The publishing house they worked for was bought out. The new owner introduced himself and let them know, in detail, a much more authoritative book by Helen Hunter was being written. This would be followed by a pleasant afternoon, sometimes rolling into the evening, as they fleshed out a project the author was excited about. Even more excited when they were offered an advance much bigger than the likely loyalties for their Elouise book, and got a better cut of the proceeds of their new project, which had an impressive marketing plan all set out. Paul liked helping people. And when he did, he wouldn't let them fail. These authors, once they settled on their subject, received the same kind of blossoming list of contributors and collaborators to make their own books something they had always hoped for. A little nudge here and there to help make that happen. Thanks to Barrion. Who didn't exist.

Apart from these interventions, the publishers of these businesses went unmolested. If it ever looked like the businesses were sold, they were simply being bought by another arm of Paul's convoluted empire. He liked books and a certain history professor and war historian had written seven now. His publisher suggested he try his hand at historical fiction. He had a wife who loved him, and whom he adored. It had taken a great deal of research to find her. Three children and they had won a nice house in a lottery for a charity. His wife had bought the one and only ticket from a persuasive man on the street. She never usually bought such things.

T-Day

Finally the day arrived. Based on what Chrona had been able to learn the virus had been circulating in the human population for years. It must have been if Paul had it in his blood. This was another uncertainty. He was firmly ensconced in the bubble he had never left since returning to make those fateful telephone calls, adjusted by Corona to be transparent. It gave people a strange sensation when they entered Paul's personal space. Which he rarely allowed to happen. He was uncertain that if Elouise had destroyed the carrier in the new version of the earth Timeline, whether he would he be the single person on earth to go insane with violence when the day came.

On that fateful day, those who had no history of aggression simply became violent and tried to kill anyone nearby. However, the toxin had been carefully designed and tested, so those with the skills killed en masse with guns and military hardware and would take their time to do so. It was as if whoever loaded the toxin onto Elouise's carrier had been to his lectures. Eradicate mercy. Magnify aggression. Be effective. He never watched what happened to Helen in the original Timeline with no interventions from Chrona. He was sure if he watched her go on a killing spree, unless she was killed early, like everything, she would be good at it. He had killed more people than anyone in history. As a killer he was probably in an intergalactic class of his own. Which was a concern if he was going to be switched on by the toxin. He believed he'd get at least a few seconds warning, so he chained himself to the wall and got some cyanide pills and had them ready to bite down on.

Paul had spent hundreds of hours in a rifle range he built on the ship, which he was now only ever leaving for a few hours at a time, quite taken with the idea of not ageing and enjoying stasis. It was like very deep meditation without any effort. If the toxin was released, he would probably leave earth. Unwilling to sit around looking at his species rot while he waited for the next important date in his calendar. And that date wouldn't be so important if humanity did exterminated itself. If the toxin didn't appear, he would have a decision to make.

He was on the roof of the building that looked out over their driveway. Helen would go first, cleanly this time. Followed by Artie and the girls. He would then get in his car, drive as fast as he could, and kill Jerry and Lissa, they having moved back home. They would be there because a friend of theirs had been given a nudge to line up a breakfast. They'd be dead before breakfast. He had a tablet with various news services in tiles. He had watched this piece of earth history so many times from so many perspectives. Trying to find a way to stop the toxin being released. So he knew the media announcements intimately.

They followed the sunrise heading west as the toxin was trigger by the arrival of daylight all around the earth. After a few islands that never transmitted any news of the drama that unfolded in their small populations, the first populous country it hit was New Zealand where reports started coming out of insane acts of violence. Reports came out for an hour before the entire country went offline however the reports; initially thought to be a hoax were confirmed when the nearly twenty million people on the Eastern Seaboard of Australia started a killing spree around the same time as one occurred in Siberia. Killers were streaming their successes onto their social media pages while they ran looking for victims. By the time the phenomena was taking root in Asia it was wall to wall news in the Western Hemisphere where people were being roused to see it. He wasn't going to wait for the panic to take over the Americas. He'd arranged for both Artie and Helen to be home that night via a few nudges and planned to call them as soon as the news started to break. He planned to tell them he had a helicopter arriving for them and they needed to wait out the front of the house for a car to get them.

He looked at the seconds tick by on the most expensive watch money could buy as a fitting way to tell the End of Days. Dawn broke across the Dateline. There were no reports of strange happening in New Zealand nor Australia. The channels he monitored in Australia carried the news about the Federal government handing down its budget. The Japanese revealed plans to significantly expand its miliary again. A boring day. A normal day. He'd decided to wait until Mumbai. This had been where some of the most grim and poignant reporting and analysis had commenced. People may not have understood why or how it was happening. But from Mumbai west, it was generally understood who was next. The pre-dawn suicides began in Africa and the Middle East and became a huge phenomenon in parts of Europe. The West Coast of the USA had as much time as any large populous area to have the news disseminate through the community. By then there was mass suicides in addition to an orgy of violence, rape, and looting of the any items that could give or symbolise luxury or pleasure or indulgence. However briefly.

Paul surprised himself by slumping down and starting to cry when nothing came out of Mumbai. He had killed so many. Slaughtered them. Let those that survived suffer so badly. And no matter how much that outcome might have retrospectively suited Chrona, it had still happened, in a now non-existent Timeline or not. And he would never say there was some moral equivalence because of this, because those killings would never rest easily in his mind. But now what he'd done was not for nothing. Humanity would have its chance. Right up until the planet was torn to pieces. And though she'd never know it, he was pleased that Elouise, cold and distant as she might appear, did not undo her benevolent genius, because she took a risk she believed vanishingly small. He knew even Basilica would be at least conflicted about the results. He thought of here often.

The waves of relief were tinged with fear. He sat. Waiting for sunrise on the rooftop. He had torn down a house and built a small apartment block to both overlook Helen's driveway at a distance from which he could confidently use a sniper's rifle but also stand such that when the sun crested the horizon the rays hit him directly. It had been pleasant to have the resources to fund these small acts of symbolism. In the seconds he had he would accept his fate, but he would die with regrets about things left undone, as well as those he had done. He saw the light coming and stood up so the rays struck him full in the face. Nothing. He spat out the pills and lay down on the roof and cried again. Finally. It was over.

Extra Judicial Killing

He went back to the ship and felt a kind of numbness. The ship's unknowable capacity to predict probabilities was now at ground zero because this future had never happened. It had to build the future from a new moment in planetary history. It would take a few years of reality to see weeks and then months in advance of the passing time. And then at variable probabilities. It was strange that the first thing Paul thought of was that he needed to take a defensive position in his vast and complicated finances because now he didn't know what the markets were going to do. It was the week Helen launched her book. The reaction could not have been more gratifying. People forgot for a while about 'Helen'. The book stimulated a fascination with Elouise and soon a global, belated gratitude for the brilliant enigma emerged. The US Government was newly minted a month before, and relieved to be on the right side of the aisle when the book came out.

Paul started to practice stasis as if it was Buddhism. He wanted to go somewhere two hundred years away 'in this old clunker' as Chrona had called it. 'Elouise's original ship was much faster, and the one that Hope of the East loaned to Kirby was amazing. 'This'll get you there though.'

'And in style.' he'd said.

'Correct.' She replied.

He would miss the closest thing he'd known to a family since the nuclear family of three he was born into had split apart when he finished university. His parents having fulfilled their duties separated amicably in a divorce he never saw coming. Now he was getting to be like an uncle to Helen's girls and was often being drawn into some activity with any one or all of the Hunter clan. Artie liked Helen's name better than his, so he'd changed it to Hunter.

The ship was starting to slowly develop probabilities, and near-term high probability viewing of a few days ahead was already available.

Paul decided to return to his habit of killing people on a grand scale.

Was it because he missed it? Was it as a gesture to Chrona? Who gave her life, cynical as she pretended to be, to save some Sororibus from abuse. Perhaps the result of reading the early drafts of Helen's next book about David Garrett. And how late in life he was exposed to one of the most terrible crimes humans commit. Maybe it was really about what he'd said to Lissa. How could someone with God like powers stand beside atrocity. Mute. Passive. When they had power. He carefully scoped the criteria, methods and means for a long campaign of extrajudicial killings. He had time to kill before the last big date. Albeit what he did on that final day in earth's orbit would be fleeting.

He built a well-paid network. Who knew there was another a well-paid network watching them, while each had their own assignment. They all believed a different story as to how the program was resourced because they all met different contacts who knew nothing of the man because he caused them to forget him. A class of people began to be afraid. The old women who made girls feel safe to travel across borders. With promises of jobs as maids or nannies only to be handed over to the proprietors of the worst kinds of brothels on a street corner. They were shot on those street corners just as the girls were taken in hand by their new owners. Who were also shot. The hapless girl taken in by a charity in that country, who paid families to give the girls a home. The family member who'd sold them; dead. As were so many pimps who were notoriously nasty to their street walkers, the peddlers of paedophile porn, film makers who filmed rape, or people like the twenty-seven men on a child molestation tour of Asia. All were dead in the most public way possible.

He accepted the role of judge, jury and executioner. He was happy to do it because he could be a first-hand witness to the crime in the future. Always. The ship could predict accurately now a few weeks ahead everywhere, months in less dynamic enclaves of the future. The more he witnessed the more sickened and the angrier it made him. And sometimes surprised that the outward persona of people could be so different when they believed they were unobserved with the vulnerable. The people they put no value on. He would go into the grey limbo for days. Making careful preparation. Compiling evidence to be dumped in front of police stations, or court houses or if he couldn't trust these sent to newspapers. They all had to get a signature shot though the forehead. Clean. He wanted it to become a global phenomenon. He wanted the people who were going to do things like that to be afraid. Thousands died. All around the world. A few in the network he created were caught. They all signed up to take the risk and the reward. They knew nothing of value about how the system worked.

Because Paul could use the ship to go forward and look back it was easy to remove every loose end they may have left and get good at not leaving any more. So as time went by no one was caught and those had been made remarkable escapes. And he saw the future changing. Maybe not a panacea, but the people who abused others were starting to get scared. Thousands of people from all walks of life were turning up with a neat bullet hole in the head. Others confronted with an incredibly detailed brief of evidence. Some he didn't want to kill. Some high profile people he wanted dragged through the courts. He knew he was starting to trip on this God like power, getting addicted to the strategy, designing the minutia and then achieving that through a short, nuanced instruction. He spent more time in stasis and his primary occupation beyond business and planning killings was with Helen and her family. Still, time itself started to drag. He wondered if he should simply go. But he decided to see out the decade. He rationalised he would be a long time on the journey to come so he should finish everything he'd planned. He got very good at stasis and finally the waiting was nearly over.

Revelations

Helen asked him to dinner. He was unaware that Artie was on location. Producing a movie about the Graceland Challenges. Which, thanks to some funding from a foundation was a full-scale re-enactment with drones and camera's mounted on hundreds of the actors. They had to live every moment as the real Challengers had, so they had to go through auditions, by the thousands, just as brutal. Helen had told the girls that night, even though they'd been expecting to have dinner with 'Uncle Paul' that they needed some sister time and were sent off to a movie. Amanda now twenty and Rebecca eighteen. Both could still fall under a spell of compulsion of a mother with whom the teen years had not always been easy. Artie was the steadying influence who smoothed things out.

Once Paul realised he was dining alone with Helen he suspected what he was in for. 'Congratulations on the Biography about David. Every bit as good as the work on Elouise.'

David Garret had died six years earlier and again there was a range of people willing to come forward and speak about a personality who was in a way akin to Paul. Ultimately seeking to do what he believed was good on a grand scale yet comfortable with what appeared to be expediency to get there. 'Such a curious a story. A

325

much more polarised opinion about the subject. And who am I writing about next Paul. Blondie maybe.' She was a notable hold out for Helen's book. '*ReOriented*.'

'Not quite ready for that one. She told her story once in a Department Store. Never again. Not someone to cross by writing an unauthorised biography I'd speculate.' Paul would not give Blondie a nudge. He had a great deal of respect for her and she was integral to his final grand endeavour.

'You seem to be blessed with foresight Paul. One of the many talents you've been able to resort to. While you curated our lives.'

This caught Paul out long enough for Helen to continue. 'When I'm twenty-nine, someone I deeply respect gets a dream job which makes me realise I was living in a collaboration. I had to be brought to the realisation that it went beyond an earpiece. And then a dream job falls into my lap and a rich lady with a mansion says we can use this as a starter home. She loves Artie's films so much she sells it to us for a song because she wants him to focus on 'movies that mean something'. And he does that.' Helen could see she was opening a door that Paul had thought was kept shut. But listening to this, he realised he'd been rather clumsy. 'I love Merc's and I win one in a raffle. Not my favourite colour. You don't want to be too obvious do you Paul. But when I pick it up they tell me I can have cerise if I want. The dealership had one painted specially but the buyer… disappeared. What's *very* strange is I have never told anyone that was my favourite colour.'

'I'm in a bar in Byron Bay in Australia. Wandering the countryside catching up with friends and relatives of Kirby. I nearly make a terrible mistake. One that I would regret my whole life long. I'm drinking too much with a handsome Aussie I'd been interviewing, and I am struggling to bat off yet another handsome man. But someone who 'went to school with Kirby' sits down between us and says she and Kirby were 'good mates'. She's getting on a bus to Lismore in a few hours if I want to catch up. Turns out she didn't really know Kirby, but she drinks me under the table at a different bar, or at least that's what it looked like. She takes me to my room before I make that big mistake.'

'The girls get scholarships, discover what instruments that are best suited for them. Friends and boyfriends that we have that bad feeling about tend to up and leave town. Their parents get some opportunity of a lifetime. I've had the door opened for me on two of the most fascinating personalities I could write about after writing what's been called the 'Definitive Work' on the Graceland Challenges.' She put her chin on two closed fists with elbows on the table and gave a penetrating but grateful look. 'Don't think I'm complaining Paul. The door opens. But it has to be by volition we walk through. Right? I appreciate everything. You would have the same question for me though Paul. Why.'

He hoped he could extract himself simply. 'Helen fixation. You see it all the time I know. Though mine is of a different quality I hasten to add.'

'The Helen fixation is a *thing* I grant you. I don't understand it.' Her eyes narrowed. 'Though I suspect you do. I *also* don't understand why I have to spend so much time trying to look and act older than I…am. Anyone else with that kind of problem you know of?'

'It's the dividend of a healthy lifestyle and a positive outlook.' He laughed. He suspected he knew what was next.

'Or maybe from living in a Rocketship. Although strangely; I don't.'

'Rocketship?'

'Yep.' He didn't look into Helen's eyes often. She reminded him of someone he would never get over and never want to. And there was the slightly uncomfortable fact that he'd been deeply infatuated with Helen himself in another Timeline and then shot her, twice, in the head. 'I get the strangest vibe from you sometimes Paul. I'm pretty sure once you show me your Rocketship a whole bunch of things are going to fall into place.'

'Yes. It seems I wasn't nearly as clever as I thought I'd been.'

'Journalist of my age. And someone who put a *very* high end and *very* tiny GPS tracker in your coat lining. I was somewhat surprised to notice that you take the elevator to the roof of your building which has an unnecessary wall around the top of it fifty feet high and you leave the stratosphere or troposphere or whatever in rather a hurry so that the little tracker isn't worth shit. Until it comes back to earth.'

Paul shook his head. Wistful but Helen wasn't sure why. The ship would never permit a tracker. Unless somehow told the ship to ignore it, *depending on who put it there.* And if the ship's enquiries identified that it was Chrona's daughter he would be none the wiser. He smiled. 'How about you come across to my Rocketship. Wednesday for dinner. We should make it a regular thing.'

'I'd like that Paul. But look me in the eye and tell me you won't be gone by then.'

He looked her in the eye. Which was difficult. 'I won't be gone by then.' Helen kept staring at him. 'I'm leaving the day after. I have an important meeting here and then a sort of rendezvous.'

'Paul, if it's not a personal question, are you an Alien. I mean rocket ship. No aging. About to leave earth for…'

'My plan is to go where Kirby went.' He relaxed. It was time. 'And no. I'm not alien. I'm human. *You* on the other hand are an alien. Or half alien at least.'

'Which half?'

'Why don't I take you somewhere with a nice view and I'll tell you all about it. Except the unpleasant parts of course which I ill-advisedly tried to shield you from the last time around.'

'The last time.'

'All will be revealed.' Paul furrowed his brows. '*Some* will be revealed.'

Helen didn't say much on the journey to the building Paul disappeared into for long periods. They walked into thin air and Helen was inside a spaceship which she found disconcerting in spite of her predictions. It turned out to be a 'small freighter' the size of a mansion. It flew out into space and docked with nothing she could see until they walked into an impossibly large spaceship of which one third was a giant orb with the hemisphere facing a substance so clear as to be invisible. It was empty but for a suspended platform. She was silent. Drinking it all in. She had only come up with the Rocket Ship theory a few months before after finally getting a drone which could follow him and film him vanishing. Also something the ship would usually warn him of before he came anywhere near the freighter. They walked out on a bridge suspended in mid-air to the control station and beyond this a platform a dining table on one side and some comfortable couches on the other so they had an unimpeded view.

Helen was more reflective than Paul had ever seen her. In either Timeline. 'I didn't think I'd ever see that. It's so beautiful. And what lies beyond it. Meeting all those people from the Challenges. I knew I would have been one of them if I'd been old enough. I envied them. To at least have had a chance. Most people thought Helen Hunter envying them was crazy. But Jarhead understood. And writing about Elouise and how her genius 'left the building' and was then despoiled by the ignorant. I got quite a bit of feedback on that book from people saying they enjoyed it, but it made them sad, because their chance at something they so longed for was gone forever.'

She gave that smile that in everyone else, except for Artie, broke down every barrier. 'So when do we leave.'

'A two-hundred-year journey. I was told that allows for the universe expanding in front of me. Don't expect me know anything about that side of things. I was given enough skills to drive a bus.'

'Apropos my question. When do we leave.'

'You mean when do you leave your family behind?' He hadn't needed to say it out loud. The first tears were halfway down her cheeks. 'I'm sorry. I knew you'd be torn. Let's go for a spin. Or would that make things worse.'

She wiped the tears off with her palms. 'Once around the moon Jeeves?'

'I don't know how to drive this thing in space believe it or not and I'm not sure I should take a freighter so far away. So it's once around the Earth Jeeves. More fun in the freighter because you can get closer to things. Like Niagara falls or the pyramids or whatever iconic place you want to go. El Capitan is always nice.'

'Surprise me. And don't leave without saying goodbye.' She was trying hard to sound cheerful. She had thought she was content with her life. Like it or not, she never would be again.

Paul tried to create a diversion from what he knew she was feeling. 'Artie and I had planned a surprise dinner for the family next week when he's back. And a I was going to propose a potential new project.'

'Do tell.'

'Sex Slavery. The inside story. The big fish. Government and international agency apathy. Incontrovertible evidence. Illegal to gather. Inconceivable that it could be gathered in the first place. So that would also need to be navigated.'

Helen looked up. He eyes open wide in surprise. No one had been able to comprehend how any person or organisation could pull something off at such a scale and no one caught. Or at least not for long. And not the slightest clue of who was behind it. 'That's you. *Twenty-seven thousand* people?'

'That's the number for the headshots. They were chosen as the ones which would have the most impact on behavioural change. There was another twenty or so that had plausible accidents, were encouraged to commit suicide or disappeared. Too much risk to give them the public treatment.' Paul laughed. Completely relaxed. 'Even the journalist of her age couldn't crack that one.' He waited and she said nothing. Digesting this. 'Helen Hunter unable to craft a follow up question. Here are a few answers. I've slaughtered *billions* of good people Helen. Innocent people yet an enemy species as far as humanity was concerned. Primarily women and children. Then fifty thousand more because I've had a Godlike capacity to witness their crimes firsthand then wind time back and have them killed. Judge, jury and executioner. And it doesn't bother me. Partly...I was filling in time until next week.'

He motioned they should get going. Helen said. 'And I thought you were a stratospherically rich...enigma, when your real hobby is mass murder.'

'The first was a genocide I...thought was necessary to win a war. Embarrassingly it was a pointless genocide. The others, as you know, are extrajudicial killings. A euphemism I like to shelter behind. Like I say. When you've killed as many people as I have, one becomes a little blasé about it. I even killed you once.'

'You even...'

'Yes. You can be sure it hurt me more than it hurt you.' Helen was quiet again. Soon they were in the freighter and flying over iconic places at breakneck speeds. The Sahara, the Amazon, pyramids, Golden Gate Bridge and Ayres Rock in the middle of Australia.

'Ever wanted to see the Titanic.'

'Not especially.'

'Too bad because you're going to. Somewhere I haven't been. And it's not a long list. I believe it's one of those 'see it before it's gone' places. Degrading rapidly now. Not that I'll care.' Even though they'd seen the footage of the grand ship they both found the visit strangely moving.

'I'd drop you home, but I'd end up crushing some of the neighbours, so it'll be the school ground.'

'Being a mass murderer I guess lying to me that you'll come to dinner next week won't cause the slightest twinge. You'll have your meetings and go off in search of what I would assume to be a long dead Kirby.'

'I'd never lie to *you* Helen. Ha. Not since you caught me out anyway. So it's dinner Wednesday. Then I take my Bubble and go.' He thought of Chrona. He thought of such a long life being lonely and longing for that beautiful slice of love. 'I hope you don't think 'curating your life' was intended to be a deception Helen. Or patronising someone who had no need for those opportunities. I thought some of those things would be good for you. But I thought of the wider world also. What you could contribute. And Artie. Lasting contributions which I believe you've made. Not least via your influential journalism of the last fifteen years. And your collaboration with Artie to raise such delightful young women.'

She gave him a big smile and he was relieved. 'Not one single complaint Paul. And all those killings; forgiven. Though I would like an explanation as to why you killed me. Please come and say goodbye. For all our sake's.'

'Wouldn't miss it. I'll see you there.'

Blondie

A week later he was sitting in front of someone he truly admired. She was accustomed to people treating hers as a story of incredible hardship and resurgence. Many people she met for the first

333

time could not conceal the judgement that what she achieved was due to David Garret. It was true David had saved her from an unimaginable endless horror and then helped her on a path she could never have followed. However she had made her way in a world no amount of help could replace individual capacity. And her mentor was someone not well liked by many in the business. Highly regarded or hated. David Garret had had a polarising effect on Wall Steet and beyond for over forty years since he'd been barely nineteen. So she was a little taken aback at the sincerity Paul conveyed in his greeting. 'It's such a privilege and honour to meet you Ingrid. Thanks for taking the time to see me.'

She smiled warmly. Appreciative of the man's admiration which he gave the strange impression was grounded in a great deal of detail. 'Paul I wish I could return some of your kind words, however I know nothing about you, only that I was given compelling advice by those I trust to make as much time for you as was needed. I'll admit I tried to do some research as to who I was meeting with.' She laughed. 'I ran into a wall of…opacity. And please. It's Blondie.'

She had had to give Blondie away as an epithet in the corporate world. Those who worked closely with her, and her friends still used it. He smiled and said. 'Thankyou. And the opacity is certainly something I cultivate. It's remarkable how much it costs to maintain. I'll come to the point. I know that's what you like.' He slid a piece of paper across with thirty numbers on it. 'These funds come from thirty sources and are set up as long as these facilities can be legally maintained in a Trust environment, however instruction are in place to renew them in seventy years. Provided there is still a legal framework to do so. The annual interest on these sums will be paid via a trust as a monthly sum the Foundation so that it's a predictable cashflow, adjusted annually.'

She looked at the thirty numbers which was all there was on the page. Her eyebrows raised. 'This is a very substantial contribution. Paul, I don't think I could adequately convey to you how much this means. You'll know that David left a remarkable legacy in the creation and core funding for this Foundation. However as I can see from your generosity you appreciate the scale of the task we face to rescue and try to create a new life for the women and children in our society being continuously raped. And caring for those liberated are where the real costs begin if we want to give them any hope of not ending up where they were all over again. Which, in a way, is worse than if they'd never known freedom.' The Foundation didn't use the phrase 'Sex Slavery'. It was 'Continuous Rape'.

'It's an unimaginable horror to me Blondie. I've only ever known certainty, safety and generally privilege.' It was something Paul had to remind himself as he'd watched the monstrous behaviours of so many men who, though many had power or privilege, some, sadly, were playing out the vices they'd been taught. That made no difference to their fate however.

Blondie knew people. Good people. Bad people. Expedient people. Ruthless people. She knew that people could be a mixture of all those things and a dozen more. She had learned much from her experiences and from David. So when she looked into Paul's eye's she knew. 'The truth is Blondie. I'm only the messenger. I spent...' His eyes started watering despite of himself. 'I got to spend a little sliver of time with someone. For which I'm thankful. Every day. This cause was very close to her heart and in...another time and place, she saved a great many women from the kind of abuse your work helps, even to a degree, to expunge from our society.'

'We try to help those caught in a terrible trap and make their freedom permanent.'

This was a good segue for Paul. 'Yes. And few people appreciate the effort and cost to create a reliable structure around that. My… investigations into the problem, helped me appreciate that donations of money could only be part of the solution. However it is not easy for you to spend donations on capital projects when there is so much need simply to spend on freeing the abused and maintaining that freedom.'

Blondie had run corporations and knew spending on capital projects, even in a profit motivated company with carefully justified paybacks took considerable effort to get approved. She nodded. 'We could spend some based on the latitude David gave us.' She shook her head 'It's tough to advantage one location over another, so our model is to support local organisations and we pay the rent, employee costs and audit them, or have our own people delivering the services. But you know everything about us already don't you Paul.'

He slid two pages stapled together. It had an eyewatering amount of money. Paul brought his gold into play at the end. 'Capital projects. And it takes away your need to decide or justify whether it should be spent on Capital or not. It would be conditional in the Agreement. Though it's not too prescriptive on the project details.' She looked at the second page. 'It provides for immediate and longer term care for those rescued in facilities the Foundation owns. Good quality, simple accommodation in a precinct where victims would access long term, professional rehabilitation services.

It's understood that some of these initiates will fail, as with the investments in any business.'

Paul didn't want to create unrealistic expectations. 'Partly because of the necessary risks which is inherent where some of the locations these centres need to be. Those who have a chance of success could make a progression through to purpose-built schools with a vocational dimension. There's also an allocation for three small universities which would be located on the best balance of geography, host nation tolerance, stability, and affordable running costs. No point to having capital without operating costs so projects are fully funded with the operational funds via the same interest on principal arrangements. There is also some assistance for victims demonstrating the capacity and drive to study elsewhere. There is a provision for a small team at each location to seek further funding from governments, foundations, the wealthy or anyone who wants to support an expansion of the long-term rehabilitation part of the process and work on placements for graduates. There's a list or organisations my interests have relationships with which are willing to sponsor scholarships, host trainees, interns or graduates.'

Blondie had been a businesswoman for years in some of the larger companies on the Street although never in the top fifty. David had insisted she get a grounding in business for ten years before coming to run the Foundation he'd started. The kind of money Paul was putting in front of her to build and operate rescue accommodation and education facilities on top of the other donations surely put him near the top of the global rich list, yet she had never heard of him before this meeting. The tech titans could barely have funded this.

He smiled. 'The opacity is going to need to continue to some degree. So the Capital initiatives will need to be announced and rolled out over fifteen years. However these facilities don't have precedents, and the learning process will be vital to their success.'

Blondie gave what they both knew was the right answer when she said. 'Only way to do it properly.' Blondie reminded him of another person he had so admired. She was aging however and still looked like the singer she got her nickname from as she also had aged. And she could read people. That made him a little uncomfortable. 'There's something else you're a bit reluctant to raise. What might that be.' She said.

'This is purely a suggestion. Something to consider.' He moved a little in his chair. 'Your succession plan.' Which he should have known nothing about. 'Naturally it leans to those with a talent for administering a complex business in a challenging environment.' He slid across a final piece of paper. 'The names on the list are people who…while there's no one like you Blondie…are people who've suffered some of the experiences you did. Some as boys, most girls and women and, based on my research, have the capacity to take senior roles in an organisation like this. Like you they'd need to be put in a business management environment or achieve a leadership level experience in NGO's or Universities. I've made a carefully study of these young people. Some still recovering, but they have immense capacity given the opportunities to fulfil it.'

Blondie was surprised again. However she also felt a sudden shame. David met her in a glass booth in Amsterdam, then saved her from brutal sex slavery to introduce her to a level of business management she expected she could only fail at. He believed in her. She became a highly regarded CEO on Wall Street. Thanks to the man who everyone thought merciless but who's judgement was impeccable. And now she realised she had mentored no proteges from where she'd come from. She'd developed some of the same prejudices as everyone else even for all her first-hand experience of degradation. She should have been the first to recognise there were no limits to the opportunities some deserved and were capable of achieving. She was now looking into eyes that were an impossible combination of compassion and remorselessness. It was now he who said. 'You have a question you're reluctant to ask?'

She shrugged. 'What does it feel like. To have so many people…killed.' The killings had led to a great deal of scrutiny of David's Foundation. But the evidence trail, what there was, always led elsewhere.

He laughed at that. Which surprised her given he was such a generous man based on his charity. She could see a man for whom killing the abusers and helping the abused was not incompatible. 'Some people build model airplanes. Play chess. Or write bad novels. Ha, or history books. It became a hobby.' He shrugged. 'In the beginning it was fuelled by outrage. Suffering is universal but this was a kind of suffering I could reduce, even to a small extent. That phase is over.'

'Brought quite a bit of business through our door.' She said. 'For a hobby.'

He looked her in the eye, 'Killing the abusers had a much more immediate and personal justification in your experience.' Blondie stiffened. There were only four men in the room that had survived *her* foray into extrajudicial killing all those years ago. David and

339

one of the mercenaries were dead. The other two men worked for her, and she would trust them with her life. The authorities found none of the dead men, nor the brothel keeper. Whom she also shot 'My information doesn't come from anyone you've ever met. And what became a hobby for me was something very different for you on that day. I'm certain you have no regrets. At least I hope not. And neither do I.'

He was standing as he said this. Blondie was usually the person to close a meeting. As David had been. Now Paul wanted to move on. He had spent decades building fabulous wealth and hiding it as the greatest inside trader and thief in history. All to honour the memory of one who was never far from his thoughts. Now all of the great occupations of his life were over. Stopping T-Day. Curating Helen and her family's lives, killing those in various parts of the sex slavery supply and demand chain and delivering his wealth as a testament to the one he loved. All done. Except for one long awaited rendezvous after a farewell dinner with the Hunter family. Then a long journey, mainly in stasis. But alone.

'Our first and last meeting Paul?'

'Yes. Believe it or not Blondie, this has been one of the highlights in a long life in which I've had the good fortune to interact with many fine people. Goodbye.'

She wasn't going to try to craft a superlative in kind. 'Goodbye Paul. And thank you for...your generosity in all its forms.' She smiled.

Back on the ship he was tempted not to turn up to the dinner which Helen had demanded everyone come to. 'And don't make any plans for later either girls.' Helen didn't demand things usually. Her cubs

340

had grown up. If they needed something they usually went to Artie. Though like so many others, they enjoyed the proximity to Helen, who treated them like friends. Usually. She was often preoccupied by some story she was writing as a journalist, or a biography or fiction. She was pleased the books in her pen name enjoyed a modest following. At the lower end of the modest spectrum. But they weren't contaminated by the 'Helen Thing'. She hoped Paul had not been buying them all. Ultimately, she had a marketing edge that most other authors lacked. Her publishers used every old and new platform to launch and market her books. She wasn't going to spend time feeling bad about good fortune. That would be the worst kind of ingratitude.

He'd given the last instructions. No more contract killings, But the second phase of major surprises was about to start. And for these his evidence gathering had been meticulous. As with many things he worked on, like Chrona he'd disappear into the grey limbo to work on things in peace for days or even weeks with no distractions and return a second later. He had no idea how old he was in chronological time. The people he laid out the evidence about didn't deserve to die. They were senior politicians and government officials, businesspeople, religious leaders and even those involved in the NGO sector. They had not directly abused anyone. But they were enablers or those who covered it over or who failed to investigate things they should have. They deserved to live and have their stories trawled through by the courts. His training as a historian and someone who wrote non-fiction plus the ability to observe the crimes firsthand allowed him to build immensely powerful dossiers. He'd found it fascinating, disturbing and ultimately depressing. He was starting to inhabit a very jaded place, even for a man who had killed billions, so he'd wound up the project a month early. It was now time for couriers to get their instructions to pick up and deliver hundreds of packages all over the world.

He'd given control of his finances to a suite of very discrete bankers and funds managers; none of whom knew he had any other holdings He spoken personally with them but they remembered little of how he looked. They had a deep and abiding inner compulsion to treat his affairs with probity. As if it was life preserving that they do so. He didn't want to face his last goodbye with Helen and her family. When he got there though, his smile was as genuine as it ever had been.

The family were relaxed. She wasn't a demanding or intrusive mother to her daughters or as a partner to Artie. She and her husband had fallen into a habit living more like friends. They were intimate. But less than they might have been which Helen found a little strange. Although Artie might have been pleased he was sleeping beside someone with an early twenties body trying to look fifty-five, while he tried hard to keep young as he approached the sixty mark. Her mind had matured; however it was still youthful and so sharp she could become frustrated by those friends around her who were naturally slowing down or becoming more conservative which age brought to many. They didn't talk about the 'age thing'. Except once. When she said she never wanted to talk about the 'age thing'. She'd had no idea what was going on and had given up trying to find an explanation. When Paul was invited closer into their orbit, she knew he had one. It was one of the things that had led her to make a detailed study of him. Including stalking him and putting beacons in his apparel. He was trying to look old the same as she was. Though she thought his starting point was more early forties which meant he should be mid-sixties. He didn't even know that chronologically he was over a hundred years old he'd spend so much time in the grey limbo studying what shares to buy, which he found fascinating, what opportunity might suit one of his 'nieces' or who to kill, which was a hobby that eventually became a burden. As with Lissa when in God mode he had to observe a lot of nasty things.

Bunny

It was a pleasant meal. In a welcome edict, for the girls at least, Helen had said a few years before they might as well have a drink at the table rather than 'sneaking off to get hammered like I did when I was sixteen'. Artie was sanguine about such pronouncements. The girls came to him for the 'important shit'. However when Rebecca wanted to exchange names with her pet cat at age twelve, she knew who her ally would be. So the cat became Rebecca, and she became Bunny. Helen had looked up from the meal when this was announced by her daughter and said casually. 'Okay. Bunny it is then. Oh and Heff called.'

'Who's Heff.'

'Google him sweetheart. I shouldn't have said anything because I like Bunny. Your name came *so* close to being Basilica. I have no idea why. Your wise father talked me out of it.'

It had only been a little nudge in case Artie loved it. But her husband was a little underwhelmed when a post-natal Helen told him. He was important so on the important things they worked through them together. All for nothing now that she was Bunny.

At the time Artie might have appreciated greater parental analysis as their daughter cast away his mother's name on a whim. However he knew when to be philosophical about some things. If Helen was okay with it his mother would be. Everyone loved Helen. And it was something Rebecca had been both tentative and excited about. He was glad she was able to choose. He thought it would last a week. However they both signed the papers so she could be legally called Bunny four years later. 'You can always change it back. But I love *Bunny Hunter.*' Helen had said at the time.

Rocketship

On this night they had picked up on the strange mood of both their mother and the man they'd called Uncle Paul for years. So the girls had been drinking a little more than Artie was comfortable with. Paul was surprised how sad the girls were to hear that he was going to be involved in a hands-on venture in South America to keep his 'mind young' and it might be a year before he was back in the States. The desserts were brought out. The two sisters having collaborated on a selection of options they were very proud of. Helen casually said. 'Actually Uncle Paul is leaving earth forever in his rocketship.'

'What's it called Uncle Paul.' Said Bunny, wanting to be the first to roll with whatever her mother and adoptive Uncle were up to. Before Amanda could get in. Her sister was the unrivalled master of understatement and never being fazed. Like Slater and Peabody. Who in this Timeline finished their scotch in the wilderness uninterrupted by a spaceship, got home from their adventure and went on to enjoy many more.

'You know it's only now that you mention that, like Elouise's ship, it didn't have a name when I took it over.'

'I think Bunny would be a good name for a Rocketship.' She was on a roll while her sister had taken a moment to process things.

Helen laughed. 'Why don't we get a bottle of Champaign, and we can christen it when we go up there after dessert.' She looked at Paul as she made the comment, giving him permission to laugh it off. Yet he realised it didn't matter if this family knew about it or not. He'd be gone, and who was going to believe them anyway. And so what if people did believe it. So they all walked to the school oval. The girls seeing who could make the lamest refence to TV space travel shows. They went quiet seeing Paul and their mother disappear into thin air. Then they were in a boring, functional environment. However they were inside of something that they hadn't seen from the outside.

They came onto the small bridge. 'This is the little freighter that takes us to the big ship. Would either of you like to fly this little baby up to the mothership.' He realised what every parent knows. Don't offer something to young people that they will both want. Even if they're adults. Amanda got in first. Fortunately Bunny wasn't one to pout.

Helen helped out. 'Looks like you're flying us home Bunny.'

'Okay Amanda. Press that button.' She did that. 'Well done.'

Soon they were gathered on an impossibly free-standing platform. Amanda needed some help to get across the walkway, not being fond of heights. A concern in this case Artie and Bunny shared to a lesser degree. For Helen walking suspended in mid-air into a giant glass orb twenty stories in diameter didn't challenge the senses.

She sat in one of the command chairs. 'Beam Scotty up would you please Bunny.' Amanda and Artie were mesmerised. Bunny had always been the sensitive one. Amanda the more perceptive. Bunny was a girl who was much fonder of her Uncle then anyone realised. He always wanted to listen to what she was up to. If advice was appropriate, he'd say. 'Bunny. I'm going to go away and think about what we talked about and then let's get together again.' If the problem hadn't been fixed as if by magic, he would come back and talk about the whole thing with her. Presenting perspectives but not quite advice. She started to cry. 'You really are going away forever.' He was soon holding a sobbing eighteen year old in a fond embrace. Something he'd never done with the girls. Partly because of the very strange experience of being part way into Elouise's bubble. She stood back and offered a lopsided smile. Bunny returned to her generally cheerful mindset quickly after most upsets. A trait many were envious of. In addition to a general admiration she and her sister inspired to a somewhat unusual degree. 'It won't be the same.'

'And not for me either Bunny. I'm frightened; to be very honest. To have said farewell to the people I've been closest to and strike out alone. But it's an opportunity I believe I have to take.'

'Why don't you take the girls for a tour around the ship Paul.' Said Artie.

The two men knew each other well. Not enough for Artie to have guessed his friend had a Rocketship, but enough to know the dynamics of their relationships. One relationship in particular. Artie's eyes held a question, and Paul's tiny nod supplied the answer.

'Aren't you two coming?' said Bunny. Amanda was more intuitive.

'They'll catch us up Bunny. I think they want some…*private time*. While looking at the big blue and white ball. Shits all over the mile high club right.'

'Eeeeew. Do they still do that?' Bunny said to her sister. As if her parents weren't there.

'Thanks for blowing that right out of the water.' Said Helen.

When they were alone Helen was surprised at what she heard. 'You've been waiting for a Rocketship your whole life Helen. And now it's going to cause this… loss. Whatever you choose.'

She turned and looked at him, having been gazing, not at the earth, but past it. 'Whatever I choose?'

'I remember when you'd only begun the adventure of morning television with me. And you mentioned the disappointment that you'd been too young to join the Challenges. It was your one chance. To do what you were made to do, which is to fly further. Assuage a curiosity that one planet is too small to satisfy.'

Helen could be warm, playful, occasionally imperious, but she wasn't often deeply emotional. She was her mother's daughter in that way. The tears were streaming down her cheeks as she stood in silence looking at the man who revelled, even now, in the fact that she would be torn between him and their family and the great ambition that fully revealed itself now. 'You want to cast me out into a heartless void I see.'

'I'm sixty now Helen. I don't want to be eighty with someone in their twenties caring for me. I've had the years of my prime and to say I'm grateful doesn't do it justice. Your prime, your life of adventure, who knows how long it will last. It still lays before you. You'll

347

be torn if you go or stay.' They were both crying at each other now. 'I love you Helen. So much. I want what's best for you. And it's this great adventure, even though you might need to carry with you some pain and regret. Though not for too long I hope.' He could see she was going to start talking about the girls. 'They love you as much as I do, and they understand the same things I do.' They both knew that might take a bit longer for Bunny. But she would get there. In some ways she was the stronger one.

'I can't believe I'm even thinking abandoning my family.' She was almost angry with Artie and a fleeting thought was to respond with. *Do you think I care so little.* But that would only be game playing. *Protesting too much.* She thought.

They were both silent for a time. 'There is one thing I'd like you to do for me Helen. Don't misunderstand it. I'd like to say goodbye here. Now.' He looked out at the silver blue sphere which made him feel so small. And that made him feel good. 'While you're standing in front of your magnificent launching pad. I have thousands of good memories of you. And this memory Helen, it's…fitting.' He laughed. 'Helping you pack your suitcase and waving you off. No. This will for me be one last memorable, beautiful moment of togetherness.'

She hadn't even decided. She knew *he* had to decide for her. For all of them. She held him close and said. 'I love you. And I'm glad that's going to last a really really long time. You deserve that kind of love.'

'And you'll be cherished in all the minutes I have. I'll find the girls.' He positioned her ever so gently and stood back, the earth shining behind her; turned and left.

Meanwhile Amanda knew she had a lot of work to do and not much time to get it done. 'Where do you keep the booze Uncle Paul.'

'By pure coincidence we're passing by there for the start of the tour. One of the places I keep some anyhow.'

'And pills? A joint maybe. Magic Mushrooms'

'I'm a Baby Boomer. Only barely. So it's booze. *Lots* of booze.'

When they arrived Amanda realised Paul wasn't exaggerating. There was wall to ceiling glass fronted refrigerators stretching out for a few hundred yards. 'Who gives a fuck about looking at some washed out ball from a shitty Rocketship. *This* is what I call out of control amazing. It's like a booze data farm.'

'I had to carry all of this in myself. It's taken years. Plus all the less interesting but essential necessities in the main storages.' Eventually Paul had given up and got some burley men to help because there was so much to have delivered and carry in. They were well paid and then a nudge made them forgetful of the whole episode.

'Woah. How long's the trip.'

'Two hundred years I was told. Depends how fast the universe has been expanding in front of me. I don't fully understand it, but the previous owner said you can't outrun light, so you have to outrun time. I have no clue. She programmed the ship.'

'Lucky I'm not coming, or this would run dry in a decade.'

'Fortunately I can go into a kind of stasis.'

Amanda had given her sister a six pack of the beer they both liked. 'Not that we're indifferent to you imminent departure Uncle Paul. But we need a bit of *sister* time. Y'know.' Bunny looked at her sister perplexed. She wanted to go on the tour.

'There's a nice lounge not far from here. I suspect the ship was designed so that the passengers drinks were still cold when they got to the lounge. It looks out at the stars.'

'Just what we need to see. We'll come and get you if these run out.'

'Come back to the orb when you're ready.'

He pretended to smile and left them. He was in a strange mood. His mind had always been so taken up by creating a varied pasture for their lives to choose from, plus making money, stopping people killing each other and later killing people himself again. He had not fully appreciated how close he was to this family and how much he had needed that. Now only one thing was left to him. A reminder of the sliver. And giving her an explanation which would be awkward. Then empty space. He knew where Artie would be. At the Freighter he'd come out of. Paul took him home to pack a few bags.

'Wow.' Said Bunny. 'No smog and no light pollution. The stars are amazing.' They had each opened a beer and had a quiet drink. 'We're still going to have a tour aren't we Amanda.' Bunny would ultimately do what Amanda thought best. And looking at these stars with a beer was a good start.

The older of the two put her drink down and took her sister gently by the shoulders, and told her, essentially, what her father had just told her mother. Bunny was upset for a long time and the bounce back was not pronounced. 'I know it's the right thing. It makes sense she was from another planet and needs go back out in space.'

'I saw her naked not that long ago. You can't have tits that perky at her age without being an alien. Obvious in hindsight right.' This was Amanda's way of agreeing with Bunny. And ironically it was Amanda coaching Bunny on how to be caring on this occasion. 'Sister. I think this is something we don't want to drag out and we have to suck it up and not make it hard on our alien mother. If I know dad, he's said his goodbyes and he's gone to pack her bags. We'll know she's where she belongs. Having some kick ass adventure.' This sent Bunny into another cycle of emotion then acknowledgement and acceptance. They had a beer in silence. Paul returned to them after taking Artie back to the oval. Before he could try to navigate what was about to happen Amanda said casually. 'Dad's gone to pack a bag for mom I imagine. Bunny's going to pack a bag for me. So get ready for a black hole in your little booze stash.' It took Paul a second. He knew Amanda would never come. The two sisters had a bond. Unusually strong. 'Of course I'm going to stay on earth Uncle Paul. It will be nice to finally say goodbye to that…' She threw her head back '…biiiiitch of a mother or mine.' Bunny wished she could say things like that.

At the Orb Amanda needed to go into confidence overdrive to maintain her equilibrium as she walked over the bridge. They met a woman they barely recognised. Never having seen Helen vulnerable and confused. 'Girls, you father and I were talking…about…' She was losing her resolve.

Her elder daughter pulled her up into a rare embrace. They were similar and they clashed occasionally however much they understood one another. 'You're out of here and that's it. And you need to skip over the feeling bad part. It's pointless. Skipping that part *is not negotiable*. If you're going to abandon us the least you could do is the only thing we ask of you. Feel good. I know you can do it. Hell. By this time tomorrow I will have forgotten I even had a mother.' This was the daughter who understood her. The daughter who would manage her emotions later. Supported in private by her sister. The other daughter who's love was more uncomplicated, joined a three-way embrace. Amanda let go of her mother and Bunny didn't try to not cry.

She wanted the same thing for her mother as her father and Amanda did. But she wasn't going to pretend she could appear casual about it. 'It's going to take me a week. Maybe two before I catch up with Amanda.'

They were all drained. Amanda, ever the pragmatist said. 'Dad will be turning the packing into a complete shambles. We'll get the car and start dumping piles of your crap at the door. So Uncle Paul load it all in with time to go and do whatever the thing is he's been getting nervous about. Will we have enough time to move all of her crap?'

'Twelve hours.'

'We'll get half of it in maybe.'

'It's a *carload* Amanda. If that.' Helen was proud of her frugal habits.

'Yeah. Whatever. Don't forget to write.' The first daughter was gone in the way that was easiest for her. The second ran back for one last hug.

Paul had been unsure what he should tell them. 'I always knew something was up with mom. This confirms my suspicion. So we're aliens too.' Amanda opened up the dialogue once in the smaller craft.

352

'One quarter alien. Mostly human. And don't ask about your family tree. And I don't know if you'll have the 'stop ageing' thing in your twenties although you'll be having some degree of admiration over and above what might normally be expected.'

'That's true but not because of the alien part.' Bunny knew this would be her sister's reply, so she got in first.

Paul was serious. 'Either way, some people like to trap beautiful, rare things and control them. Put them on display or make them into something that suits their needs or wants. You're smart young people, but the world's a different place now compared to when your parents and I were your age.' They could see Paul was a man worn out by saying goodbye to a life double its length in years. And double in identity.

They walked home to help their father finish loading all three of the cars in the garage. 'I think that's it. She has more stuff than she likes to believe.' Said Artie. It all got unloaded into a bay near the elevator door on the freighter within an hour. There were final handshakes and hugs.

Travelling Companions

He went to find Helen at the console in the orb and dropped down in the command chair next to her. She reached across and squeezed his hand. 'They told me to skip over the sad part so that's what I'm going to do. From what you told me it sounds like you're leaving behind two lives. This one being quite intense I imagine. Maybe you'd like some alone time.'

He smiled across at her. With some strategic stasis, they would get along fine on such a long trip. 'Some sleep would be good. Let's meet here for breakfast tomorrow morning at nine. I'll bring the breakfast. It's the last time we'll see this. I'll take you to your cabin.' He took her to the door and gave her a welcome hug. 'You'll find everything you need in there.' He had already gone when she realised this wasn't a cabin. It was a mansion which had been arranged and furnished as if he had an intimate understanding of her tastes. He didn't need to. She had taken over Chrona's quarters.

Paul thought he'd feel relief and an excitement about a journey only a handful of humans had taken. Albeit that he would be travelling more slowly than Kirby and spending long periods in the stasis which Helen would need to learn from the ship where Chrona stored many useful things. Paul took a pill to get to sleep which was rare.

He awoke feeling good. Today was the last day and he had a pleasant and erudite travelling companion to share stories with, some perhaps unbelievable, play board games, learn instruments, spend hours cooking meals if they felt like it. And he was certain they wouldn't get under each other's feet. On a journey like this they would decide a on pleasant phrase that conveyed the simple message 'leave me alone' and the recipient of this phrase wouldn't feel slighted. They could use it with impunity as much and they wanted. It was one of the first things they talked about over breakfast. Helen said. 'Easy. We'll make it - *Leave me alone.*' Paul had a pang of nostalgia. He missed Chrona but he had the next best thing.

After breakfast, the ship pointing at earth, confident as Helen might have been, it was not easy to say goodbye to your planet. Forever. She looked up and smiled and he said something that made everything easier. 'I feel so much better about this journey to have you come with me. I was getting a little more than apprehensive about whether I could keep my sanity for two hundred years. Though the stasis the ship will teach you is very calming.' Paul thought it might be good to share a few stories. 'You know Helen, you lived dozens of lifetimes on that planet. You don't remember them because they ceased to exist in time and space. But you still lived them. In so many other Timelines.' Paul wondered how many records of these Helens the ship kept of her. It would make fascinating movie nights.

'I can see there is going to be a massive pestering campaign from me to figure out what you're talking about. Perhaps we skip that, and you tell me everything.'

'How about I tell you everything, except what the previous owner would want me not too. I understand some of what she went through now. Even though I've experienced only a tiny sliver of what she did. The many and varied histories of Helen are, I expect, somewhere in the ships records of all those civilisations that came and went from existence.' He said quietly. 'But first, a farewell to our beautiful planet. We have to be somewhere not too far out in the solar system, but I want to be ready.'

He spun the ship around and took off into space. No expressions of a fond farewell. They understood each other. The ship parked several million miles away, facing away from the earth.

'And we are waiting for?'

'An old friend. At least from my perspective. I've brought us out here a few hours early to answer some of your questions before you feel the need to ask them. And know that if some are unanswered, that is how they will stay.' He told her almost everything. She was a 'changeling'. The grief her mother felt at leaving her to be brought up with humans and the years in the grey limbo studying and selecting the best possible parents for her. She needed a break for half an hour to absorb this news. Finding out your parents weren't your biological family was a shock. Mitigated a little by the fact they didn't know either.

She returned with a coffee for each of them, which further cemented Paul's certainty all would be well. She thought she knew Paul. As she heard about the Sororibus and their final Timeline, and the partnership they shared in navigating Barrion, who Helen minted as their 'nemesis'. She was surprised how close they had once been. Paul came to how they joined Basilica and realised he could hardly stop there.

'You killed her? The alluring Alien woman.'

'Yes.

'And?'

'Remember I can drop you back home if you'd like.'

Helen covered her open mouth with her hand as the story progressed. 'You killed *me*. You even said so that last time…I thought you were joking.'

'I'm not proud of it. I concluded it might have been poor judgement afterwards. However you must understand the decisions were made under immense pressure.' He didn't put enough thought into what he said next. 'Now that I think about it, you're still down there. I left the rest in a beautiful pasture. Except Basilica whom, I think in poetic justice, took part in Barrion's demise.'

'Down there?'

He tried to divert this subject by launching into a description of his initial interactions with her mother. And the reluctant pact she entered into. Although the degree of reluctance may have been less fulsome than he thought at the time. His descriptions of the slow, ghastly death of some of the children and youths beside their dead mothers and the quick destruction of every living thing in the range of the Pulses was arduous for both of them.

'I changed my mind late in the process. Having even the reluctant interaction with your mother and having grown to know the young alien woman she would characterise as the finest Envoy she ever had…I believed them. About the terrible violence caused by a virus. Which ironically escaped from a Bubble in time and space created by Elouise. Which, also ironically, we're sitting inside of now.'

Helen, who everyone thought impossible to disorient, was suffering from improbability fatigue. But motioned he should continue. She wanted it all. At the end of the story of the genocide Helen surprised him by saying 'You did the right thing Paul. Um…maybe. These people admitted to taking over the planet and why should you be expected to believe what did sound like a convenient story. And yes Paul. I don't think I could have stomached it. Even if I agreed with you.'

He was quiet for a long time. 'You can't imagine what that means to me.'

'Though I do want to visit myself later.'

'Of course. You can take that little journey on your own and…a bleated apology is in order.' Her eyes narrowed. 'You'll see what I mean.' He said.

He described how his relationship with Chrona thawed and then 'became warmer' which Helen passed no comment on. He described the 'sliver of joy' her mother experienced, the birth of her daughter and the desperate hope of saving the girl she adopted. And living with all of that for thousands upon thousands of years as the Sororibus cycled through realities to avoid the Event Horizon taking all of them. He finished with Chrona's retirement to live with the Nouveau Balinese.

'I'm glad we're sitting in a big impressive rocketship Paul. Or I'd be telling you that you are so full of shiiiiiiit.'

They laughed and then sat quietly for a time until a giant Chrona appeared on a large portion of the Orb. 'Hi you two. Time's weird right. This file got triggered based on my forecast which was that there was an eighty nine percent chance you would have a certain passenger join you Paul. How about you stretch your legs while I belatedly talk to my daughter. I spent months in the grey limbo answering every question she might pose, to the extent my failing memory permitted me. They are liberally sprinkled with a bunch of 'mind your own business' type responses. We'll only be here a few hours Paul. Plenty of time before your *other* predictable engagement. Make sure you say hello to her for me.'

Paul returned, expecting to find perhaps a sombre or further confused Helen. He found someone who had had an entirely cathartic experience. 'She adopted *my* parents on earth. After so much research. The same as you Paul. You put so much into caring for me and my family and I've even made a bit of a joke about it. You should know how much it's meant to all of us. Our lives have been so enriched by someone who gave us compelling choices to make. But always good.'

A Curious Reunion

He was about to make an expression of appreciation when a different Chrona came on the screen. While they'd been talking a ship had appeared in front of the bubble. It was like looking at a mirror. Identical to the ship they were in. In fact it *was* the ship they were in. Chrona's ship was in the original Timeline where she arrived fourteen years after T-Day expecting to find a devastated earth and not having conceived a thing like a Bubble existed. Paul's life and the ship had persisted because he was always in the Bubble of time and space created by Elouise. Never found or manipulated by *this* Chrona because she had only visited briefly and she could find no way to remedy the people of earth's self-destruction. She found the Bubble years later because it was left open.

'Hello.' An extraordinary mind was analysing an extremely improbable reality. 'I thought you were one of my kind. However that ship is very familiar and…not.'

'I can imagine you're feeling disappointed on a few fronts. We didn't take this ship from one of your species. *You* gave it to me. If you examine it carefully it's the ship you're in right now. Though you made quite a few modifications and it's a little worse for wear given it's been on duty for at least a few hundred thousand years. Since today.' Even having her observe the ship was creating a strange dissonance all around that part of time and space.

'Quite a story I imagine. Yet for all my experience with

Time I'm at a loss…'

'You found something that Elouise, who you heard about from one of your species, created. A Bubble in time and space. Your ship detected it, and you used it when the Sororibus you're resettling now discovered that a Back Holes can in fact turn up unexpectedly in your back yard. So the time they had as an established civilisation was less than you'd hoped for, and you stayed longer and found a way to take a new group of settlers fifteen hundred years into the past and start a new Timeline.'

Chrona, like her daughter was difficult to disorient for long. 'Clever aren't I.'

'A genius.'

Helen waved 'Hi mom. It's great to meet you. Though I was only talking with your hologram a few minutes ago, which now seems a little weird.'

Disorientation passed across that face that was not so much beautiful, rather it was anything it wanted to be. The same face could be haunting, witty, disdainful, alluring, confused in forgetfulness. And all perfect portrayals of those things. Galvanising and captivating always.

'Quite the story it would seem.'

'I'm having the ship send across its full history since this moment in time when the earth should have been covered in dried out human bodies. I realise this leaves you with a bit of a logistics pro…' They all started to scream and hold their hands against their ears as if their heads were about to explode. Which would have happened had the ship shut down the feed.

'Looks like if I let anything out of the bubble time and space get rather annoyed and want to tear the whole anomaly to pieces. You said if I ever had a problem like this it would disappear when I was far enough away from earth. Outrunning time instead of light you said. That's why you would never return for a new Timeline before Kirby left after her visit. She'd be destroyed leaving the bubble of a new Timeline. You can go into it, but you can't come out unless the Timeline is the same. We're kind of stuck in here now that I think of it.' He didn't realise Kirby had left earth, even on the first occasion, in *his* new Timeline.

'I don't remember that being explained to me.' Said Helen.

'It was in the Ts and Cs you scrolled through but didn't read.' This was the best he could do until he figured out an answer to that question. He turned his attention to a sharper but now somewhat deflated Chrona. Being the saviour to a hundred thousand of Sororibus could be tiresome 'I imagine you're wondering where to go now that colonising the earth isn't…as desirable an option.'

'This is somewhat of a disappointment.' The Chrona of that time had other objectives pursue after what she assumed to be a short 'settling in' period for her latest cargo.

'Over the centuries you were able to dramatically expand and improve on the Sharing the Sororibus have developed. It does need blocks to stop it propagating into a mass state of unconsciousness.'

Chrona had a natural curiosity that surpassed the need for information on the foibles of the Sharing. At that time, quite seminal. 'Something of, at least tangential interest is…what happened to me. And the Sisterhood I carry with me who have been so ill used by their males.'

'Ah.' Said Paul. 'That.' He realised after all this time he was less prepared for this meeting than he ought to have been.

Helen came to the rescue. 'They had who knows how many fifteen-hundred-year cycles. More than a hundred.' She turned to Paul. She looked back to her genetic, though not biological mother. 'And I got to be in about fifty of them which I'm looking forward to watching. A shame we can't get together for that. It came to an end when an evil nemesis arose among the Sororibus. A man pretending to be one of the Sisterhood. He triggered events that led to the… annihilation of the Sororibus.'

She digested that. 'And even I was annihilated by this evil being.'

'Hmmmm. Can't really help you with that one. From what I can tell things got a little ah…complicated between you and my friend here…' Paul didn't want to place something so special to him before someone who could only be made awkward by it.

'You…were having trouble with your memory by then. And naturally a bit upset by the whole annihilation incident. Sort of. So you went to live with these…ah Monkey People who had evolved into quite a delightful species of matriarchal sentient beings. They adored you.'

Chrona, able to be light-hearted or imperious in the space of seconds said. 'So if I had your…Bubble I could go and visit…myself.'

'Well no. When I returned here, I came before your first visit… this one. By creating a new Timeline, that sort of terminated the Timeline you…the other you…were in and you…ceased to exist. You even made a recording of yourself to taunt me about that.'

Paul's Chrona came on the big screen so that they all could see her. 'I imagine Paul's doing a ham fisted job of explaining this. And my wayward daughter is being a little flippant. It's a shame we would probably be ripped apart by time and space which will simply not brook such flagrant abuse of the simple, easy to follow rules they think are universal. Chow.'

'Oh.' Said the Chrona in the other ship.

The somewhat more time worn Chrona appeared again. 'Continue with your tale Paul. You wont have long. And why not try bouncing the history of the ship, *not the technical stuff* off a planet on your way out. By the time it gets here you might have outrun time enough. Chow.'

'I do that a lot?' The other said.

'It's always good to see her…you. Anyway, although you and those whom you've rescued haven't experienced it Chrona, your undertaking was a *huge* success. Over a hundred and fifty thousand years of peaceful, productive, creative civilisations. Even though none of it, sort of, technically ever existed, it's not so different as if it had happened in the past. Which also doesn't really exist either.'

'Unless you have a Bubble apparently.' She observed.

Paul nodded. 'Good Point.' He could have visited his aunt on the forgotten journey now their he thought about it. 'But it can only go back to the Timeline it's on and start another one if one wanted to. Can't visit any of the other Timelines.' Chrona didn't get confused often. In this case she thought it was okay to be. Paul continued. 'Anyway, we're going to where Kirby went. You recorded the visit she made to earth in detail and where she went.

Sounded very pleasant.'

Chrona responded while distracted by an emerging sensation. 'Yes. She had some role in a war that killed billions. I heard that from a one of my Species. Her presence catalysed an improvement in the plight of females throughout that galaxy. Hence if I interfered with that it would be the height of hypocrisy.' Chrona looked at her hands. 'Diverting as this is, unfortunately even with your ship in...a bubble...I'm starting to feel the fabric of time and space starting to tear around me. Which might not bode well for those aboard or indeed for the planet.'

'Damn.' Said Helen. 'I wanted to let you know I have the coolest mother in the universe.'

'Oh. That's nice. I was good mother?'

'I've...never actually met you. Until now as a hologram a moment ago. It's a long story. Still a very cool mother.'

Paul knew enough about time to be afraid. For everyone. 'Chrona. I'm going to bounce a tiny ping of Neptune on our way out. It will be followed by the ships history bounced *away* from the solar system in the opposite direction to that which we're going. If the ping doesn't cause problems you might be able to go and load the database when we're safely a long time away. It's been so good to see you. Maybe we'll see you in Li. It'll take a while to get there but it sounds like a galaxy that might have the kind of place you're looking for. You'll learn Statis which would help you all get there.'

Paul hit the button which had Kirby's ships trajectory loaded in and fled. He made the voice command to the ship to bounce the tiny energy burst and then send out the data package.

Chrona appeared. 'We're lightyears past Neptune Paul. Space is rather big and there's a lot to pass through. The ship already had the 'idea' you had. Younger me will get a few laughs out of it and know her Sororibus vision was fulfilled many times over. Maybe she'll decide that's good enough and evacuate the oxygen out of the ship and eject the remains. It's probably what I'd do. Enjoy the ride. And *don't* go and look in the freezer Helen.'

The Visitation

'That was weird.' Said Helen. 'The more I think about time the more it makes my head hurt. It seems you and my mother predicted everything that happened right up to this point.'

'Broadly. Provided Elouise emptied the Bubble.'

'And now we're moving like…really fast.'

'Yes. In time…and hence space.'

'Really really fast.'

'Yep.' Paul was facing her. Wondering why she needed more clarification.

'So my question is…what are *they* doing there.' She pointed with her eyes across the orb. Paul looked around. A spacecraft was sitting a few hundred yards off the upper right-hand portion of the orb. 'As if we're both standing still.' Helen finished.

Paul had seen that ship before. Or recordings of when Kirby made her last visit.

The two entities had been watching the drama of the departure since the same ship arrived only to find itself already parked in space. This incident had sent a strange ripple across untold light-years to where they were. In time. Not dangerous to them or the galaxies it passed through. However completely unprecedented. And it came from a place one of them knew very well. They had decided never to visit their home planets again as all the beings in Li and the entire galaxy it was situated in had been extinguished in a massive pandemic before Elouise and her companion emerged from the long process of genesis which they had designed for themselves.

A beautifully marked fur covered entity with an expressive face said. 'Not many individuals can claim to have singlehandedly wiped out their entire species.'

'It's regrettable, and indeed I know of no precedents.' Said a voice that over centuries had grown warmer.

'And via the propagation of extreme violence.' Her partner could not help himself sometimes.

'The consequences, unintended as they were, were shocking and the misery unimaginably awful. I am chastened.' The Li's mind had not yet followed the connection hers had already made.

'And then, all unintended, to have the events repeated again and again because of this truly unprecedented resetting of time in the… Bubble which was….'

'My contrition is heartfelt, and I believe nothing is to be gained by belabouring what's apparent.' He had gone a little too far on what was clearly a sore spot now. Rare as they were. 'It's to the strange entities credit that she achieved her ends while mitigating the suffering of humanity prior to the virus's propagation. And then to free those in her charge of the emergence of a Black Hole, its arrival another occasion of which we know of no precedent.' Something much larger than the self-annihilation of the people on her home planet was beginning to propagate in Elouise's mind. A related, and much larger tragedy.

Hope of the East stated the obvious. Which she sometimes found trying. However Elouise was entering a state of grief and guilt she never thought there could be a reason to touch her life. 'Had the entity been less scrupulous and delivered her charges prior to Kirby's departure…'

'Indeed.' Elouise said. 'What Kirby catalysed throughout the galaxy would not…exist. But alas. All those great works had their potential truncated, perhaps by tens of thousands of years, because Kirby acquired something on earth unlooked for in addition to my father. She carried with her a toxin developed by the ignorant set in a carrier which persisted due to my unforgivable carelessness. By the time we emerged it had spread to every planet. Kirby died of natural causes, but not so those alive on the day the carrier was activated.'

Her partner realised the momentous consequences of the virus having spread far beyond earth. 'Yet we owe our existence to her. Had the original Timeline been changed on earth and Kirby not arrived back, my father would not have provided the essential insights that allowed us to…metamorphosise into this new form.'

Elouise took the cue to focus on what was now mundane by comparison. 'What that entity did with my crude protype of what she calls a 'Bubble' if mismanaged, or misused, could be catastrophic.' Her voice trailed off. 'Or even more so.' They were sitting in a ship that presented the very same risks to the universe. That someone might take it and create havoc across time and space. However like Chrona's, only more advanced, it had an array of biometric and AI monitors such that if any other entity launched a weapon or approached it with hostile intentions the ship would automatically reel backwards in time and turn them to ashes before the approach started. The future be damned. In the unlikely event of the immortal occupants dying, the ship would go into the grey limbo and destroy itself.

'We must disable and permanently eradicate the Bubble around that ship and its occupants.' This situation; essential, though not urgent, helped distract Elouise's mind from the awful truth.

'Indeed. We need to address the fate of these two and of the Sororibus, who have journeyed a century, in experienced time, only to find disappointment. That ship, or an earlier version of the same ship, is slower than the upgraded version. To find a new home might be a challenge. Earth is so far away from anywhere. We must address the Sororibus before the trader species individuals makes any decision.'

Paul and Helen. Gazing at the ship, smaller than their freighter, disappeared but only for an eyeblink as they returned to the ship captained by a more youthful Chrona, though she looked little different, and Elouise cast a Bubble around it so that all within became fixed in time. She had refined these. They would brook no interference and would both devolve to nothingness and take the interferer with them should they be tampered with.

They had returned to their former station in less than a second after experiencing an interval of half an hour. 'The occupants of the ship before us are becoming stressed at our arrival. We should assuage their concerns.'

The entity who had invented it would never usually deign to call it a Bubble. As with the spaceship she built, she distained giving things a name. However she and the furry entity with her travelled in a bubble, in this case more advanced from the brilliance of a few thousand lived years of genius. That after many years in the insubstantial form the Li keep loved ones in. They did this so that by holding a hand of a much-loved relative there a soft sweet echo. In the case of Elouise it was far more than an echo.

When they materialised on the Orb, Paul and Helen felt a calming insinuation enter their minds. 'All is well. Be calm. Our intentions are benign.'

Helen broke though the mild restraints filled with excitement. 'Elouise. No way. I can't *believe* this. You're supposed to be dead. Do you know I spent years writing a book about you.'

Elouise found such a rapid recovery from what her partner insisted on calling a 'gentle embrace' when they introduced themselves to entities that way, made it difficult to compose the reply she might have preferred to make. 'Oh. How…nice. I must make time to read it.'

Her companion found this most amusing. She had never read prose of a non-technical nature in her long life. Whereas he now consumed huge quantities of fiction, biography and history from throughout the array of Galaxies they 'provided support to'. She had never uttered a mistruth so she would read the book and probably find it most unsatisfactory.

'If you'll excuse me for a moment. She vanished as did the ship for an eyeblink and returned. 'Thank you for the efforts you made

369

in preparing your book.' It had been unsatisfactory but there was hardly any point spending the time to correct errors of fact and the unnecessary conjecture. Then she thought of Kirby. During the Challenges and during the mission. And the things the girl from Northern New South Wales she was able to draw out of her and later Hope of the East who would have been insufferable without Kirby showing him how to 'chill out' as she put it. So she added. 'If the opportunity presents itself, I would be pleased to provide some…further context.' Helen had spent time with her holographic mother, the person who was her genetic mother and now one of the people she admired most. She was positively beaming, and this had a peculiar effect on Elouise. She was reminded of Amazon. Her favoured Challenger.

Helen knew enough from her research not to give Elouise the hug she wanted to. Paul had come forward to shake Hope of the East's paw. Paul was also ecstatic to be meeting both of them. 'You can only be Hope of the East…sir. I watched the whole duration of the visit of Kirby and Ted and young Manion and the noisy child… Amazon. And the things they said about you. Even the partial history I was able to learn of. Quite amazing.'

Hope of the East had softened considerably over the centuries. Once at least as imperious as Elouise, if not more on occasion, he was now gratified. Even a little embarrassed by the remarks. Elouise was ready to move on. She went to the control panel and navigated through menus in a blizzard of motion, apparently being able to circumvent the need to sign on as a controller. Paul felt the very slight settling indicating the ship had 'stopped'.

Elouise looked at her partner of centuries. 'I'll return shortly.'

She disappeared and reappeared thirty seconds later.

'More challenging than you expected I see.'

'It took me a week to understand what those…individuals had done to corrupt the carrier I left in…' She needed to use a name whereas she and Hope of East communicated via complex and exacting thoughts. '…my Bubble. It demonstrates the infancy of my understanding of many things at that time.'

'I think Bubble's quite a good shorthand.' Said the entity Kirby had given the unlikely nick name of Smatypants to.

'Thank you for that perspective.'

'I find such separations difficult.' Hope of the East was entirely sincere.

'My experienced time away was three weeks. As this interval progressed, I grew more aware of your absence.' Paul recognised the smile of pleasure on the Li genius's face. He'd experienced it with Chrona and had seen it many times on the face of Artie with Helen.

Elouise moved on from the moment which for her, was one of considerable tenderness however this did not create the need for a reflective pause. 'We have business to attend to. I see the entity who vested this ship into your possession linked its existence to your heartbeat. Very wise. You are now suspended in space and time.' She had cast another of her more recently perfected Bubbles around the ship and its occupants. It's our intention to return and take you to…what we hope will be a pleasant place.' She looked at her partner and shared a thought.

They vanished. Helen frowned. 'Did you pick up on the fact that she said they *intended* to return and that where were going was going to be nice…hopefully.'

Paul looked at the control panel. 'I was a little distracted by the fact the ship, from any kind of 'going somewhere or some*when*' perspective; is disabled. And Chrona's Bubble is no more.' Elouise's was imperceptible.

'Oh.'

'However the ship is supplied with a magnificent selection of booze, movies and books.'

'Lead on.'

Can the Past Catch Up

Elouise decided a remedy was required. They had taken their ship to visit exactly the same ship when Kirby was using it to visit earth. In France. Elouise resolved the 'Space Time Dissonance' problem that Paul and the younger Chrona had experienced by hiding them both from space and time in a Bubble.

The much-upgraded version of Kirby's ship was hovering not far from the Eiffel Tower where Kirby had wedged it deciding to fly through the gap at the base as a final flourish before leaving earth forever.

Elouise had said nothing as they until she had cast the Bubble around the ships. 'I am heartbroken. This corruption of an idea mutated through the Nautilus Galaxy until nothing survived. All surrendered to violence, studied or mindless.' The Hope of the East came and wrapped his long furry arms around her. There was little he could say. Kirby and Manion had carried the virus to

The Nautilus Galaxy. 'I put a chronological trigger in a harmless virus as a carrier.'

Hope of the East could offer nothing. He squeezed her a little tighter.

'It would have been my mother's eightieth birthday. An age I calculated she would have lived to were it not for exposure to a virus. A condition I had cured within a *year* of her passing. After that date it defaulted to a century later. It was an arbitrary point in time I chose to sustain the thing, locked in the…Bubble…in case I ever…' She gave a little shrug. 'Went back to earth. I had built incredible safeguards around it. I didn't fully apprehend the capacity of AI, brought to bear on a massive scale. And…the coopting of poor Ryker. They didn't respect its purpose. It was to carry a cure to all humanity and trigger on a certain day as the sun made it's apparent journey around the earth.'

She took note of where they stood. Hope of the East thought it would be 'fun' to give them the injections at that moment when they were stuck in plain view of earthlings and the younger Li, whom Kirby had named Manion, was welding up the tower to stop it toppling all over their goodbye gesture. They were frozen in time.

Manion sat calmly in a wheelchair. Happy about any kind of outcome now that he'd seen at least one of the Graceland Challengers had made it. He'd been enjoying the excitement of the farewell lap. Elouise glanced fondly at her father. Kirby's son was looking up giving his mother some advice about what the pitch of an aircraft meant while he used remote arms to weld the broken struts of the tower, only ever intended to be there for the 1889 World Fair and then it was to be taken down. Then Parisians found it was rather good to put antennae on. So they kept it. Shimmering Light, now known as Ted, was trying to soothe Amazon who, only learning to walk, was demanding to help her half-brother. In the Li culture she was too young to learn stasis. However Ted was determined to try to teach her for the return journey.

Elouise brought out the antiviral doser. There as one for each, in case it has mutated to host in the Li or in the half human, half Cyanne which Amazon was. She came to Kirby first and hesitated. Uncharacteristically anxious. 'If the Li civilisation were to persist, we would still emerge because no activities on the surface would change. The two of us, as in the past, will emerge. But in this case, those manifestations of *us* in time and space may not depart our galaxy, as we did, having found it a dead and forlorn place the... last time.' Even Elouise was finding it a little confusing. They had spent nearly two millennia visiting places and 'making things better' for whatever entities lived there. It was rewarding and stimulating because they used every kind of science and engineering. 'With this dose in their bodies, all that we've done...will be gone. We can exist within our...bubble. But once these travellers have their cure, what had been our past will...cease to have occurred. Reset to a new present and future without *what we've done.*'

Hope of the East had been coming to a similar conclusion with a different starting point. He said. 'They don't need that.'

She looked up. A little annoyed by now. Nothing in her life had ever go so badly off track from her plans. Except perhaps Gaspar's ill-fated fiddling with the controls of the first space craft she built.

Hope of the East looked at Elouise sadly. '*This* is the *only* time that Kirby visits earth and picks up your father. Because the *first time* she did it no longer exists. That man Paul came and convinced you to do something. Which you caused yourself to forget. Via a telephone we learn. Quite the persuader.'

Elouise's mind was embarrassed at its lack of comprehension of the consequences of what they'd learned from Paul such that she'd spent an experienced three weeks making an antidote she didn't need to. Then the other consequence emerged into her mind.

Hope of the East's mate was reflective. 'We never called our changes Timelines because we didn't need to conceive it as such because we didn't ever create an alternate from the same starting point. We never went back and changed things. That remarkable example of the 'trader' species did. We have only heard rumours of them as they usually travel; invisible and pulse some target and take their plunder. During an uncharacteristic act of altruism, she found and used my Bubble to create alternative Timelines. And the man she gave her ship to convinced me to destroy what was in it. So Kirby, your father and her family never caught it. Because the humans never carried it. Hence it did not spread either on earth nor as a pandemic on the Nautilus Galaxy.'

Elouise moved the medidoser away from Kirby's arm. 'Only one Kirby goes back to Li. This one. And she had no virus.'

Hope of the East was following a thread of thought. 'And as with Chrona do a different Elouise and Hope of the East. At a great distance in space and in far the future from where we stand now. Or as likely, are we them however our past is very different. We are at a great distance from it and we have disobeyed the rules of time and space. Rules it, our past must obey to find us.'

She nodded. 'Now we have a different past. The details of which we know nothing.' Elouise's whole conception of her life was changing. 'We're standing in a time many centuries before we emerged from our metamorphosis deep in the ocean. And millennia before we most recently roamed a different corner of the universe. We never once revisited the past except to visit the source of an anomaly. We never changed it.'

'Until today.'

This event caused a kind of reflection in Elouise she didn't usually partake in. She lived in the present. Designing and imagining for the future. 'I...I...' He saw tears glide down cheeks he had thought would ever be innocent of them. Of course there was something else in her past that had caused her to cry herself to sleep many a lonely night as a child. That was so long ago now. 'I... treasure my past. My past with you. I don't want to lose it like...'

'What happened to Paul's aunt.'

'I've never needed to imagine such an affliction. Such a...loss.'

The ancient Li genius, now kept in his magnificent prime by the ship they travelled in, had moist fur at the corners of his eyes. 'It would seem we need to keep away from anywhere we...ever went or ever might go.'

'We can only try. While not knowing who we were or are going to be if out past ever catches us.'

'Time's weird.' Was all he could offer. He walked over to what was and uncertain Elouise, a state he had never imagined her to be, and said. 'We'll flee our past. Any past. To where we would never go. It cannot scale or dive through the leaps and jumps we've made through time and space because it does not have our ship to do it in.'

'Yes. The lines we make much never cross an earlier path we took. We of an alternate Timeline as we've learned to call it.' She was looking at Kirby. Initially the realisation that the pandemic had never happened had caused Elouise to ponder a visit to Kirby. She could only imagine the excitement the Australian, who would always be young at heart, would show wanting to know all about what 'Princess Bubblegum and Smartypants' had been up to. Now she could never go near any of the thousands of places they had been, many times in some cases, and shared their genius and enthusiasm and received the same in kind from so many species through so many galaxies. She had never much valued memories. She didn't realise that it had been a comfort to here that had she ever had the desire, she could revisit anyone, anywhere. Even if only to see them and not visit. And now, unlike Paul's aunt, she was aware of what she had lost. And a visit would rend them to shreds.

What is Emma Doing There

They were both adjusting. They would make a new life. In some part of the universe it might take an ordinary lifetime to get to even in their incredibly fast ship so that they were quarantined forever from their past. She looked at her partner and could see his eyes telling her it would be a good life. *Again*. However all at once they felt a strange presence as they pondered. It was only for an eye-blink. Elouise cried out in pain and looked down at her forearm. The pain was transient, however what had appeared on her arm was most objectionable. The chance of Elouise ever getting a tattoo was infinitesimally small. The probability of getting this specific tattoo voluntarily were certainly down at absolute zero. The person who had written the words had only ever used a tattooing gun as a part of an elaborate Project via which she repaid in kind a very evil man who had misused her. Her tattoos were supposed to be ghastly to any professional's eye. Such untidiness drawn on her tormentors body was yet another pronouncement of the Total Control she had wrested from him.

Once she had learned everything there was to know about Elouise and was then asked to go and tattoo a message on her arm she had tried to make the writing as neat as possible, which she could do very well now on paper. However she had never tried to write nearly over human skin. Hence it was with both surprise and displeasure Elouise was able to read;

Come to Cecil Court. West End. London. 30th November 2054. Noon. I'll be waiting. Everyone needs you. Please come. Emma.

Hope of the East was looking at her forearm, he assumed, in a way as confused and confounded as Elouise. However Elouise wasn't confused. She had experienced a second existential shock in the space of less than an hour. A hand had rested upon her shoulder in that eyeblink. She knew everything about the young detective from Essex. And Elouise also knew that that Emma knew everything about her.

He had to repeat himself as Elouise seemed transfixed by the message. But it was the revelation she'd been given that had caused this disappearance into contemplation.

'Is Cecil Court somewhere any of our possible pasts would

be likely to go?'

'I think not.' Whispered Elouise.

'A good place to start then. Where's London.'

'It's only some hundreds of miles from here. And half a century hence.' She said quietly.

'Looks like time got weirder.'

'That's not the half of it.' Said Elouise in a whisper now. Which he thought a strange thing to say. He knew she had been the subject of a profound revelation when she finished with. 'My love.'